Unequally Divided
A vibrant novel portraying difficult choices of love and life's direction during the tumultuous Vietnam era

Jane E. Harper

PUBLICATION
CONSULTANTS
We Believe In The Power Of Authors

PO Box 221974 Anchorage, Alaska 99522-1974
books@publicationconsultants.com—www.publicationconsultants.com

1464658

DEC 11 2018

ISBN 978-1-59433-723-9
eBook ISBN 978-1-59433-724-6

Library of Congress Catalog Card Number: 2017952121

This book is a work of fiction. Names, characters, places, and
incidents are the product of the author's imagination or are used
fictitiously. Any resemblance to actual persons, living or dead, or
locales is entirely coincidental.

Manufactured in the United States of America

DEDICATION

To my family, close and far.

ACKNOWLEDGEMENTS

U nequally Divided has been quite a journey, from the beginning to the end. I couldn't have completed this voyage without the help of my family and friends in varying capacities. First, I am thankful for the support and patience of my husband, Michael. He was the best shoulder to lean on when I needed encouragement. Next, my friend and colleague, Phyllis Fast, led me through this process. Without her persistent reinforcement and direction, I never would have finished this novel. As well as a longtime friend, she is the author of Northern Athabascan Survival, Half Bead of Fundy, Midnight Trauma and two children's books. I am also thankful to Darlene Candee for her motivation and constant inspiration and help in the development of the character, fourteen-year-old, Nora.

Many others also contributed to the completion of this novel. I am grateful to Clela Reed, who provided support and insight into the essence of good writing. As a poet, she has authored: Bloodline, Dancing on the Rim, and The Hero of the Revolution Serves us

Tea. I also appreciate Beth Cromie Howlett for her input, spending over five hours on one long distance call making suggestions. Many others have also contributed to the completion of this novel, including: Johanna Harper, Tanya Gularte, Rosemary Mosby, and Jan Harper Haines, author of Cold River Spirits. I also received words of encouragement from Alice Smith, Larean Pierce, Nancy and Ron Whitten, and Judy Bergheim.

I thank Publication Consultants who helped in producing this novel. I also thank Darcy Ruppert for her excellent editing skills which enhanced Unequally Divided. Peggy McMahon also added her editing skills and found errors no one else could find. She is the author of Abba, Hear My Prayers, plus two children's books.

Not to forget my good friend, Ann Chambliss, I wish I could have shared this experience with her, but sadly she has passed on. I do appreciate that I have been able to share this with with my daughter, Kristi, and eventually with my granddaughters, Sheila and Sky. A final thank you to my husband and his eternal patience.

Chapter 1

Columbus, Georgia, October 1969

J orden stopped pacing for a moment and stared out the picture window. An unfamiliar white car caught her attention as she watched it maneuver slowly around her apartment complex for the third time. She figured the driver must be looking for the right building. A gust of swirling leaves blurred her vision, causing her to focus on her current dilemma.

What was she doing? "A date, of all things, is not what I need," Jorden mumbled as she resumed pacing. How did she let Darby talk her into this? Alex had been off to this gut-wrenching war for five months—and she was going out. "What's wrong with me?"

Tapping her fingers, Jorden turned up the radio. The catchy lyrics to the tune "For What It's Worth" made her think about the Vietnam War and the terrible uncertainty it had created. She picked up her momentum as the tempo of the song increased.

"Stop pacing! You're making me nervous," Darby called out. "I heard what you said, but I don't think of this as a date, only a dinner. Besides, you deserve a night out," her roommate stressed as she applied her makeup. "Hey, I'm looking out for your welfare."

"My welfare?" Jorden stopped. "How do you figure?"

"Look, you're twenty-two and not officially engaged."

"Just because I don't have an engagement ring doesn't mean I'm not marrying Alex next summer."

"Yes, but the point is—you're not married now. I don't doubt your loyalty to Alex. I'm just worried about you! You've been cooped up for the last five months. I think you need to get out."

"Need to?" Jorden scoffed. But, Darby had struck a nerve. She looked at her roommate, realizing she did miss the fun of an innocent date: a movie, a football game, and even a dinner out with friends. Besides, she wasn't married. Jorden valued Darby's companionship and support; she had become her confidante. To think of it, Jorden even let Nate, Darby's boyfriend, sway her on the decision to go out.

Jorden watched Darby apply blush to her high cheek bones. She had to admit her roommate, at five feet, eleven inches, looked more like a model than a teacher.

Darby seemed to sense Jorden's distress. "Remember, Nate says the guy's an American Indian, so this should be an interesting evening."

Jorden couldn't help but smile. "Yes, it should be."

A moment later the doorbell rang. "Can you get the door? It must be Nate," Darby replied. "I need to get dressed."

Jorden opened the door in one quick movement. Her jaw dropped; it wasn't Nate. An Asian-looking young man stood before her. Her wary blue eyes took in the details. He was dressed casually, displaying a lean build. He had close-cropped jet black hair with thick eyebrows arched above familiar army issued eyeglasses. In contrast, soft brown eyes gazed back at her through clear lenses.

Jorden had not seen anyone like him at their door before. The unfamiliar face alarmed her. He didn't look like an American Indian. She wasn't sure what to say, finally she stammered, "I'll be right back."

Jorden sprinted back to Darby. "It's not Nate!"

"Well, who is it?" Darby asked, adding the last touches of mascara.

"I've never seen him before!"

"Where is he?" Darby's voice rose in alarm.

"In the hallway."

"He has to be Nate's friend," Darby instantly replied. "You have to let him in."

Jorden knew she had used bad judgment and dashed to the door. She could feel the muscles in her shoulders tighten when she didn't see him. Guilt hit. Panicking, she opened the door wider. Relief overcame her when she saw him standing at the hall window with his back to her.

"I'm so sorry! Please come in," Jorden blurted out.

He turned around casually and appeared to study Jorden. A slight grin formed as if he were about to make a clever remark, but instead he introduced himself. "I'm Matt Ulster, Nate's friend. You must be . . ."

"Yes, I'm Jorden Marshall," she replied, trying to soften her voice. She couldn't help but be impressed with his good-natured attitude. "Come in. Can I get you something to drink—a Coke?"

"I'm fine . . . thank you."

Again, the doorbell rang. This time it was Nate. A huge smile spread across her face as she opened the door. "Come on in. Darby's almost ready."

"Hey, don't you look nice." Nate's eyebrows went up as he noticed her red dress.

"Thank you." Jorden could feel herself blush. The dress wasn't even hers. Emma Lynn, her other roommate, had let her borrow the classy outfit.

Nate looked at Matt. "Sorry, looks like you beat me here."

"No problem," Matt stated. "I like cooling my heels in the hall." Matt laughed, Jorden cringed, and Nate looked confused. He started to reply when Darby entered the room.

"Hi y'all. I'm ready."

"About time," Nate replied. He pulled Darby into his arms. Her long blonde hair swayed back and forth as he kissed her. Embarrassed, Jorden looked away. At the same time, she thought about Alex. She missed those times with him.

After an awkward silence, Nate apologized, "How rude of me. This is my office mate, Matt Ulster; we keep Fort Benning Army Base running smoothly."

"Sure you do," Darby said, "just like Jorden and I keep the school district in good shape."

"We'll make an excellent foursome," Nate replied. "Now, let's head to dinner."

Nate had a sleek, 1969 sapphire blue Pontiac GTO. Jorden could see he was eager to show off his new car as he steered smoothly through the Julian Apartments. The complex was composed of six separate buildings shaped into a horseshoe. Her eyes swept to the borders of the complex, which were outlined with a mixture of oak, maple, and tall swaying Georgia pines. Then, to her surprise, Nate revved up the motor in front of the exit sign, popped the clutch, and let the engine rip. Like a burst of lightning, the GTO sped forward and flew onto Buena Vista Road.

Jorden gasped, but no one seemed to notice. She held onto the backseat to keep from flying forward as the Julian Apartments vanished from sight. She flashed back to Alex. She remembered the first time she met him. It was here last September. Nostalgia hit like an aching pain.

Jorden's stomach churned watching Nate trying to impress Darby with his driving while scaring the wits out of Jorden. She looked over at Matt. He seemed to take it in stride—more power to him, she thought. After Nate parked at a local popular restaurant, her stomach settled down. At least he hadn't chosen Amore's, which was Jorden and Alex's favorite choice.

Jorden and the others decided on the dinner special, two beef tacos and nachos with everything on them. Nate placed the order and added to it a large pitcher of beer.

Darby turned to Matt. "Where are you from?"

"Iceland." Matt didn't crack a smile.

"You're kidding?"

Nate interrupted, "Don't listen to him; he's trying to shock you. He's from Alaska. Don't forget it's our forty-ninth state, and the reason he managed to get drafted into the army."

Watching Matt's deadpan face, Jorden allowed herself to become amused by him. "Be honest with us, are you really from Alaska and all those freezing temperatures?"

"Yes. I confess I really am," Matt replied.

By then, Darby couldn't hold back, and she proceeded to bombard Matt with every conceivable question she could think of about Alaska.

After ten minutes, Matt called a halt to the questions. "Enough! You're wearing me out." His eyes wandered around the table and settled on Jorden. She couldn't help but smile to express her sympathy.

Near the end of the meal, Jorden jerked in her seat. She noticed something moving on the window ledge high above their table.

"What are you staring at?" Darby focused on the window. She squealed, "Look!" A tiny mouse raced across the ledge. Jorden barely saw it as it ducked into a crack in the wood. All eyes were riveted to the spot.

Darby got up. "Time to go!"

Jorden was right behind her. The two young women shivered outside of the restaurant while Nate and Matt paid the bill. Darby leaned into Jorden for warmth and a break from the wind. "What did you think of Matt?"

"He's okay," Jorden answered. Inwardly, she had to admit she found Matt witty and entertaining, but right now she didn't feel like sharing this with Darby. Thoughts of Alex held her back.

"Only okay? Aren't you finicky?" Darby teased.

"Hey girls," Matt called out, "the restaurant's manager assured us they have only one pet mouse, and his name is Harry. He accidentally got out of his cage tonight. No need to worry; Harry is under control now."

"You're right." Nate slapped Matt's shoulder. Both men laughed.

"You're not fooling us," Darby hooted. "Where there's one, there are more. And, they're all named Harry, and none of them are under control! My suggestion: the next time we do this, how about a different restaurant?"

"Fine with me," Nate replied. He looked from Matt to Jorden. "Come on and be a good sport. This was fun; don't you agree?"

"You bet!" Matt replied.

Jorden didn't know what to say. She liked Matt, but right now she wasn't thinking about another outing.

Matt seemed to sense her hesitation. "This was fun, but shall we let the future take care of itself."

The tightness in Jorden's chest eased. She liked his reply. She knew what her future held—Alex.

Chapter 2

October 1969

The sun was setting when Jorden noticed Nate approaching their apartment building. He and other young soldiers visited Darby and Emma Lynn most weeknights. Jorden had to admit life wasn't dull in apartment 206. Tonight, though, she didn't feel like joining the mini-gathering of constant chatter and music.

Jorden decided not to write Alex about the visiting soldiers. There was no reason to share; the gatherings didn't really affect her. Instead she would often retreat to her bedroom to work on lesson plans, grade papers, and eventually write to Alex. Weeks earlier she had written to him she hadn't gone out since he left—she was bewildered with his recent reply. She reached for his letter to reread his comment.

> *It makes me happy you haven't dated, but it is okay to go out. I know it won't mean anything. It gets old for you to sit around and just watch TV. I'm sure you'll go to parties. If you go out I want to know, but at the same time, I don't want to know. We have something unbelievably wonderful. I get nostalgic just thinking about the apartment—it brings back fantastic memories. We have memories we haven't even made yet . . .*

Jorden stared into space. Alex's reaction wasn't what she expected. After reading the passage a zillion times, she began to realize he was simply giving her space. She hoped he really meant it. As she thought about her recent outing, she knew it was of no consequence, most likely she wouldn't see Matt again.

Later that night, Darby returned to the apartment glowing. "Come see what Nate just gave me."

"What is it?" Emma Lynn stepped out of the bathroom with cleansing cream smeared all over her face. Jorden had been writing to Alex and carried her pen and paper to see what the commotion was about.

Darby stood at the entrance of the hallway and stretched out her left hand. The glitter of the diamond ring on her finger reflected off the light from the lamp in the living room. Emma Lynn rushed forward to get a closer look. "Wow! What a rock!"

"He asked you tonight?" Jorden gasped.

"Yes! I can't believe it. We'll have a Christmas wedding! I have to call Mama and Daddy."

"Slow down. Tell us more," Emma Lynn insisted. "It's beautiful!"

Jorden looked down at her own ring-less left hand. Alex wanted to wait—wait until he came back from Vietnam. He didn't want to rush into marriage, and she didn't want an engagement ring until he returned from this war. She didn't plan on dating, but she didn't want to feel completely restricted at twenty-two.

"I've got to call home first. I hope Mama will make my wedding gown—you two have to be in the wedding! Oh, save Friday night for us. Nate and I are planning a gathering at the Officers' Club around five thirty to celebrate our engagement." Darby hugged both girls before she closed off the kitchen to make her call home.

***

Friday evening, Nate arrived a little before five still wearing his Army greens. Jorden opened the door after his first ring. "Don't you look nice!"

"Thank you. It's the uniform," Nate replied. "I should wear it more often."

Jorden gave him a gentle hug. "Hey, congratulations to you and Darby."

Emma Lynn looked like she couldn't contain herself; she jumped up and gave Nate a hug and a kiss.

"Hey there, watch out you're hugging my guy," Darby replied while laughing. Her teaching attire had been replaced by an elegant black sheath dress.

"We're going to be late. No need for you girls to drive onto Fort Benning. Why not come with us?" Nate suggested.

"Who's going to give us a ride back?" Emma Lynn teased, batting her dark brown eyes.

Nate tossed his keys upward, catching them in midair. "Don't worry, we'll give you a ride if you can't lure one of those nice soldiers to take you home."

"You're awful! Darby can have you," Emma Lynn joked, appearing to be insulted.

Jorden followed Darby into the Officer's Club with Emma Lynn on her heels. Nate led them through a maze of tables before they reached the one reserved for the engagement party. In no time, recently commissioned officers joined them. Three bottles of Champagne along with bowls of nuts were on the table. Emma Lynn gleamed while flirting with the young soldiers close to her. Looking around the room, Jorden wondered if Matt would come, but then she forced the thought away.

Nate stood up to propose a toast but stopped himself. "Wait, here comes Matt." Nate pulled out a chair from the table behind them while Matt wound his way through the room, reaching Jorden's side of the table. She was glad Nate had put the seat next to her. She couldn't help finding Matt funny and interesting.

By then, all the Champagne glasses were filled. Nate continued his toast. He tipped his glass toward Darby. "To the love of my life, to the woman who will soon be my bride." He beamed as he pulled Darby next to him. "Cheers!" Glasses clinked. "Age of Aquarius" played in the background; Darby and Nate swayed to the music.

Jorden could hear Emma Lynn laughing. She appeared to dazzle the two officers on either side of her. An hour later, the gathering began to thin out. An officer named Kyle must have won over Emma

Lynn as Jorden watched him lead her to the door. A few minutes later, Jorden and Matt also walked outside the Officers' Club under the cover of the awning. Well-groomed shrubbery and trees were planted next to the entrance.

"Do you need a ride?" Matt asked.

"I do. Thank you." Jorden pointed to the building across the street. "This looks familiar."

"Maybe you've seen it on television. Lieutenant Calley has been in the news a lot. His military inquiry is going on right now. I've even seen him coming into our building."

"You're kidding." After a moment it came back to Jorden; she had seen it on television. Scott O'Brady, the local newscaster, carried the latest details on the events surrounding the My Lai tragedy. Lieutenant William Calley had been charged with killing over one hundred civilians in the hamlet of My Lai in the Quang Ngai Province of South Vietnam. The story finally broke early in September, almost two months ago.

Jorden had thought of Alex when the Calley inquiry made national news. O'Brady spoke of all the killings of innocent civilians which had been hushed up for over a year. She wondered if Alex had seen anything similar—she hoped not.

Jorden continued to stare at the building. "I can't believe the inquiry is actually happening here. History is in the making."

"I promise you it is."

"Can we go in?" Jorden asked.

"Why not." Matt caught her elbow. "Watch the curb. Hey look, the lights are on, and the entrance is still open."

Matt steered Jorden through the door and pointed toward the stairway. "Let's go up to the second floor, where my office is." The hallways had portraits of generals, battlefields, and military scenes going back to the American Revolution. His office complex was still open. The reception area contained several chairs and a large old wooden desk. Behind the desk was a row of cubicles.

"My cubicle is the fourth one, and Nate's is two down from mine. Look, you can see the Officers' Club. Now look straight down.

I saw Lieutenant Calley being escorted in from there, followed by the press."

Jorden bent over to look. "This is quite a view." She stood up, and thought she saw him glancing at her legs. Shame on him. She tugged at her dress, trying to straighten it.

Matt appeared to notice her unease and led her back to the reception area. "We better go before the cleaning crew kicks us out."

Jorden looked down at the wooden desk. A nameplate caught her eye–Eloise Butler. Next to it, a white porcelain frame held a picture with the face of a girl probably about ten, with long straight black hair, and dark brown eyes. The face looked familiar.

"What are you staring at?" Matt asked.

"This picture." Jorden picked it up. "I've seen this girl before, but she's too young to be one of my junior high students." Puzzled, she placed it back on the desk.

"That's Eloise's daughter. This poor woman has such a sad story. Her husband threatened her so many times at the textile mill where she worked they had to let her go. Her supervisor felt responsible for her losing her job, so he helped influence the head of our department to hire her."

"How awful, but fortunate she got work here," Jorden replied.

Matt led Jorden out of the building and down another block to his white Dodge Dart. The car looked familiar to Jorden. She stretched her mind, then she smiled. This had to be the same car she spotted driving around her apartment complex the other night.

While pulling out, Matt glanced in Jorden's direction. "The night's early. How about dinner?"

Jorden shifted her position to get a closer look at Matt. While he was different from anyone she had ever met, she found him curiously attractive. For this reason she should say no to dinner. Meaning, no one could come between her and Alex.

"No response. I assume you must mean yes?"

Jorden wavered, "I don't think so. I have a lot going on this weekend." She really didn't, but she thought she should explain in some way.

"Aren't you hungry?" Matt's eyes met hers with an open smile. "I sure am."

Say no! Jorden could hear her mom's voice reverberating in her mind. She knew Mom would be rooting for Alex. Even subconsciously, her mother was always trying to control her. But, she then thought, Mom was over a thousand miles away up north in New Jersey. Put her out of your mind! Jorden remained silent for a half second, then she smiled. She couldn't resist his appeal, and besides, it was only dinner.

"Why not? I am hungry!"

Chapter 3

October 1969

M att parked across the street from Amore's. He gestured toward the Italian restaurant. "I've heard they're good."

"They are good, but I'd rather not."

"Why not?" Matt looked confused.

Jorden quivered. She tried to collect her thoughts. She didn't want to talk about Alex. He was a separate part of her life—one she didn't want to share. So she just blurted out, "You do know . . . I'm getting married next summer?"

"Yes. So, what does this have to do with Amore's?" Matt turned down the radio.

"We used to go there a lot—Alex and I. It doesn't seem right."

"I know you're getting married. Nate explained your situation. I also know I'm probably going to Vietnam within the next year. There will be no commitments or attachments between us. That makes seeing you much easier—if you'll see me. Just think of me as an escort, not a date."

Jorden exhaled. "Sounds reasonable." Simple and uncomplicated. She didn't need to say anything to Alex.

"Good," Matt said, as he grinned. "Shall we have dinner with Harry again?"

Jorden laughed. "Never!"

"Okay. How about Fiona's? It's across from Columbus Square. I've never been there, but it looks nice."

"Let's try it. I haven't been there either." Jorden relaxed and leaned into the car seat.

Fiona's turned out to be a small, cozy Greek restaurant. Matt checked the menu. "How about a pepperoni pizza and a beer?"

"Sounds good," Jorden said with a nod.

"Great." Matt stepped up and placed their order. "It should take ten to fifteen minutes—time for you to tell me about yourself. You don't sound like you're from Georgia."

"I'm not, but my family's roots are in the South. I actually grew up in New Jersey. My father was transferred to Trenton when I was three. My sister and I were raised in the North." Jorden laughed, "I'm the baby; Bobbette's two years older. Can't you tell from our names, my Dad wanted a boy? But he seems happy with us." She kept talking even after their pizza and Heinekens arrived. After her second slice she paused. "Now tell me about you."

"Not much to tell." He brushed several crumbs off the table.

"I don't believe you."

Matt looked out the window. "My parents died soon after I turned two."

"I'm so sorry."

"I barely remember them. My grandmother raised me—the Athabascan side of my family."

"Ath-a-bas-can?" Jorden had never heard the term before.

"Athabascan, my Indian side, comes from the interior region of Alaska. My roots are along the Yukon River." Jorden looked at him with a blank expression.

"You don't know much about Alaska do you? Let me start over and make it simpler. Ma—I mean Grandma is my Indian side. Her husband, my grandfather, is my Irish side. He was born in Ireland but migrated to the States as a young man. Eventually, he made his way to Alaska which is where he met and married Grandma. After having several children, they moved from their village on the Yukon River to Fairbanks. My grandfather died long before I was born. I never knew him."

"So your last name, Ulster, comes from your father's side of the family—right?" Jorden asked.

"You got it. He's my Irish side. After my parents died, Grandma took care of me, and then we moved to Anchorage where I grew up."

"Anchorage." The city sounded familiar to Jorden. "I remember the gigantic earthquake. Were you there when it happened?"

"No, I was at the university in Fairbanks. We felt it, but the quake's center was almost four hundred miles south of us." Matt looked at the pizza. "Do you mind if I take this last slice?"

"Go ahead, I can't finish this one." Jorden looked at her third slice—she had hardly touched it since Matt started talking.

Matt peeled off a piece of pepperoni and plopped it into his mouth. Jorden sensed he was relieved he wouldn't have to go into more details about his background. Talking about the 1964 earthquake seemed much easier for him, for whatever reason.

Jorden had seen coverage of the earthquake televised on the news. "When did it happen?"

"Back in March of 1964. Um . . . March 27 sticks in my mind. They called it the Good Friday earthquake. It was a big one—close to 9.2."

"I remember lots of destruction from the news." Jorden pushed aside her plate.

Matt reached for his beer. "Oh there was. Downtown Anchorage got hit the hardest, along with the rest of Cook Inlet. Some families lost their homes into the inlet, but worse tsunamis followed, damaging Seward, Kodiak, Valdez and Chenega Bay."

None of those names sounded familiar to Jorden, but she could picture the annihilation. "How many died?"

"I'm not sure. Um . . . one hundred and thirty sticks in my mind but don't quote me." Matt looked at his watch. "Can you believe it's after ten?"

"Can't be," Jorden said, checking hers. "Oh, you're right." She reached for her purse to pay for her share.

"Put your purse away. This is my treat!" Matt whipped out his wallet.

Jorden's palms flew up to stop him. "Remember, you're my escort—your words. I want to pay my portion."

"Well, this escort pays for outings. My rule." Matt smiled, pushing his chair back.

"Whose rule?"

"Mine." Matt winked and strolled off.

An irrepressible smile spread across her face. Jorden had to admit she liked him. Spotting the ladies' room, she stepped past Matt as he paid the bill. "I'll be right back."

After leaving the restroom, Jorden stepped outside. "There you are! I thought you had left."

"Never," Matt replied. "It was just too crowded in there. I needed some air."

While they walked back to his car, Matt changed the subject. "Do you remember the poor woman I told you about earlier?"

"Yes, what about her?" Jorden asked.

"Well, I promised I would help her find housing tomorrow morning. Eloise, her friend Lisa and maybe her daughter, will be coming along. Why don't you come with us? You could help."

"I don't know." Jorden still wasn't sure if she should see Matt again. Then she remembered the picture of the young girl.

"Right now Eloise and her daughter are staying with her friend, but she wants to get her own place. Come with us—another opinion will help."

"I guess I could try." Jorden's curiosity about the young girl was taking over her good judgment.

Matt concentrated on the road, maneuvering the curves smoothly. He parked directly in front of Jorden's apartment building. "Hold on, I'll walk you up." At the landing her eyes met his. "Are you on for tomorrow?"

Jorden hesitated before she opened the door. She paused before saying, "I'll try."

"Good. I'll pick you up in the morning at nine thirty."

Chapter 4

October 1969

Jorden never heard Darby or Emma Lynn come back to the apartment. She had fallen asleep with her pen, paper, and Alex's letters still on her bed.

"Where are you going at this hour?" Darby yawned as she crossed paths with Jorden, leaving the bathroom Saturday morning.

"It's almost nine. I'm going with Matt to help his receptionist find an apartment to rent."

"Oh!" Darby replied.

"Take that silly look off your face. This isn't anything special. I'm just doing him a favor."

"Sure you are—and my name's Marilyn Monroe." Darby smiled. "I'm going back to bed."

Jorden ignored Darby's comment and headed to the kitchen to start the coffee. Fifteen minutes later, Matt's sleek Dodge Dart pulled up. She heard his footsteps on the stairs. This time, she opened the door with a smile.

"Are you ready?"

"I need to get my purse. Come in." Jorden's index finger went up to her lips and she whispered, "Darby and Emma Lynn had a late night—they'll kill me if we disturb them." Moments later, Jorden and Matt slipped out the door and into his car. "Where to?"

"I'm going to pick up Eloise, her friend Lisa, and maybe her daughter."

Jorden looked at the backseat. "Can three fit in there?"

"They can squeeze in." Matt assured her.

"If you say so."

"I called just before I left. Eloise said they'd be ready." Matt tapped his fingers to "California Dreamin" as he drove through an older neighborhood.

"There it is." The two bedroom house was set back off the street. Jorden watched as a middle aged blond woman stepped out, followed by a younger, dark haired woman, and a teenage girl. The girl looked like a replica of her mother, only taller.

"What's wrong? You look like you've seen a ghost."

"That's Nora, my student! I mean, she was last year." Jorden rolled down the window to get a better view. "I can't believe it's her."

At the same time, Matt got out and greeted them. "All set to go?"

"Ready as we can be," Eloise replied. "This is my daughter Nora and my friend Lisa."

Matt smiled. "The more the merrier."

Lisa leaned over and looked at the back seat of Matt's two door Dodge Dart. "Not much room. Why don't we follow you?"

"Fine, but let me give you directions." Matt huddled with Eloise and Lisa and gave them the list of apartments he planned to show them.

Nora turned and did a double-take when she looked in the car. "Miss Marshall . . . Is it you?"

"Sure is."

"I can't believe it. Mama, look who's here. It's Miss Marshall. You have to meet her."

Jorden stepped out onto the curb. Eloise turned toward Jorden.

"Miss Marshall, this is my mother, Eloise Butler."

Jorden extended her hand. "It's so good to meet you. Nora was one of my favorite students."

"Oh, she was always talking about you. She and Cheryl had a great time with your stock market project."

"Those two were the best! They outdid me. I'm proud of them."

Nora's face lit up. "Can I ride with them, Mama?"

Eloise looked at Jorden. "Nora's welcome," Jorden replied. "I'd love to hear about her high school classes."

"Are you sure it's not inconvenient?" Eloise asked.

"Not at all," Matt intervened, "she can keep us straight with the directions."

"See, Mama? It's okay."

"It's settled, Nora's coming with us." Matt waved for Eloise and Lisa to follow him.

Jorden looked back at Nora as Matt started driving. "You know, my roommate teaches at your high school. Maybe you've seen her, Darby Simms?"

"I can't believe it. Cheryl and I have Miss Simms for third period English. She's cool! I wish I could say the same for my math teacher. He's a dud! You ought to teach high school math. You'd like it."

"I bet I would," Jorden agreed.

Matt drove while Jorden bombarded Nora with questions. He kept one eye on the road and the other on the rear-view mirror looking for Lisa's car. A large sign for Buena Vista Apartments loomed before them. He put his arm out and motioned for Lisa to turn right. This was the first of four apartment complexes he had chosen.

By five, Eloise had decided on the first one. The others were too small, too run down, or too expensive. Eloise met Matt back at Buena Vista for one more look.

Lisa agreed with Eloise. "I think you're right. Buena Vista fits you the best. It's close to the base, and Nora can catch the school bus." Jorden agreed with Lisa's assessment. There were two fair-sized bedrooms and a living room with a tiny dining area. The kitchen was small but compact and overall it was well kept up.

"For the price, you can't beat it," Lisa declared.

"You're right. I can afford sixty-five dollars a month, even though it will be a squeeze. My savings will help. Thank goodness Sam didn't have access to my bank accounts back then."

Jorden listened to everything Eloise said about Sam. She could only imagine how bad it must have been.

Eloise looked at her daughter and asked, "What do you think?"

"Take it, Mama. It's the best. I just hope Sam doesn't find us."

"We have a restraining order, for what it is worth. If we have to, we'll call the police." Eloise hugged her daughter. "We'll make it work. I promise."

"Amen!" Lisa replied.

Eloise touched Matt's hand. "Thank you so much for all your help."

Matt squeezed her fingers. "Any time."

Eloise smiled at Jorden and said, "I'm so glad I got to meet you, Miss Marshall."

"Same here, but please call me Jorden." Then, Jorden turned and caught Nora's attention. "You and Cheryl remember to stop by and see me. I'm in the same classroom."

"We will. I can't wait to tell Cheryl about today. She won't believe it."

"Now let's get moving," Lisa said as she nudged Eloise. "You have to sign the lease and finish up the paperwork." Nora and her mother planned to move in the first of November.

Matt waved as they drove off. "I hope this apartment works out for them."

"I do, too. She's lucky to have your help."

"Eloise is a good person with a tough story. Thanks for coming."

"I didn't do much," Jorden protested.

"Enough for me to at least treat you to a hotdog. I think the Snack Shack is still open. What do you say?" Matt offered.

"I'm up for it." Jorden chuckled as she couldn't remember the last time she'd eaten a hotdog.

"Let's do it." It took less than twenty minutes to drive there, fill their order, and consume the chili-dogs and Cokes.

"Unbelievable. It was delicious!" Jorden licked the excess sauce off her fingers. "I haven't had anything that tasty in ages."

"Me too," Matt agreed, throwing their cans and wrappers in the trash. "How about a walk? There's a park around the corner."

"I'm in," Jorden replied. They reached the park in minutes and walked along a path lined with pines, oaks, and maple trees. She spotted a near-perfect maple leaf. Unable to resist, she picked it up and twirled it in circles. "I was shocked when Nora showed up today. You know, she stomped out of my fifth period math class last September."

"You're kidding. What happened?"

"It was a Friday afternoon. The day had been hot and humid—in the high nineties." Jorden remembered she had just put a math problem on the overhead projector. "Nora wouldn't stop talking. I had been explaining a lesson on multiplication and division of rational numbers."

"Yuck!" Matt teased.

"Don't give me a hard time. The students didn't like it either. Anyway, I went over the problem again. Nora kept talking. I cautioned her."

"Did she listen?"

"Nora quieted down a few minutes, but it didn't take long before she was back at it. Nothing I did seemed to work. Finally, I'd had enough and gave her an ultimatum: either she stopped talking or go to the principal's office!"

"And?" Matt's eyebrows went up.

"Nora rose, picked up her books, and stomped out. I thought I saw a hint of tears in her eyes before she marched down the hall. She certainly looked like a troubled thirteen-year-old."

"I hear you." Matt pushed an overhanging branch out of the way.

Jorden ducked and continued. "I went down to the school counselor's office during sixth period—which was my planning time. Edna Brown had her door open." Jorden twirled the maple leaf several more times before she let it float to the ground. "Nora told Mrs. Brown she wanted to be transferred to another math teacher. But what Nora really needed was someone to talk with about her problems at home, especially with Sam, her step-father. Edna did her best to settle her down and assured me she would be back in class on Monday."

"Was she?" Matt asked.

"She was. I never had any more problems with Nora. Actually, she became a joy to have in class. Did you hear what Eloise said today about a restraining order against her husband?"

"I heard. Sam, at times, has made her life feel like a nightmare," Matt replied.

Jorden kicked at the leaves, angry Nora had to deal with a man like Sam. "At least now I have an inkling of Nora's problems."

"I'm just glad Major Hawkins could get Eloise work in our office."

"Can you keep me updated on Nora? I'd like to know what happens to her."

"Of course I can." They walked in silence until they reached a clearing. Jorden noticed Matt eyeing the tennis courts off in the distance.

"Do you play?" Matt asked, pointing toward the courts.

"A little. Tennis was my last P.E. class at the university. I got an A, but still it doesn't say much."

Matt's eyes widened. "These look like clay courts. They're great. The clay helps slow the ball down for better control."

"I've never played on clay." Jorden squinted to get a closer look.

"Want to try? What about Wednesday afternoon around five thirty? Look, they even have bleachers. I bet I'll have to get a reservation."

"I'm not the best," Jorden said.

"I'm sure you're better than you think," Matt assured her.

"I doubt it."

"Well, I'll translate your answer into a yes." Matt smiled as he bent over and picked up an oak leaf. "This one looks flawless," he said as he handed it to Jorden.

She rolled the leaf around in her fingers. "I think you twisted my words. I didn't say I would go this Wednesday? Did I?"

Matt winked. "I'll pick you up at five fifteen."

"You're awful, but okay." Jorden had to admit she was looking forward to playing again. "Here, take your leaf back."

"No. It's for you. Save it for posterity. I guess I'd better take you home and be a good escort."

"I guess you'd better," Jorden replied with a smile.

Chapter 5

October 1969

At last Nora felt secure. Mama sealed it, signing the lease to move into the Buena Vista Apartments. Lisa had been good to them, letting Eloise and Nora share a bedroom in her home over the last year. Lying on her bed, Nora thought about her mother. She looked a lot like her, only her mother was a couple inches shorter with a slightly darker complexion. Otherwise, Nora had the same straight black hair and large brown eyes. Eloise had given birth to her at nineteen, but Nora never knew her father.

Lying quietly, she could hear Lisa and her mother's voices. Tonight she didn't have the urge to eavesdrop. She knew they were talking about the move and the new apartment. Her thoughts shifted to the nice surprise of seeing Miss Marshall. She never forgot the day she stormed out of her class. If only she could take it back—still, she was thankful for Mrs. Brown's help.

Nora went even further back in her memories when she and her mother made the hardest move ever.

***

April 1966

It happened in the spring of sixth grade. Nora had spent March and April working hard on a science project. Mrs. Welch, her teacher, paid close attention to her progress, and said so as she stopped by Nora's desk, "You should enter your project into the District Science Fair. It's good."

"It's not."

"Don't doubt yourself! Using a windmill to create energy is inspiring. Write up a good explanation, and you have a chance of winning an award."

Nora hesitated before saying, "You really think so?"

"I do."

Those two simple words inspired Nora to enter the competition. Several weeks passed and she had almost forgotten about the Science Fair until her teacher received the results. To Nora's surprise, she came in third place. She couldn't believe it.

"Congratulations! I knew you could do it," Mrs. Welsh said as she patted Nora's shoulder.

Nora grabbed her hand. "Thank you."

Mrs. Welsh smiled and squeezed Nora's fingers. "Be sure and invite your mother to the Awards Assembly."

Hurrying home after school, Nora couldn't wait to tell her mother. "Mama, I can't believe it, I won an award. It doesn't seem possible, I came in third place in the Science Fair. There's an Award Assembly tomorrow at two; please say you'll come."

Her mother threw her arms around Nora. "Terrific! I'm so proud of you." Happy for her daughter, Eloise didn't want to dampen her spirits as their lives were about to change again.

Bad news had come earlier in the afternoon. Eloise couldn't forget the foreman's words. "I'm sorry we have to let you go. With business slowing down, we need to cut back. You're our latest hire and the first to go."

Besides being fired, her landlord threatened to evict Eloise from her apartment. This was the third month she had been late and behind in rent. Either she made the payment by tomorrow or she was out. Eloise was overwhelmed. The only solution was to leave during the night as she and Nora had been forced to do in the past.

Eloise and Nora had grilled cheese sandwiches and leftovers for dinner. While they ate, Eloise's thoughts spun out of control.

Unaware of her mother's dreadful mood, Nora chatted happily about tomorrow's award assembly. "Mama, what should I wear? How about my blue and white dress? It's my favorite. What do you think?"

Eloise hesitated before she answered. She knew the news would destroy Nora.

Nora looked at her mother. "Don't you like the blue and white dress?"

"It's not the dress. I wish it was. I've dreaded telling you this since you got home." Eloise couldn't look directly at her daughter.

An alarm went off in Nora's mind. She stared hard at her mother. "We're moving again, aren't we? When?"

"Tonight!"

"We can't. I won't—it's not fair!" Tears streamed down Nora's face.

Eloise tried to explain the circumstances, but her daughter wouldn't listen. Backed into a corner, Eloise's only way out was to leave town before dawn. The more she struggled to defend her situation, the harder Nora cried as they left early in the morning. She never received the science award or saw Mrs. Welsh or her school friends again.

***

Nora stirred. She raised her hand to her cheek, surprised to feel real tears on her face. Even in the safety of her bed, her other hand was balled into a tight fist. She vowed she would never let herself be set up for such disappointment again.

Eventually, Nora's eyes grew heavy. She hoped all would be better at the new apartment.

Chapter 6

October 1969

Leaves dotted the landscape with reds and yellows. The weather was warm for the last week of October and good for a tennis game. Jorden and Matt sat on the bleachers near the tennis hut. He had reserved Court Three for five thirty.

Matt pointed toward Court One. "Look at them. They're good. The rhythm of the ball is smooth with quick, even strokes, and their forehand and backhand appear strong. The players on Court Two are also good, but Court Three is having problems."

"I'm not any better than they are." Jorden's eyes settled on Court Three.

"Watch Court One. They're a good example to follow," Matt suggested.

"They make it look so easy. Maybe we should just watch today," Jorden proposed.

"You're no fun. It'll be fine. Remember, you said you made an A," Matt replied.

"But, it was my sophomore year of college. I haven't played much since then."

"Tell you what, today we'll just volley. Next week we can play a game. What do you say?"

Jorden's frown turned into a smile. "Good, I agree."

"Come on, let's warm up and do some stretches," Matt announced as he skipped down the bleachers.

"I'd much rather run. How about a couple laps around the track?" Jorden countered. "We have ten minutes before our reservation."

"Bet I can beat you," Matt said as he ran in the direction of the track.

"Hey, wait for me!" Jorden raced down the bleachers and caught up with him.

Matt looked over his shoulder. "What are you up to?"

"Making sure we start at the same time," Jorden said before sprinting past him. "Two can play at this game." She watched him catch up with her. "Cheater!"

"Hey look at the couple on Court Three, they've given up. Come on, let's go." Matt motioned to Jorden. She watched Matt wave to the attendant in the tennis hut, who signaled them onto the court.

Matt swung with ease, lobbing the ball over the net.

Jorden hit it with gusto. The ball went out of the court.

"No home runs in tennis. Let's try again. Keep your eyes on the ball, bend your knees, and swing your racket back to anticipate the ball."

"That's too much to remember." This time Jorden hit the ball easier. She soon began to get it over the net in a reasonable fashion. The feel of the racket started to come back. The clay court did play slower and gave her better control. The hour ended before Jorden was ready to stop.

Matt checked his watch. "We've got to go."

"I love these clay courts. Thanks for your patience."

Matt winked. "You aren't too bad. I'll give you a C."

"Humph! How about a C+?"

"You need more practice. How about next Wednesday?" Matt countered. They made their way up to the tennis hut. "We'd like to reserve a time for next week?"

"You need to put down a deposit," the attendant replied. "It's three dollars." Jorden noticed he had traces of grey sprinkled throughout his dark brown hair; he looked like he might be retired military.

Matt turned to Jorden. "What do you think?"

"Sign us up. I had fun."

Matt pulled out his wallet and gave him three dollars.

"Remember, if you don't show up, you don't get your money back."

"A deal. We'll be here."

The sun was beginning to fade as Matt drove past the tennis courts. The road paralleled the park and ran into a residential area. A young woman and two small children walked along with a German shepherd. Seeing the dog, Jorden started to smile. "Tell me about your sled dogs. Were they anything like the dog we just passed?"

"What are you talking about?"

"Don't remember, do you?"

Matt kept driving. "Oh, you mean the dog team Darby asked me about. No comparison."

"Did you even have dogs?"

"No. I admit I was teasing Darby, but my neighbors did have a dog. They had a big mutt named Lucky. But Ma, I mean Grandma, didn't believe in keeping dogs unless they were smart and useful. She grew up where dog sled teams were used for transportation along the frozen Yukon River."

Jorden's jaw dropped. The rivers in New Jersey almost never froze. Milder temperatures, and also pollution, kept them open. "You're not kidding this time, are you?"

"No. Back in Grandma's youth frozen rivers were how her family traveled in the winter. They used frozen rivers like we use roads. Of course, in the summer they used boats."

Jorden knew from his tone he wasn't being playful; he was talking about a very cold place. "How does anyone live up there?"

Matt patted her hand. "Believe me, they have for thousands of years. Don't you think you'd like to try it?"

"No way! I'll take the green grass and warm temperatures over frozen rivers."

"Too bad. You're missing a lot of fun."

Matt drove up to a major intersection, stopping at the red light. He leaned over and turned up the radio when "Crystal Blue Persuasion" started to play. "I like this one."

Jorden sat back and tapped her feet to the music. Soon, Matt pulled into the last parking spot on her side of the apartment complex. "Remember, next Wednesday. Same place—same time."

"It's a deal," Jorden replied.

"Hold on. It's dark, I'll walk you up. Have you seen *Butch Cassidy and the Sundance Kid?*"

"No."

"Want to go Saturday night?"

Jorden hesitated. Her inner voice said no. Instead she replied, "Sure. I haven't seen a movie in a long time."

Loud voices and laughter boomed out when Jorden reached the second floor. She looked at Matt. "It's always like this. Want to come in?"

"I think I'll pass. See you Saturday around seven."

A voice from inside called out, "Who's out there?"

"It's me and Matt."

"Come in and join us," Emma Lynn shouted.

Matt shook his head, waved, and skipped down the stairs.

"Where's Matt?" Emma Lynn asked as Jorden stepped inside.

"Gone."

"Too bad." Emma Lynn turned back to Kyle.

Not wanting to join the group, Jorden covered the distance to her bedroom in mere seconds. She closed the door and stood there a moment before she plopped down on the bed. Her room in no way compared to the spacious bedroom she had stayed in at Alex's home last May. She remembered the large canopy bed and the pleasant sunroom off to the side. Alex's mother, Margo Whelan, had sent her a note soon after her visit to Albany. Politely, Mrs. Whelan thanked Jorden for the porcelain flower vase she had given her.

Jorden had written to Mrs. Whelan several times since then but Alex's mother was short on replies. Jorden would keep trying— she wouldn't give up. Alex wrote often, almost daily. Five months had passed since he left for this war. She still debated whether to write Alex about Matt but again decided against it. Matt was a safe distraction. They had been up-front with each other right from the start. Soon enough, Matt would be off to Vietnam, and Jorden and Alex would be married.

Chapter 7

November 1969

Alex's latest letter mentioned trying to get R&R (rest and recuperation) in Hawaii. Jorden pulled his letter from the top of the stack.

> *I heard back from my application for R&R. None in December. I don't know the right people to pull those strings. I'm trying for January and if not then, maybe in February. I'm looking forward to it, but we can't count on anything. We'll have to wait and see. Hon, I want to be with you . . .*

Jorden put the letter down and stared at the ceiling. She wanted the same, to be with Alex—he never left her thoughts especially since he left for Vietnam. She wanted to believe in the war ... she had to, or how could she justify Alex being there?

Madison, her best friend, had encouraged her to get Alex to apply for R&R. She and her husband, Luke, took advantage of it in Hawaii last year. According to Madison, the five day break was like a piece of heaven, getting away from this hated war.

Lost in her thoughts, Jorden barely heard the burst of laughter from the living room and the knock on her door.

"Jorden. You have a call," Darby called out.

"Thanks. I'm coming." Jorden managed to step around a couple of guys sprawled on the floor—two others were on the couch. Someone started playing "Light My Fire" on the stereo.

"Why don't you join us? There's plenty of room on the couch." A guy waved at Jorden, then patted the cushion. He had a beer in the other hand.

"Thanks," Jorden said as she gestured toward the kitchen. "But I have a call."

"What's going on?" Madison exclaimed on the other end of the phone line.

"Something, huh? It's like this most weeknights. I do get peace on the weekends when my roommates are out on dates. Hold on, I'll close off the kitchen." Jorden slid the pocket door out of the wall.

"Much better. How are you doing?" Madison asked.

"Busy."

"What kind of answer is that? Come on, be honest with me," Madison pressed.

"I'm missing Alex!" Jorden declared. She could imagine Madison standing there with the phone in one hand and the other one on her hip.

"Have dinner with us Friday night. Luke has a study group at seven, so we'll have time to catch up."

"You bet!" Jorden's mood instantly improved; Madison was a great sounding board. "I'll come around five."

Jorden was true to her word; she arrived on time. Luke was full of questions about Alex, the one topic Jorden loved to talk about. After dinner, Luke grabbed his backpack and was off to his study group.

"Delicious dinner," Jorden commented after Luke left. "It's great to get out of that apartment."

"Anytime. How about a walk?" Madison suggested.

"I'm up for it." Jorden reached for her sweater. The evening air was cooler since it was the first of November.

"Can't believe Halloween is over. Did you get many kids?" Madison asked, opening the front door.

"None, our apartment complex isn't much of a kid's place. Of course, we did have a pumpkin party. Did you get many?"

"Almost sixty. Luke kept count. He's so funny." Madison broke out in a huge smile. Tall and willowy, she kicked the leaves as she swept her long, shiny black hair behind her ear.

Jorden watched her friend with envy. "You look happy."

"I am. Having Luke back means everything to me. I don't know what I'd do without him." Madison looked directly at Jorden. "Now, tell me what's happening with Alex. Has he heard anything about R&R?"

"December is out. It's impossible. Maybe January or February, but nothing's definite yet," Jorden replied.

"He'll get it. It just takes time. I'm so glad Luke is back from this awful war."

"I wish Alex were back." Jorden swallowed hard, hesitating before she spoke. "I need to ask a favor?"

"Name it."

"If Alex gets R&R, I'll need birth control pills. You know, doctors won't prescribe them to single women. I can't go through the worry of this past summer. Those were the longest months."

"You've got it. My doctor just gave me a prescription for a year's supply. A couple months' worth should work for you."

"Great!" Jorden sighed in relief.

"Now you're getting smart. Have you said anything to Alex?"

"I'll wait until we know if he gets R&R. I'm not sure how he'll react." Jorden skipped forward to miss a pothole.

"You don't have say to anything. He won't have to know."

"Trust is important. I have to say something." Jorden's hand brushed against a tree trunk.

"You're right. Without trust—what do you have? Since Luke and I have known each other so long, I hope we can always trust each other."

"You already do. You made a formal commitment. I wish Alex and I had. If we were married, I wouldn't be playing tennis with Matt."

"Who's Matt?" Madison caught up with Jorden and grabbed her arm.

"No one." Jorden broke loose from her grip.

"Don't hold out on me." Madison increased her stride. "Slow down, will ya!"

"Sorry," Jorden replied as she stopped.

This time Madison took Jorden's arm and led her to a nearby bench. "Here. Sit down and tell me what's going on."

"Nothing really. Darby's boyfriend set me up for a double date with them. He was up-front with Matt and told him I was getting married next summer so no strings attached. I have to admit, Matt is nice. He then asked me to play tennis . . . which we did. But, no strings attached."

"There's nothing wrong with playing tennis. Remember, you're not married. What's this Matt like?"

"Madison, you're terrible. Listen to you. Matt's a good guy. I like his company. I've even reminded him I was getting married next summer. It suits him fine, so he poses no threat to Alex." Jorden stood up, getting impatient.

"Calm down. I didn't mean to upset you. Just tell me, have you written to Alex about him?"

"No. There is nothing to it—so I'm not going to mention it."

"Smart. I think it's good for you to get out. Take advantage of it while you're still single. It will make the time go by faster. Before you know it Alex will be back, and you two will be married."

Chapter 8

November 1969

Darby and Emma Lynn were out on dates when Jorden returned from dinner at Madison's home. Glorious peace prevailed. It was Friday night, and the apartment belonged to Jorden for the next few hours. Twirling around, she threw her arms up, jubilant to be alone. Thirsty, she poured a tall glass of iced tea with a wedge of lemon. Next, she picked an album by "The 5th Dimension" and tapped her toes to the rhythm. She had to admit she was excited about going to a movie Saturday night. She hadn't told Madison about the date—she didn't want to know her reaction.

Guilt had spurred Jorden to shop for a care package for Alex. He mentioned he had access to paperbacks, but there was a hardback he would like to have: Michael Crichton's latest thriller novel, *The Andromeda Strain*. Anderson's Book Store was her first stop. A hardcopy stood out on the display counter. It was expensive, but he was worth it. She wrapped the book and other items carefully with plans to mail the package in the morning. Relieved, she set the parcel on the dining room table and sat down to write Alex.

Thirty minutes later the phone rang and broke her concentration. It turned out to be Emma Lynn's mother. Her roommate's aunt had been in a serious car accident, and her mother wanted Emma Lynn to drive home the next morning. Jorden paraphrased her mother's words and taped a note to the refrigerator.

Jorden woke late Saturday morning. Her first thought was to mail Alex's package. She glanced in the mirror and decided not to apply makeup. Sunlight streamed in, reflecting off her smooth skin and clear blue eyes. For an instant she noticed the similarities to her mother—she quickly dismissed them, remembering the package.

Jorden slid into her jeans, jerked a sweatshirt over her head, and pulled her light brown hair back with a hair clip. She dashed into the kitchen and immediately noticed her note was missing.

"Where are you going?" Darby asked.

"To the post office, I want to get a package and letter off to Alex."

"Will you mail some letters for me?" Darby asked.

"Sure. Looks like Emma Lynn got my note?"

"She did. It really scared her. Thank goodness her mother talked her out of driving home last night," Darby said with a sigh.

"Is it serious?" Jorden asked.

"Her aunt is still in the hospital with a fractured arm, but she should be all right. They might release her today or on Sunday."

"Good. You remember when Emma Lynn told us about the awful car accident she was in which almost killed her? It's scary." Lost in her thoughts, Jorden almost forgot the package. "Oh, I better get going."

"Wait!" Darby retrieved her letters and placed them on the table. "Before I forget, there's a party in 209 tonight. Nate and I are going. Want to come?"

"I can't," Jorden answered.

"Why not?"

"I'm going to a movie."

"Oh. Could it be with Matt?" Darby smiled with her knowing look.

"You guessed it but don't read anything into it. It means nothing," Jorden insisted.

"Sure. How many times have you seen him?"

"Not many. Besides, he knows I'm getting married." Jorden swirled around to leave.

"Forget something?" Darby asked.

"What? I've got to go."

"What about your package and my letters?" Darby replied with a huge smile.

Jorden grimaced. "You distracted me." She grabbed the mail and hurried out.

Saturday night the doorbell rang at six forty-five. Matt was ahead of time. Jorden checked the peephole; he glared back. She jumped. After she regained her composure, she opened the door.

"Gotcha. Didn't I?"

"Never!" Jorden laughed. "What kind of escort are you?"

"The best! See, I'm even early. Are you ready?"

"I am. I haven't seen a show in ages." It dawned on Jorden, she and Alex rarely went to the movies. Most of the time, he arrived too late.

Jorden noticed Matt looking in her direction. Her shoulder length hair shined from the shampoo and conditioner Emma Lynn had lent her. The pale rose sweater she chose went nicely with the dark brown wool skirt which flared slightly above her knees.

"You look great!"

"Thank you." Jorden couldn't help but blush. She had now become used to Matt's distinctive features. His thick dark eyebrows arched upward to give him his Asian look. Together, they were an odd looking couple in this southern community. They drew looks of curiosity and a few rude stares. The rude ones irritated her. She wondered if Matt ever noticed them.

Butch Cassidy and the Sundance Kid turned serious in the end but was hilarious at other times. Many of the scenes got the audience howling at Paul Newman, Robert Redford, and Katharine Ross. At the end, Matt pushed open the theater's door and held it for Jorden. "What did you think?"

"Loved it." Jorden moved past Matt, thinking about how she enjoyed the characters and the South American countryside, especially in Bolivia.

"It's only nine thirty, want to grab a beer?" Matt suggested.

"Why not," Jorden replied.

They ended up at Delroy's. It appeared to be a cross between a small restaurant and a bar, with light contemporary music playing in the background. Matt ordered two beers and nachos with cheese.

"Hey, I saw your former student today."

Jorden looked up. "You must mean Nora."

"Right," Matt replied.

A smile lit up Jorden's face.

"I helped Eloise and her daughter move into the Buena Vista Apartments today."

"How nice of you."

"It wasn't just me. Major Hawkins and two other men from the office also pitched in. The major seems to be in our office a lot more since Eloise joined us. Rumor is he lost his wife a number of years ago."

"So sad. Does he have children?"

"I don't think so."

Their server appeared with a tray of drinks and their order. The aroma of the hot cheese drifted toward Jorden.

Matt lifted his glass. "Cheers."

"Cheers," Jorden replied. Hungry, she dug into the chips and drank her beer. Customers were lined up for tables; the noise level peaked, making it difficult to hear.

"Shall we leave?" Matt stood as he picked up the bill. Jorden followed behind him, trying to avoid the rush of people who wanted their table.

"Whew! What a stampede."

Matt held Jorden's arm to stop her from getting swept backward. After he paid the bill, they dodged the crowd trying to get outside, only to find a raging storm of wind and rain.

"Let's run to the car."

It took Matt over thirty minutes to drive to her apartment. Jorden could see the outline of the complex through the fogged windshield while rain resonated against the car's roof. "What time is it?"

"It's almost eleven. Don't worry, you won't turn into a pumpkin. Come on, let's make a dash for it."

Jorden's eyes adjusted to the dim light. "You're on. I bet I can beat you to the entrance."

Matt was out of the car before she had reached for her door handle. Jorden couldn't believe it when she watched him arrive at the entrance seconds before her. He held the door open with a slight bow.

"How did you beat? You tricked me!"

Matt laughed. "Don't be a sore loser." He caught Jorden's elbow and guided her up the stairs. "It's quiet."

"Weekends always are. They're the most peaceful time. Tonight it should be even quieter since Emma Lynn went home, and Darby and Nate are at a party. Want to come in?"

"Sure." Matt helped her with the door.

"Would you like something to drink?" Jorden checked the refrigerator. "All we have are Coca Colas and orange juice. What's your pleasure?"

"I'll have a Coke." Matt reached for an album by Kenny Rogers.

Jorden pulled out two bottles, popped the metal tops, and poured them into glasses. Matt stepped up behind her. She froze when she heard the silver chain reverberate against the glass. Alex had given her the bracelet last winter. The sound caught her off guard. For a second a shiver traveled down her spine as Alex's image flashed before her. What was she doing?

"I didn't mean to startle you." Matt backed away.

Matt's voice brought Jorden back to the moment. "You . . . you didn't . . . I'm fine." She twisted away before she handed him a glass.

"Thank you." Lightly, he touched her hand. "Come on, let's sit down and enjoy the music."

Jorden and Matt sat in a companionable silence on the couch, listening to music, and sipping their drinks. He reached for her hand. She could feel his fingers envelope hers with a soft stroke. To her amazement, her fingers responded in a swaying motion to the rhythm of the music. It was as if her fingers took over, longing for the feel of another person.

Matt moved closer. Their shoulders touched while he reached for the softness of her face. Slowly, their lips met.

In the background, footsteps and laughter rang out. A key turned and the door opened. Jorden scooted over. Darby and Nate's eyes widened when they saw Jorden and Matt opposite them.

"We didn't realize . . . you were here," Nate stammered. "The spillover from the party ended up in my apartment so we decided to come back here. We can leave."

"No. It's almost midnight," Matt replied and stood up.

Jorden rose and walked out of the apartment with him. "I'm sorry."

"It's okay." Matt's longing look seemed to say otherwise. "Well, are we still on for tennis this Wednesday?"

"I'm up for it," Jorden replied.

"Excellent." Matt kissed her cheek and sprinted down the stairs.

Jorden stood at the hallway window and watched him run to his car. The remnants of rain steamed up from the pavement.

Chapter 9

November 1969

Jorden wrote Alex a long letter. She needed to shake off any sense of regret. Matt Ulster wouldn't intrude on her life—she wouldn't let him. But, she would let him help her pass the time. At the end of May they would go separate ways. This approach seemed simple.

Still—sleep eluded Jorden. When she got up at ten, she found her roommate in the kitchen sipping coffee. A smile danced on Darby's lips.

"Don't give me that grin," Jorden sighed.

"What about you and Matt seated so cozily on the couch?" Darby's eyes lit up.

"There's nothing to it! I need some coffee. I didn't sleep well." Jorden reached for a cup when she noticed the empty pot.

"Nate had some this morning. I guess I'm finishing the last cup," Darby replied.

"Oh, he stayed the night?" This time, Jorden turned the focus onto Darby.

"No. Not here. We went back to his place later. Nate walked me back this morning, and I made us coffee." Darby looked down at her engagement ring and tilted it into the sunlight—no other explanation was needed.

Frustrated without her morning coffee, Jorden decided to have hot tea. She put a kettle of water on the stove and turned it on high. "Have you heard from Emma Lynn?"

"No. She said she'd be back around seven tonight." Darby took another sip before she got up and rinsed her cup. Of the three roommates, Darby always cleaned up after herself. Jorden tried and Emma Lynn rarely did. Darby stopped drying the cup and turned to Jorden. "I have a couple letters for you."

"Wha . . . what?" Jorden stammered.

"Look, Nate and I were in a hurry early last night, and I didn't notice it was your mail. Sorry, I just stuffed it in my purse on the way out and forgot about it." Darby's eyes turned downward.

A burst of annoyance flashed across Jorden's face.

"I'm sorry. I'll get them."

"Thank you." Jorden trailed behind Darby. The kettle began to whistle. Hot steam shot out with a deafening pitch.

Darby spun around and yelled, "Get the kettle!"

Jorden crashed into Darby.

"Ouch!" Darby grabbed for Jorden. Losing their balances, they ended up on the bedroom floor. Jorden looked at Darby and started to laugh. Soon they erupted into uncontrollable laughter while the kettle shrieked.

Nate banged on the door. "What's going on?"

"Come—on—in. It's not locked," Darby blurted out while she tried to catch her breath.

Nate pushed open the door. He raced to the kitchen and yanked the kettle off the burner. The siren ceased but laughter continued to bellow out from deep in the apartment. Nate followed the raucous sounds.

"What's going on?" He looked down at both roommates. They looked up at Nate and howled even harder.

"What's so funny?" Nate looked around the bedroom as if searching for clues. One side was neat, the other in utter chaos. Jorden and Darby were sprawled on the messy side. Seconds later, they calmed down.

Nate held out his hands to both Darby and Jorden and pulled them up. Darby proceeded to explain what had happened.

"Well, give Jorden her letters." Nate's eyes crinkled with mischief as he looked at Darby. "Shame on you."

Darby immediately reached into her large handbag and produced two letters; one letter was thicker than the other but both were in Alex's familiar handwriting.

"Thank you." Jorden left for her bedroom in order to savor the letters contents. Today, she yearned for assurances of Alex's love—words to ease her unrest about her possible feelings for Matt. She found a passage.

> *It's funny how sometimes you remember a person in so many different ways. One of the ways I remember you was a night late in March. I can see myself knocking on the door and there you were. You opened the door with sleep in your eyes. You were so soft and warm. It really was wonderful. I sound like an idiot, don't I? But the night stands out. There are so many other ones, but I especially like this one.*

Jorden smiled when she remembered the weekend. Easing back onto the bed, she propped up the pillows to read the second letter.

Chapter 10

November 1969

The Buena Vista Apartments worked out well for Nora and Eloise. Their furnished apartment, 12 B, was at the end of the second section of four buildings. They had two bedrooms—a welcome change from having to share one room at Lisa's home.

Every Friday night Lisa traveled across town to have dinner with them. Tonight they were having a basic dinner of meatloaf, potatoes, and green beans. The doorbell rang at six.

"It has to be Lisa. Nora, can you get the door?" Eloise stood next to the stove while she balanced a hot dish between two pot holders.

Lisa hugged Nora. "Yum—it smells good." Straightaway, Lisa stepped into the small kitchen. "What can I do?"

"Sit yourself down. You've done enough for us. Now it's our turn to take care of you. We can at least feed you dinner," Eloise replied. "Nora, Honey. Come set the table."

"Knives, forks, and spoons?" Nora asked.

"The works. We'll need them all. I even bought a pie."

"What kind, Mama?" Nora scanned the countertop but didn't find any sign of the dessert.

"Your favorite."

Nora opened the refrigerator. A lemon meringue pie with fluffy peaks of meringue brought a grin to her face.

"I swear, Nora, you look more like your mother each day."

"Don't even mention it. At fourteen it's not a compliment—more like an insult." Eloise warned Lisa.

"Oh Mama!" But, there was a ring of truth; teenagers don't like to look like their mothers.

Eloise filled their glasses with freshly brewed iced tea. After an enjoyable dinner, Nora excused herself. She knew how Lisa and her mother liked to talk.

"I'm going to call Cheryl." Nora and Cheryl had been best friends since seventh grade. They were as different as night and day. Nora's long, straight, black hair contrasted with Cheryl's bright blond curls which fell down to her shoulders and brought out Cheryl's clear blue eyes. At fourteen, both girls had almost reached their maximum height with Nora towering over Cheryl.

Without thinking, Nora dialed Cheryl's phone number. She let the phone ring at least ten times before she remembered, Cheryl and her family had gone off for the weekend. Disappointed, she returned to the kitchen.

"Careful, Nora. You've got the phone cord caught on the planter."

"Sorry, Mama." She carefully moved it to hang up the phone. Her mother and Lisa were standing at the sink doing the dishes with their backs to her.

Nora stepped back to the small dining room. She dragged her schoolbag up to the table and pulled out a couple of books to make it look like she was doing her homework. Her ears strained to listen to her mother and Lisa's conversation.

"I don't know what to do," Nora could hear her mother saying.

"Keep your distance," Lisa warned her. "You don't need to get involved with anyone just yet. Remember, your divorce still isn't quite final. Has Sam given you any more problems?"

"No, not since I got the restraining order. I'm not sure he knows where we live. Has he been by your place?" Eloise rinsed the last two glasses.

"I haven't seen his truck at all."

"It's been good for us, not having to deal with Sam. I know Nora is happier."

"Amen!" Nora mumbled to herself.

"How's your job going on base?" Lisa asked.

"Good. I'm so fortunate to have it. The office staff is great. You remember how they helped me move in here?"

Lisa nodded and said, "I do. Tell me more about this Major Hawkins."

"There's not much to tell. I've just noticed him around the office and heard some rumors."

"What kind of rumors?" Lisa appeared puzzled.

"Seems he's around the office more than usual. I'm not sure why."

"Well, you don't need to get involved with anyone at this point in your life. Look at all you and Sam have been through. You need a break. I'd hate to see you get hurt again."

"I know. I'm grateful for your concern but really, I'm okay. Not to change the subject, but I have to forewarn you, Major Hawkins and Matt talked me into inviting them for Thanksgiving dinner. Can you handle that?"

Lisa threw up her arms up as if in disbelief while a smile rose up on her face. "It's fine, but promise me you won't jump into another relationship just yet."

"Don't worry, that's the last thing I need." Eloise pushed away from the sink.

Their words set off fears in Nora. She met the major the day she and her mother moved in. He seemed nice, but she didn't trust men. After two terrible years with Sam, she wasn't ready for more turmoil. She recalled the major's image. He had a sturdy look—strapping shoulders which carried his six-foot frame with distinction. He looked a few years older than her mother, with gray hairs sneaking through his thick auburn hair.

Nora gathered her books and papers; she had heard enough.

Chapter 11

November 1969

I t was late November. The trees, nearly barren, had shed their leaves for dormant, darker times. Alex's latest letter caught Jorden off guard. She didn't know what to think. She read the first page again.

> *I hope I haven't upset you. My being Catholic seems to present problems for us. The Pre-Cana sessions I mentioned I feel troubled you. That wasn't my intention, but it's important to me for you to go. Ideally, we'd go together, but it can't happen with me over here. They're meant for engaged couples planning to be married within a year. We can work this out. I love you. Most important, I will marry you. There's no other woman for me. There are no problems we can't overcome. We're okay.*

Alex's words troubled Jorden. In her own defense, she tried to do her part and saw a Catholic priest when she flew home for her sister's wedding in June. A friend of Jorden's mother had suggested Father Capello. Jorden had made an appointment to meet with him—she remembered liking him . . .

***

June 1969

"Welcome. Please have a seat." Father Capello extended his hand.

"Thank you."

"How can I help you?" His deep brown eyes penetrated Jorden's but in a kind way.

"My fiancé, Alex Whelan, is Catholic and we plan to marry next August. Right now he's in Vietnam," Jorden explained.

"I'm sorry to hear he's over there. I'll include him in our prayer list at St Joseph's," Father Capello offered.

"Thank you. A few more will indeed help. Alex comes from a devout Catholic family, and we want to be married under Catholic vows. I'm Protestant, a Methodist, this is a problem, right?" Jorden shifted in her seat, wondering how he would answer.

"Yes and no," The young priest replied.

"I do plan to convert. I've also agreed to raise our children under Catholicism. This has been a hard decision, but I want to make this marriage work." Jorden looked solemn. "What's the next step?"

"First, I'm glad to hear you will convert. This makes quite a difference. There are classes for you and your fiancé to attend together. You will have over a year to plan and schedule your wedding. Are you considering marrying here at St Joseph's?"

"Yes. Right now I'm teaching in Georgia, but Trenton is my home."

"Not a problem. Are you coming home for Christmas?"

"I am. I get two weeks off."

"Good. Give me a call in December. You and Alex need to decide on a date for your wedding. I'll have time to see what we can work out to get you two set up for classes. Where is Alex from?"

"His home is in Albany, New York. "Will this cause a problem?" Jorden asked.

"No. You may not be able to take the sessions together, but he should be able to set them up at his diocese in Albany. You don't have to take them together, so it shouldn't be a problem." Father Capello reassured Jorden all would work out for their summer wedding.

Jorden felt pleased to have the details coming together. The priest never used the term Pre-Cana, but she figured the sessions he referred to must be the same ones Alex had written about. She assumed Alex's mother must have made the suggestion.

Tearing herself away from the memory, Jorden's eyes slid back to Alex's letter.

> *Let me try and explain. Pre-Cana conferences are for engaged couples planning to marry. I really want you to go. It's important to me. They have a lot of good information about Catholic doctrines and general information to prepare for marriage. The sessions will be valuable to you—to us. The Catholic Church considers us a mixed marriage. Doesn't that sound awful?*

The words stung. Jorden sat up and straightened her shoulders. Unbelievable. She would never have thought of them as a mixed marriage. They were both Christians, only on different spectrums of the same religion. Her eyes darted back to his letter.

> *These sessions involve a group of people. There will be a priest, a doctor, a married couple and someone else, all of the Catholic faith. The group will present helpful information on finances and other issues we will face as a newly married couple. They will talk about birth control. This is where we could have a problem. The church only recognizes one method. We'll try and make it work. With you I'll be practical. We'll be careful to space out our children— two to three kids. I wish I was there so we could go together. It's important to me for you to go.*

Jorden twisted around and sat up on the side of the bed. Her thoughts went back to their previous times together. Alex had never suggested they attend a Catholic Church service. At the time she found it strange, since she had agreed to convert to his faith. She had a sinking numbness. Why didn't they go to those sessions last January, when they talked about marriage? She would have gladly gone. Still, she planned on going, but not down here—back in New Jersey at St. Joseph's.

Jorden decided to write Alex to try and clear up the misunderstanding. She didn't see how he could have a problem with her decision—she hoped not.

Chapter 12

November 1969

Nora had never seen her mother so excited about Thanksgiving. Monday evening, several days before the holiday, she and her mother zipped over to the Piggly Wiggly supermarket, buying much more food than Nora thought they needed.

"Mama, a twenty-five pound turkey. It's huge! Will it fit in our oven?"

"Of course it will." Eloise opened the freezer door wide enough for Nora to lift it out.

"Whew, this is heavy. Grab the other end, Mama," Nora pleaded, trying to hold up her end. "I'm dropping it. Help me get it into the shopping cart." Finally, they set it down. Nora laughed, "We look like we're feeding an army, not five for Thanksgiving dinner."

Over the next two evenings, Nora helped prepare side dishes. By Wednesday night, her mother had crossed off most of the items on her list, but still she seemed anxious. Eloise's voice rose as she patted the excess flour off her hands onto her apron. "Check the turkey, Nora, and see if it's thawed."

"I can hear you, Mama. You're only a couple of feet away. It's pretty much thawed; it should be fine by morning. You need to stop worrying so much."

"You're right, I just can't help it. Go on to bed, Nora, it's after ten and we need to get an early start," Eloise replied in a softer tone.

She sunk down at the kitchen table, wiped her brow and looked up at her daughter. "Thank you, you've been an angel this week."

"It's okay Mama, I know you want tomorrow to be perfect. It will be." Nora leaned over and kissed her mother's cheek, tasting bits of flour. "I'm going to bed."

"Thank you." Eloise patted her hand.

Nora puffed up her pillow and scooted up in the bed. She was worried about her mother. Deep down, she knew it had to do with Major Hawkins. Why didn't Mama follow Lisa's advice? It was too soon to get involved with anyone after Sam. Nora was happy now without a man in her life. Can't Mama leave it alone?

Thursday afternoon, the doorbell rang at one forty-five. "That has to be Lisa," Eloise uttered as she lifted the turkey out of the oven.

"I'll get it, Mama," Nora called back as she opened the front door. It wasn't Lisa. Major Hawkins and Matt stood there. "Oh, you're early, I thought Mama told you dinner was at two. Come in, she's in the kitchen." She never heard her mother come up behind her.

"Don't be rude, Nora," Eloise intervened. "We're happy you're here."

"Smells delicious!" Major Hawkins inhaled the tantalizing aromas while he handed Eloise a bouquet of carnations and baby's breath arranged in an elegant crystal vase.

"How lovely, thank you." Eloise smiled at Major Hawkins and Matt. "Nora, please put them on the dining room table."

"Sure, Mama." Nora obeyed, putting the vase in the middle of the table which was completely set with everything in place. She knew her mother had been up since six, not stopping until the doorbell just rang. Ten minutes later, Lisa arrived to take over and orchestrate the dinner. Nora decided Lisa was her savior, as her mother now seemed preoccupied with entertaining Major Hawkins.

Still, Nora had to admit this was the best Thanksgiving she could remember. The dinner went well, with scrumptious turkey, stuffing, and all the other fixings. At the end of the meal, Nora served pumpkin pie a-la-mode and coffee. She had fun listening to Matt banter back and forth with Major Hawkins; they were funny. During a lull in the conversation, Nora turned to Matt. "Why didn't you bring Miss Marshall? You two look cute together. Besides, I can tell you like her."

"Nora, don't be impolite, asking Matt such a question. You should apologize," Eloise chided her daughter.

Matt laughed. "Nora's fine. I don't mind answering her question. I do like Miss Marshall, but we're just friends. I believe she has other plans for today."

"Well I just wondered. I like her too and wished she could have come." Nora gave Matt a knowing smile—he wasn't fooling her.

Suddenly, a truck started back-firing. The relaxed atmosphere quickly changed as Nora saw fear in her mother's eyes. Eloise jumped up, rushed into the living-room, and jerked open the curtain. A black Ford pick-up had pulled up behind Lisa's car. Seconds later, one fist after another hammered on the front door, rattling the light fixture in the entryway. Nora and the others hurried to the front room.

"Open this door . . . right now . . . you're still—my wife!"

"It's Sam!" Eloise cried out.

Major Hawkins pushed Nora back along with Eloise and Lisa. He lunged for the side of the front door, pulling Matt with him, as if he figured Sam had a gun.

"Get out of here!" The major yelled. His strong male voice must have taken Sam by surprise.

Moments later Sam began pounding again. "You ain't scaring me. She's my woman!"

"I'm calling the police. You're violating your restraining order! You'll be arrested if you don't leave now," the major yelled again, motioning to Eloise to call the police. She dashed to the kitchen and dialed the number she had taped to the phone.

Matt had stretched upward to look out the side window. "Looks like Sam is going ballistic," Matt muttered loud enough for Nora to hear. "He's glaring at the door as if he wants to kick it in."

"I'll . . . show . . . you," Sam thundered.

"He's staggering backward—losing his footing. Oh no, he's yanking a gun out of his waistband. Run—get back," Matt shouted at the women.

The next moment Nora heard a huge blast. It almost shattered her eardrums. Lisa screamed, blood was spraying from the side of her calf. Luckily, the bullet had only grazed her leg before it buried into the opposite wall.

Despite the ringing in her ears, Nora thought she heard something off in the distance. Each second the sound seemed to get louder. The roaring of Sam's engine soon became muffled by deafening sirens.

The major flung back the drapes. Flashing red and blue lights temporarily blinded Nora. She tripped over Major Hawkins trying to see out the window. The police had Sam sprawled against the side of his truck while he shouted obscenities. They patted him down, handcuffed him, and led him to the squad car. Afterward, an officer came in to check on Lisa and order an ambulance. He took statements while another officer investigated the entryway.

Thanksgiving for Nora and her mother had started out well until Sam arrived and shattered it—just like he had tried to destroy their lives in the past. Nora hated him.

Chapter 13

November 1969

Jorden looked forward to the peace of the four-day Thanksgiving weekend. Her roommates were going home for the holidays. Darby was taking Nate to meet her parents. Jorden got a chuckle out of the couple as they left Wednesday afternoon.

"Come on. We need to get going. It's at least four hours to reach your home," Nate called back to Darby in her bedroom.

"I'm coming. Just give me a few more minutes. Mama and Daddy know we'll probably be late. Don't worry!"

Nate turned to Jorden. "Women!"

"Hey—watch your tongue," Jorden warned him.

"No. Not you. You know I meant Darby. She's always late."

"I heard you!" Darby dragged herself into the front room with three bags, one over her shoulder and the other two in her hands.

"Where are you going?" Nate's jaw dropped.

"What do you mean? Home, of course!" Darby put the two bags down.

"Are you moving out? Our wedding's a month away."

"Men! Come on, Nate. Give me a hand, I need all of them!"

"If you say so," Nate replied.

"See you late Sunday," Darby said as she waved from the door. Jorden watched them from the window while they struggled to get the suitcases into the car. Nate planted a kiss on Darby's cheek before he opened the door for her. Their happiness made Jorden smile.

The next day Jorden carried a vase of vibrant pink tulips to Madison's home. Her mother answered the door. "How sweet, let me take those delightful flowers."

"Hey there, Jorden. I was about to call you. This gorgeous turkey is ready to eat. Luke, take those flowers. Mama, come help me with this," Madison called out orders.

"I've got two hands; let me get my coat off and help."

The smell of roasted turkey and the trimmings engulfed the apartment. Jorden hadn't eaten since last night and the aromas made her hungry. After finishing their turkey feast, they had apple pie with whipped cream and coffee.

"What a great dinner. I don't have to eat for a week." Jorden stood next to the door, patting her waistband.

"Stop by for leftovers this weekend. We have plenty," Madison offered as she waved goodbye.

Jorden had a hard time finding a parking space at her apartment complex. It was a day to celebrate for the soldiers, their families, and friends. Her hand automatically reached for her key to check the mail, but of course there was none today. She thought she heard a phone ringing and soon realized it was coming from her apartment.

"Hi. I didn't think you were home."

Jorden couldn't help but recognize Matt's voice. "I just got in. I had Thanksgiving dinner at Madison and Luke's. How about you?"

"Not the best. I really need to talk with you. How about going out for a couple beers?"

"Sure," Jorden replied. Her curiosity was peaked. Matt didn't sound like his typical jovial self. "Are you okay?"

"Fine. I just need to talk to you," Matt replied. "Will seven work?"

"Okay. See you at seven," Jorden agreed, though somewhat puzzled. She had a couple hours of free time. No need to change. She decided to write Alex to ask what he did for Thanksgiving. The doorbell rang as she completed the address on her letter. It had to be routed through an APO number in San Francisco, California. Alex should get it within the next ten days. Jorden placed it in her top dresser drawer. She glanced at the mirror and smoothed her hair back before going to the door.

"Come in, I'm ready. Is there any place open at this time on Thanksgiving?"

"There is one place, a section of the Officers' Club on Fort Benning. Is it okay with you?"

"Fine." Jorden still wasn't sure what was up with Matt.

The ride down Victory Drive took only twenty minutes. The Officers' Club wasn't crowded. Matt ordered two Heineken's before he began to explain. "I had dinner at Eloise and Nora's apartment. Major Hawkins and I joined them along with her friend Lisa. You remember the Saturday we helped them look for an apartment?"

"Of course I do."

"I know you want to keep up on Nora. This is the main reason I asked you out tonight."

Jorden listened as Matt took the next fifteen minutes describing the afternoon in detail. Finally he concluded, "The dinner started out well, but after Sam crashed the party it became dangerous!" Matt looked at Jorden's astonished face. "At least Lisa is fine, and thankfully no one else was hurt."

Dazed, Jorden looked at Matt. "I hope Eloise pressed charges."

"Yes! Sam's in jail with numerous charges against him. At least he's off the streets."

"Thank goodness!" Jorden sighed.

"I'm sorry, I should have forewarned you or waited until after Thanksgiving," Matt apologized.

"Oh no, I'm glad you told me. I want to know how Nora and her mother are doing. The major sounds like quite a guy."

"He is. I'm proud to know him."

"I can't believe this is happening to Nora and Eloise." Jorden looked off. She could only imagine how this was affecting Matt.

"I didn't mean to upset you—thanks for coming," Matt replied.

"I'm glad you called. Nora and her mother mean a lot to me." Jorden touched Matt's hand. "This is scary."

Chapter 14

November 1969

Nora trembled as she lay in bed. Thanksgiving shouldn't bring fear—but terror is what Sam always brought. How could her mother have married him? Then she thought of that horrible day, a year ago. It reminded her of today.

***

November 1968

Nora met Cheryl after school—they always walked home together. She wished her life could be more like her friend's. After ten minutes, they reached Cheryl's house.

The Barkers had recently painted their home a cheery light yellow with a dark chocolate trim. The house was nestled between huge pine and maple trees. Nora loved the warm, cozy kitchen, where she and Cheryl spent afternoons after school.

"Hi, girls." Cheryl's mother waved while raking the remnants of fall leaves. Nora and Cheryl waved back. "Hey Cheryl, your piano teacher called to change your lesson to this afternoon. You better get over there."

"Okay, Mama." Cheryl dropped off her school pack and dragged her bike from the adjacent shed. "Sorry, Nora. See you tomorrow."

"Why don't you stay and visit? I'm at a stopping point," Mrs. Barker suggested to Nora.

"Thank you, but I'd better get home."

Most afternoons, Nora stayed at Cheryl's until five doing homework. She liked to get home after her mother returned from her job. Today she would be early, but Sam should still be at work.

Nora's house was seven streets past Cheryl's. Using the alleyway, she took a short cut. The homes became smaller and shabbier the further she walked. Minutes later she reached Star Street, only it wasn't anything like a star. The houses on her street were worn, and her home was in the worst shape. Still, it provided a roof over their heads which was important to Eloise for Nora.

Nora stepped closer to her house and noticed Sam's truck in the driveway—a bad omen. She was glad she came by the alley; it made it much harder for Sam to see her. She tiptoed up to the side window, peeked in, and saw a bottle of bourbon on the dining room table. Sam staggered as he paced back and forth—she heard him shouting.

"What a useless foreman; he had no right to fire me! He's a lazy, worthless bum. I'll show him . . ." His voice trailed off.

Sam could do a lot of damage if provoked. Frightened, Nora decided to wait in the shed behind the house until her mother came home. She would warn her mother as she knew there would be trouble. Eloise had been very protective of Nora and, so far, Sam had left her alone.

Shivering in the cold shed, time seemed to stand still as the light of day dimmed. Nora continued to peek out the door. At last she heard the sound of a car, it had to be her mother. She stepped out and waved.

Eloise saw Nora and abruptly stopped the car and got out. "What are you doing out here?"

"Mama," Nora whispered, "I'm scared! Sam is drunk—he lost his job."

Eloise lifted her finger to her lips to silence Nora. "Let's get out of sight." Eloise led her into the shed. Nora quivered while she explained to her mother what had happened.

"You did right to hide. Here, take my jacket." Eloise hugged her daughter to help warm her.

"Mama, what are we going to do?"

"I need to see what's happening. Promise you won't leave the shed!"

"Please, Mama, let me go with you."

"No! You stay here! No matter what happens, don't follow me. Do you understand?"

"I have to go with you," Nora stammered.

"No arguments!"

Nora didn't utter a word.

"I'm counting on you to stay back. If something happens, Sam will have no idea you're out here. You'll be safe."

The shed was set approximately thirty feet behind the house, close to the alley. Eloise crept up to the left side of the house, peering into the same window Nora had. Sam was sprawled on the couch with an empty bottle of bourbon next to him. She studied the situation and decided to take the risk of going inside to retrieve her hidden cash. Over the past two years she had saved almost four hundred dollars for a day like this.

Eloise had built up cash from the money Sam doled out to her to buy groceries and household items. Since the beginning of their marriage, he insisted on managing their finances. Reluctantly, she gave him her paychecks, leaving her in the dark as to how much money they had. Never would she have agreed to this if it hadn't been for Nora. Keeping a roof over her daughter's head was her main priority.

Eloise's hiding place was in the back of their bedroom closet, behind the baseboard. She would pry it away from the wall with a kitchen knife, slip in the cash, and tap it back in place with a hard-soled shoe. Old shoe boxes covered the spot. The money had never been disturbed, so she assumed Sam didn't know about it.

Eloise hoped to get in and out of the house as fast as possible. He was a violent drunk. She climbed the three steps to the back door and slipped into the kitchen. Peeking around the living room, it appeared Sam was out cold.

Eloise tiptoed backward toward their bedroom, turned to the right and stepped forward to reach the closet. Brushing against the waist-high dresser, she bumped a small glass vase. It fell and shattered on the well-worn hardwood flooring. She stood perfectly still, not hearing a sound.

Eloise slid into the closet, bent down, and found the spot. She didn't have the kitchen knife, so instead she used her car key to pry the baseboard up and retrieve the cash. Using the familiar shoe, she lightly tapped the baseboard back into place. Swiftly, she stuffed the money into her bra and pulled down her sweater in one quick motion. Backing out of the closet, she stopped when she heard a sound. Trembling, she turned around. There was Sam.

"Going . . . somewhere? I . . . I don't think so," Sam said, garbling his words. "I can see a bulge under your sweater. Got the money didn't you? Thought I didn't know. I've been waiting for this day."

Eloise froze with fear. She forced herself to act normal. "You were asleep, and I didn't want to disturb you."

Sam lunged at her. He was so drunk he lost his balance and fell to the floor. Eloise decided to make a run for the back door. She scrambled over Sam, but he caught the heel of her shoe and slammed her down to the floor.

"No way! You're not leaving me. This time I'm going to teach you a lesson you won't forget!"

Eloise's head hit the door frame, stunning her for a moment. Sam was upright again, kicking her. She fought back, grabbed his foot and knocked him off balance. Using all her strength, she pulled herself up and ran. This time, she reached the back door. Sam picked himself up and staggered after her.

"I don't think I'm going to make it," she muttered under her breath.

Nora heard crashing sounds. In a panic, she grabbed a three foot piece of a two-by-four and ran to the back of the house. Crouching down, she watched her mother fly out the door and down the steps.

Sam's footsteps were right behind her mother's. Adrenaline raced through Nora as she jumped up and slammed the two-by-four into Sam's back, knocking him down the steps. She heard his head hit the ground. Shaking, Nora gripped the club with all her might. Slowly, she approached him. Hearing a groan, she stopped.

Sam struggled to get up before slumping back down. Nora caught a glint of hatred in his eyes.

Her first impulse was to clobber him again, until she heard her mother call out her name. The sound of her voice stopped her.

"I'm coming, Mama! I'm right behind you."

Eloise and Nora raced to the car. The motor roared to life. Putting the car in reverse, Eloise backed out. The tires sprayed gravel as she straightened the car and raced down the alleyway. She drove like a crazy woman until they reached town.

What should she do? She thought of Lisa. Eloise had worked next to her friend over the past two years, during which time they became close. Lisa was the only one who knew about her situation with Sam.

Eloise looked at Nora. "I'm going to call Lisa. I hope she'll take us in." Driving around another five minutes, she spotted a payphone at a Texaco station.

She watched her mother hang up. Soon, her fists raised up as a victory signal. "It's a go. Lisa said to come over," Eloise shouted as she stepped out of the phone booth. She got in the car and sat still for a long time.

"Mama, talk to me. Are you okay?" Nora waited, but her mother didn't say anything. "You're bleeding. Please, let's go to the police first."

"I can't—not yet anyway." Eloise feared what Sam would do. "The police always give the man the benefit of the doubt. They would tell us to go back home and work it out. I will never do such a thing. Lisa's home is the best place for us. Please try and understand."

"Anything to get away from Sam!"

***

Nora shuddered in bed. She turned over, unable to sleep. Memories from a year ago continued to shake her. She hated Sam. What better day than today, Thanksgiving, for the police to arrest him! With those thoughts, her eyelids became heavy.

Chapter 15

November 1969

Alone letter arrived in Jorden's mailbox the day after Thanksgiving. Usually Alex's letters came in batches of two or three. Maybe the holiday had something to do with it. She tore open the envelope.

> *I already feel remorse for the last letter I sent you. I'm referring to the one about my being Catholic and the Pre-Cana classes. I haven't even heard from you but I feel I have upset you which wasn't my intention. I shouldn't write this, but I will. I want you to know my religion won't interfere with our marriage. Honestly, it won't come between us. I want to make you happy. I can shut my eyes and see your face. I love you. You're most important.*

Jorden closed her eyes. She had to be more understanding of his Catholic faith. The doctrine anchored him to his family and upbringing. Like breathing, this was part of his life. She would honor her commitment to convert to his Catholic faith—but she was happy he was also willing to bend. Her eyes darted back to the page.

> *Now the good news! I got my R & R in Hawaii. It's not the date I put in for but I hope we can make it work, January 17 through January 21. A couple months gives us some time to work out the details and get reservations. I can't wait to see you, just to hold you in my arms.*

"Yes, Yes, Yes!" Jorden danced around the kitchen. She stopped to look at the calendar; January 17 was a Saturday. She had to call Madison.

"Guess what?"

"I don't have a clue. Spit it out," Madison demanded.

"We're going in January!" Jorden stammered.

"Going where?"

"To Hawaii!" Jorden exploded.

"You and Alex?"

"Who else! I can't believe it." Jorden twirled around again.

"Great! You two deserve it. Now—get yourself over here and pick up those birth control pills. When did your last period end?" Madison quizzed Jorden.

"Yesterday."

"Good. You can start them right away. Now you'll be protected," Madison said with a sigh. Silence followed. "Jorden, are you there? You still plan on taking them—don't you?"

"Definitely! I just don't know what I'll tell Alex. You know he's Catholic and against birth control."

"So what, he doesn't need to know."

"I have to tell him," Jorden mumbled. "But no matter what he writes, I'll take the pills."

Jorden wrote Alex right away, but waited until the end of her letter before she mentioned the pills. She tried to be positive and read her words out loud.

> *"I have great news. Madison is giving me birth control pills so we can be together. We won't have to worry. I'm doing this for us. I hope this is all right with you. Please let me know what you think. I love you and want to be with you."*

She hoped Alex wouldn't be upset. Even if he was, Jorden wasn't taking chances.

The next day, Madison handed Jorden two circular disks. "It's crazy you can't get birth control pills from a doctor. You're twenty-two—more than old enough to make this choice. I guess it's one way the state of Georgia pushes the issue of morality down our throats."

"Amen! I wholly agree." Jorden turned one of the disks over to read the directions.

"They're easy to take—one pill every morning until your period comes. Repeat after your period is over."

Jorden held onto the disks. It was hard to believe these little pills gave her the power to take charge of her body. Whatever Alex thought, her mind was made up. She looked up at Madison. "Got a glass of water?"

"You bet! You're making the right decision."

Jorden pushed out the first pill and let it rest on her tongue. She reached for the glass and downed the water. "I've done it—started the process."

"Have you written Alex?"

"I wrote him last night. I hope he approves or at least he's happy for us." Jorden figured it would take a couple weeks before she would know his answer.

"He shouldn't upset you so much. I think Alex is being selfish. Don't have any regrets."

"I won't. Thank you, Madison."

"Any time." They heard the front door open. "Luke has to be back. Hey Honey, we're in the kitchen," Madison called out.

Jorden slipped the disks into her pocket.

Luke gave Madison a kiss. "What are you two conjuring up?"

"We're solving the world's problems," Madison replied.

"We sure are," Jorden agreed. "Now I better get going."

"Stay for dinner. We're having turkey sandwiches."

"Again? Let's go out for a pizza," Luke shot back. "I'm sick of turkey."

"You poor thing!" Madison leaned into Luke to push him off balance, only he didn't budge.

"I'm not cutting into this high-powered debate," Jorden declared as she headed out of the kitchen.

"Come back here!" Madison shouted at Jorden.

"I'll call you next week. Enjoy the pizza!" Jorden could hear them laughing as she opened the front door.

Chapter 16

December 1969

Emma Lynn had just completed her student teaching and would graduate in one week. On top of this, the principal at her school had already offered her a job. One of the second grade teachers had to take maternity leave. This delighted both Emma Lynn and Jorden. After Darby's wedding, they would still be roommates.

With Thanksgiving over, the Christmas decorations started coming out. Darby and Emma Lynn had their hearts set on a live Christmas tree, not an artificial one. They recruited Nate and Kyle to help them. Emma Lynn had been seeing Kyle since Darby and Nate's engagement party in October.

Jorden couldn't believe her eyes when she swung open the door. "Wow! What a tree!"

"Turn it around. The treetop should go in first," Emma Lynn insisted. "Honey, move it the other way."

"Make up your mind," Kyle stammered under the weight of the tree.

"Hey, I got it." Nate picked up the mid-section. "Darby, you and Emma Lynn pick up the top portion, and we'll get this in quicker."

"Ouch! It's prickly," Emma Lynn cried out.

"I'll get it." Darby stretched and lifted the top portion. "Got it. Let's move it in." They lifted it through the door and plopped it into the tree holder.

"Too far to the right, no more to the left," they taunted Nate. Five minutes later, the tree stood as straight as it was going to get.

"It's a beauty. We did well!" Emma Lynn exclaimed.

"We?" Kyle looked up at Emma Lynn.

"Yes, we! Hey, let's have a decorating party."

"Great idea," Darby agreed. "We can partially trim it Thursday night, and Friday night we'll have a popcorn stringing party to finish it up."

"Jorden, you've got to invite Matt," Emma Lynn proclaimed. "The more the merrier."

Jorden wondered if he would join them. They usually saw each other only on Wednesday and Saturday nights. To her surprise, Matt accepted when she asked him Wednesday night.

Thursday night, after they partially trimmed the tree, Emma Lynn blew a kiss to Kyle. "Where's the mistletoe?" she asked.

"We don't have any," Darby answered. "I'll put it on my list."

"We can put it over the kitchen doorway. Here—right here." Emma Lynn pointed up to the spot. She looked at Kyle with a devilish gleam in her eyes. "Now, who can show me how it's done without the mistletoe?"

All eyes were on Kyle as he swept Emma Lynn off her feet and planted an amazing kiss on her lips.

Nate, not to be outdone, pushed the couple out from under the empty spot, and swept Darby into his arms for his version of a dramatic kiss.

Jorden watched the couples while longing for Alex. She wished he could sweep her up in his arms.

By Friday night, the Christmas tree had two sets of lights, ornaments, and the sparkle of tinsel. Emma Lynn bent down and plugged in the tree's lights. She gazed at the tree while the popcorn popped in the kitchen.

"Our fifth batch is almost done. Think we have enough?" Darby asked.

"Plenty. We can always pop more if we need it. Come look at the tree."

Darby looked up. "Wow! It's incredible! Now all we need to do is to string the popcorn. Did you get needles and thread for everyone?"

"I took care of it after school today," Emma Lynn replied.

"Good. We're set. Hey, Jorden, get back out here," Darby called out.

"I'll be there in a minute." Jorden was writing Alex her latest news. At the end of the school day, she finally got the courage to ask her principal for leave for the trip to Hawaii. It was a delicate matter. She stretched the truth and told him both of their families were going to meet in Honolulu. He granted his approval; but she doubted he believed her story.

"What can I do?" Jorden asked.

"Fill these bowls with popcorn. I want everyone to try their hand at stringing some," Darby answered.

"How many?"

"At least twelve. We'll have a full house. Is Matt coming?"

"Surprisingly, he is," Jorden said with a smile.

"You two look cute together. Matt's a sweetie!" Emma Lynn smiled. "Come on, Jorden, help me set up the mistletoe—I don't want to fall." Jorden held the ladder while Emma Lynn climbed up and pounded in the mistletoe. "Got it."

Thirty minutes later, the party began. Spiked eggnog and beer flowed freely. It was a full house. Jorden made sure each person received a needle and thread, a thimble, and a bowl of popcorn to string. The doorbell rang around eight.

"Whose there?" Emma Lynn jumped up to get the door. The spiked eggnog flowed through her veins. "Hi, Matt. We thought you'd never get here." She gave him a big hug.

"Jorden, look who's here." Emma Lynn steered Matt toward the kitchen, grabbed Jorden's arm, and centered them under the mistletoe. "Jorden helped me put this up just for you." Everyone laughed and clapped while Matt and Jorden stared at each other.

"Go on. Give her a kiss."

To play along, Matt took Jorden in his arms. Dramatically he arched her back and planted a kiss on her lips. No one realized sparks were flying between them.

It was quite a night. Jorden and Matt strung two long laurels of popcorn which they placed impressively over the lower limbs of the tree. Many smaller strands were placed above theirs, emphasizing the number of people who had added their contribution to the tree. Matt was the first to leave around midnight.

Jorden walked him out to the hall. "Thanks for coming."

"My pleasure," Matt replied. "How about seeing *Easy Rider* tomorrow night? I haven't seen it since it was released."

Jorden didn't hesitate. "I'd love to."

"Good. Pick you up around seven."

Jorden waved as Matt disappeared down the stairs.

***

The next morning, Jorden looked up as Emma Lynn dragged herself upstairs after the night of partying.

"Where have you been?" Darby teased while she sipped a mug of coffee. Jorden stood in the kitchen pouring milk over her cereal.

"Nowhere—and everywhere," Emma Lynn sighed.

"What's up with you?" Sometimes Darby acted like an anxious mother hen, probing to find out more. "Are you okay?"

"I'm great. Never better. Do I look different?"

"What's that supposed to mean?" Darby looked directly at Emma Lynn, awaiting an answer. The three roommates had become close; each watched out for the other.

"Nothing."

"Nothing, my foot! I can see it in your eyes. Do you know what you're doing? You hardly know Kyle." Darby looked worried. "Now sit down and tell us what happened."

Jorden forgot about her cereal and concentrated on the conversation as she stepped into the living room.

"I don't know—only last night was heavenly. Maybe I'm getting in too deep, but I don't care. Besides, you haven't known Nate long, and you're getting married in a few weeks." Emma Lynn tapped her fingers on the couch, circling the ribbing on the upholstery. "How can you be an expert on timing?"

"I'm not. That's true, but it's different with us. Nate has already served his time in Vietnam. After two tours, he doesn't seem worried about going back. Kyle, on the other hand, is probably worried about going over there," Darby replied, trying to make her point.

"So! What does that have to do with how long you've known Nate?" Emma Lynn's fingers stopped. She scowled at Darby.

"I can't explain it; the deep feelings Nate and I have for each other."

"And I don't have the same feelings?" Emma Lynn protested.

"I didn't mean to imply you didn't. I just don't want to see you get hurt." Darby said with a compelling voice.

"Let's have a truce," Jorden exclaimed, sitting across from Emma Lynn and Darby. "Neither of you is making sense."

Both roommates glared at Jorden as if she had no right to talk. Emma Lynn got up and retreated to Kyle's apartment. Darby got up and went to her bedroom.

Jorden sat there bewildered. She didn't mean to cause trouble, but she knew this would blow over. Her mind shifted to pleasant thoughts. She couldn't help but smile when she thought about Matt's kiss under the mistletoe.

Chapter 17

December 1969

T he holidays approached swiftly. This year, Jorden planned to fly home to New Jersey. She had also made airline reservations for Hawaii, making her spirits soar at the thought of seeing Alex in Honolulu. He had sent a copy of the hotel reservation confirmation, making her smile—but the smile soon faded when she read some of his latest thoughts.

> *In your last letter you asked me what I thought about Madison giving you a supply of birth control pills to begin taking before you come to Hawaii. I can't really tell you what I think. I'm mostly concerned for your health. Some women have suffered blood clots and even strokes. I would never ask you to do anything to endanger yourself. Jorden, you know I love you and want to be with you. I know how much you love me. Believe me—it makes me feel good.*
>
> *I suppose if you don't take a chance, you'll be taking a lot of other chances, such as getting pregnant. I don't think you are awful, you are beautiful. I guess what you're doing is all right. I think it's okay. If you have any doubts, please write and tell me. I promise we can be strong. I don't want to do anything to hurt you.*

Tears welled up in Jorden's eyes. At least Alex halfway gave his approval. She would interpret his answer as a yes, but she knew birth control would continue to be a problem between them.

On the bright side, Darby's wedding preparations were going at full speed. She had been speaking with her mother on a daily basis since the beginning of December. The long distance phone bills were expensive, but she needed to get the details of the wedding in place.

"Don't worry, Mama. We're driving down this weekend. You can fit my dress and make the alterations then. The church is reserved, and the invitations are ready to send."

"I'm sure Mama worries more than I do," Darby announced to Jorden and Emma Lynn after she hung up with her mother. "I'm bringing your dresses back to make sure they fit. They're dark green velvet with matching lighter green satin bodices. You'll love them."

Jorden knew Darby wouldn't hear whatever she and Emma Lynn said. The wedding plans mesmerized her and dwarfed all else.

The doorbell rang at seven. Jorden got up to answer it. She checked the peephole and there stood Nate. No surprise. He was like another roommate, only he didn't live with them. She ushered him in and called out, "Darby, its Nate."

Darby came out with a long list. "Come on Nate, you can help me check these off. Mama's driving me nuts over all the wedding details. I told her we were driving down for the weekend, but she still worries."

Nate watched Darby clear off the dining room table top to make space for him. Instead of joining her, he stepped back toward the door. "Come on, Darby—let's go for a drive and clear our heads of all these wedding preparations."

"Okay, but there's still a lot to do before we leave on Friday."

Jorden noted how Darby reluctantly got her coat and put the list in her pocket. At the same time, she saw how Nate's eyes scanned the room, noting the Christmas tree and all the decorations before he opened the door.

Kyle skipped up the stairs as Darby and Nate walked down.

Darby yelled at Emma Lynn, "Kyle's coming!"

"Where are they going?" Kyle asked while giving Emma Lynn a hug.

"For a ride."

"Nasty night out. Looks like it wants to snow. I'd rather be in here." Kyle's eyes darted from Emma Lynn to the mistletoe. Jorden took the hint and left.

Darby returned around nine thirty.

"Where's Nate?" Kyle asked.

"Gone."

"You didn't ask him in? Did you have a fight?" Emma Lynn raced to the door to call his name.

"I told you, he's gone." Darby threw her coat down.

"Gone where?" Emma Lynn looked puzzled.

"Away. The engagement—the wedding is off." Darby looked down at her left hand—the engagement ring was no longer on her finger. "It's over!"

Jorden heard the commotion and peeked out of her bedroom.

"Why?" Emma Lynn asked.

Darby ignored her question. On the verge of tears, she rushed by Jorden. Darby didn't say a word, entered her bedroom, and slammed the door.

After Kyle left, Emma Lynn approached their room. She could hear Darby sobbing. "Let me in—please. Tell me what happened."

"Leave me alone. I don't want to talk about it!" Darby called back.

Softly, Emma Lynn spoke, "Remember it's my room, too. I need to get ready for bed. Please let me in."

Jorden could hear them from her room and stepped out into the hall. Little by little, Darby opened the door. Her eyes were red. Emma Lynn held out her arms. At the same time, Jorden joined them. The threesome stood together until a sob broke the silence. Emma Lynn led Darby to her bed. "Tell us what happened."

The words began to spill out as Darby caught her breath. "Nate . . . he . . . thinks he's going to be sent back to Vietnam. Rumors are going around, and he's scared. This would be his third tour. He's even received medals, including the Purple Heart. He didn't think he would be sent back again and wants to postpone the wedding. I've never seen him so distraught." Darby's voice cracked with another sob.

"Maybe he's wrong. Has Nate gotten his official orders?" Jorden asked.

"I don't think so. But . . . even the possibility is putting him over the edge." Darby sobbed along with a hiccup.

"You know my friend, Madison, she married Luke before he left for Nam. Lots of couples marry before they're sent over there. Can't you talk some sense into Nate?" Jorden persisted.

"I tried! He says he can't go and feel responsible for a wife back home. He's seen the horrors of war and other things which happen. He wants to postpone the wedding. We went back and forth. I couldn't budge him. Exasperated, I finally called it all off—the engagement, the wedding, everything!"

"Is that what you want?" Emma Lynn looked directly at Darby.

"No!—Yes! I don't know what I want . . . only . . . I felt like I was put on hold with no end in sight. I hate this! It's killing me!" Darby's hands flew over her face.

"What do we say? You know people will want to know," Emma Lynn asked.

"Just tell them there won't be a wedding and the engagement is off. If they ask more, tell them you don't know anything else." Darby looked from Emma Lynn to Jorden.

"Okay. We can do that," Jorden agreed.

The next day, Jorden and Matt changed their plans from tennis to see a movie, *The Sterile Cuckoo,* starring Liza Minnelli. The outside temperatures were in the twenties, too cold for tennis. Jorden had forewarned Matt on the phone about Darby and Nate's broken engagement. She could tell he was shocked. After Matt arrived, Jorden tried to persuade Darby to join them but she declined— wanting time alone.

"Did Nate say anything at work about the broken engagement?" Jorden asked as Matt drove away from her apartment.

"Not a word. They seemed happy. Do you know what happened?"

"Darby didn't say much—just the engagement and wedding were off."

The movie turned out to be depressing. The story centered around two freshmen college students who fell in love then the relationship turned sour. The young couple split in the end. Jorden was relieved Darby hadn't joined them. She didn't need the same message again.

Matt pulled into a parking space close to Jorden's apartment entrance. He looked up at her second floor window. "Do you think there's a chance Darby and Nate might get back together?"

"I—I don't think so. Darby seemed final about the decision."

Matt reached for Jorden's hand and wound his fingers around her delicate ones. "Life is short." He touched her cheek and pulled her close. Their lips met.

Chapter 18

December 1969

Jorden's good mood was spurred by the coming holidays. When she returned from New Jersey, the trip to Hawaii would be on the horizon. She hadn't told her parents about it; she would when she got to Trenton. They may not approve, but the decision rested on her shoulders.

The phone startled Jorden. "Matt here. Are we still on for tonight?"

"I am. How about a movie?"

"How about something a little more exciting?" Matt replied.

"Like what?" Jorden looked up, wondering what he was thinking.

"A night of dancing on base at Custer's Rendezvous."

"Great! I feel like dancing." She tapped her fingers to the radio playing "Solitary Man."

"Good. I'll pick you up around seven thirty."

The doorbell rang at seven fifteen. Jorden threw her robe over her slip. She looked out the peephole, and there was Matt.

"Hey. You're early. I'm only half-dressed," Jorden managed to reply.

"Are you going to make me wait out here?"

Jorden smiled at the first time she had kept him waiting. She turned the doorknob and peered out.

Matt could see her rose-colored robe. "Hey, nice outfit."

She opened the door wider. He swept past her. By eight o'clock they were on their way.

"You mean they have a dance spot on base?" Jorden couldn't believe it.

"Sure do. My roommate, Chip, told me about it. He said we should check it out." Matt rounded the curve, and the lights lit up Custer's Rendezvous. "There it is."

They danced several sets to a live band. The final song to this set was "Holly Holy" a slow one. Matt held her close as he hummed the words and swayed to the rhythm of the music.

"I don't want to, but we'd better go," Jorden whispered. "I'm flying out of here early tomorrow."

"You're right. Let's go."

When Matt drove into the Julian Apartment complex, Jorden noticed most of the parking spots were empty. Few Christmas lights illuminated the windows since most of the tenants were on holiday leave.

"It's eerie," Jorden exclaimed.

"Come on. I'll go in with you." Before he got out of the car, Matt lifted a shopping bag out of the backseat.

"What time is it?"

"It's a little after midnight. Not too late." Matt walked her into her apartment. He turned toward the tree and plugged in the lights, adding to the aura of the night.

Before Jorden knew it, Matt had stepped into the kitchen. She heard an explosion followed by a crackling fizz.

"What's going on?"

Matt held up a Champagne bottle. "Let's celebrate. It's close to Christmas, and our last night together. I thought bubbles would be appropriate. Why don't you put on some music? We'll share a toast—for you and me."

Jorden stared at Matt—then she grinned. "Why not? It's a special occasion and you're right—we never have this place to ourselves. I'll put on an album."

He poured Champagne into two small juice glasses.

"Here's to you—to us—and this Christmas season and . . ." Matt stopped and didn't finish the toast.

And many more, Jorden thought. She knew that would never be the case. This Christmas was it.

"You know . . . what I mean," Matt hesitated—their eyes met.

Jorden clinked his glass as they sat down to enjoy the sparkling wine, the music, and the warm glow of the Christmas lights. A mischievous gleam seemed to shine from Matt's eyes.

"What are you up to?" Jorden knew the look. He only meant trouble.

On the sly, Matt reached to the side of the couch and brought out a shopping bag.

"What's do you have there?" Jorden tried to peek inside.

Matt grabbed the bag and lifted out a box wrapped in Christmas paper and placed it on the tabletop.

"But. . . I didn't get you anything!" Jorden responded.

"Just open it."

Excited, Jorden lifted the box by its ribbon. It felt light. She shook it—no rattles. She sniffed—no smells of chocolate. She tore into the Christmas wrap and yanked off the top of the box—a pink and white plastic football.

Matt howled, "You should see your expression. Fooled you. Now we can play touch football. What do you think?"

"You're crazy." Jorden laughed and juggled the lightweight football in her hands. At the same time she stood up and stepped into the kitchen. Twisting, she threw a fast pass at Matt. Agile, he caught the ball in midair but caught his foot on the coffee table and ended up sprawled on the floor.

"I'm sorry. Are you all right?" Jorden ran back to the couch and leaned down to help him.

Matt lifted his head—their eyes locked. "You're too late."

Hearing the tease in his voice and seeing the smile on his face, Jorden shoved him further down with her foot. "You're awful." She picked up the pink and white football and rotated the dual colors in her hands.

"Now I don't feel bad I didn't get you anything." While Jorden played with the ball, Matt reached deeper into the bag and pulled out a much smaller parcel. Before she knew it, Matt placed another gift on the table.

"What's this?" Jorden was captivated by a silver box. It was topped with an elegant bow; no Christmas wrap this time.

"Open it."

Jorden picked up the box and slid the bow off. An inner box rested inside. On the top were the words, "Today is the Time to Shine." Carefully, she pulled open the lid and there lay a small gold pendant.

"It's beautiful." Jorden looked at the satin backing of the jeweler's box—Yukon Gold. Slowly, she lifted out the pendant. Her eyes strained to read the tag, Alaska Gold Nugget.

"I've never seen anything like this." Jorden turned it over. The backside was smooth while the front was rough.

Matt watched as she turned over each side. "The front is gold nugget, panned like the Alaska pioneers did. I hope you like it."

"I love it. It's so different." Jorden slipped the chain over her head. It stood out on her soft wool sweater.

"I called my cousin in Anchorage, and she picked it out for me. She did a great job of getting what I described. I thought about a heart, but it didn't seem appropriate for an escort."

Jorden reached for his hands and gave them a squeeze. "Thank you."

"This you can wear without any explanation, but I hope it will carry a special meaning."

Jorden raised her hand to touch the pendant. The silver bracelet, the one Alex had given her last winter, crossed paths with the gold pendant—it went unnoticed as Matt pulled her close. She swayed to the music, leaning into him.

A lone car's backfire startled Jorden. She looked at Emma Lynn's crystal clock and realized it was after two o'clock. "It's late."

"Can't I stay? No one's here. No one will know."

"I will."

Matt seemed to sense the answer in her clear blue eyes. "All right. I'm going . . . but at least let me drive you to the airport tomorrow. Deal?"

"Deal. Thank you."

Matt pulled Jorden close and kissed her—a lingering kiss.

Chapter 19

January 1970

The Christmas holiday flew by. The two weeks in Trenton with Jorden's family seemed too short and now she was already in a cab, riding back to her apartment in Columbus, Georgia. The cab driver never stopped talking.

"Where are you from?" He asked. "You don't sound like you're from Georgia."

"No. I'm from New Jersey."

"Thought so. What brings you here?"

"I'm a teacher."

"Oh. You look too young. I thought you might be a college student."

Jorden didn't say anything. The cab driver's constant questions irritated her. She watched him turn into the Julian Apartment complex.

"Where to?"

"Apartment number 205." Jorden didn't want him to know the exact number. "Drive to the right." She put her arm up to stop him. "There—there it is. Just pull over here."

Jorden glanced at her watch, surprised to see it was after eleven. The cab driver hopped out, retrieved her two bags, and hauled them into her apartment entrance before she could stop him.

In the lighted area, Jorden noted he appeared to be in his late thirties. She watched him sweep his unruly hair back while his eyes followed her legs. She felt uneasy.

"Up?"

"I can get the bags from here," Jorden replied.

"No problem." He pointed to the stairs and lifted the luggage with ease.

Jorden didn't know what to say.

"Here you go." The cab driver placed the suitcases at the top of the second floor. He smelled of cigarettes as he moved closer to Jorden.

"I'm at the end of my shift. How about going out for coffee?"

Her palms began to sweat. She stepped back to increase the distance between them.

"It's late. My roommates are expecting me." They weren't due until tomorrow, but he didn't need to know they weren't there.

"Oh." He sounded put off as she watched him stare out the hall window.

At this moment, all Jorden wanted was Matt by her side. Her safety net.

"Well then, it will be five dollars and sixty cents," he countered.

Jorden rummaged through her purse and came up with seven dollars. She decided the amount was more than enough.

A surly look came over him. He tromped down the stairs without uttering another word.

Jorden held her breath until she heard the main entrance door close. She sighed and watched him turn his taxi around and drive out. Usually Jorden cherished a quiet apartment—but not tonight. She entered the kitchen and reached for the wall phone. Without thinking she dialed Matt's phone number. No answer. She missed him.

While at home, only once did she mention Matt's name. She felt her family wouldn't understand their relationship. Too complicated, especially with her plans to marry Alex next summer. Thinking of it, her father never seemed to like anyone of the opposite sex she brought home.

Both roommates returned on Sunday afternoon. Emma Lynn arrived first, around three o'clock.

"I'm back. I can't wait to start teaching tomorrow. My first real job." Emma Lynn was taking over a second grade class for a teacher who was in her second trimester of pregnancy. This time the government's position was in Emma Lynn's favor, but she knew the teacher she was replacing was terribly upset at being forced to take a leave of absence. Though sympathetic, Jorden knew Emma Lynn tried not to dwell on the other teacher's misfortune.

"Hey, Jorden. Is Kyle back yet?"

"I don't know. The apartment complex was quiet last night. I got in after eleven."

"How was your holiday?" Emma Lynn asked, dragging her suitcases back to her bedroom.

"Good. How about yours?"

"Great. I had fun ... but I missed Kyle. Tell you what—I'm going down to see if he's here. These suitcases can wait."

Darby drove in around six. Her entrance contrasted Emma Lynn's boisterous one. Jorden figured the return home must have been hard. She came from a small town where everyone knew she had called off her wedding.

"How are you?"

"Okay. It was difficult, but Mama and Daddy were great. It was refreshing to have them treat me like an adult."

Several days went by without a word from Matt. He knew she was going to Hawaii to see Alex, so Jorden figured he was wisely backing off. Still, it hurt—but she knew she needed to let go.

Move on! Jorden told herself. The visit with Alex took precedence over all else. She couldn't wait to see him. Her scheduled departure was set for seven thirty Friday morning. Madison promised to take her to the airport.

Chapter 20

In-Flight to Hawaii,
Friday, January 16, 1970

A bright day greeted Jorden on her journey to Hawaii. She had waited eight months for this moment; she could already picture a Hawaiian sunset. The first leg of the flight took her to Atlanta, then to Chicago, over to Los Angeles, and ultimately on to Hawaii.

The aerial view of Columbus was stunning. Gazing out the window, Jorden watched the city vanish from sight. Her mind drifted back to the fall of 1968, more than a year earlier. She remembered the first time she met Alex. It was a Wednesday night late in September. A party was underway at the Julian Apartment complex. She didn't want to go, but Madison, her roommate, and a couple of neighbors insisted.

***

Previous Year – Columbus, Georgia – September 1968

"Come on, Jorden!" The tall girl insisted.

"We don't want to walk in by ourselves," the short redhead piped up, "we need you."

"You don't need me. It makes no sense," Jorden retorted.

"Think of it as helping out friends," Madison replied.

"I said I don't want to go," Jorden reiterated.

"Yes, you do. I want to listen to music and write Luke in peace and quiet," her roommate declared.

Jorden shot Madison an outrageous look as the two girls swept her out of the apartment. "I hope you're happy!" Jorden called back.

"I am. Thanks." Madison laughed. "Take her away! She needs to get out."

"Hey, where's the place we're going?" Jorden asked.

"It's in the recreation room. Straight ahead."

Jorden heard voices and laughter as she stepped inside. The two girls she came with disappeared into the crowd. Looking around, she didn't recognize anyone.

"Hey Jude" played while couples danced. Jorden swayed to the rhythm of the music as her eyes shifted to the doorway. While already planning her departure, a young man came into view. His smile slanted slightly, accentuating a strong jawline. He had a sense of aloofness—yet his hazel eyes brought out a softness, eyes looking directly at her as he moved closer.

"You aren't leaving, are you?"

"Why would you ask?" Jorden looked perplexed.

"Your eyes haven't left the door. I'm Alex Whelan. And you are?"

"Jorden Marshall."

"Good. Now I know someone—at least someone's name. I didn't mean to come off so blunt, but the way you were eyeing the door I knew you wouldn't be here long."

"I was dragged here by my friends who have now vanished." Jorden glanced at a swirl of people dancing.

"I seldom come to these parties, but I was also talked into it by my roommate. There's Tom." Alex pointed to him in the crowd of dancers. "Now I'm glad he did."

Jorden relaxed to the tone of Alex's voice. He sounded like a New Yorker.

"Can I get you something to drink?"

"Thank you. Sounds good."

Jorden watched Alex's easy gait carry his trim but solid frame past the couples dancing. He looked close to six foot with a head of dark brown hair. A few minutes later he returned with two tall, bubbling glasses.

"I'm not sure what we have here. The bartender's hands flew pouring the drinks. Let me try it. Hmm . . . ginger-ale, lime, and some gin. It's good—not too strong." Alex slipped the other glass into her hand.

Jorden took a sip. "It's good. Thank you."

"You don't sound like a southerner. Where are you from?"

"New Jersey. And you?"

"Albany. In New York," Alex replied.

"I knew it. You sound like a New Yorker!"

"Have you ever been there?"

"I've been to New York City—I had a great time." Jorden couldn't help but blush under his steady gaze.

"Albany can't compare to the big city, but its history makes it an interesting capital. Where's your home in New Jersey?" Alex asked.

Jorden smiled. "It's also the capital. Know it?"

"Of course, it's Trenton." Alex's eyes crinkled with triumph.

"I'm impressed."

"What else do you want to know?" Alex laughed. "Still, I'm curious, what brought you to Georgia?"

"My family's from the South. After four years at the university, I thought Columbus seemed a logical place to begin my first year of teaching."

"Makes sense," Alex replied.

"I take it you're in the army." Jorden assumed most of the men at the party were.

"Right. The draft caught me. I have another eighteen months before I'm out, but I'm sure Vietnam is on the horizon."

Jorden didn't know what to say. Saved by the music "Gentle On My Mind" began to play.

"Want to dance? I like this one." Smoothly, Alex led her around the floor for three more songs.

Dancing to a slow one, Jorden glided past a wall clock and noticed it was after eleven. "I didn't know it was so late. I need to go."

"I'll walk you back." It took only a couple of minutes to reach Jorden's second floor apartment.

"I had fun. Can I call you?"

"Please do." Jorden gave him her phone number—then she thought of her boyfriend, Justin. She hadn't dated anyone except Justin since her senior year in college. She still saw him on weekends at the university, but they were having problems. They had opposite beliefs. Jorden was pro-civil rights; Justin was anti-civil rights. Their differences were driving a wedge between them.

***

The following Friday evening, Justin drove over to Columbus from the university. He and Jorden were sitting on the couch, talking and listening to music when the doorbell rang around seven. Tentatively, Jorden rose and opened the door. To her surprise, there stood Alex. She hadn't heard from him since the party.

"Hi." Jorden's fingers drummed against the doorknob. She tried to sound pleasant, but she was annoyed Alex hadn't called first. He seemed to hesitate as he peered around the door and saw Justin sitting on the couch.

"I'm sorry, I . . . should have . . . called." He left abruptly. Jorden closed the door and tried to erase the image of his face. She went back to the couch with a nervous smile. Of course, this didn't sit well with Justin.

Life carried on. The next week, while Jorden and Madison were grading papers at the dining room table, the phone rang.

"Hi. This is Alex. I want to apologize. I was a fool . . . I should have called first."

"It's okay," Jorden responded, not meaning it. She and Justin had fought over Alex's visit.

"I hope you'll accept my apology. I'd like to see you again. How about this Thursday night for dinner?"

Jorden hesitated but eventually accepted. Why not? She and Justin were always arguing. After she hung up, she turned to Madison. "What do you think about me going out with Alex?"

Madison shrugged her shoulders. "I guess you know what you're doing. Dating two men could be tricky."

Before Jorden knew it, Thursday night arrived. A ball knotted up in her stomach. Madison had the stereo playing in the front room. As Jorden changed, she could hear "Up Up and Away." The music had a calming effect. Fifteen minutes later, Jorden stepped into the front room. "How do I look?"

"Terrific, but you can't wear those shoes. Wear your light blue heels; they're sharper."

Jorden made a face. Those shoes were too tight, but she put them on anyway.

"Alex said he'd be here at seven and now its seven thirty. Where is he?" Jorden assumed anyone in the military would be on time.

The phone rang. Jorden answered it. She could hear Alex's voice in the background.

"Jorden. Are you there? I've got a disaster going on with the troops. I'll be late. Sorry. I'll call you back." Alex's voice faded out. She could hear yelling in the background—words not to be repeated before he hung up. Two hours later, there was still no word from Alex. She fumed. "Looks like I've been stood up." Irritated, Jorden decided to change into her sweatshirt and jeans.

At nine thirty the phone rang, startling Jorden. Didn't he know this was a school night?

"I'm on my way. Be there in fifteen minutes," Alex stated and hung up.

"How dare him." He didn't give me a chance to say a word. It was late; Madison had already retreated to her room. The doorbell rang at nine forty-five. Jorden stood still, thinking about what she would do. It rang again. She looked out the peephole, and there was Alex in his Army fatigues. She relented and opened the door.

"I wouldn't blame you if you didn't let me in, but I wanted to explain in person." His fatigues were rumpled and stained with smudges appearing to look like blood.

Jorden's eyes widened as she surveyed his condition. "You're a mess! Have you been in a fight?"

"Sort of. It's a long story."

Jorden's features softened. His rugged appearance did have a certain raw appeal.

"Do you have time for a short ride?" Alex asked. "I know it's late, but I'd like to explain."

Jorden looked at her watch. "It's almost ten."

"You're right. I'll leave." Alex turned to go.

"Wait. I'll get my coat." A slight smile lifted her face.

During the next hour, Alex did most of the talking. "Tonight a bad fight broke out in the barracks. Two officer candidates got into a knock-down blowout over a woman. Mayhem broke loose."

"And?"

"I had to step in. It's my job to lead these men. In this case, thirty-two of them. It was bad. All of the men had to be disciplined. I ordered a low-crawl—five times each way up and down the barrack's hallway."

"How awful." Jorden studied Alex's face. The creases tightened around his mouth. She sensed this was not easy for him to talk about.

"One of the candidates, Ben, a nice guy, but on the chunky side has trouble with physical challenges. The low-crawl is hard to do and, for him, almost impossible. His belly dragged along the floor, holding him back. It took more strength than he had. Some of the candidates had to go around him. In their frenzy, a few plowed over him."

Jorden visualized Ben being crushed. It made her stomach turn.

"Finally, Ben couldn't take it. He stopped in his tracks, choked up, and turned red. Tears rolled down his face. I yanked him out. He isn't meant to be an officer candidate."

"How cruel. I'd hate your job. How can you do it?" Jorden twisted in her seat.

"I don't like it, but its part of the job. It's a weeding out process. In the long run, Ben is better off getting out now."

"What will happen to Ben?" Jorden asked, pressing her fingers against her temples.

"He'll go back into the Army as an enlisted man. About half of the candidates either quit or can't meet the challenges."

"And go where?"

"Anywhere." Alex shrugged his shoulders. "My guess is, he'll end up in Vietnam like most of us."

"I don't want your job! Think I'll stick to teaching," Jorden replied.

It was around midnight when Alex drove Jorden back to her apartment. "Can we try this again? How about Saturday night?" Alex asked as they climbed the stairs to her apartment.

"I'm not here on weekends, but weekdays will work," Jorden answered without any other explanation.

"Okay. How about next week for dinner? I'm not on call Tuesday night. I hope you'll give me a second chance?" Alex asked at the top of the landing.

After Jorden unlocked the door, she turned around with a grin. "It's a date."

"See you next Tuesday. I'll pick you up around six." Alex skipped back down the stairs to the parking area.

Chapter 21

January 1970

Turbulence rocked the plane. Jorden looked out the window to see if they were near Atlanta; farm lands dominated the view. She closed her eyes and remembered her first official date with Alex.

***

Previous Year—October 1968

After a weekend at the university seeing Justin, Jorden thought little of Alex.

"What are you doing making a sandwich? Don't you have a date tonight?" Madison asked.

"What are you talking about?"

"It's Tuesday. I thought Alex asked you out."

"Oh my gosh. I thought we were going out tomorrow night. What time is it?"

"A little after six."

Jorden threw down the sandwich. "Want this?"

"No. It looks awful," Madison replied as she made a face.

Staring at her closet, Jorden tried to decide what to wear. She selected a green and white striped cotton-blend dress with short sleeves. The hem hit right above her knees, showing off her legs. Marching into the front room, she confronted Madison. "How's this?"

"Great for such fast work! Shall I tell Alex how quick you are?"

"No. Don't you dare embarrass me," Jorden replied. Looking out the front window, she caught a glimpse of Alex's red Mustang. The convertible top was down. Her fingers slipped through her loose flowing hair. She could imagine it flying in all directions. "Men never think!" Running back to her bedroom, she grabbed her comb and pulled her thick hair back with a designer hair clip, tucking in a few light brown strands, before she gave it a strong dose of hair spray. Her lucent blue eyes stared back from the mirror in approval.

The doorbell rang. Madison answered it and looked at her watch. "You must be Alex. I see you're not late tonight."

"Good observation," Alex replied.

Jorden overheard her roommate. She never knew what could come out of Madison's mouth, so she dashed to the front room.

"Hi, Alex." Jorden did a double take. He looked nice out of his army fatigues, wearing gray slacks, a casual shirt, and a light tan sports coat. She looked from Alex to Madison. "I see you two have met."

"Yes, we have," Alex responded.

They went to Amore's. The waiter, Antonio, introduced himself. He looked and sounded Italian, which added to the atmosphere. "I recommend the chef's special, Linguine' Ai Gamberi'. Delicious black tiger prawns are tossed with sun dried tomatoes and red pepper flakes in a white sauce. It's excellent."

They both couldn't resist his enticing description. Antonio was true to his word; the meal was outstanding. They lingered a bit longer over glasses of Chardonnay.

Alex leaned forward. "I'm sorry about last Thursday."

"Those were tough circumstances. Why don't you tell me about a typical day," Jorden suggested.

"It's pretty dull. I hate to bore you."

"Try me. I'm curious." Jorden tried to listen, but her attention soon faded. She watched his lips move and his expressions change. Her eyes drifted to his. They looked smoky brown—no they were hazel. The change in his tone made her realize she missed half of what he had said.

"I'm sorry. Can you repeat what you were saying about breakfast?"

"See? I've already lost you."

"No you haven't. Tell me more."

"All right. As I said, the officer candidates go to breakfast about six forty-five. There is a pull-up bar in front of the mess hall, and each candidate has to do three pull-ups before entering."

"If they can't do them, do they miss breakfast?"

"No. Most of them can't at first. I'll have them do push-ups instead. At some point, they'll gain the upper body strength to do the pull-ups. After breakfast, each platoon runs in formation to class, followed by PT around ten. It's exhausting. I get worn out just like the candidates."

Jorden looked surprised. "You lead these exercises?"

"Most of the time."

Jorden was glad she couldn't be drafted into the army. "And?"

Alex shrugged and continued. "After lunch, each platoon runs in formation to afternoon classes. Field work begins around three, with map reading, weapons training, shooting machine guns, grenade launchers . . ."

Grenade launchers caught her attention as her peripheral vision took in his strong shoulders and the strength in his upper arms. He was slim but in a well-built way.

His voice filtered back. "After dinner, the candidates return to their barracks for study hall. Lights are out at nine thirty, ending a typical day."

"Wow, sounds like a lot of work." Jorden shifted in her seat to get a better look at him.

Antonio interrupted them. "Would you like to order dessert?"

"Not for me." Jorden placed her napkin on the table.

Antonio turned to Alex. "Not tonight, maybe another time." Jorden liked what the words implied.

The drive back took about fifteen minutes. Alex turned the Mustang into the apartment complex and parked near Jorden's entrance. Gently, he pulled her close. "Are you free Thursday night? Maybe we could go for a soda? Thursdays aren't the best for me, but I'd like to see you again."

"Thursday's fine. But . . . call me first to let me know when you can get off."

"I will." Alex leaned over and lightly kissed her.

Jorden watched him from the living room window. He sat in the Mustang a moment before he drove off.

The next morning Madison was full of questions.

"How was your date?"

"Fine," Jorden said with a nod.

"Really? You sound like one of my second graders! Fill me in on the details."

"I had a great time. Alex is fun." Jorden flipped up the switch on the toaster as she checked her toast. "I may see him Thursday night."

"You may? What about Justin?"

"What about him? It can't hurt to see Alex during the week." Jorden looked away to avoid Madison's scowl. On purpose, Jorden changed the subject. "How about you? Have you heard from Luke?"

"I got several letters yesterday. He seems to be doing all right. I can't help but worry about him."

Jorden touched Madison's shoulder. "I'm sure he's okay." She knew Madison's thoughts centered on Luke. He would be in Vietnam for another ten months.

That afternoon, Jorden got home before Madison. She turned on the five o'clock evening news. Scott O'Brady, the local newscaster, began to highlight happenings in the Vietnam War, both at home and in the warzone:

> *"The United States is in turmoil with rallies against the Vietnam War. The anti-war sentiments have been fueled by the Tet Offensive and the battle of Khe Sanh."*

Madison had a map of Vietnam on the dining room wall for reference. She liked to see where the fighting took place. So did Jorden.

> *"The Tet Offensive was put into action by the North Vietnamese on the lunar New Year, January 30, 1968. The North Vietnamese attacked over thirty of South Vietnam's provinces and caught the South Vietnamese off guard. U.S. troops were also unprepared."*

Luckily, Luke didn't get over there until after the battle.

> *"The drawn out battle of Khe Sanh was also in late January of 1968 and took quite a toll on U.S. Marine troops. Many were injured and others killed. Morale here in the United States dropped. Americans were becoming unhappy with the war."*

If Madison had been here, she would have automatically tried to locate Khe Sanh on her map. The battle was situated in the northwest mountainous area of Vietnam. Air was the only way in, isolating the Marines.

> *"Continual rallies and demonstrations were made against President Lyndon B. Johnson and his cabinet members for their policies in Vietnam. The Democratic Party was divided. Senators Robert Kennedy and Eugene McCarthy, both, challenged President Johnson in the early months of 1968 for the Democratic nomination."*

"Amen! I hope we don't get more of the same after President Johnson. Anyone would be better than him!"

Startled by Madison's voice, Jorden pivoted to face her. "You're so late. Are you okay?"

"I'm fine. We had an unexpected faculty meeting which went way too long. There are problems on the playground. The principal wants to set up new rules no one likes. You're lucky you don't have to worry about such things with junior high kids."

"You had me worried."

"Oh, I'm good." Madison slipped off her shoes. "Now we need to worry about dropping off our rent checks. I can't believe they raised the rent to one hundred twenty-five dollars a month. Last year, I just paid one hundred dollars. You'll need to make your check out for sixty-two dollars and fifty cents. Don't forget to date it the first of November."

"I've already made it out." Money was tight for Jorden. She had signed her first year teaching contract for $5,800. The agreement covered nine months of work but she chose to spread it over twelve payments. Her monthly paycheck after deductions amounted to $374.50.

Madison continued to complain. "Can you believe gas is now thirty-six cents a gallon? It was only thirty cents six months ago."

"Let's drown our woes in cheeseburgers and french-fries," Jorden announced with a laugh.

Madison threw up her arms. "Let's do it!"

Chapter 22

January 1970

The plane touched down in Atlanta. The flight to Chicago was on time. Jorden walked past a number of gates and became confused when she looked up and saw Gate 15. She had gone too far. Without thinking, she back-tracked to Gate 12 and spotted an empty seat.

Forty minutes later, a voice from the loud speaker boomed out, "Boarding will begin for Chicago."

On the plane, a man with graying hair helped Jorden put her carry-on in the overhead bin.

"Thank you."

He winked and took his seat next to her. Not wanting to chat, she closed her eyes. Memories of her fight with Justin and her time with Alex last November flooded back.

***

Previous Year – November 1968

Throughout November, Jorden continued to see Justin on the weekends, and Alex during the week—but Thanksgiving weekend ended in disaster. On the drive back from Justin's family's home, she had a heated argument with him over Martin Luther King Jr.'s assassination in April. Justin was behind Governor Wallace's ideologies whereas Jorden was pro-civil rights. The division was tearing them apart.

Jorden slept little Sunday night. She knew Justin was using his finals as an excuse to avoid seeing her. Two weeks seemed like a long time to be apart, especially before being separated by the Christmas holidays.

"Get up, you're going to be late," Madison shouted at Jorden for the third time.

Jorden bolted up and looked at the clock. "Why didn't you wake me?"

"What do you think I'm trying to do? You wouldn't budge."

Jorden dressed in seconds, pulled her hair up, twisted it into an attractive topknot, and secured it with a hairclip.

"How was Thanksgiving?" Madison asked.

"The weekend at Justin's home was great, but the drive back was a disaster. Let's talk tonight." Jorden hurried out the door carrying a stack of her students' papers.

Monday flew by. Jorden was glad she had prepared a week's worth of lesson plans before the holiday weekend. After school she mounted the stairs to her apartment. The phone rang; she was surprised to hear Alex's voice instead of Justin's.

"Hi. I hoped I'd catch you at home. How about having an early dinner? I know its spur of the moment, but, at last I have some free time. What do you think?"

She didn't know what to say. "I wasn't expecting to hear from you until later in the week."

"Should I call back, say Wednesday?" Alex responded.

"Don't be ridiculous. I'm tired, but I'd enjoy dinner with you tonight. What's the occasion?"

"No occasion. I've missed you. I know of a small French restaurant I think you might like. I can pick you up around five. Can you make it?"

"Sure. I hope you don't mind if I don't change; you haven't given me much time." Jorden checked out her school attire and decided it would do fine.

"Perfect. Now I can see the other side of you; just don't bring your ruler."

"Aren't you full of it? See you when you get here." Jorden really didn't want to go out, but Alex lifted her spirits. A glance in the mirror told her to leave her hair up. She was busy re-doing her make-up when Madison came in.

"Are you going somewhere?"

"Alex called. We're going to dinner."

"Well aren't you something?! You just spent a long Thanksgiving weekend at Justin's and now you're off with Alex. What gives?" Madison asked.

"Nothing. It's not a crime to go out. Besides, Justin and I got into a fight on the drive back. You know how we're always in disagreement over racial issues. Well this time, it was a terrible argument." Jorden went on trying to explain as she finished her makeup.

"So, Justin's not going to see you for the next two weeks. Sounds serious."

The doorbell rang. Jorden jumped. "Let's talk later. I'm sure it's Alex." She smoothed her skirt and gave herself a look of approval in the mirror.

***

Chez Antoine, a cozy French restaurant, served gourmet French cuisine. After a delightful main course, Jorden and Alex had a light dessert of raspberry sorbet.

"How was your Thanksgiving?" Jorden asked.

"Good. I had dinner with Captain Hudson and his new bride. It was fun, but it would have been nicer to spend the day with you. Now, tell me about your weekend."

"There's not much to tell. I spent it at my friend's house," Jorden replied. She couldn't remember how much she had told Alex about Justin, probably not much.

"You did, but how close is this friend?"

"I've dated him about a year."

"And? What does that mean?"

"Nothing. The weekend turned sour on the drive back. I won't see him again until after Christmas, if then. But—I really don't want to talk about it." Jorden looked away.

"Okay—we won't, but it's good news to me. Now we can spend weekends together if you'll have me?"

"Thanks for letting me off so easy. It'll be fun to have extra time together."

"Oh, I'm not letting you off too easy. I still have to compete with your so-called friend."

Jorden watched Alex as he caught the waiter's attention and paid for their dinner. He was smooth and handled himself well. She admired this about him. Right now, she wasn't feeling she could find much to admire in Justin. She couldn't understand how a man she thought she knew so well could still be opposed to the civil rights movement.

"Let's go for a ride." Alex took her hand.

"Why not?" Jorden smiled and forgot about Justin.

"Where to?" Alex asked.

"Surprise me."

The night was clear but cold, in the upper thirties. They listened to music as Alex drove out of the city limits. "Look, there's a sign to Calloway Gardens. Have you ever been there?"

"Several times." Jorden remembered swimming in the lake area of the resort last summer with Justin. She wondered what it would be like with Alex.

"I have an idea. Why don't we go on Saturday? We could make it a day trip." Alex shifted in his seat. "Wait. I forgot I have a basketball game on base. I promised my platoon I'd root for them. Why . . . why don't you come with me?"

"Sounds like fun. I'd love to," Jorden replied. She enjoyed a good game.

Fifteen minutes later, Alex drove back and parked in front of her apartment.

"Would you like to come in? Madison's probably gone to bed."

"I wish I could but I have to be up by five. The candidates have a special drill starting at six." Alex pulled her closer. "We could get together Wednesday night. Can you fit me into your schedule?"

"I can." Jorden's heart leapt as he leaned over and kissed her.

* * *

"What's up with you and Alex?" Madison demanded. "He calls and comes over every night. I haven't seen you this cheerful in a long time."

"Alex is amazing. Tomorrow I have a full day with him. I can't wait!"

He even arrived on time Saturday for the basketball game. Jorden noticed Madison smile when she opened the door. Her roommate was starting to like him.

Jorden watched Alex drive carefully onto Fort Benning, winding through streets until he finally found a parking place. A light rain started. As they made their way to the gym, she stumbled over an uneven spot, and Alex caught her. A church steeple emerged from the mist. Fog lightly hovered over the area and enveloped her. She felt peaceful. This seemed to be a good sign, an omen for the future—perhaps her future with Alex.

"Are you all right?" Alex reached down to help her up.

"I'm fine." Jorden stood up and took a step forward to balance herself. She searched for the church, but it had disappeared in the mist.

"Come on. We're going to miss the game if we don't hurry."

Jorden noted how old the gym appeared to be. Several rows of bleachers lined each side filled with only a handful of people. She looked on as the players moved swiftly up and down the court. During the first quarter each team traded baskets to keep the score tight. Cheering exploded at the end of the second half. Jorden clapped as hard as anyone else when Alex's platoon won. The final score was seventy-eight to seventy-four.

Jorden looked up as they walked back outside. The sky appeared even grayer and suddenly opened with drenching rain.

"Let's make a run for the car," Alex called out. After Jorden settled into his Mustang, he confessed he still had work he needed to finish. "Would you mind if we take a break and get back together tonight?"

"No, but first how about a ride home?" Jorden joked.

That evening Alex arrived around seven thirty. Madison had gone home for the weekend. They had no special plans besides listening to music—which was fine with Jorden. They'd have time and space to themselves.

"A Coke or a 7UP? Our selection is small," Jorden offered.

"A Coke is fine."

Alex followed Jorden into the kitchen. He put his arms around her as she poured the Cokes. Startled by his touch, she overfilled the glasses and watched the foam slide down spilling onto the counter. His powerful arms enclosed her. She became oblivious to the drinks, turned, and slid her arms around his waist. Electricity flowed through her as he pulled her closer, and his hands glided down the narrow of her back. Her knees buckled when he kissed her. Caught up in the moment, she barely noticed him lead her to the couch.

Chapter 23

January 1970

The aircraft touched down at the Chicago O'Hare Airport. Jorden was worried she wouldn't make her connection to Los Angeles. In the open concourse, she checked the flight schedule. Departure time was at one thirty. She looked at her watch—one fifteen. Yanking up her carry-on, she rushed down Concourse A. She gazed up, and noted she had just passed Gate 6—her stride increased to a sprint. Gate 12 loomed in front of her. Passengers were in the boarding line; she got out her ticket and joined them. Rejoicing, she eventually slid into her seat. After take-off, her mind shifted back to last December.

***

Previous Year – December 1968

Justin kept his word. He didn't call until after finals. Jorden decided he must have figured she would relent and call him. Often she did so, calling to apologize but not this time. She knew he was upset with her since he didn't drive to Columbus before he went home for the holidays. Instead, Justin invited Jorden to spend Christmas with him and his family. Of course she declined since her parents expected her home.

But, Justin had been far from her thoughts the last two weeks. Time with Alex had been intoxicating. Topping it off, Alex had offered her a ride home to New Jersey on his way back to New York. The two planned to leave right after her last day of school.

Jorden became excited every time she thought about the trip. She wondered how long it would take to reach Trenton. One or two days? Alex came over Thursday night to go over their travel plans. They had a road map spread over the dining room table; their heads were bent in deep discussion.

Madison walked in. "What are you doing?"

"Planning our route to Trenton. Want to come with us?" Jorden replied.

"No way! You can have that cold weather. Macon's fine for me. Besides, I wouldn't want to get stuck in a snowbank."

"Hey, sounds like fun!" Alex laughed.

"Fun my foot. You don't really think we'll get lost in a snowstorm?"

"It's not possible with me at the wheel. Look at these great directions." Alex waved them in Jorden's face.

"I'll leave you two to bicker while I make a sandwich. Want anything?" Madison called out as she left the room.

"We're fine," Jorden replied.

"Well I'm not. Let's go for burgers. It'll give us a break. Besides, I need to fill up the car," Alex piped up.

"Okay. Give me a second, I'll get my coat." Jorden caught Madison out of her peripheral vision. "We're going for hamburgers. Want anything?"

"No thanks. I'm good."

A half hour later Jorden and Alex were finishing their Cokes and burgers in the car.

"That hit the spot." Alex reached for her hand. "I'm excited. Let's get an early start. How about six?"

"Too early! How about seven?"

"Too late! But for my special girl—let's go for six thirty."

Jorden laughed and pushed him away. "Okay—six thirty."

Jorden finished her teaching duties later than usual for a Friday afternoon. She wanted to get home and finish her packing, but she had more papers to grade when the bell rang. Students scurried down the halls to get to their lockers before they left for Christmas break.

Jorden was concentrating on checking answers when she heard a voice call out her name. She looked up and saw Nora.

"Miss Marshall, aren't you going home?" Nora asked.

"Soon. I'm trying to get these papers checked. Actually, they're for your fifth period class." Jorden flipped through them and found Nora's. "Here's yours. Looks good. You're doing much better. You might get an A if you keep this up."

"If you say so, I bet I can." Nora eyed her paper and smiled. "I just came by to wish you a merry Christmas."

"Thank you. Same to you."

"Gotta go." Nora waved and vanished.

Jorden sat and thought about what a puzzle Nora was, but she was sweet to stop by. Then thoughts of Nora evaporated when Jorden looked at the rest of the papers. She didn't reach her apartment until five. She couldn't wait for tomorrow. Thinking of the trip with Alex gave her goosebumps.

Madison had already left for home. Scott O'Brady's news forecast came on when the phone rang. It must be Alex; he planned to come over around seven.

Jorden reached for the phone on the second ring. "Hello?"

Jorden heard anxiety in her mother's voice. She couldn't imagine what was wrong. "Don't worry, Mom. I'm still leaving early tomorrow morning."

"Oh, I'm so glad I caught you. I've been calling and calling. . . Uncle William, he . . . he died Wednesday night."

"Oh Mom, I'm so sorry." Jorden paused for a moment, taken aback by her mother's words. Next, she stammered, "How?"

"Jeanette said it was a heart attack. It happened Wednesday night in his sleep. She couldn't wake him the next morning."

"I'm so sorry. What can I do?"

"Come to the funeral with us."

"Of course . . . of course I will. When?"

"Your dad and I are already on the way. We should reach Grandma Marshall's home early tomorrow. Please drive to Lockton in the morning and meet us there. We'll all drive to Selma Saturday afternoon for the funeral on Sunday."

"I'll be there. I'll leave early tomorrow morning." At times like this, Jorden would do anything she could to help her Mother.

"Good. We want you to drive home with us to New Jersey."

"What about my car?"

"You can leave it at Grandma Marshall's. She won't mind. It would be a big help to us."

"Anything, Mom. I'm so sorry. I'll get there first thing tomorrow morning."

"Thank you—we'll see you then."

Jorden could hear the relief in her mother's voice. Still, she couldn't believe her uncle had died. She remembered Uncle William suffered a severe heart attack several years ago. He survived and had been doing well. Jorden and her uncle weren't close, but she knew how much he meant to her mother. Growing up in New Jersey had separated Jorden from her southern relatives.

What was she to do? Jorden's thoughts went in all directions. She couldn't feel the grief her mother was experiencing; she hardly knew Uncle William. And, at the same time, she worried how she would tell Alex.

Arriving at seven thirty, Alex stepped into the apartment with a huge smile and swept Jorden into his arms. "I've been thinking about you all day. I can't wait for this adventure to begin."

Jorden didn't say anything.

"Are you all right?"

"No." Jorden sat down on the couch. Alex joined her. "Mother just called with sad news. My uncle had a heart attack . . . he died Wednesday night. Mom and Dad are driving down right now and should be at Grandma's home tomorrow morning. My mother is so upset. I could hear it the instant I heard her voice. The funeral is set for Sunday in Selma."

Alex leaned forward with his hands on his knees as he listened. He didn't say a word or move a muscle.

Jorden didn't know how to react. She sensed his irritation. How could he be angry and not sympathetic? Leaning forward, she unsuccessfully tried to make eye contact. What was wrong with him? The only thing she could do was apologize. But why did she always have to say she was sorry? She paused before she looked at Alex again. "I really want to be with you, but I have to make this trip to be with my family. I hope you understand."

"I do. I'm sorry about your uncle." A muscle seemed to twitch in Alex's neck as he spoke. "You don't have a choice but to go to his funeral and be with your family." His words were right, but they lacked any emotion or empathy. He stood up. "I have to go."

"You just got here. We still have plenty of time." Jorden had never seen this side of Alex. He had always been caring, thoughtful, and affectionate toward her. Who was this person? Her back stiffened while her lower lip quivered. "Please stay. It's still early."

"I have a lot to do." Alex barely kissed her cheek as he stepped out the door.

Shocked by his actions, Jorden followed him into the hallway putting her hands on her hips. "My folks are going to drive me to Trenton. Are you going to still give me a ride back from New Jersey? I could get a flight back—maybe that's a better idea."

Alex never paused on the stairway. She could hear his words as he rushed down the stairs. "The ride is still on. I'll call you from New York." Seconds later, the main entrance door opened and closed. She watched his red Mustang pull out and flash around the bend.

"My uncle just died. Where is his compassion? Do I really want to see him again?" Jorden cried, hugging her chest. She looked around the stairway, hoping no one had heard her.

Chapter 24

January 1970

Jorden shivered in the plane's seat. Alex's icy reaction stirred up intense emotions. "Fasten your seatbelts, turbulence ahead." The pilot's voice vibrated over the intercom. The airplane shook. "We're going to change our altitude to try and reach a smoother flight path. Bear with us."

After a few minutes, the plane stabilized. Jorden turned her head toward the window with memories of her family and her uncle's funeral during the Selma trip.

***

Previous Year – December 21, 1968

Jorden left for Lockton, Alabama at nine Saturday morning. As she drove across the border from Georgia into Alabama, she seethed over Alex's insensitivity. He wasn't worth it. Right before she arrived in Lockton, she vowed to put him as far from her thoughts as possible. It was almost eleven thirty when she coasted down Grandma Marshall's driveway. Her parents and grandmother were out in the yard looking at the pecan trees.

Jorden rolled down the window and waved. Her spirits lifted. Looking at Grandma Marshall, Jorden could see a resemblance. They had the same light cream complexion and oval face. Strands of gray hair drifted out from her grandmother's darker locks. She remained slim; the years had treated her well.

Her grandma greeted Jorden with a huge hug. She had prepared a scrumptious meal of southern fried chicken, mashed potatoes, gravy, turnip greens, and cornbread. During lunch, the conversation dealt with Uncle William's death and the upcoming funeral. Jorden's mother was quieter than usual.

For dessert, Grandma Marshall served Jorden's favorite, banana cream pie. "You did it this time, the best meal I've had in months," Jorden exclaimed. She noted even her mother lightened up while she finished her pie and iced tea.

Afterward, Jorden's father drove them to Selma. The day was sunny, clear but cool and in the forties. Jorden remembered visiting Uncle William several times in Selma. He owned a grocery store in the poorer section of the city, where the population was predominately Black. The store was a one story, rectangular, wood-framed building. The exterior looked worn but the interior appeared well-organized. The cash register and checkout stand stood at the front of the store. She remembered the large wooden candy counter encased in glass. It was her favorite section.

Customers wandered in during the day to make purchases, oftentimes charging them to their accounts. Although unusual for the time, Uncle William extended credit to many of his customers by keeping an informal ledger.

Racial problems were stirring up in Selma, which prevented many of his Black customers from registering to vote. The practice of segregation was rampant. This reminded Jorden of a paper she had written in college titled "The Voting Rights Act of 1965." At the last minute she had thrown it in her bag and now pulled it out on the ride to Selma.

"What do you have there?" Jorden's mother asked.

"An old paper I wrote about Selma."

"Read it to us. It should get our minds off Brother and the funeral." Her mother frequently referred to Uncle William as Brother. This was her affectionate name for him.

"It's pretty dull," Jorden replied. She had brought it along to refresh her memory of Selma's recent history, not to read it out loud.

"I don't care, maybe we'll learn something."

"All right. If you insist."

"'Selma was the county seat of Dallas County, Alabama. This county's population was over fifty percent Black people and most of them lived in poverty. Only a small percentage of those in the Black community were registered to vote; not by choice, but by the negative influence of state and local officials.'"

"Are you sure of your facts? Seems pretty tough," her dad declared.

"Believe me, Dad, its right. I did my research. It gets worse." Jorden thought of Justin. He probably would have thought the restrictions were necessary. She couldn't understand his reasoning. Putting her opinions aside, she read on.

"'There were only two days per month citizens could go to the courthouse and apply to register to vote. One of those days, October 7, 1963, was called, Freedom Day. Over 300 Black people from Dallas County organized and stood in line all day in the hot sun to apply at the registration office. Individuals were arrested for trying to give them water. At the end of the day, only a small number were allowed to fill out the voter registration applications. Most were turned down because they had to pass a literacy test to prove they could read and write. Other pressures were applied, even threats of violence to stop the Black people from voting.'"

"Oh, I remember Brother talking about that day," Jorden's mother spoke up. "He wrote a long letter describing it. One of Brother's customers, Etta May, had been there. He described her as a large colored woman with four children. She took her oldest son to stand in line with her. The day proved brutal. She told Brother she wished she hadn't brought him along to witness such unbelievable behavior. She never made it to the courthouse door—but the event ignited a fire of determination in Etta May."

Grant glanced at his wife. "I've never heard of Etta May. Are you making this up?"

"No! You just don't listen to me. I'm sure I mentioned her to you. I may even have Brother's letter. Go on Jorden."

Jorden glanced at her mother and continued.

"'The passage of the Civil Rights Act of 1964 made segregation illegal, but it was difficult to enforce in Selma. By January of 1965, Martin Luther King Jr. had officially started the Selma Voting Rights movement. A plan was set up to march from Selma to Montgomery, the State Capital, to ask Governor Wallace to protect Black registrants. The Governor denounced the march and called it a threat to public safety. Governor Wallace said they would take all measures necessary to prevent the march.'"

Grant glanced toward his daughter. "Quite a long march. I know I saw it on the news, but how many days did it take?"

"Grant, keep your eyes on the road; you're going to kill us!" Jorden could hear her mother call out to her dad.

"I'm not going to kill anyone!" Grant barked back. "I'm just curious. A march from Selma to Montgomery is quite a hike. Don't you think?"

Jorden felt the car accelerate.

"We don't need to pass the car ahead of us," her mother yelled.

Jorden smiled at her parents. They always bickered. Alex came back to mind. At one point she thought they might have had something special between them, now she wondered. She scolded herself for thinking about him and tried to answer her dad's question.

"Dad, I think it would take almost a week. I'll read on and see what I've written."

"'This was followed by Bloody Sunday, on March 7, 1965. John Lewis and Hosea Williams, under the leadership of Martin Luther King Jr., led a group of over 600 people on a fifty-four mile march to Montgomery. They made it only six blocks to the Edmund Pettus Bridge. They were brutally attacked by state and local lawmen and forced back into Selma. The media was present during the peaceful march and images of the brutal attack were on the news. This stunned the nation, awakening the U.S. civil rights movement. The Selma march made international news.'"

"Mom, do you think Etta May marched with this group?"

"I know she did. Brother told me Etta May marched each time they tried to cross the Edmund Pettus Bridge. Due to her weight she couldn't move as fast as the others. She didn't sustain injuries, but she had friends who were badly hurt. After the march, Brother said the tension in Selma boiled over." Her mother paused before saying, "Please, read on."

"'Right after Bloody Sunday, Martin Luther King Jr., organized a second march for Tuesday, March 9, 1965. He called for support. Over 2,000 people responded. This time an attempt to get a court order to prevent the police from intervening was denied, and a restraining order was issued to stop the march. Instead, they held a ceremonial march. They led the large group of marchers to the Edmund Pettus Bridge for a short prayer session and then turned them around to march back to Selma.

The night after the prayer march, three white ministers who had come for the march were attacked and beaten by white bigots. One of the ministers died. A week later, a federal judge ruled in favor of the freedom to march.'"

"I remember. It was awful they killed a white minister. It stirred up a lot of trouble," her dad commented.

Justin popped into Jorden's mind. She knew he would have surmised the white ministers shouldn't have been there supporting the cause whereas she hoped Alex would have cheered them on encouraged by their support.

"'The third and last march prevailed and they made it to Montgomery, Alabama. It took five days before they reached the State Capitol Building on March 25, 1965. Martin Luther King Jr. delivered his speech "How Long, Not Long" standing next to the State Capitol building.'"

Her mother turned around and interjected, "You don't have to ask. Etta May made it to the State Capitol. Brother said she beamed every time she talked about it."

Jorden continued with a final highlight.

"'Within five months of the third march, President Lyndon Johnson signed the Voting Rights Act of 1965.'"

"That's the end. By the way, I got an A on the paper."

"Thank you. It brings back memories of Brother during those hard times. We forget too soon."

***

The funeral began at eleven Sunday morning. Jorden looked at the crowd as the last people arrived. Most of those attending were family and friends, with a sprinkling of his customers from the grocery store. After the service, quite a few people lined up to share their condolences with Jeanette and Uncle William's two grown children and grandchildren.

Jorden noticed a heavy set Black woman with three children and a young man, in uniform, waiting in line to pay their respects. Jorden watched them out of curiosity as they moved up the line and stood face to face with Jeanette. Jorden was close enough to hear their voices.

"I'm so sorry about your husband. He was kind and helpful to my family. I'm Etta May and these are my children."

"I know you!" Jeanette exclaimed, "William mentioned you often. You were one of his favorite customers. It's so good to meet you and your children. This young man, is he your oldest?"

"Yes. Jeremy is eighteen and has just joined the army. We're very proud of him."

The chatter continued a while longer. Jorden looked on and realized it would take time to heal the barrier between the races, if ever, but she was delighted she got to see Etta May and her family. She tried to catch them, but they were gone before she could reach them.

Jorden stood there looking at the crowd while her thoughts digressed to the XIX Olympic Games in Mexico City. Her students went crazy over the Olympic events, especially the 200 meter race. A date stuck in her mind—it was October 16, 1968. Two Black athletes—Tommy Smith won the gold medal and John Carlos won the Bronze medal. She remembered the local newsman, Scott O'Brady, and his words describing the two Black men.

They stood on the Olympic Podium shoeless, wearing black socks, with their heads lowered and at the same time each raised a black gloved fist showing a symbolic move which displayed rebellion and was eventually labeled the Black Power salute.

O'Brady implied this act was brought on by racial and political unrest in our country.

Jorden couldn't forget how Justin went crazy when he watched it on the news. They had quarreled over it. Alex, even though she was angry at him, would likely applaud the athletes for their courage.

The thought of politics also made her think about the straw poll she had her students do right before the presidential election. It was a close race between Richard Nixon, Hubert Humphrey, and George Wallace. Nixon managed to win—but by a small margin to become the thirty-seventh president. Most of her students voted for George Wallace, who carried five southern states: Alabama, Arkansas, Georgia, Louisiana, and Mississippi.

Justin voted for Wallace, Alex for Humphrey, and Jorden for Nixon, representing three different political views. She could tolerate Humphrey but couldn't understand how Justin could give his vote to Wallace. The world was changing, and Justin seemed to want to stay in the past, while Alex seemed to push for a more united future.

Jerked out of her thoughts, Jorden heard her mother calling.

"Come on, Jorden, we're going to be late. They're just starting the processional to the cemetery."

Today, her mother's wish was her command.

Chapter 25

January 1970

The longest leg of the trip to Hawaii lay in front of Jorden. She gained three hours when she touched down at the Los Angeles Airport; she was now on Pacific Standard Time.

The waiting area of Gate 4 was packed, but Jorden managed to spot an empty seat. A family was seated across from her and appeared to be in a deep discussion about their Hawaiian vacation. The two teenage girls seemed to know what they wanted and scoffed at their parents' plans. Jorden smiled as she thought about her own family last Christmas.

***

Previous Year – December 24, 1968

The trip from Selma, Alabama to Trenton, New Jersey took two days. They reached their doorstep minutes before the start of Christmas day.

"We did it. Good driving Dad!" Jorden clapped, with her mother joining in. Grant Marshall looked tired, but he was fit for his fifty-six years.

Bobbette, Jorden's sister, greeted them at the door. She had the flu and hadn't gone to Uncle William's funeral. "I'm so glad you're back. Come on in. It's cold out."

"How are you feeling?" Mary asked her older daughter.

"Much better. Mark made the best nurse."

"I bet he did!" Jorden quipped.

"What's that supposed to mean? You're hateful!" Bobbette covered her mouth to cough. "I should give you the flu!"

"Girls, you haven't been together two minutes and listen to you bicker!"

"Mom, we're not fighting. Jorden just has to get in her digs."

"Well, enough! You hear me?"

"Got it!" Jorden gave her sister a look which said, "We're not kids anymore!"

"Where is Mark? I thought he'd be with you on Christmas Eve?" Jorden asked.

"He left early to join his family for the midnight Christmas service. His family opens their presents Christmas Eve and he couldn't miss the excitement."

"I think this is the first time we've missed a service on Christmas Eve." Jorden's mother sighed as she flopped down on the couch.

"You missed even more. Mark and I watched the most spectacular coverage of Apollo 8 circling the moon. The three astronauts showed tremendous views of the moonscape."

"I would have loved to have seen them," Jorden spoke up.

"It moved me to tears. At the end of the program each astronaut read from the Book of Genesis. Remember how the verse goes? 'In the beginning God created the heaven and earth . . .' The hairs rose up on my arms during those readings."

"Hey everyone, it's late. We need to get to bed!" Grant shouted as he carried the last piece of luggage into the room. "I'm tired! Remember, Santa's got to come."

"Oh Dad, don't worry. Mark hauled in the presents and put them around the tree. He wouldn't even let me peek."

"Good guy, but now my girls need to get to bed."

"Come on Jorden, let's go." Bobbette pulled at Jorden's arm.

On the way up the stairs, Jorden grabbed her sister by her shirt-tail to get her attention. "What's happening with you and Mark?"

Bobbette stopped at the top of the stairs. "I love him—plain and simple. I know this is it." Her voice softened before she continued, "Mark hasn't asked me to marry him—but he's dropping hints."

Jorden hugged her sister. "I bet it won't be long."

Christmas day started off with a blanket of snow. Jorden, half asleep, could hear her mother stirring. Her voice floated down the hallway. "It's Christmas! Wake up, it's almost ten." Jorden groaned and rolled over.

An hour later, Jorden's family managed to gather around the brightly decorated tree, eating cookies, and drinking steaming mugs of coffee. This year Mark joined them; he acted as Santa and gave out the presents. "This one's for Mr. Marshall." He tossed it across the room. "Good catch! You must have played football in your younger days."

"Oh, call me Grant. You're at our home so much I forget you're not part of our family."

"Dad!"

"What?"

"You're embarrassing me," Bobbette said in a low voice, nudging her father. Jorden winked at her sister, watching her reaction.

It was a fun-filled day but Jorden couldn't help but think about Alex and Justin. Neither had called. She needed to make sure she had a ride back to Columbus—but refused to call Alex. After dinner she helped her mother with the dishes.

"Where's your mind? What's wrong with you?"

"Nothing!" Jorden retorted.

Bobbette yelled from upstairs, "Jorden, a call for you." She put the pan down and ran upstairs. They had two phones, one in an alcove between the living and dining rooms and the other in the upstairs hallway. The upstairs phone had more privacy. Breathlessly, Jorden answered.

Justin came on the line to wish her a happy holiday. Jorden's shoulders slumped. She had hoped to hear Alex's voice.

Sunday morning they all went to the Methodist church. Jorden couldn't keep her mind on the sermon. She wondered why Alex hadn't called. With little time left, she thought about getting a plane reservation. Early evening, the phone rang several times. "It's for you, Jorden," Bobbette called out.

Jorden answered warily. "Hi. It's Alex."

Jorden's heart skipped a beat. At the same time, she thought about hanging up. But no—she still needed to know if she had a ride.

"I hope you had a good Christmas."

"Yes." She kept her answer short. He didn't have a clue how upset he had made her.

"I'm sorry I didn't get a chance to give a call before now. We had a house full of family, and it was hard to find time. I'd like to make it up to you. Let me take you to dinner after our drive back to Columbus, most likely Friday night."

Jorden hesitated. She had been so upset with Alex she had told Justin she'd meet him Friday night at the university. She began to peel the nail polish off her fingernails. She should say no. What was wrong with her?

"Jorden, are you there? I have a small gift for you and wanted to give it to you after dinner. Am I persuasive enough to get you to spend Friday evening with me?"

"I can't . . . it would be fun . . . but I . . ." Jorden faltered.

"I'll take your answer as a yes, because it will be fun. I didn't hear I can't."

"You've twisted my words. I didn't say yes."

"Sounded that way to me. Now you have to honor it. Besides, I really want to see you."

Jorden gave in. "Okay." She couldn't believe her own ears because she was still upset with him. Quickly she changed the subject. "When are you picking me up?"

"Good question. My roommate, Tom, will be driving back with us. We'll pick you up in Trenton on Thursday, the second of January. It should be somewhere between two and four that afternoon."

"Fine. I'll be ready."

Jorden's stomach churned. She knew it wasn't fine. She had to call Justin and explain it to him. Oh, how she dreaded the call.

Despite her unrest, she spent New Year's Eve with her parents watching television as the crystal ball dropped at the stroke of midnight, ushering in 1969. Bobbette and Mark went out celebrating on their own. The next morning her sister waltzed into Jorden's bedroom. She held out her left hand. Jorden screamed when she saw the dazzling diamond.

"Mark did it and you accepted! Congratulations!" Jorden gave her sister a big hug. "Tell me all."

Bobbette went on and on—Jorden suppressed a surprising surge of envy. She wished she had someone like Mark in her life.

Later in the morning Jorden remembered she had to call Justin. She had put it off long enough, and when she made the call, it was a disaster. Tears rolled down her cheeks. Justin had hung up on her!

Chapter 26

January 1970

"Flight 198 to Honolulu is now boarding." Jorden jumped up, grabbed her carry-on, and joined the crowd lined up at the departure gate. She settled in a window seat near the rear of the plane. Five more hours and she would be with Alex. Closing her eyes, the memories of the extraordinary trip from Trenton, New Jersey to Columbus, Georgia flooded her senses.

***

Previous Year – January 2, 1969

The clock struck four. Alex and his roommate hadn't arrived.

"Stop pacing. You're going to wear out the carpet," Jorden's mother warned.

"I'm just anxious. I want to get on the road before it gets too late. It's going to be a long trip." Jorden had taken pains to dress casually but stylishly. Today she wore a pair of dark brown wool pants with a rose-colored, loose-fitting turtleneck sweater.

Jorden fled to the bay window when she heard the sound of a motor. "They're here."

"I'll get some coffee. I know they'll need a break," Mary Marshall offered.

Jorden watched Alex drive slowly up the driveway to her family's two story red brick house with white wooden shutters. In her opinion, she thought it was an attractive home nestled into a nice neighborhood. She wondered what Alex's home was like and how it compared to hers.

As Jorden opened the front door, she could hear their voices.

"Come on, Alex, we're running late," Tom barked.

"Be nice! I don't want to make a bad impression!" Alex snapped back.

Jorden called out as they approached the front door. "You're here at last." She couldn't help but smile at Alex. "I'm glad you made it."

Jorden introduced her mother to Alex and Tom. Graciously, Mary served them coffee and peach cobbler around their large oak dining room table. Jorden watched her mother talk with such vitality; she did envy her easy manner with people.

Tom spoke up, "We'd best be going. We have a long drive ahead of us."

Alex lifted his cup to Mrs. Marshall. "Thank you. The coffee and cobbler hit the spot—just the break we needed."

"I'm glad you liked it."

Mary Marshall appeared to be an innocuous, pleasant woman, but Jorden knew her mother was assessing the two young men as she spoke with them. Jorden could almost read her thoughts and body language. She figured her impression of Alex was positive as he had a refined look and spoke well in spite of his New York accent. Jorden knew her mother hoped she would meet and marry a nice southerner.

"Mother, we need to go."

"I know," Mary replied.

Jorden gave her mother a hug. "Love you. Tell Dad and Bobbette goodbye for me. I'll call you when I get to Columbus." She knew she would follow through—she always did when it came to her mother's wishes.

"Love you too. Take care." Mary stood in the doorway and watched them load the car.

"Jorden, why don't you sit in front with me? All Tom does is complain or sleep." Alex put Jorden's bags in the trunk.

"I don't mind sitting in the back." She didn't want to sit back there—but why did she said it?

"Don't I have any say in this?" Tom piped up.

"No," Alex scoffed, showing his irritation. Tom grunted and got in the back. Jorden noted their exchange and wondered what it forebode for the rest of the trip?

"You know, you have taken us out of our way and added hours to this trip. Does this make you happy?" Tom called out to Jorden from the back seat.

"Sorry. Alex did offer me a ride."

Jorden looked at Alex. "Didn't you tell Tom you were coming to get me?"

Tom answered, "Yes, he did, but I had no idea it would take us almost one hundred miles out of the way. Besides, we got lost and spent a couple hours trying to find your house. How's that make you feel?"

Jorden watched Alex snarl at Tom through the rear-view mirror. At first she thought Tom was kidding, but soon she realized he wasn't. Unrelenting, he complained non-stop. She had never been around anyone so rude and decided to ignore him and keep her mouth shut.

Alex drove out of New Jersey into Pennsylvania. After thirty miles, Tom drifted off to sleep. A quiet peace fell over them. Jorden assumed Alex planned to drive through the night.

"Sorry about Tom. I never expected he'd give you such a rough time. I'm impressed you didn't blast him."

"I felt like it, but what good would it do? Besides, I'd be down at his level, and I'm not reaching so low."

"Good for you!" Alex slid his hand over hers. "I've missed you."

Jorden didn't know what to say. She was still upset with him. Their last parting was awful. Had he forgotten? She sensed Alex was holding back. Maybe he did know what she was feeling, but she couldn't tell.

"I hope your uncle's funeral went well," Alex said.

"It's always sad when you lose a family member, but yes, it went well." Jorden wanted to know why he had acted so cold and left so abruptly after she told him about her uncle's death—but something held her back. She really didn't want to ruin the moment. Instead she asked, "How was your Christmas?"

"Good. We had a full house. My two brothers and their families were there which is why I didn't get a chance to call you sooner. My little niece and nephew never left me alone. But it's okay; they're cute and fun to be around. How was your holiday?"

"Fun. Good to get back home. Bobbette, my older sister, kept me entertained like old times."

A piercing snore interrupted them. They both laughed.

"Tom's definitely asleep." Jorden felt Alex's gaze linger on her before he turned his eyes back to the road. His fingers continued to caress her hand—this was the side of Alex she cherished.

Large flakes of snow started falling. Jorden watched Alex concentrate on the road while his thick eyelashes blinked faster as the snow increased. At the same time, he turned up the speed of the windshield-wipers and blasted the defroster. Now, he used two hands on the steering wheel. The roads were slick. Slowing down, he stepped lightly on the breaks and the Mustang fishtailed—Tom woke with a start.

"Wow, what happened? What time is it?"

"Almost eight," Alex replied.

"Where are we?" Tom belted out.

"Virginia."

"You're kidding. We haven't gone any further then Virginia. Well, we know whose fault this is." Jorden could feel his eyes boring into the back of her head. She didn't say a word.

"We're getting low on gas. Keep your eyes open for the next exit. Think you can do that, Tom?"

Jorden could feel the tension when Tom ignored Alex's question. Two miles later, a large sign appeared advertising gas at 39 cents per gallon. Alex turned off and pulled up to the gas pump as the attendant walked up to the car. "How much?"

"Fill'er up," Alex replied.

"We need a break. Let's go in and get some snacks. Those should hold us until morning." Alex waited for the car to be filled while

Jorden and Tom went straight to the restrooms. Next, they each picked out drinks and a variety of munchies to eat. "What a lousy dinner," Jorden mumbled, but not loud enough for the others to hear. She didn't want to complain.

While they waited in line Jorden couldn't help but overhear the conversation between the man in front of them and the store clerk.

"Roads are awful. Have you heard the weather report? Sure isn't good. I wouldn't be out if I didn't have to," the man remarked as he paid the clerk.

"I agree. We might close early. I hate the thought of driving home."

Jorden, Alex, and Tom paid for their individual items as the clerk continued to talk about the weather. "The forecast says it's going to get worse. Better be careful!"

On their way out, Tom turned toward the clerk. "Well, we're going on. We can handle anything!"

Alex grinned at the clerk. "He just wants to make sure he gets back in time for a hot date."

"So? I've been thinking about this woman for weeks. I don't want to blow it because of Jorden and the weather." Jorden could see Tom give Alex a killer look.

"We'll see how far we can go. I hope we can make it through the night."

"I'll drive," Tom offered.

"No way! I don't want you to wreck my car!"

Jorden wondered what he would say if she offered to drive? She was a good driver, but the idea of driving his car seemed off limits.

Alex drove another five hours. The roads became slicker and deadlier. This time, Tom stayed awake. All eyes were glued to the road. Right and left cars had skidded off the Interstate.

"It's after one thirty. I'm exhausted!" Alex declared. "We're pulling off at the next exit. Hopefully, we can find a place to stay for the rest of the night."

Tom didn't argue. Several miles down the Interstate Jorden noticed a lighted billboard advertising the Chelsea Retreat Motel. Open 24 hours a Day—One Mile Ahead. Alex turned off at the exit. Four minutes later, Jorden saw the motel off in the distance.

It looked run down, but that didn't matter at this point. A Vacancy sign flashed dimly.

Alex went in—Jorden assumed to get two rooms. When he came out, he shook his head and threw up his arms in disgust. "They only have one room left. It's a single with a double bed. I took it."

Tired and beat, she watched Alex open the door to the room. It was garish with a grungy overhead light fixture and a small lamp which put out little light. At least it featured a small bathroom, its one redeeming feature.

"This will have to do."

Jorden started to laugh. "Hey, Tom, look what you have to tell your hot date. This should spice up your evening—a threesome!"

They started laughing and couldn't stop until someone in the next room banged on the wall.

"Hey, keep it down! It's after two!"

"These walls are paper thin. It's good we're in an end unit," Alex muttered.

"Why? What are we going to be doing?" Jorden asked. This made them howl even louder. They had to force themselves to stop when a second bang came with stronger language.

The laughter released tension; even Tom seemed to mellow out. "I'll take the chair. You two can have the bed."

"You're crazy," Alex stated. "The three of us can manage in the bed."

"Okay," Tom replied.

Jorden could see Tom's shoulders relax. She thought he would be perfect under the bed.

Tom proceeded to lay down fully dressed on top of the bedspread. There were a couple of blankets on top of a rack over the bed; Alex pulled them down and draped them over the three of them. Tom lay on the outer left side, Alex in the middle and Jorden on the right side. Alex turned toward Jorden's back with no space between them as Tom quickly began snoring. Alex placed his arm over Jorden's small waist. She felt him squeeze her hand while he brushed his lips against the back of her neck . . . then he promptly fell asleep.

Jorden could hear his shallow breathing become deeper and slower. She couldn't believe they were sharing a bed even if it included Tom. The men slept while Jorden lay awake. Tom's snoring drove her nuts. She had the urge to leave—but where too?

She turned her thoughts to her last conversation with Justin. How could she have broken their date? It wasn't right. Maybe she'd stop by the university tomorrow. She didn't know what she'd say . . . Jorden's eyes became heavy as she tried to decide what to do.

"Jorden, wake up! It's almost seven. We have a long drive ahead of us." Alex's voice seemed to come through a fog. She heard a toilet flushing. Where was she? She opened her eyes and it all came back.

They took turns in the bathroom. Jorden checked out her disheveled hair in the mirror and quickly pulled it back, securing all with a hairclip. Since they hadn't undressed, it didn't take long to get back on the road. As often happens in the southern states, overnight the temperature had warmed up forty degrees. It was now in the upper fifties, and the roads were much better.

They stopped for gas and spotted a diner. After eating a scrumptious breakfast of crisp bacon, eggs, pancakes, and steaming coffee, they were ready to get back on the road. Jorden couldn't get over the change in Tom. He looked relaxed and wasn't even harassing her. The catchy tune "Respect" by Aretha Franklin, bolstered her spirits and helped her drift off to sleep. An hour later, Tom started snoring. The sound startled her, making her body jerk. Alex put his hand out to catch her. "What's going on?"

"It's Tom."

Jorden pushed herself up. "I didn't realize I fell asleep. You must be beat driving the whole way."

"I'm better now after getting some sleep and a decent breakfast helped. How about you?"

"I'm okay—just tired. It's hard to sleep through Tom's snoring."

"Lucky me," Alex replied. "I never heard him last night."

"You were out when your head hit the pillow."

Alex smirked. "Well, what are we going to do now?"

"What are you talking about?"

"We've already slept together." Alex grinned from ear to ear.

Jorden slapped his hand. "Never! You slept, and I laid there with my eyes wide open."

"Not this morning. I had to wake you up."

"I'm not counting it as a wakeup call. Besides, if you want to be technical, I slept with two men."

"Okay, you win. At least admit it was nice to be close. The storm made this quite an adventure."

Jorden reached over and squeezed his hand.

Tom slept in the back seat until they reached the outskirts of Lockton. Alex stopped for several red lights, waking Tom with the change in momentum.

"Are we in Columbus?"

"No. We're three hours away in Lockton, Alabama." Alex looked at Tom in the rearview mirror. "Be patient, we're getting closer."

"You should have taken my offer to drive." Jorden watched Tom lean forward to make sure Alex could hear him. "You know, we'd be in Columbus by now."

Alex ignored him as he approached the turn for Jorden's grandmother's home.

"It's the next one on the right," Jorden said as she motioned to Alex.

Jorden could see her Volkswagen under the large pecan tree. She looked for her grandmother's car; it was nowhere in sight. She got out of the Mustang and knocked on the front door. No answer. Perfect. Alex and Tom could drive on and she would stop by Justin's to make amends.

Satisfied with her plan, Jorden threw up her arms up to indicate no one was there. "Why don't you and Tom go on to Columbus? I'll wait for Grandma in Lockton."

"We'll wait with you."

"Come on, Alex, I want to get back to Columbus. Jorden can drive on later." Tom looked like he was ready to spit fire.

"No. We're waiting. I'm not budging," Alex muttered

Tom swore and slammed his hands against the dashboard.

"Go on. There's no reason to wait for me," Jorden called back.

Alex glared at Jorden. "I'm not leaving without you."

"It's okay," Jorden said, gritting teeth. "Go on for Tom's sake."

"Yeah. Yeah! Hear that? Let's go," Tom barked.

"No!" Alex adamantly stated, leaving no room for rebuttal.

"Look—Grandma may have gone to dinner at my aunt's home, so it's futile to wait. I'll leave a note." She silently cursed his stubbornness. Now what would she do? She couldn't have Alex following her to Justin's.

"Good. We'll follow you on to Columbus." Alex proceeded to start his car while Jorden walked over to her Volkswagen. She would try and outrun them.

Chapter 27

January 1970

Jorden shifted positions in the plane's window seat. She glanced out to look at the ocean, only to find the view obstructed by clouds. She made a face somewhere between a frown and a smile when she remembered the trip from Lockton, Alabama to Columbus, Georgia.

***

Previous Year – January 3, 1969

Jorden tried to outdistance Alex, but his Mustang was too fast and powerful for her Volkswagen Bug. Two hours later, she approached the university's city limits. Soon there would be a number of traffic lights. After the first one, there was a shortcut to Justin's. If she timed the light right, Alex would have to stop. Luck was on her side. She slid through the yellow light while the Mustang screeched to a halt.

"Hooray!" Jorden continued a half mile, then turned onto a side street. She was in familiar territory with no sign of Alex behind her. Justin's apartment was off to the right. Driving slowly, she noticed Justin's car in the parking lot and lights on in his living room. She couldn't forget Justin's angry words the last time they spoke at her home in Trenton. He had given her an ultimatum. Either Jorden let him know she hadn't broken their date, or he didn't expect to see her again. Justin had vehemently hung up! Even today, a shiver ran down her back as she drove closer to his apartment. She never made that call. Surely, there was still time to explain and make him understand.

Jorden scraped the curb as she parked. Anxious, she stared at the familiar walkway to Justin's apartment. Why couldn't she move? Her arms and legs seemed paralyzed. Minutes passed, then a half hour as she remained in the same position. Tingling sensations ran up her calf. She felt the beginning of a spasm and knew it would soon develop into a painful cramp. Trying to stop it, she stamped her left foot, kicking her knee up and hitting the steering wheel. As she clenched the wheel, a figure crossed into her peripheral vision.

Jorden honed in on a young lady moving quickly up Justin's walkway. She seemed familiar—of course, she had seen her at parties she and Justin had gone to. Jorden couldn't stop looking at the classy young woman who was pulling back her hair with one hand and straightening her skirt from under her coat with the other. Then, she pressed the doorbell.

Spellbound, Jorden watched Justin open the door, greeting the woman with a hug and a light kiss. Jorden's fingertips flew up to her own lips, feeling deceived. But, how could she condemn him? Look how she had acted. The young woman walked inside and Justin closed the door behind them. Jorden felt wounded! Tears slipped down her cheeks.

Without thinking, Jorden turned the key in the ignition, pushed down on the gas, and eased off the clutch. She reached her apartment an hour and a half later, around seven thirty. In a state of denial, she almost didn't hear the phone as she climbed the stairs. The ringing stopped—only to begin again. She answered on what she thought was the fourth ring.

"Where have you been? You had me worried." Alex's voice cracked. "I've been calling and calling. I thought you might have been in an accident."

Startled by Alex's tone, Jorden hesitated. "I'm . . . I'm fine." She wasn't sure what to say. She couldn't explain the situation with Justin, but still she wanted to be truthful. "I stopped by the university but didn't stay long—which is why I'm late."

"I thought you might have, but you really had me worried. How about the dinner I promised you?"

"I'd . . . I'd like that."

"I'm leaving now."

"Wait! Give me thirty minutes. I've been in these clothes the last two days. I've got to shower and change." But Jorden wanted more—she needed to clear her mind.

"See you in a half hour." Forty-five minutes later, the doorbell rang. She'd try to put Justin out of her thoughts.

"Are you ready?"

"Quite."

Alex reached for his keys. Out of habit he checked for his wallet. "Sorry, we need to make a detour. I'm pretty sure I left my wallet at home."

Fifteen minutes later, they reached his place. "It's cold out here. Come in with me."

"I'll wait. I'd rather not see Tom."

"He's gone. Remember his hot date?" Alex laughed.

"I'm fine here."

"I'll be right back." Alex left the engine running and dashed inside. To Jorden's relief he soon returned, waving his wallet as he got back in—but by then the Mustang's engine had stalled.

"I don't know what happened. The engine just sputtered and quit," Jorden replied.

Alex tried a dozen times, but the engine wouldn't start. "Don't quit on me now after two thousand miles! I think I've flooded it. Let's go inside; it should start in a few minutes."

Jorden focused on the wall clock in the kitchen—it was after nine. "Aren't we too late for dinner?"

Alex paused, appearing to study the clock. "I know, what if I make us something?" He opened the refrigerator. "Let's see . . . there's ham, eggs, and cheddar cheese. How about an omelet?"

"I can help."

"No, I'm an expert. Just watch." First, Alex pulled out a pan and gathered what he needed from the refrigerator and cabinets.

"This is new! I've never had a man cook for me. How about coffee? I can at least start it brewing."

"We're out. I didn't have any to make the morning I left for New York. Tom pisses me off. He drinks coffee all the time but never replaces it."

"I'll drink whatever you have."

Alex opened the refrigerator again. "We have lots of beer. I know it doesn't go with an omelet, but it's all I have."

"Whose beers are they? I won't touch Tom's!"

Alex grinned. "Here. Have a beer. It's on the house—and don't worry about Tom." He flipped the metal caps off with a bottle opener and handed her one. "Sit back and relax. I make the best omelet ever."

Jorden took him for his word. The beer tasted good. She relaxed and watched Alex whip the last six eggs. He diced up the ham and grated the cheddar cheese. Then he poured the egg mixture into a well-oiled heated pan. Meticulously, he moved the skillet back and forth on the stove's burner to set the mixture. Rich aromas filled the tiny kitchen as he added salt and pepper, ham, and cheese before he flipped it over at the perfect moment.

"Smells delicious. Yum. I could eat it all."

"No way! We'll split it right down the middle." Alex proceeded and divided the omelet with the spatula and served it up on paper plates.

"Yum! It's perfect." Devouring the omelet in no time, Jorden licked the remains off her fork. "Delicious—the best. Thank you."

"Told you I was good. Here, have another beer." He popped off two more caps and handed another one to Jorden before she could protest. "Let's sit on the couch in the living room. I'm tired of these hard stools." The furniture was sparse with a couch, one side chair, and a television perched on an end table.

"Aren't you tired? My legs feel like lead weights," Alex stated with a sigh.

"No wonder, you drove straight through. You've earned the right to feel beat."

Alex pulled Jorden closer as they slid down on the couch. "Now that feels better, doesn't it?" He kissed the back of her neck and held her gently. Shivers ran up her back as she felt the soft pressure of his lips on her neck. He buried his face closer to hers while three simple words rolled off his tongue: "I love you."

Light headed, Jorden pressed in closer. His arms encircled her. Jorden responded, reaching for his hand and weaving her fingers between his. Before she knew it, she murmured the same words back to him. They were still for a long time, captured by the moment.

Around two in the morning, Jorden sat up with a start. A car had driven up in front of the apartment. The motor sputtered and clanged, sounding like firecrackers.

"What's going on?"

"I can't believe it! It can only be Tom's car." Alex jumped up.

Next they could hear voices and laughter as the car door slammed. "Watch your hands," the woman yelled. "At least wait until we get inside."

"Get me out of here! Tom is the last person I want to see."

"Too late!" Alex replied. The door opened and Tom and his date waltzed in draped over each other.

"What are you doing here?" Tom blurted out, trying not to slur his words.

"No fear. We're leaving," Alex replied.

"While you're here, you might as well meet Ruby. She's the prettiest girl this side of heaven." Tom gave Ruby a squeeze. A young woman, nineteen or twenty, in a skimpy, tight black dress stood there leaning against Tom for support.

"Pleased to meet ya." Ruby smiled, batting her light blue eyes at Alex.

"Ruby, go grab us some beers. Couldn't wait to see me again, could you?" Tom looked at Jorden with a silly grin.

"We're going." Alex opened the door.

"You're no fun! Ruby, just bring two beers; let's go to bed and forget them."

Alex apologized as they walked to the car. "Tom can tie one on. He'll be a pain to be around tomorrow. Glad I'll be working."

Jorden noted the Mustang's engine fired up and there were no problems on the drive back to her apartment.

"I didn't mean for tonight to end like this, but I meant what I said earlier. I love you." Alex leaned down and kissed her.

Adrenaline rushed through her veins as she stepped into the apartment. Before she could think, the words flew out: "Please stay."

Alex paused.

"Just lie down next to me until I fall asleep. There's not much left of the night. It's almost three."

"Let's do it."

Jorden took his hand and led them to her small bedroom. He touched her arm and slid the quilt over her.

Jorden woke around nine the next morning. To her surprise, Alex was next to her with his leg halfway off the bed. It struck her as funny, but she suppressed the urge to laugh. It amazed her how different she felt from just a month ago—now she was convinced she did love him.

Her eyes settled again on Alex's leg. The small bed barely had enough room for one, much less two. She couldn't control herself and started to giggle. Alex woke up and pulled himself further onto the bed. "What's so funny?"

"You are. Look at you."

"Well, you don't look much better." Alex propped his head up on his elbow. "Well Miss Marshall, what do you have to say for yourself this time? Two nights in a row!"

"You were supposed to leave after I fell asleep. But . . . thank you. I didn't want to face the apartment alone, especially after Tom and his girl showed up last night. Madison will be back tomorrow and things will go back to normal."

"Are you inviting me for a third night?" Alex looked at her with mischief in his eyes.

"No!"

He reached for her. "What if these nights could go on and on?"

"What are you talking about?"

"What does it sound like?" Alex asked.

"I don't know. You tell me."

"It's simple. Will you marry me?"

The words startled Jorden. "Now I know you're crazy."

"No, I mean it. Will you marry me? Shall I get down on my hands and knees?"

Jorden looked at him like he lost his mind. "No."

"You mean you won't marry me?" Alex frowned.

"That's not what I said."

"Oh. You will marry me."

"You're the Devil!" Jorden lay there, speechless.

Alex slid off the bed. He got up on his knees and reached for her hand. "Well then—will you marry the Devil?"

Squeezing his hand, she startled herself with a slight rasp in her voice, before she answered. "No . . . Yes."

"Which is it?"

"No. I won't marry the Devil."

"And?"

Jorden continued, "You really shouldn't kid about marriage."

"Can't you hear me? I'm not kidding. I want you to be my wife."

Alex pulled her close. Their lips met. "I promise to make you happy. Look at me—I'm waiting for your answer."

Jorden looked one way then the other and, finally, directly at him. "Yes. . . I'll . . . I'll marry you." She couldn't believe her words.

It was happening so quickly! Was she being influenced by her friends' marriages, even her sister's recent engagement, or was Justin part of this? Right now, she had no answers. At the moment, she didn't care—she felt happy.

Chapter 28

January 1970

Jorden knew she wasn't far from Hawaii, maybe another hour. Closing her eyes, she drifted back to the weekend Alex proposed.

***

Previous Year – Saturday, January 4, 1969

A lot had happened since Jorden left her home in Trenton, New Jersey. The past few days had changed both Jorden's and Alex's lives. She couldn't believe Alex had asked her to marry him. Even more unbelievable, she had accepted. Her spirits lifted even higher at the sight of him pulling into the spot next to her Volkswagen. She had the door open when he reached the top of the stairs.

"You're on time."

"At your service. I even brought Champagne to celebrate later."

"Great. I'll put it in the refrigerator."

"Are you ready?"

"You bet!" Jorden waltzed towards him.

"You smell delicious." Alex wrapped his arms around her. "Want to delay dinner?"

"No way! You do have your wallet—don't you?"

"Let me see," Alex said as he pretended to go through his pockets.

"You're terrible." She reached into his back pocket. "Here it is." She grinned and shoved him toward the door. "Now, I'm ready for the dinner you promised me."

"Can't break my promise," Alex said with a bow.

They went to Amore's. Antonio waved them over. "You two look happy. Is this a special occasion?"

"It is! This beautiful young lady agreed to marry me."

"Congratulations!"

"Thank you," Alex replied.

"Have you set a date?" Antonio inquired as he pulled out a chair for Jorden.

"Not yet."

"Well, with such good news, can I interest you in our special, Shrimp Fettuccini Alfredo? Antonio asked in an upbeat tone. "It's delicious."

"Perfect," Alex agreed.

Jorden nodded in agreement. "Good choice."

"For this special occasion, two glasses of Chardonnay are complimentary, if you'd like?"

"Sounds wonderful," Alex replied.

Jorden enjoyed the dinner and Antonio's attention to detail. "Can I tempt you with one of our delectable desserts?"

"Not for me, I can't take another bite." Jorden dropped her napkin on the table.

"Thank you, Antonio. We'll linger awhile longer."

"No rush. Take all the time you want."

Settled in, Alex reached into his pocket and pulled out a rectangular box wrapped in Christmas paper.

"What do you have there?"

"Remember, I said I had a present for you."

"Yes. You wouldn't take no for an answer." Jorden wanted to forget Justin's phone conversation. Her shoulders slumped when she thought of him hanging up on her.

"I see a frown; maybe I should save it for later?"

"No. You can't keep me in suspense." Jorden took it from his hands and tore off the wrapping. She opened a jeweler's box. At the center lay a silver bracelet. A delicate heart dangled from the silver chain. It was outlined in gold with an emerald in the center.

"It's beautiful! Here! Help me put it on."

"First, look on the back."

Gently, Jorden turned it over. Their initials were finely engraved with the date, 1/4/69. Jorden looked astonished. "When did you have it engraved?"

"I found a jeweler this afternoon. I wanted to give you something special to remind you of this date. Each year I want to add another heart so it will grow with us."

Jorden held up her wrist for Alex to latch the silver chain.

"It's lovely." The heart dangled freely, the emerald reflecting the light from a vase of cut flowers.

"I love it," Jorden said while kissing him. "Thank you."

Jorden was quiet on the ride back to her apartment. She couldn't keep her eyes off the bracelet. "It's amazing we ever met. Do you think we're a good fit?" Jorden squeezed his arm.

"Getting cold feet?" Alex joked. "Oh, we have differences. Everyone does. Like we said this morning, we should talk."

"You're right. This is a good time—Madison won't get back until late tomorrow afternoon."

Alex enveloped Jorden in his powerful arms after they entered her apartment. She shivered.

"Are you all right?" Alex asked.

"Just cold."

"Are you sure that's all?"

"Yes, but . . . I still worry we may have too many differences."

"I don't think so. Come sit with me."

"First, I want to say how much I love you. I know it seems like we made this decision too quickly, but it feels right. After those crazy two days on the road, I knew I wanted you for my wife. Tom acted so terrible, and you took it so well. You're beautiful. I hope you don't want to back out?"

"No. I just want it to be right between us."

"It will be. We share the same value system. What are you worried about?"

"Religion. I know you're Catholic, and I grew up Methodist. They're very different. The church was a big part of my life." Jorden and her family had gone to the same church ever since she could remember. She never thought about changing faiths.

"Yes, I'm Catholic, and I have to be honest with you; I can't leave my faith. It would break my mother's heart. Growing up, our lives were immersed in the church. I want my children, I mean our children, brought up in the Catholic faith." He squeezed her hands. Their eyes met.

Silence followed. Jorden kept hearing the phrase "Break my mother's heart." It continued to play in her mind. Lowering her eyes, she stared at her hands nestled in Alex's large ones. The emerald on the bracelet sparkled as she moved her wrist. It reminded her of his earlier words: "Each year I want to add to this so it will grow with us." She wanted that too.

Jorden looked up. "I know there is quite a difference between our faiths, but maybe I can bend easier than you. I'm . . . I'm willing to convert and bring up our children in the Catholic faith if it means that much to you." She wasn't sure she could ever go along with all the Catholic doctrines, but she would try.

Alex's eyes brightened. "I want that more than you can ever know. You makes me a very happy man."

"I'm glad you want children. I'd hate to fall in love with someone who didn't want a family." Jorden hesitated before she continued, "I also have to be honest—I only want two children, three at the most. I do believe in birth control." Jorden looked directly at Alex. "Is this going to be a problem for you?"

"I'll be practical. We won't be able to afford more than two or three kids. We can follow the Church's acceptable rhythm method or at least give it a try. If it doesn't work, we'll have to figure out some other plan. I know we can make this work."

An alarm went off. She knew the method accepted by the Catholic Church wasn't reliable. She wondered how he thought they could make this work, but she pushed the thought aside.

"When shall we get married?" Alex asked.

"This all feels so—overwhelming. I haven't even had time to think about it."

"I think I'd like to wait until I return from Vietnam. That will give us more time. It won't be like we rushed into marriage. What do you think?"

"All right for now—we still have time to make up our minds." Jorden thought about Madison. They married before Luke went to Vietnam. But, they shared the same religion. Maybe Alex is right— it would be better to wait.

"You make me so happy! Let's break out the Champagne and celebrate our future." Alex squeezed her shoulders.

"I'll get the glasses. Hey, all we have are water glasses."

"They should work." Alex popped the cork and poured the sparkling wine.

"Whoa!"

"You're no fun!" Alex laughed and raised his glass. "To the future Mrs. Whelan."

Jorden shivered as she clinked his glass.

Alex put on an album by Neil Diamond. "Kentucky Woman" began playing. "Let's dance—I like this one."

They glided to the rhythm of the music. Jorden felt him nuzzle her neck, smelling the fragrance of her perfume. He held her tightly, touching the softness of her skin. Several songs later, Alex led them in the direction of her bedroom. Piece by piece the remnants of their clothes ended up on her bedroom floor. He kissed her, gently at first. A quiver went down her back when he lifted her like a feather and placed her on her bed. A flurry of emotions intensified. She felt herself lift out of reality. Then—it was over.

Jorden lay quietly. "I hope I haven't hurt you?" Alex asked.

Jorden didn't say anything.

After a few minutes, Alex left for the bathroom.

"So that's it," Jorden murmured.

He had his briefs on when he returned to the bed. Lying next to Alex, Jorden realized she could get pregnant. It hit her like a ton of bricks. Surely, she wouldn't. She reached for her underwear before tracing his steps to the bathroom and looking into the mirror. She touched her face to see if she looked different. The reflection appeared to be the same, but she felt changed.

"Are you okay?" Alex called out.

"I'm fine." Jorden walked back and slid in next to him.

She had to say something. "We . . . can't . . . do this again! I can't get pregnant, at least not now."

A long silence. Jorden clenched her fists.

"I know I shouldn't have, but I couldn't stop myself," Alex replied.

"We could have used something." A condom was what Jorden meant to say, but didn't.

Alex gazed at her. "I promise I can be strong."

Well, he sure closed the door on using birth control. "We both have to be strong," she corrected him.

Silence fell over them. Fortunately, she didn't get pregnant.

Chapter 29

Flight Arriving in Hawaii,
January 16, 1970

"**P**repare for landing. We are on our final descent to Honolulu." Jorden raised the window shutter. Bright lights dotted the landscape below. She wondered if Alex had already arrived. After landing, she hailed a cab to their hotel. She looked out and caught the moon shining over the horizon. She really was in paradise.

Jorden had lost her concentration when she realized someone had spoken to her.

"Miss. Your name please."

"Jorden . . . Jorden . . . Whelan," she stammered as she signed the hotel's register. She could see Alex hadn't signed in. What if something happened, and he couldn't come? She barely remembered the hotel attendant taking her luggage to Room 418. Her fingers shook while pulling out a tip. She gasped as she realized she had drawn a five dollar bill. She saw his smile and knew she couldn't easily exchange it for two ones. Reluctantly, she handed him the larger amount.

Jorden focused on the room. A queen bed dominated the space with a television, double drawer dresser, and the bathroom off to the right. She slid open the balcony door. The sea air renewed her spirits. The view heightened her awareness she was in Hawaii. The lights from the hotel picked up the white caps of ocean waves as they rolled toward the beach.

A key turned in the door. The sound seemed to explode in her ears even though it was actually hard to hear. Alex. He dropped his duffle bag, rushed forward, and grabbed Jorden. Tears flowed down her cheeks. "What's this?" He tilted her chin upward and kissed them away. "No time for tears, we have much more to catch up on."

The next morning, room service knocked at nine. Alex clambered out of bed and asked them to come back later. He showered while Jorden slept—the sound of the running water soon roused her. Last night seemed like a dream, but thankfully it wasn't. Alex had lost weight, but he still had his boyish smile, the one she loved.

She twisted the fake wedding band on her left hand—it felt strange but in a good way. How she wished it was the real thing. She and Madison had gone to Montgomery Ward to purchase a cheap, gold-plated band. She wanted to make the adventure appear authentic. Now, the ring brought a smile to her face. Why had she worried so much? The hotel clerk never even questioned her marital status.

"What are you smiling about?" Alex asked as he stepped out of the bathroom with a towel wrapped around his waist.

Jorden lifted her ring finger. "I'll keep wearing this to keep us looking honest."

"We'd best put it to good use." A sly grin spread across Alex's face.

Saturday flew by. They had a late lunch and drove around the island. Jorden was determined to hold onto every minute and not let time slip away.

On Sunday, their second day, Jorden was surprised Alex never suggested going to church. Pre-Cana classes hadn't been brought up nor the subject of birth control. She was glad she was now on the pill—taking control of her life. They spent part of Sunday at a large shopping mall. Jorden lost herself in all the unique pieces of art work. She purchased wooden salad bowls for her mother and a hand-blown glass vase for Bobbette. She couldn't forget Madison or her roommates and selected small, hand-carved wooden jewelry boxes for each of them.

Monday morning, before seven, Jorden and Alex went for a long walk on the beach. She wore shorts, soaking up the sun's rays while the waves lapped at her feet. Few people were out, making it a peaceful time. The tide was low as they searched for shells. Jorden looked up and saw the morning mist lift. It reminded her of the church steeple at Fort Benning and the basketball game they had attended last December. The mist had swept in and surrounded the steeple. The moment was surreal. It was one not to be forgotten— like this morning.

On Tuesday, clouds formed over the horizon. The ocean's waves grew in strength as they pounded the shoreline. Alex led Jorden to breakfast at the hotel's glass-enclosed terrace restaurant. The aroma of coffee filled the air, accompanied with crisp bacon, eggs, fresh fruits, and pastries spread out on the buffet table. Jorden and Alex helped themselves to the assortment of island delicacies.

"Two days left," Jorden said softly as she sipped her coffee.

Alex held her hand as he reached out to comfort her.

"What's it like over there? You haven't said one word about this war."

Alex looked away before he spoke. "You try and get through each day—thankful to reach the next one. Like the waves, they keep coming and receding—that's how this war feels. You gain ground, but it's a matter of time before it's taken away or abandoned. Over there, it's a no win situation. But—I don't want to talk about Nam. I just want to carry you off—back to our own private world." The corners of his mouth edged upward. Jorden knew the look and reached for his hand as they strolled back to their room.

Hours later, they emerged refreshed. The skies had darkened, and the rain pelted down.

"Let's walk on the beach," Alex suggested.

"Are you crazy? It's pouring out there."

"So? Don't you have any spunk?"

Jorden couldn't resist the challenge. She slid on a lightweight jacket, pulled on her wrinkled blue shorts, and stepped into her white flip-flops to give her feet support on the sand.

"We'll have about an hour before the sun sets. By then our appetites for dinner will be back." Alex winked at Jorden. "For dessert we'll end our day on the sweetest treat ever." She looked up and slapped his back in jest, knowing full well what he implied.

Wednesday morning, the sun poured into their room and woke them early. Jorden stretched out, enjoying Alex next to her.

"What shall we do today? We could go for a drive and explore the northern shores," Alex suggested.

"Let's take our snorkeling gear—maybe we'll find a nice quiet area." Jorden sat up and looked at Alex before she spoke. "One day left, let's enjoy it! I'll do my best to have a tearless day." She leaned over and kissed him.

After a relaxed breakfast, Alex drove them away from the city. Jorden spotted a quiet cove where people were snorkeling.

"Let's go down there."

They gathered their gear, strolled down to the sandy lagoon, and found a spot to put on their flippers. After assembling their snorkeling gear, Jorden entered the calm water. A new world opened up. The reflection of the sun turned the lagoon into an array of colors—reds, yellows, and greens. Schools of fish whirled in and out of the coral reefs and rock formations. Jorden and Alex floated on top of the water, bobbing back and forth with the push and pull of the gentle waves.

Jorden almost forgot this was their last day. After an hour, Alex was ready to leave. She pulled herself out of the water and took off her flippers, before walking up the beach. They toweled off and sat on their beach towels to let the hot sun dry their suits. She watched others soaking up the sun. Unexpectedly, her eyes fell upon a man who looked like Matt. She did a double take and couldn't take her eyes off him.

"What are you staring at?" Alex's eyes followed hers. "Do you know him?"

"No. He looks familiar." She averted her eyes toward the lagoon.

"He looks like a local, not a tourist."

The man came back into view as he slipped into the water. She could hear the smack of his flippers.

Jorden laughed. "I don't know him, but he's kind of cute." She winked at Alex and made him laugh. She then gazed at the lagoon again. The stranger was no longer in sight; that's the way she would keep it with Matt.

Wednesday evening arrived too quickly.

"It won't be long now," Alex kept saying, "The month of May will be here before you know it, and we'll be back together." Neither wanted the night to end. They made love knowing the morning sun would soon come up. It didn't seem fair to be so close and then to be torn apart again.

Jorden tried to hold back tears as she boarded the plane. Alex had driven her to the airport for her ten o'clock flight; his flight to Vietnam would leave later in the afternoon. Tearfully, unable to stop them, she waved goodbye.

Jorden reached her seat and sank back into the cushion. Closing her eyes, she could see them riding the waves and rolling back to the shoreline. That was life, high and low with space between. Hawaii was one of the highs.

Chapter 30

Return to Columbus, Georgia, Thursday, January 22, 1970

J orden sat on the runway at the Honolulu airport, wishing it was five days earlier. She and Alex had such little time. It didn't seem fair they were leaving each other again. She had a great time, five carefree days and no controversy between them—much better than this time last year. The rose-tinted illusions of romance had dimmed sooner than she had expected.

***

Previous Year - Columbus, Georgia, January 1969

Jorden wished they had more time together. Alex's life seemed to be consumed with work. He complained there were too many meetings, with never enough time for his regular work. He even maintained he skirted the job to fit time in for her. She found his excuses hard to believe.

With extra time, Jorden and Jim Stone, a fellow teacher, decided to start a new math project. They would add a section on the stock market. The general premise was to teach the students how to buy and sell shares of stock in order to make a profit. Jorden remembered Jim's enthusiasm.

"This is a great idea—only I don't know much about the stock market," Jorden confessed.

"We'll learn it together, starting at the local library."

Jorden thought he was out of his mind, but why not give it a try? She and her students would be learning it together. "Okay, let's do it. Shouldn't we say something to Mr. Rinehart? Seems like we'd need the principal's approval."

"I'll talk with him tomorrow. I don't think he'll mind as long as we don't disrupt our regular math curriculum," Jim replied.

Jorden figured she could work with the stock market at least one period a week, probably on Fridays, over the course of several months. Instructions could be adjusted to fit each class level. She took the next three weeks to gather data while developing lesson plans and coordinating her efforts with Jim.

At last, the day came for the first presentation. Jorden looked out at her students. "Let's start with the basic history of the stock market. Does anyone know when the Dow Jones Industrial Average was established?"

Blank faces stared back at her.

"I'm not crazy. This has been around for a while. Someone make a guess." Jorden scanned her students' faces. Jimmy's arm shot up.

"Go ahead. Give it a try," Jorden encouraged him.

"The 1920s. You know, with all the flappers dancing around."

"Good try. You're close. The actual date was May 26, 1896. In the beginning, twelve prominent companies were involved. During this time period, the average started at zero. Today, in 1969, the Dow Jones Average is around 950."

Nora raised her hand. "What's the average mean?"

"Good question." Jorden checked her notes. "Here we go: 'The Dow Jones Industrial Average is a price average of thirty blue-chip stocks of companies which are generally leaders in their industry. It has been a widely used indicator of the stock market since October 1, 1928.'"

After reading, Jorden looked up at the class. She saw one hundred percent confusion and forced herself not to laugh. "Don't worry.

I've made a handout for all of you. There's nothing in your math book about this."

After the introduction, Jorden continued with the rules. "Each of you will receive ten thousand dollars of bogus money to buy stocks."

Ben called out, "I think it should be real money."

"I wish!" Jorden couldn't help but smile before she continued. "A list of twenty-five high-quality companies will be given to each of you. From the list, you can choose which ones you want to invest in and become a stockholder."

Nora's hand flew up. "Why can't we pick our own companies?"

"Yeah," Jimmy piped up. "Why not?"

"We, Mr. Stone and I, thought it would be easier for you to have a list of trustworthy companies. You can select your companies to be a stockholder at any time during the next couple months. All stocks will be sold on a designated day, and then a test will be given."

Boos and hisses filled the classroom. "No fair!" Pete shouted.

"I have to see what you've learned. Besides it'll be fun. Now for the good part . . ." Jorden paused, getting their attention. "Prizes will be awarded to the top four students—meaning those who make the most money. There will be two winners from my classes and two winners from Mr. Stone's classes."

"How much? Will it be fake money?" Cheryl asked.

"We sure don't want play money," Jimmy blurted out.

Jorden stepped forward. Her eyes roamed from student to student. "The prizes will be paid in actual money. First place will receive $25, second $15, third $10, and fourth $5. The prizes will be paid from a specific fund provided by the Parent-Teacher Association."

"Let's win this!" Nora sent Cheryl an excited look. Nora started following the twenty-five companies from Miss Marshall's list. Cheryl clipped out the New York Stock Exchange from the daily newspaper and kept track of the data for each company in a separate notebook. Nora then ran comparisons and chose the best three stocks which continued to increase in value. The two girls decided to enter the competition under their combined names.

After school, Nora spent each afternoon in Cheryl's cozy kitchen, strategizing over their stocks. Cheryl's mother often listened while cutting up vegetables for dinner. Nora could tell Mrs. Barker was as caught up with the planning as the girls were plotting their strategy to make money.

Chapter 31

January 1970

They reached cruising altitude. Jorden's destination was Los Angeles—ultimately Columbus, Georgia. She pulled out the airline's magazine from the seat pocket in front of her. Leafing through the pages, she noticed an article on the "Twelve Days of Christmas." The title reminded her of the Twelfth Week party Alex had organized on Fort Benning Army Base. It was a celebration of the officer candidates' success and their halfway passage through the training program. Those candidates who made it this far usually completed the course and became officers. The night came back with clarity.

***

Previous Year – Saturday, February 15, 1969

Jorden wore a stylish, ankle-length and sleeveless apricot-colored silk dress. The front bodice was trimmed with a lattice of tiny colorful flowers on a silver backing. For a finishing touch, she draped a matching shawl over her shoulders to keep the chill off the evening air. Her hair, pulled back in a Grecian style, topped off her elegant look.

Madison clapped as Jorden emerged into the living room. "You look tremendous. Alex doesn't deserve you."

"Thank you." Jorden smiled and looked at the clock. It was six fifteen. "Alex should arrive by six thirty."

For the first time, Alex came early. Madison opened the door. There he stood in his full dress uniform. "Well aren't you handsome! I never would have recognized you."

"Thank you," Alex replied.

The dress blues gave Alex a stately appearance. He seemed to catch his breath as he spotted Jorden and reached for her. "You're lovely." Caressing her face, he kissed her. Her knees weakened.

"Hey you two, save the fireworks for later." Madison laughed.

The evening began smoothly but soon became long and tedious. Alex was in charge. He had to make sure the evening ran well. During their single dance, he remembered he needed to check on the drink set-up.

"I'm sorry Hon. I'll be right back."

Minutes stretched well beyond an hour. Jorden made polite conversation with anyone who came her way. Her feet hurt; she wasn't used to standing in three inch high heels for such a long time. No one asked her to dance. She guessed the officer candidates wouldn't dare since she had come with Alex and the others had dates.

But one officer, a striking young man, walked toward her. His prominent cheek bones, dark brown eyes, and angular nose made him look distinctive. "I've been noticing you. I figured you must be here with Alex. I'm Noel Jackson, a friend of his."

"Yes, I'm with Alex. I'm Jorden Marshall."

"We were in the same OCS class. Alex is a good man. Looks like he is awfully busy," Noel replied.

"It certainly does."

"Would you like something to drink?"

"I'd love something. A 7UP would be great."

"You've got it."

Noel returned with a Coke. "I hope this is all right? They ran out of 7UP."

"It's great. Thank you," Jorden replied.

Noel drank a beer while they chatted with a group of officers. He introduced Jorden as Alex's date. After a break in the conversation,

Jorden thanked him again. "If you'll excuse me, I need to find a place to sit down."

"Look, there's a small table. Let's claim it. I could use a break myself . . . if you don't mind my company?"

"Please do." Jorden sighed with relief. The small round table had a white covering which fell close to the floor. She couldn't pass up the opportunity to slip off her shoes. She and Noel entertained each other the next half hour, making it nearly two hours since she'd last seen Alex.

Fifteen minutes later, Alex spotted them. He waved. Jorden was laughing and didn't notice him.

"Here you are. I thought you'd deserted me," Alex teased.

"I believe you're the deserter," Jorden replied.

Alex seemed to ignore her comment as he spoke to Noel. "I see you've met my fiancée."

"Yes. You're a lucky man." Noel smiled at Jorden.

Alex's wary tone caught Jorden off-guard. He pulled up a chair and joined them. The night wound down after the colonel left around midnight. One never left until the top ranking officer made the first move, in this case the colonel. Noel then excused himself, shaking Alex's hand and touching Jorden's shoulder.

"Aren't you on the clean-up committee?" Jorden asked.

"No, I'm done for the night."

Tired and ready to leave, Jorden got up to find her shawl. She spotted the line to the cloakroom. Before long, she felt a tap on her shoulder. "Are you looking for this?" Alex handed her the shawl.

"Where did you get my shawl?"

"Remember, I organized this. You could have asked me, and I would have gotten your shawl. I'm not that bad. Let's go. It's been a long night."

"It sure has," Jorden muttered to herself, not saying a word on the drive back to her apartment. Alex walked her up and gave her a perfunctory hug and kiss.

"Aren't you coming in?"

"I'm exhausted. Some things didn't go as I planned. Sorry, I'm in a lousy mood."

Jorden didn't say a word while shrugging her shoulders with resignation. She could see Alex's wall forming.

"Don't be upset. I'll call you tomorrow."

"Fine." Jorden's voice shook. How could Alex leave like this? At the least, he could have given her a better explanation. What's wrong with him? Jorden wanted to shout.

Chapter 32

January 1970

Wedged into the window seat, Jorden looked into the dense cloud coverage. She shifted her position lifting her wrist to check the time. It was almost two—Alex had already left Hawaii going in the opposite direction to Vietnam. Coming and going seemed to be part of their lives.

***

Previous Year – March 1969

After the Twelfth Week party, Alex seemed to bounce back to his cheerful self—until he announced his latest news. She watched him pull into the parking lot and dart in to avoid the wind and rain. She had the door open when he reached the top of the stairs.

"Hi . . . how's my girl?" Alex looked past her, but not at her.

"What's happening?" Jorden sensed something wasn't right.

"I got my orders for Vietnam. I'm scheduled to leave at the end of May."

"I knew you were leaving, but we still have three months."

"I wish." Jorden followed Alex's gaze out the living room window. The wind carried broken twigs over the parking lot—twirling them in the wild currents before they dropped. He shifted his footing to face Jorden.

"And? What aren't you telling me?"

Alex seemed to hesitate. "It means I have two months of training and it won't be here."

"W–w–where?" Jorden stammered.

"It's in North Carolina."

"How many miles from here?"

"It's about four hundred miles from Columbus."

"When are you leaving?"

Alex was silent.

"When?" Jorden glared at him.

"Next Sunday."

"Why didn't you tell me before now?" Jorden sat down onto the couch.

Alex looked sheepish. "I just found out the details."

"You mean you knew about this and didn't tell me."

"Don't push me, Jorden!" A sharp edge crept into Alex's tone. "I'd hoped it would be here. I just got the news myself." He sat down next to her and focused on her face. "You are beautiful. I never wanted to hurt you, believe me." He leaned forward and kissed her.

Jorden kissed him back. Tears sprung up, ready to spill over.

"Please don't be mad," Alex pressed.

"I'm not mad. I'm upset. We don't have any time left. At least now we're together almost daily—even if it's only a couple of hours."

"I promise, we'll be okay. We can get together for a few weekends, plus I have a month's leave in May. I checked my training schedule, and it looks like I can get off at the end of March. It'll take eight hours to drive over here, but it will be well worth it. Why don't you drive up to see me for a weekend in April?" Alex held her tighter.

"You can drive it in eight hours; it'll take me much longer. Besides, I have to clear it with my principal. What if he says no?"

"He won't say no if you stretch the truth."

"You're awful. Listen to you corrupt me."

"Better than not seeing you."

After Alex left, Jorden poured time into school activities. She and Madison did more together. Jorden even called home more often. An earlier call to her mother about Alex came to mind. It was when she and Alex had decided to be married back in January. She was so excited she had to call home.

***

January 1969

"Hi. What's up?" Mary Marshall recognized Jorden's voice right off, as she always did.

"I have great news. Alex and I are going to be married." Jorden didn't hesitate or let her mother persuade her differently.

Silence.

"Mom. Are you there?"

"Yes, I'm here. Isn't this a quick decision?"

She could hear the alarm in her mother's voice, which didn't surprise Jorden.

"Do you know him well?" Her mother asked with concern.

"I know it seems sudden, but it's not really. I've been seeing him since September. At least you met him in January." Jorden sighed, trying to get her words out without wavering. Sometimes she wondered how she made the decision so quickly. But no, she made the right choice.

"When is this happening?"

"Not for another year, Alex wants to wait until he returns from Vietnam." Jorden knew this answer would please her mother. She heard Mary heave a sigh of relief.

"Thank goodness! You're not rushing into this. I think you're wise to wait."

"There is a drawback." Jorden sucked in her breath before she continued. "Alex is Catholic, and I agreed to raise our children in the Catholic faith. I know Dad won't be happy, but somehow it will work out."

Another silence. Jorden waited for her mother's response.

"Thank you for letting me know. Your dad will come around in time. I'll spread your news." And . . . her mother did.

***

March 1969

Bobbette, Jorden's sister, recently called with a warning. "Don't tell Mom you talked with me, but I had to forewarn you."

"About what?"

"Mom called Aunt Stephanie after she talked with you this past week. The two sisters are scheming to get Mom down to Atlanta."

"So?"

"So—looks like you're going to have a visitor. You shouldn't have told Mom about Alex coming to see you at the end of March."

"You mean Mom is coming to Columbus when Alex is here?"

"You got it."

"I can't believe it!" Jorden snapped back, slapping the countertop.

"Well you better believe it. Not even you can change her mind. Mom's determined to get to know Alex better," Bobbette stated as she ended the call.

Frustrated, Jorden ran her fingers through her hair. In the five years she had been in the South, her mother had only come to visit when she graduated from the university. She paced the room, then stopped and looked at Madison.

"I can't believe it. How can Mom even think about coming when Alex is here?"

Madison returned Jorden's look. "She's your mother, so she's concerned. When's she coming?"

"Friday night. I assume she'll return to Atlanta on Sunday. She knows I have to teach on Monday."

"Well when does Alex get in?"

"Late Friday night. With Mom here, we won't have any time alone."

"You shouldn't get so upset. She just wants to get to know Alex." Madison tried to lessen Jorden's fears but seemed to upset her more.

"She will ask Alex every possible question. I dread it. I wanted this time for us—not to be shared with my mom."

"Jorden, look at yourself. You're a mess! Your mother is coming, so accept it. Tell you what, I'll go home for the weekend, and your mother can use my room."

"Thank you." Jorden smiled.

"Where is Alex staying?" Madison asked, with a curious look.

"I assume he'll stay at Tom's place. There's no way he can stay here. Mom would never approve. She would assume a lot more is going on between us."

"I know it's none of my business, but have you and Alex worked out your differences on birth control? I'll be blunt. Is Alex using a condom?"

"No. We don't even talk about it. Nothing has happened since January. I can't fathom Alex's logic on not using protection except he's Catholic." Jorden knew without birth control, she'd probably get pregnant—and right now this wasn't an option for her. "He hasn't pressured me, but I don't know how long we'll be able to hold out."

"You should discuss it with him."

"Alex won't touch the subject. It's his Catholic doctrines. I have to assume these beliefs are behind his silence." Jorden respected his religion, but she didn't have to agree with it.

"What are you going to do after you're married?"

"I don't know." Jorden gazed out the window. "Contraception is a subject we can't seem to agree on."

Chapter 33

January 1970

Jorden squirmed in her seat as she strained to look through the clouds. She had at least three hours before her flight reached Los Angeles. A slight smile formed as she remembered her mother's visit to Columbus last year.

***

Previous Year - March 28, 1969

Jorden made sure she got back from school before her mother arrived. Mary Marshall drove into the Julian Apartment complex late Friday afternoon. Jorden had given her explicit instructions, so she wouldn't get lost. She figured it would take about two and half hours to drive from her sister's home in Atlanta to Columbus.

Standing at the picture window, Jorden watched as her mother got out of her car. Mary was a couple inches shorter than Jorden with a trim figure. Strands of gray ran through her short, naturally chestnut-colored hair, giving her a sense of warmth. She vowed to follow Madison's advice and treat her mother well.

Jorden hurried down the stairs to help her mother with her things, but first she gave her a huge hug. Minutes later she had her settled into Madison's bedroom. Mary then spent the next thirty minutes filling Jorden in on the family's latest news. "Now, tell me about Alex. This all seems so sudden."

"I will, but let's have dinner first." Jorden decided to take her to Amore's for old times' sake. Antonio was in rare form, flirting with both of them. Mary couldn't stop laughing. "Don't tell your dad, but I'd like to take Antonio home with me."

On the drive back to her apartment, Jorden relaxed. Her mother's sense of humor was contagious and lightened the mood. At last, she was ready to answer her mother's questions. She hit the highlights—how she met Alex, her trip to Columbus after Christmas, and a shortened version of his marriage proposal. Of course her mother had other questions, and Jorden did her best to answer them.

By ten o'clock, Mary looked exhausted. "Thank you for having me. I know you cherish your time with Alex. I just want to get to know him—and I promise not to ask him a thousand questions."

Jorden squeezed her mother. "I'm glad you came. Alex also wants to get to know you. I think you'll like him."

"I'm sure I will." Mary embraced her daughter and went to bed. Jorden read until midnight. Alex still hadn't shown up. She cleaned her face, changed, and put on her robe. By then it was almost one. She wished he'd call. Lying on the couch, Jorden's eyes became heavy. A sound woke her. She heard knocking, got up and looked out the peephole.

Alex was beaming! He embraced her, kissed her lips and neck. "I've missed you. I can't believe I'm finally here. You smell so good." There was sleep in Jorden's eyes and a warm glow on her face. He lifted her up and hugged her again. Jorden melted in his embrace.

"Is your mother here?" Alex whispered.

"Yes. She got in late this afternoon. She's in Madison's room."

"Good. The three of us will have to do something special tomorrow." Jorden and Alex talked into the night. The late hour didn't faze either of them.

Jorden's mother did her best not to dampen Jorden and Alex's short time together. Saturday morning, Alex drove them to the picturesque Callaway Gardens. The majority of the spring flowers were in full bloom, displaying a breathtaking view.

"It's almost twelve thirty. Who's hungry?" Alex piped up, "I sure am."

Jorden nodded in agreement. They had a tasty lunch of sandwiches and chips at the Callaway Gardens Lodge. Mary had quite a way of telling stories. When she wanted to, Jorden's mother could be hilarious. Alex couldn't stop laughing; he was almost howling. Jorden loved this side of her mother. Maybe she should have been a comedian—even the waiter was cracking up.

After lunch, Alex drove them to Warm Springs to take a tour of President Franklin D. Roosevelt's Little White House. Jorden suggested it since it was close to Callaway Gardens. After arriving, Alex checked at the admission desk; the next tour began in a half hour. He led them along the paths while Jorden read from a display of the historical information aloud.

"'This was the personal retreat of Franklin Delano Roosevelt. He had it built in 1932. Roosevelt first came to Warm Springs in 1924 to take advantage of the eighty-eight degree natural spring water to ease the pain of his paralysis. He had contracted polio in 1921. The hot springs helped him to engage in physical exercise. By 1927, Roosevelt purchased the springs and a surrounding 1,700 acre farm.'"

The sound of chimes rang out. Jorden figured they must be signaling the next tour. A group had already gathered next to the admission booth. When Jorden, her mother, and Alex arrived at the booth, they rounded the number up to ten.

"Greetings. Welcome to the Little White House." A cheery, grey haired woman greeted them. "My name is Helen. We're so happy you joined us." She had a twinkle in her eyes making Jorden smile.

"The house opened to the public as a museum in 1948, and the State of Georgia operates this historic site. Franklin Delano Roosevelt died here of a stroke on April 12, 1945. Most of this property has been willed to the Georgia Warm Springs Foundation."

"As you can see, the design is a miniature version of the Washington D.C. White House. We're going to walk through the rooms as they looked the day President Roosevelt died. Please listen—but don't touch. We want to keep this site preserved as it is now." Helen led them in.

The tour began in the entrance hall, with doorways to Eleanor Roosevelt's bedroom on the left and the kitchen area on the right. Straight ahead, a passage led to the living room. Jorden first entered the kitchen behind the others and then proceeded into the living room. She could see a large sun deck which spanned the width of the rear of the house.

Next, Helen led them to the right, and Jorden entered the secretary's bedroom with its own bathroom. Reversing her steps, Helen crossed the living room to the entrance of Franklin Roosevelt's bedroom. As they entered, Jorden listened to Helen explain the details of his bedroom and the events which occurred the day of Roosevelt's death. At the time, Jorden found it strange Eleanor and Franklin didn't share the same bedroom, but who was she to question it?

Jorden trailed the end of the tour group as Helen took them through the bathroom Franklin and Eleanor shared; it was between their adjoining bedrooms. Helen stopped in Eleanor's bedroom and continued to describe the details of the room. Before exiting to the entrance hall, she turned and looked at the group. "Any more questions?"

A loud voice from the back of the group boomed out, "What about Lucy Mercer? Wasn't she here when he died?"

"I wondered if someone would ask about Lucy. I usually don't mention it unless someone brings it up," Helen replied.

Another voice rang out, this time it came from the center of the group. "Who are you talking about?"

"We're talking about Lucy Mercer. She was an attractive young woman Eleanor had hired in 1913 as her personal secretary. Sometime between 1913 and 1918, Lucy and Franklin began an affair. In the fall of 1918, Eleanor found love letters between the two after Franklin returned from a trip to Europe. To put it mildly, Eleanor was furious. She wanted a divorce."

"Go for it Eleanor!" shouted an older woman. Jorden couldn't help but laugh along with the others.

Helen continued, "Divorce wasn't in the cards. Franklin's mother, Sara Delano Roosevelt, threatened to disinherit him if he divorced Eleanor. Franklin didn't want to put his political career in jeopardy, so he pledged to never see Lucy Mercer again. But in the end, it wasn't quite the truth since Franklin did see Lucy in later years. To the first question, yes, Lucy Mercer was here the day Franklin Roosevelt died. Franklin's daughter, Anna, had arranged for Lucy to be here. The family tried to keep this quiet when Roosevelt died, but it became public three years ago, in 1966. Are there any more questions?" Helen asked once more. Seeing no hands raised, she exited into the entrance hall where she smiled and curtsied. "Thank you for your interest and all your questions. Come again." Her smile broadened as they clapped.

Mary looked warmly at Jorden and Alex. "Thank you. What a treat!"

"Shall we head into Warm Springs and get something to eat?" Alex suggested.

Mary demurred, "I've had a great day, but I'm tired. What about taking me back to the apartment, and you two go out and get something. Maybe we could stop and pick up a sandwich for me?"

"Are you sure, Mom? It won't take us long to get something in Warm Springs."

"No, I'm sure. My feet hurt!"

She knew her mom was trying to let them have time together. Jorden couldn't help but smile. They picked up a hamburger, fries, and a chocolate milkshake for Mary. Jorden got her mother settled in before Alex drove them off to Amore's for dinner.

"I like your mother. She's fun."

"I know she liked you. Mom was on good behavior—thank goodness! She could have put you under the microscope."

After a nice dinner, Alex steered them towards their favorite park. Jorden prized these special moments, talking and snuggling with Alex. She hated to return to her apartment.

"Come on in. It's almost two, I'm sure Mom is asleep."

"When's your mother leaving?"

"Tomorrow—I think around eleven."

"Then, I'd better go. I'll drive over before she leaves."

"I know she'd like to see you again."

"How about nine? I'll treat you and your mother to breakfast?"

"Good. Maybe we'll have some time after Mom leaves."

"You bet we will." Alex leaned over and kissed her.

They ended up having a mid-morning brunch. Jorden had to admit she'd enjoyed her mother's visit.

"This has been a real treat. Thank you." Mary gave Jorden and Alex bear-hugs. "I'm so glad you're going to be a part of our family."

"Me too," Alex replied.

Mary waved as she drove off. A tear slipped down Jorden's cheek. Alex put his arm around her when they walked back to her apartment.

Chapter 34

January 1970

J orden stretched her legs as far as she could. There were two more hours of flying over the Pacific Ocean before the plane landed in Los Angeles. There would be flowers in bloom in California but not now in Georgia. She would have to wait for spring when the dogwood trees would be lush with delicate pink and white blossoms. She closed her eyes and visualized the array of colors she'd seen on her trip to North Carolina last April to see Alex.

***

Previous Year – April 1969

After a week of procrastinating, Jorden worked up the nerve to ask for Friday off. She cleared it with her principal, but she didn't tell him the complete truth. Her grandmother in Lockton, Alabama didn't really need help moving; she wasn't going anywhere. The innocent white lie, pulled at her sense of right and wrong, but she considered it necessary to get the day off. If she left at seven in the morning, she could get to Alex around five.

Jorden drove off as Madison began to dress. Accompanied by a sunny day, she made three stops: the first for gas, the second to grab lunch, and the third at Stuckey's, a chain store to get a Coke and a bag of chips. She rolled onto base at five thirty, following Alex's detailed directions to his housing. To her delight, he was waiting outside talking with a few soldiers. She couldn't take her eyes off him as he walked toward her.

"Give me your keys. You're a beautiful sight!"

Jorden threw her keys into the air, aiming them at the center of Alex's palm. She couldn't stop smiling.

After a short drive, they checked into the Sawyer Inn. Alex encircled Jorden, pulling her into him, causing quivers to run through her. She felt warmth through his fatigues and the strength of his arms. Each time she was with him, she felt her resolve weaken. But still, Alex kept his bargain and didn't push further.

On Saturday Alex drove them to Pinehurst, North Carolina. Jorden had been to the famous golf course once before. She remembered the U.S. Open Golf Tournament had been held there several times. From there they ventured out to Morrow Mountain State Park, where they walked, talked, laughed, and savored each other's company.

Jorden couldn't believe it was already Sunday afternoon. Alex had suggested bowling—anything to prolong their time together. Worried, she kept looking at her watch. "It's after two. If I don't leave soon, I'll be driving back in the dark which I don't want."

"Let's finish this game, and then you can go," Alex said, appealing to her vulnerable side.

Jorden knew he was using delaying tactics. She frowned but rolled the ball down the lane.

The moment they stepped out of the bowling alley; they were in the center of a superstorm. It had been sunny at noon, but now the visibility was non-existent. The skies were dark with heavy rain.

"You can't drive in this." Alex grabbed her hand while they raced to his car.

"What am I going to do?"

"Stay another night. We can check back into the Sawyer Inn," Alex replied.

Jorden looked frightened. "I don't want to lose my job. I'm not worried about where we stay, but what will I tell my principal? I'm supposed to be at Grandma Marshall's home in Lockton. Maybe the weather isn't so bad there."

"I know—tell your principal your clutch failed. You can't get it replaced until Monday, and you'll be back on Tuesday. What can he say?"

Jorden frowned. "Since I can't drive back in these conditions, I'll try it."

"Let's go back to the Sawyer Inn, and I'll get us a room. You can call him from there rather than use a pay phone. The sooner you do it; the better you'll feel."

Nervously, Jorden dialed Mr. Rinehart's number. Thankfully, she had a copy of the school directory. She hated to lie, but felt she had no other choice. Her hands shook when it was over.

"He ... he ... believed me. Mr. Rinehart accepted my explanation. He said he'd arrange for a substitute." Jorden sighed with relief.

"I told you he'd understand." Alex beamed. "Now we have another night together."

"I think you ordered this storm."

"See how powerful I am? I'll do anything to keep you with me," Alex said as he laughed.

"Don't push your luck. I'm leaving first thing in the morning."

"Good timing, my first class starts at eight. Its five thirty now. How about dinner? Because the weather's so horrible, let's stay and eat at the hotel," Alex suggested.

"I won't argue with you." Jorden leaned back feeling much more relaxed.

An early dinner of chicken and dumplings, comfort food, helped put Jorden in a better mood. Alex unlocked their door, stepped in behind her, and closed his arms around her as he leaned forward to caress her neck.

"I love you," Alex said softly. The room was dark, but lights sprung in from outside. Rain pounded against the window, lightning flashed, and thunder roared. Alex's arms tightened around her waist. Jorden stood still until Alex began swaying back and forth to the rhythm of the rain.

"It's been so long," Alex whispered.

"I know, but . . . we can't." Jorden struggled to get the words out.

"Somehow you're not making me a believer." Alex lifted Jorden gently onto the bed. It seemed natural to feel the softness beneath her. Their movements kept tempo with the rain until Jorden could no longer hear the raging winds. Afterward, they held each other a long time. Jorden slowly slipped off to sleep.

Morning arrived. It was sunny. A good day for driving. Jorden left first while waving goodbye. She drove for hours, glad when she managed to get back to Columbus just before sunset. Again, she made three stops to break up the ten hour trip.

Madison was at the apartment when she hauled her suitcase upstairs. "Where've you been? You should have called—I've been worried."

"The weather turned terrible. No way could I drive back. I'm sorry, I should have called. I'll shower, then I'll fill you in."

Thirty minutes later, Jorden rejoined Madison. "I feel better now."

"What happened?" Madison asked.

Jorden covered the details. She began with where they stayed, what they saw, and the horrendous storm. She talked over an hour—but never mentioned her intimacy with Alex. Jorden knew Madison would lecture her about taking chances—of course she was right.

Chapter 35

January 1970

A white-haired gentleman seated next to Jorden stretched his hands out. His fingers had been leafing through a stock market portfolio. She recognized several of the stock symbols and had to smile as she thought back to April of the past school year.

***

Previous Year – April-May 1969

Jorden immersed herself in the final stages of their stock market project. She and fellow teacher, Jim Stone, developed five different tests covering the material for each grade level, seventh through ninth. Jorden made comparisons and combined her results with Jim's. She wanted her classes to be fairly tested using the same questions.

"I'm ready to see what our students have learned. Friday is the big day. I'm betting on high test scores!" Jim exclaimed.

"I'm sure they'll become millionaires and outshine us," Jorden replied.

Nora and Cheryl had also been preparing. Every afternoon Nora plopped down at Cheryl's kitchen table. The two girls were quite a sight. Nora's black hair was pulled back in a ponytail, bobbing with her movements. Cheryl's long blond curls flowed forward, touching the tabletop. Lines tightened around Nora's jaw and furrows deepened between her eyes. Back and forth they covered the stock market handouts as they continued to concentrate on their notes. Nora and Cheryl were a classic balancing act, supporting each other's strengths and weaknesses.

The eighth graders walked into Jorden's classroom and took their seats for the final exam. Cheryl filed in while Nora quizzed her on the stock market terms.

"Well girls, sounds like you two are ready for this test."

Nora's face lit up. "We are Miss Marshall."

"We're going to ace this one," Cheryl added.

"Let's go for it!" Nora exclaimed.

Some of the students took the whole period and others finished in less time. Nora and Cheryl were the last two to hand in their tests.

In between classes and during her planning hour, Jorden graded tests. She had gotten through a quarter of them by the end of the afternoon. She wanted to complete them before Alex arrived next Wednesday. He would be with her through the weekend. She couldn't wait to see him.

After a marathon weekend of grading papers, Jorden was happy with the results. A few didn't do well—but she expected some low scores. At least she finished them before Alex would arrive. She stopped by Jim Stone's classroom first thing Monday morning.

"How'd your students do?" Jordan asked.

"I only got half graded and those students did fairly well. I can't believe you're done."

"I have a lot going on this week and needed to get them finished," she replied.

"No problem. I'll get mine done by next week," Jim said with a smile.

Finally, Wednesday arrived. Jorden got home from school at four and began doing some last minute cleaning.

"Jorden, why don't you try and relax? This apartment is cleaner than it has ever been." Madison laughed as she scolded Jorden.

"I need something to keep me busy," Jorden said as she wiped the countertop one more time. "I thought he'd be here by now."

"I'm leaving for Macon Friday afternoon, so you'll have the apartment to yourselves for the weekend."

"Thank you, Madison. I appreciate it."

"So—is Alex going to be on the couch or in your room?"

"My room. This time my mother isn't here!"

"Remember to be careful," Madison reminded her.

Jorden saw a red Mustang pull in and stopped listening to her roommate. "He's here."

"I'm on my way to the mall. See you later." Madison slipped out.

Light on his feet, Alex swept his duffle bag over his shoulder, skipped past the curb and headed to the apartment's entrance.

Jorden had the door open when Alex reached the top step. He couldn't take his eyes off her.

"What is it?" Jorden asked.

"You. I can't believe how beautiful you are!" He lifted Jorden and twirled her around. "I feel intoxicated," Alex murmured as he carried her into the living room.

She held on and whispered, "We're safe." Perfect timing—her period had ended yesterday.

The words were magical. Swiftly, he carried Jorden to her bedroom. Time was suspended. Exhausted, Jorden relished their closeness before she fell asleep.

Jorden woke up with hunger pains. She hadn't eaten anything since lunch. It was too late to go out, so she got up and made a couple roast beef sandwiches. She was opening the refrigerator to grab the mayonnaise when she felt two arms wrap around her.

"Thank you. That was beautiful."

Startled, Jorden almost dropped the jar. She laughed and leaned into him. They sat at the dining table eating their sandwiches while they talked about their future plans.

The next morning Jorden started her school day without much sleep, but it didn't seem to matter. The time with Alex made up for missed slumber. The weekend zoomed by and in no time it was Sunday night.

"Can't you stay a few more days? It seems like you just got here," Jorden pleaded.

"I want to, but I need to get home." Alex untangled a long strand of Jorden's silky hair. "My family wouldn't understand. Remember, you're coming to meet them soon. May 15 isn't far away. We'll have a long weekend together."

"You know the weekend will fly by," Jorden argued. "I know how important your family is, but please think about spending a couple days in Columbus before you leave for Vietnam. We have so little time left."

Alex got up and paced the small bedroom.

"I'm not asking you not to go home—just spend your last couple days with me in Columbus. Think about it," Jorden appealed to him. Why does he make such a big deal out of this? She could see a veil forming over his face.

"I'll think about it—is all I can promise." Alex held both her hands and kissed them gently. "I can't wait for you to get to Albany."

"I hope your family likes me. It makes me anxious."

"They'll love you!" Alex whispered, pulling her closer.

Alex left early Monday morning for Albany. Jorden began the week tired but happy. She couldn't wait to begin the trip to New York. She already had her airline reservation and ticket for next Thursday. She was scheduled to arrive in Albany around nine. Her principal had been good about letting her take Friday off.

Jorden was pleased the majority of her students did well on the stock market exam. Nora received the highest score with Cheryl a point behind her. The girl's bright faces brought a sense of accomplishment to Jorden. They did it! She loved seeing their sense of pride. Soon after the test, the students turned in their results from the sale of their stocks.

Wednesday, May 14 arrived. This was the day Jorden and Jim Stone would be announcing the winners of the stock market contest. Nora and Cheryl had been keeping tabs throughout day on who had received awards. Three had already been presented. The grand award still hadn't been declared.

"Do you think we have a chance?" Cheryl asked Nora as they entered Miss Marshall's classroom.

"How can we miss? All of our stocks made a profit. If we had put real money into them, we'd be rich!"

Jorden's eighth graders crowded into her classroom. She couldn't help but hear Nora go on about being rich.

"Welcome, Mr. Rinehart," Jorden greeted the principal, "I'm glad you could join us. Mr. Stone and I are honored to have you share this fine achievement with the top performer."

Nora and Cheryl were sitting on the edges of their seats. Nora bit her lip, almost drawing blood.

Jorden joked, "We need a drum roll in honor of the Grand Winner." Danny Johnson, sitting in the back of the room, started to do just so with two pencils—then the rest of the class caught on and pitched in.

Mr. Rinehart chuckled. "Well, there's your drum roll, Miss Marshall. Now for the winners!"

Jorden applauded before announcing the first place winner. "The prize for the highest profit—goes to two partners. The winners are Nora Summers and Cheryl Barker. Congratulations!" Jorden clapped while the class joined in.

"You two are to share the twenty-five dollar award, plus another ten dollars put in by Mr. Rinehart. Thank you for your generosity." The class cheered again.

Mr. Rinehart stepped to the front of the room. "Nora and Cheryl, I'm proud of you. What a fine performance. I wish I had followed your wise judgment and invested in those stocks. Well done!" He clapped again.

Jorden couldn't contain herself when she got home. "What a grand day! I wish you could have been there to see how proud my students were. Nora and Cheryl outdid themselves! It was amazing!"

"Bravo! It's good to see you so happy. What a good send off to New York tomorrow. This should bolster your confidence for meeting Alex's family." Madison gave Jorden a victory hug.

"I hope so. You know, they aren't keen on southerners," Jorden remarked.

"Remember you were brought up in New Jersey—Yankee land," Madison countered.

"But my family's roots are in the South. My parents are only in New Jersey because of my dad's job."

"Maybe they don't realize you're from the South. They'll like you; I just know it." Madison gave Jorden a thumbs up.

Chapter 36

January 1970

Jorden sat near the rear of the plane in the coach section. She remembered passing through first class where the seats had extra room and better amenities, not cramped like her area. Then, her mind drifted to last May. It was the weekend she met Alex's family. The visit made an enormous impression.

***

Previous Year – Albany Weekend, May 15 – 18, 1969

Jorden packed with care. She just had two full days in Albany, Friday and Saturday, to be with Alex and his family. This would be the last time she would see him for over a year.

"Come on, Jorden, it's almost five. We need to get to the airport. If you don't hurry we're going to get stuck in rush hour traffic," Madison insisted.

"I'm ready," Jorden declared.

The flight went well, but Jorden couldn't stop thinking about Alex and his family. She was going to do her best to make a good impression.

Jorden had spent hours trying to find something special for his parents. She walked through Columbus Square Mall both Saturday and Sunday afternoons looking for the right gift. Nothing.

Frustrated, she then spotted a pastel blue porcelain vase with violets etched around the circular rim. The colors and the intricate detail of the flower petals on porcelain lured her in.

"May I help you?" the saleswoman asked.

Lifting the vase, Jorden turned the delicate piece around in her hands. "This is perfect. How much is it?"

"It is a nice piece which just came in this week. The price is on the bottom."

Jorden turned it over. She gulped. The price was $44.95. It was thirty dollars over her limit. Way too much! "It's beautiful, but I can't afford it." She placed it back on the shelf.

"Let me show you some others. This way please. These aren't as expensive, but they're also well done."

Jorden looked at the porcelain pieces; none of them caught her eye like the pastel vase. She had almost two hundred and fifty dollars in her savings account. It had taken her a year to save this much. She was saving for her wedding—especially for her wedding dress. This gift didn't fall into the right category. On the other hand, it was for her future in-laws—she wanted to make a good impression.

While pondering what to do, two women wandered in. Their voices carried, and Jorden couldn't help but listen. "Look at this. It's exquisite."

Jorden watched the taller woman pick up the pale blue vase. Her friend also looked at the piece. "I like it, but it's just not right for Jeanie. She's only twelve. Let's try another store."

Jorden sighed with relief. Without further hesitation, she bought the vase.

Lost in her thoughts, Jorden finally realized the plane had landed. She jumped up and followed the passengers to the terminal. Off in the distance she spotted Alex. A smile dominated his face as he swept through the crowd. His arms swung around her.

"At last you're here. I thought your plane would never arrive." His New York accent sounded heavenly.

Forty five minutes later they reached the turnoff to his home. To her surprise, Alex, with a boyish grin, activated a large gate with the push of a button.

"You have a gated drive!" Jorden exclaimed in surprise.

"My Dad's creation. He had it put in years ago after they remodeled the house. I still get a kick out of it."

Jorden looked in awe at the driveway which curved back, making it impossible to see the house from the road. The silhouette of his home was of an older colonial style. Even in the darkness she could see the home's grand features. There were three floors with a series of symmetrical windows. The top of the house had three prominent dormer windows. A triple-car garage stood separately towards the back. Alex pulled the Mustang around and parked in the third space.

"Come on. Let's go in. I know Mother is up and wants to meet you. My father is in New York City—business as usual. He won't get back until next week. He sends his apologies."

"I'm sorry. I had hoped to meet him." Jorden was disappointed—she had wanted to meet both of his parents.

"Can't we sit out here for a while? I'm so nervous."

"Mother won't bite. Come on, she's looking forward to meeting you." Alex got out, opened the trunk, and lifted her luggage out. Reluctantly, Jorden got out. Together they made their way up a set of stone stairs, leading into a large warm kitchen. A dining alcove was off to the right with a table which could easily fit six. A cozy fireplace highlighted the far corner on an elevated hearth.

Jorden watched a tall, willowy woman make her entrance into the kitchen. Medium-length auburn hair silhouetted her face in a stylish cut. Jorden couldn't stop staring at her future mother-in-law.

"Oh, here you are. I thought I heard you drive in," Margo Whelan said as she greeted them.

Impeccably dressed, though casual, Margo Whelan wore navy blue gabardine slacks, a light blue silk blouse sporting a large flaring collar, and a pair of navy flats. Visible double stitching on her shoes made them stand out. She exuded expensive taste. Jorden assumed she turned heads with her classy look.

Jorden was captivated by Mrs. Whelan, but there were no hugs from his mother. The difference between Alex's mother and Jorden's were glaring. Mary Marshall was always kind, gentle, and down-to-earth. She made company feel welcomed. Those vibes weren't coming through from Mrs. Whelan.

"Mom, I want you to meet Jorden." Alex's tone seemed stressed.

"Nice to meet you. I'm Margo Whelan," she replied, extending her hand.

"Good to finally meet you," Jorden managed to squeeze out while she reached for her hand.

"Would you like something to eat? I could make you a sandwich."

"Thank you. I'm fine." Though, she wasn't really as her stomach growled. Jorden remembered she hadn't eaten since breakfast, but she would never expect Mrs. Whelan to make her a sandwich.

"I'm sure you're tired—I'll show you to the guest room." Margo nodded toward the stairs. "It's on the second floor. Alex, please bring Jorden's bags."

Alex had briefly described the layout of the house to Jorden on the drive from the airport, so she knew the home had two sets of stairs to the second floor. The main stairs were off the front entrance and the ones at the back were used as a short cut to go from the kitchen directly to the second floor. Margo Whelan loved this feature, from what Alex had told her.

Jorden followed her up the stairs and down the second floor hallway. They passed what appeared to be the master bedroom suite, followed by a third set of stairs, and then to the guest bedroom at the other end of the second floor.

"This is your room." Mrs. Whelan led Jorden into a spacious bedroom. Alex followed and placed the luggage on the rack at the foot of an antique canopy bed.

"What a lovely room!" Jorden exclaimed.

"Thank you. We had it redone when we renovated the house." Mrs. Whelan pointed toward the bathroom and an adjoining small sun room. "I hope you'll be comfortable."

"I know I will be." Jorden said, trying to make a good impression.

Mrs. Whelan acknowledged Jorden with a small smile and then turned her attention to Alex. "I have early meetings in the morning, so I probably won't be back until mid-afternoon, but I know you and

Jorden can find plenty to do. I'll see you later tomorrow afternoon." Margo retreated to her master suite.

"We'll be fine. Don't worry about us," Alex called to his mother. He relaxed and gave Jorden a squeeze.

"It's late. I'll see you in the morning. My room is on the third floor—are you okay?"

"I'm fine." Jorden stretched the truth. She actually felt like a bundle of nerves.

"Don't worry. I'm not far off and morning will be here before you know it." Alex leaned over and kissed her. In moments, Jorden could hear his footsteps on the stairs leading up to the third floor.

Jorden sat on the enticing bed and slipped off her shoes. Her eyes traveled across the room. It was beautiful. An elegant antique chest of drawers matched the oak frame of the four poster canopy bed. Her eyes moved to the sunroom. The walls were windows with little other structure. She slid from the bed and walked toward the corner alcove. She could imagine sitting there with the sunlight streaming in. Right now the white wooden shutters were closed to seal off the room for evening privacy. Jorden sat in an armchair while her eyes traveled the length of the crown moldings on the ceiling down to the hardwood floors. She wondered what it would be like to grow up in a home like this.

Nature's call guided her toward the bathroom. This room was equally well-provided with everything she needed, even a hairdryer. His mother had made an effort to make her comfortable, which seemed to be a good sign. She unpacked and hung up the few clothes she had brought. She lifted out the vase for Margo Whelan to make sure it was fine. She shook the wrapped box and heard no sounds. It was intact. Jorden debated where to put the gift and decided to keep it in her suitcase. She hoped her future mother-in-law would like it.

Wistfully, she wished she could share the room with Alex, but of course that was out of the question. Somehow, despite all her excitement, Jorden fell into a deep sleep. Just before she drifted off, she prayed, "Please, God, let Margo Whelan like me."

Chapter 37

January 1970

J orden shifted in the plane's seat. The full force of the weekend in Albany overwhelmed her. Friday morning filtered back. How could she have been so naïve and reckless? But, how could she not?

***

Previous Year – Albany, Friday morning, May 16, 1969

The downstairs clock chimed nine times. Jorden woke with a start. Then, she felt arms envelop her.

"Wake up Sleepy Head," Alex whispered.

Jorden realized Alex was in bed with her. "Where's your mother?"

"Gone! Mother left before eight this morning—the perfect time to sneak down here. She's a board member for the Hospital Auxiliary Guild. Don't worry, she won't be back until later this afternoon, so I have you to myself."

Jorden could see a pleased smile grow on Alex's face. The tips of her fingers outlined his lips. His eyes darted to her gown.

"Wait. I need to use the bathroom." Jorden hurried off. What would she do now? This shouldn't happen. The timing wasn't right— she felt like she was playing Russian roulette. But it was their last time together . . . how could she not?

Alex's clothes were on the floor when she returned. He lifted her gown as if it were air. Their desire for each other at first flowed like a meandering river, gaining speed with each turn until nothing could halt the momentum. Jorden lay quietly afterward. She couldn't have held back knowing this may be their last intimate moment before he left for this dreadful war. Still, he used no condom. She hoped she wouldn't have to pay the consequences—a baby was not in her plans.

Jorden tried to push those thoughts out of her mind and let herself enjoy the comfort of the canopy bed. It felt like they were in a sea of pillows with the soft comforter surrounding them as if it were a cocoon. She knew this day would be etched deeply into her memory.

Jorden and Alex fell asleep. The chiming clock woke her again. Alarmed, she punched Alex. "What time is it? What if your mother gets back early?" Jorden's voice cracked.

"Mother's never early. It's only eleven so don't worry. I guarantee she probably won't return until after three this afternoon." Alex kissed her and lifted himself out of the comfort of the bed. "Get dressed. I'll make coffee and toast."

"I need time to shower—then I'll come down," Jorden replied.

"Okay. See you downstairs." All was ready when Jorden appeared thirty minutes later. Alex handed her a steaming mug of coffee and a large slice of toast with orange marmalade.

"This is scrumptious." Jorden remembered she had hardly eaten anything yesterday. No wonder it tasted so good.

"Don't eat too much," Alex warned.

"Why not? I'm starving!"

"We're having lunch with Peter Hampton; he's an old friend I want you to meet. I told him we'd meet at Rodono's around one."

Jorden barely listened, instead remembering her gift for Mrs. Whelan. "Oh, Alex, I brought a present for your parents, really for your mother. I'd like to find a florist."

"For what?"

"I wanted to pick out three white roses."

Alex looked perplexed. "It's not necessary."

"I know, but I want to. I found a porcelain vase I thought she might like—I love it." Jorden wanted to put the three roses in the vase to symbolize Alex and his two brothers. "It's my way of saying 'thank you' to your mother for the weekend."

"How nice. I know she'll like it."

"Think we can find them today?" Jorden hoped the rosebuds would open before she left on Sunday.

"Sure. Just remind me after lunch."

"I will. Now, please show me this wonderful house."

Alex smiled. "Finish your toast and I'll give you a tour."

Jorden looked around the kitchen. The center island caught her attention. It was set off by the dining alcove and the fireplace to the right.

"Come on, let's go through the butler pantry into the dining room." Alex extended his hand, steering her past him. As Jorden passed through the pantry, she guessed the space must act as a buffer and a storage area between the kitchen and the formal dining area. Then, her eyes settled on a large remarkable antique cherry table which dominated the room.

"Mother loves this table. It's been in our family for generations." Alex radiated with pride. Jorden noted the pleasure in his voice.

"Come over here and check out these pocket doors." Alex pulled three foot-wide doors out of the wall, demonstrating how to close off the dining area. "I loved to play with them as a kid. Of course it wasn't allowed, but that didn't stop me or my brothers." Alex beamed.

Next, Alex led Jorden into a grand hallway. A large crystal chandelier hung above the impressive entrance.

Jorden gasped. "This is lovely." Her eyes roamed to the high ceiling where the sunlight reflected off the hanging crystals.

Across the hall Jorden could see the living room and, off to the right, an elegant staircase leading up to the second floor. Hardwood floors prevailed throughout the house, especially on the first level, with an assortment of elegant area rugs. Stepping further into the hallway, her reflection from a large heirloom pier mirror startled her. The mirror seemed to expand the formal entrance, adding to its grandeur.

"We need to move on." Alex looked at his watch as he guided Jorden into the living room.

"This is beautiful!" The fireplace captured her attention, surrounded by white marble.

"We're going to be late for lunch," Alex reiterated, "if we don't speed up."

Jorden tried not to frown. She wanted to take it all in. He led her back to the entrance and down to a cozy den. Adjacent to the den she saw an enclosed sunroom, which appeared to face the back of the house and look out on a garden.

"Let's go out."

Alex checked his watch again. "Not enough time. Later, maybe tonight or tomorrow."

"I won't forget your words."

He guided her back to the main hall, turned right and returned to the kitchen.

"Aren't I an excellent tour guide? Alex applauded himself."

"Yes, but what about the third floor?" Jorden asked, knowing she was irritating him.

"It's just three bedrooms and a bath, nothing special. Those were Eric, Scott, and my rooms."

"I'd love to see yours."

"It's not much, but . . . if you insist . . . let's take the back stairs. It's quicker." Alex led her up to the second floor, passing the master suite.

Jorden paused, then asked, "Is this your parent's room?"

"Yes. Mother recently had it redecorated."

Jorden glanced in and could imagine how grand the suite must be. She wondered how it compared to her guest room, but she figured the space was off limits as it should be.

"Hurry up!" Alex skipped up to the third floor. "Come on. My room's at the end. Eric had the first and Scott the second." Jorden stepped into a boy's simple room. Model cars, baseball cards, and sports equipment lined most of the shelves. She noticed the bed hadn't been made.

"So this is where you grew up." As she stood there, she thought about what little time they had left. She looked up at Alex, trying to decide how to put her thoughts into words.

"What is it?"

Jorden watched the muscles in his neck tighten. Why did he make this so difficult? But she wouldn't back down. She stammered, "Can't you come to Columbus . . . at least for a couple days before you leave? You will still have two weeks at home."

Jorden felt Alex stiffen. He raised his hands and slowly pushed her shoulders back until their eyes met—his were steady, unwavering. "I can't come. Those are my final words! Please, Jorden, don't ask again!"

Immediately, she recognized the abruptness of his words—the barrier was up. She saw the signs; there was no reasoning with him.

"We have to go."

Jorden watched him hurry down the hall. She couldn't speak. Her legs barely moved forward.

"I'll pick you up in front," Alex stated firmly from the staircase.

Jorden looked back at his room and shivered. For a split second she wondered about their future.

Chapter 38

January 1970

The gentleman next to her had fallen asleep and leaned toward the aisle—this gave Jorden a few more inches to stretch out. A furrow was etched between her brows as she reflected on what Alex had said to her.

***

Previous Year – Albany, Friday afternoon, May 16, 1969

"I can't come. Those are my final words!" The declaration cut her to the core. Why be so cold? All she wanted was for Alex to return to Columbus for a couple days. Was she asking too much? She stopped by the guest room and laid down on the bed. She looked up at the canopy—anything to distract from her thoughts. Would she ever understand Alex?

Jorden lost track of time before remembering their lunch date. She wouldn't let Alex spoil the rest of the weekend. "Get up—deal with it. Get some spunk," she coached herself. She touched up her makeup and regained her composure. Standing in front of the mahogany mirror, she muttered words of encouragement. "It will be all right. It has to be."

Meanwhile, Alex had parked the car in front of the house. Tired of waiting, he went back inside. From the hallway he spotted Jorden on the staircase, but she couldn't see him.

Jorden had decided to use the main staircase leading down to the entrance hall. Despite being upset, she couldn't help but grin when she looked down at the graceful steps. This was her chance to make a grand entrance—especially when no one could see her trying to do this. She stepped forward, attempting to glide down the stairs. Her cotton skirt floated up as her leather flats sailed down the steps. At the bottom, she majestically bowed her head and threw up her arms.

"Bravo!" Alex cheered, acting as if nothing had happened between them.

His voice startled Jorden, causing her to trip. She fell onto the entryway's hardwood floor.

"I didn't mean to make you trip!" Alex rushed forward and leaned over to help her up.

Jorden pushed back and looked up at him—she didn't know how to react.

He held out his hand. She wavered but slowly reached for his fingers. The tension seemed to ease—with an unspoken truce.

"You scared me to death! I had no idea you were inside."

Alex smiled. "I couldn't help myself—you were fun to watch." He squeezed her hand and led her to his car. "Now, let's meet Peter for lunch."

Jorden noted a semi-circular drive in front of the house. The outside entrance was impressive, with sidelights on either side of the front door. As he drove away, Jorden turned to get a better look. The main portion of the house had a recent coat of white paint with contrasting green shutters—a dramatic effect.

"What a beautiful home. I could just see the outline last night, but in the bright sunlight it's outstanding. I can't imagine growing up in a house like this."

"It is a great place, but it doesn't mean growing up here was beautiful."

"What do you mean?" she asked, eyeing him.

"My father was always away on business. Being an investment banker, he spent many weeks in New York City—sometimes Boston. We saw him on weekends, holidays, and vacations. Being the youngest, Dad never seemed to have time for me."

"What about your mother? It must have been hard on a marriage," Jorden blurted out. "I'm sorry . . . I'm out of line."

"You're right. It's true. It was hard on Mother. She raised us mostly by herself. He still gets home on weekends and they're together, so I guess it's a good sign. I hoped he would be here this weekend. I'm disappointed, but I'm not surprised." Alex grimaced. "I never want to be like him."

"I'm sorry, too. I wanted to meet him." Jorden wondered what Alex's life had been like. "Tell me about Peter."

Alex smiled. "I've known him forever. We were inseparable growing up—first grade through high school. Now he's a second year law student."

"Lucky for him he didn't get drafted."

"Oh he did, but he was classified 4F—he has terrible eyesight. I wouldn't mention it at lunch. Peter's sensitive about it, especially with me going to Nam."

"I won't say a word," Jorden replied.

"There's his old Ford Fairlane. I keep telling him to get rid of it. The old jalopy will break down and leave him stranded one of these days."

Jorden could see Rodono's was an Italian restaurant, but it didn't look as nice as Amore's. Still, it was cozy. Peter Hampton sat in the back corner. He stood up and waved when he saw Alex.

"There's Peter."

Jorden's first impression of Peter was surprising. He was much shorter and heavier than Alex. A beer gut hung over his belt, mousy brown hair straggled below his ears, and thick, dark glasses dominated his face. He seemed to brighten as she and Alex approached the table. After an awkward introduction, Jorden checked out the menu.

"What can I get you?" the waitress asked.

Alex spoke up. "We'll have the usual, salads and an extra-large pizza. Rodono's Special will work. Oh, and bring us a large pitcher of beer."

"I'll have a diet Coke," Jorden added.

"Got it, a diet Coke."

The salads and drinks came in no time. By one thirty most of the lunch crowd had left. Jorden was hungry and devoured her salad.

She could see why Alex had ordered a large pitcher of beer—half was already gone. Peter gulped down his second glass. The pizza arrived and vanished in minutes. Digging in, Jorden ate two large pieces.

Peter never looked straight at Jorden or addressed her. For the next thirty minutes, Alex and Peter talked over old times. Jorden tried to pay attention but soon lost interest. Getting fidgety, she excused herself to go to the ladies room. She lingered as long as possible. A group of women came in, so she decided to leave. Walking back from the bathroom, she heard Alex and Peter speaking. She didn't think they could see her, so she stopped to listen.

"What's up with this babe? Is it serious?"

Alex hesitated but leveled with his best friend. "I asked her to marry me."

"Wow! She's a beaut. And she said yes?" Peter knocked back his beer.

"She did. What do you think?"

Peter slapped his buddy on the shoulder. "She's too good looking for you. I just hope you know what you're doing. When's this happening?"

"Not until I return from Nam. Think about being my best man?"

"Anytime. It's a given. How long have you known her?"

"Long enough." Alex continued to talk about Jorden—until Peter realized he needed to meet his study group. "Give my best to Jorden. You've got a prize with her."

Jorden waited until Peter walked away before she returned to the table.

"Where have you been?"

Jorden noted an edge in Alex's voice. "I just went to the restroom. There was a line and I had to wait. Where's Peter?" She played innocent.

"He had a study group to meet."

"I'm sorry I didn't get to see him before he left."

"Me too—but no matter." Alex paused. "Let's go into Albany, and I'll give you a tour. We don't have a lot of time before we need to change for dinner."

"My own tour guide, how nice. What are the plans for dinner?"

"Good friends of mine, Rick Critten and his wife, Kim, want to meet you. They asked us to join them at The Manor House. It's a fine place with excellent gourmet dishes. I know you'll like it."

Jorden didn't know what to say. She'd rather spend a quiet dinner with Alex. After an uneasy moment she replied, "It . . . sounds nice."

"I'm sure you'll like them. They're our age and fun."

Alex spent an hour driving around Albany before he looked at his watch. "It's almost five. We need to go back and change."

Jorden was gazing out the car window and watching people scurry in all directions, when she remembered the roses. "Can we stop by a florist? Remember, I want to get three white rosebuds."

"Sure. Floramart is a couple miles from here; we can stop there. I also forgot to tell you, tomorrow night Mother is having Scott and his wife, Carrie, over for dinner. Mother also tried to get Eric and his family to come, but it didn't work out. They're over a hundred miles away and already had a commitment. Oh, and Carrie is pregnant, almost six months. This is their first, and they're really excited. You'll like them."

While Alex continued talking about his family, Jorden noticed a sign for a florist shop. "Alex, there it is!"

"What?"

"Floramart! Remember the roses?"

"Oh! Right." Immediately, he made a sharp turn to get off the main road to circle back to the shop.

Jorden held onto her seat to brace herself. "Wow! Let's make it there in one piece."

"Don't worry. You're in good hands."

Jorden picked out three long-stemmed white rosebuds for the vase. She hoped the buds would open before she left on Sunday.

"Why don't you pick out a rose for yourself?" Alex proposed.

A smile slid across her face. Her eyes gravitated toward her favorite color. She chose a yellow bud. "I want to pay for these," Jorden told the clerk as she lifted out her wallet.

"No! These are my treat, so put your money away," Alex asserted. He already had his credit card out for the clerk.

Jorden threw up her hands in defeat as she thought about tomorrow night's dinner. She hoped to make a good impression. She wanted to fit into this family.

Pulling up to the garage, Alex slid his Mustang into the last spot. Margo greeted Alex and Jorden as they entered the kitchen. She was having a cup of tea while reading the newspaper.

"Would either of you like some hot tea or a soda?" They both declined as they sat down.

"What do you have there?" Margo looked at the long shaped packages.

"Something for you and Jorden. Actually, it was Jorden's suggestion."

"Wait, Alex. I'll be right back." Jorden got up and raced upstairs. She retrieved her wrapped gift and hurried back to the kitchen.

"They're beautiful," she could hear Margo saying. "Thank you."

Upon entering the kitchen, words stumbled out of Jorden's mouth. "Oh, Mrs. Whelan, you already have them in water. Alex, you were supposed to wait for me!"

Margo tried to smooth over the situation. "What a nice suggestion with the roses. Thank you."

"But, I have the true surprise." Jorden placed the present on the table in front of Alex's mother.

"You didn't have to bring a gift," Margo said as she held the gift in her hands.

"Open it," Jorden urged her.

Long, delicate fingers meticulously removed the gift wrapping, setting aside both the paper and the large violet bow. It took Margo almost a minute to get into the box and remove all the white tissue. When the pale blue porcelain vase emerged, a large smile lit up Jorden's face. The violets etched around the rim, reflected the afternoon sun streaming in the kitchen window.

"I hope you like it!" Jorden exclaimed.

"It's lovely!" Margo turned the vase around to look at it from all angles. "Thank you, Jorden. I'll treasure this." She placed her hand on Alex's arm and smiled at both of them.

"The vase, it's for the white roses," Jorden replied.

"No. It's too nice to use. I'd be afraid of breaking it. I'll have to find a special spot for it." Margo looked as if she were in deep thought, contemplating where to put the vase.

"We're running late. We had better get dressed." Alex tugged at Jorden's hand.

"Don't forget your yellow rose," Margo called out to Jorden. "I've put it in a vase for you to have in your room."

"Thank you," Jorden replied. She couldn't help but notice the crystal vase appeared more expensive than the one she had given his mother.

Carrying the rose upstairs, Jorden felt a sense of failure. At least she tried—she just didn't rank in his mother's class. She told herself to perk up. Jorden unpacked a simple black linen dress and a contrasting white jacket. Next, she took out her short-heeled black pumps—they went well with the outfit. She stood in front of the free-standing mahogany mirror and turned around for one last look. She was pleased with the results.

Alex knocked. "I'm going down."

"I'll be there in a few minutes."

When Jorden entered the kitchen, Alex and his mother were in the middle of a conversation. They looked up, and Jorden could see could see approval on both their faces.

"Wow, you look great!" Alex exclaimed.

"Thank you."

Margo took their photo before they left.

Chapter 39

January 1970

The smell of dinner drifted through the plane's cabin. Chicken or beef were the selections. Jorden decided she would have the chicken with rice. She remembered the meal she had in Albany last May. How elegant. A restaurant she would never forget. A smile spread across her face as the evening played back in her mind.

***

Previous Year – Friday evening, Albany, May16, 1969

Jorden marveled at the Manor House as she and Alex walked toward the entrance. Looking up, she could see how the central tower stood out over the entrance with two smaller towers on either side. The dark stained wood contrasted with a slightly lighter trim, which created an enticing atmosphere.

"Unbelievable. I can't wait to see the inside," Jorden said with fascination.

"Well come on. I'm sure Rich and Kim are waiting for us." Alex opened the front door with a gentleman's flourish. Whiffs of roasted garlic and other spices stirred Jorden's appetite. Light dinner music played on a baby grand piano. The pianist was dressed in a black tuxedo. His fingers flew over the keys—it looked so simple.

The maitre d' stepped forward. He also wore a tuxedo but of a slightly different shade.

"Can I help you? Do you have a reservation?"

"Yes, we do. It's under Rich Critten."

"Your party is here. Follow me." He bowed, sweeping his right arm out to show the way.

They followed the maitre d' across the hardwood floor. Jorden was impressed with how each table had its own privacy. Amore's, their favorite restaurant, held special memories, but it could not compare to this refined dining. She was glad she had brought her best dress. Alex hadn't told her it would be this formal.

As they reached their table, Jorden could see Rich and Kim huddled together laughing. Jorden wished she and Alex could have the same intimacy instead of sharing the night with a couple she hadn't even met.

"Here we are. Madame. Let me help you with your chair."

"Thank you." Jorden sat down in an upholstered, high back chair with a soft, comfortable cushion. She took in the elegant table. Each setting had crystal water and wine glasses and starched white linen napkins folded upright in the center of the plates. Distracted, she hardly noticed the maitre d' hand her a leather-bound menu trimmed with gold. His voice brought her back to reality.

"Your server will be Ralston. Have a wonderful dinner." He bowed and left.

Jorden sat across from Kim and Rich. She envied Kim's rosy complexion. Her large blue eyes contrasted with her rich black hair. Short curly locks surrounded her face in a chic cut and her subtle curves added to her charismatic and outgoing personality. At first glance, Rich, tall and thin with a thick head of red hair, appeared to be more reserved than his wife. Jorden decided they looked like opposites.

Alex made the introductions, and they all exchanged greetings.

"Isn't this something!" Rich opened the conversation. "I've never been here before—have you Alex?"

"Once, quite a while ago. Peter and I brought dinner dates on senior prom night. We were trying to impress them, but it cost us a fortune. To top it off, my date never even went out with me again."

They laughed and began to study the menu. Despite Jorden's initial reluctance, her first impression of Kim and Rich was good.

"Where are you from?" Kim asked.

"Trenton, New Jersey."

"Oh, I thought you were from the South, but you don't have a southern accent. Alex, you misled us. I thought you said you met Jorden in Georgia?"

"I did. We met in Columbus, Georgia," Alex replied.

"I went to college in the South. Right now I'm teaching in Columbus where I met Alex," Jorden tried to explain.

"Oh—now it makes sense," Kim replied. "We have something in common; I teach third graders. They drive me nuts, but I love them."

Out of nowhere, a voice took over the conversation. "Good evening. My name is Ralston. I'm your server." He was dressed completely in white with a red rose in his lapel. "I see you don't have any water. I'll take care of it." Ralston snapped his fingers at the commis waiter.

"Have you seen the menu? If you have any questions, please ask. Can I start you off with a drink or something from our wine list?"

"A bottle of Champagne would be great. Do you have a suggestion?" Alex looked at Ralston.

"A white Dom Perignon is excellent."

Alex nodded with approval, as he turned to Rich. "What do you think?"

"Fine by me," Rich replied.

"I'll get the Champagne right away. However, first let me make a suggestion for an appetizer. The mussels are excellent. They come with white wine, garlic, parsley and cream. It's delicious, I highly recommend it."

Alex gave a nod of approval, and Ralston turned on his heels and left.

Jorden was impressed with Ralston. One word summed up this man: sophisticated. He seemed to be in his late twenties, with a sturdy build and thick black hair. His dark eyes spoke volumes, commanding respect for his expertise. Jorden could imagine him owning his own equally profitable restaurant. A man on the move.

Kim turned her attention to Alex. "Have you set a wedding date?"

"Not yet, but it'll be after I get back from my tour of duty," Alex explained.

"You mean Vietnam?"

"Right. I leave in two weeks."

Ralston came back with a bottle of Champagne. After popping the cork, he showed it to Alex. Carefully, Ralston poured the sparkling wine into a Champagne glass for Alex to sample. Alex nodded in approval. Afterward, Ralston filled the other glasses.

Rich promptly proposed a toast. "To Jorden and Alex . . . and many good years together."

The bubbles from the Champagne rose up to tickle Jorden's nose as she took a sip. "This is delicious."

Alex raised his glass again. "Let's make another toast—to Rich and Kim and our future friendship."

During the second toast Ralston brought the appetizers. The aroma from the garlic sauce drifted upwards, tantalizing Jorden. After she finished the first course, a crisp green salad with bright red tomatoes was set in front of her. Ralston served the plates with ease. Jorden noted how he limited his comments and employed professional reserve to let them enjoy the meal and conversation.

Jorden was loosening up from the Champagne. She felt relaxed as the main course was being served. Alex had talked Jorden into ordering the Maine lobster. Never had she ordered such an expensive dinner. He ordered the beef medallions. After a short while, all of the entrees had been served except for Jorden's.

Without warning, Ralston appeared by Jorden's side. His arm accidently brushed against her and accelerated her senses. Captivated, she watched him cut through the lobster shell. His hands were large and masculine, but they moved like a surgeon's, delicately slicing through the hard surface. The cracking sounds grew louder as he peeled the shell back and removed the pink and white lobster. A delightful garlic butter dip accompanied it.

"Madam." Ralston's fingers almost touched Jorden's as he set the plate down in front of her. She smiled and thanked him. He smiled back, removing his hand with a slight nod of his head. She was amazed at his intensity.

Conversation slowed down as they finished their entrees. Ralston returned with a dessert cart, showing samples of rich enticing pastries. Alex, Rich, and Kim each ordered one of the spectacular treats along with coffee. This time, Jorden simply settled for coffee. After several sips, she looked at Kim. "What a spectacular dinner, evening and time meeting you and Rich." She meant each word, she liked Kim and Rich.

Kim touched Jorden's hand. "It's been a treat getting to know you. Alex is a lucky man. We're looking forward to more times together and a growing friendship."

"Thank you. I'd like that also," Jorden said with a smile, placing her hand over Kim's.

Ralston returned and freshened up their coffees. "I hope you have enjoyed your dinner. It's been my pleasure to serve you." He placed the itemized bill enclosed in a leather jacket at the end of the table between the two men. Alex and Rich had decided to share the cost of the dinner. Jorden got a glimpse of the bill. She almost choked up when she saw the total was almost $190. To her, the amount meant at least three month's rent. Unbelievable!

On the drive back, Jorden relaxed. She reached for Alex's hand as he parked in the garage. He pulled her close. "I wish we could stay out here all night, but we better go in." He leaned over and kissed her longingly.

Jorden sighed; at least they had one more night.

Chapter 40

January 1970

J orden's dinner tray had been removed. In an hour the flight would land in Los Angeles. She let her mind wander back to Saturday in Albany—a tight knot formed in her stomach.

***

Previous Year - Saturday afternoon, Albany, May 17, 1969

Jorden was on the go all day. Alex seemed to take pleasure in taking her to special spots around Albany. First, he drove by his grade school, reminiscing about those younger years. She became immersed in his stories, laughing at his antics. At the same time, she couldn't help but notice the stately homes, almost mansions, surrounding his school. The elementary school she attended was bordered by smaller ranches and two story homes. Her beginning was quite different from his.

When Alex swung by his high school, Jorden wasn't surprised to see a similar wealthy neighborhood in the vicinity of his school. She could only imagine what his life must have been like. Maybe their children would also grow up in an area like this, but today she was content with just having Alex by her side.

Alex's last stop of the afternoon was his favorite childhood park. Jorden settled down next to him on one of the park benches, watching ducks swim gracefully by. A trail of ripples reverberated through the water behind their webbed feet. She arched back to look up at the sky as white clouds rolled in. Spring's fragrances blossomed out of the wild flowers opening along the lakeside.

"Let's stay here forever," Jorden said, while in her own fantasy world.

"I wish we could." Alex bent forward.

Jorden leaned further back, still in her own thoughts, until two young children ran by squealing in delight. Alex sat up, pushed himself off the bench and reached for Jorden's hand. "We better go. Mom will expect us by five. Remember you're the honored guest for dinner."

Jorden didn't want to leave but took his hand.

When they arrived back at his home, Jorden stepped ahead of Alex as he checked a back tire he thought might be going flat. She skipped up the steps, but stopped when she heard voices from the kitchen. She turned toward the open window to a full view of Mrs. Whelan and another woman deep in conversation. The bushes concealed Jorden, but she could see and hear them clearly.

Riveted to the window, Jorden couldn't help but listen. She decided it must be Sarah, Margo's best friend, the one Alex had told her about. It looked like Margo had spent most of the afternoon in the kitchen preparing dinner. Flour covered both Margo and the counter top.

"Why don't you start a catering business? You'd be good at it," Sarah remarked, sitting at the kitchen table and crocheting what looked like a baby blanket.

"It's not that I wouldn't like to," Margo replied, continuing to roll out dough for dinner rolls.

"Well, just do it."

"Steven wouldn't stand for me having my own business, and heaven forbid if I made any money at it. I've mentioned it to him I don't know how many times, and he just scoffs at me. He says he doesn't need the hassle, like I wouldn't be responsible for my own actions."

"He's gone all the time. Why shouldn't you be able to do your thing? The boys are out of the house so no excuses now. Get some gumption. I could help, not with the cooking but with the financial end of the business. Think about it. We'd make a great team." Sarah tied off the yellow yarn; the next color she tied on was blue.

Margo worked in silence, not replying to her friend. Sarah seemed to sense Margo's distress and changed the subject. "What scrumptious dinner are you concocting in honor of Alex's girl?"

Jorden's ears perked up as she strained to listen.

Margo jumped in to describe her menu. "I'm making thyme-roasted rock Cornish hens, steamed broccoli with béarnaise sauce, saffron rice, along with a mixed green salad, and homemade rolls. The dessert will be individual chocolate tarts, each topped with a scoop of French vanilla ice cream."

"Yum! This should impress her. What's her name? I think you told me."

"Yes, several times. Her name is Jorden Marshall. You just don't listen. Should I write it down for you?" Margo laughed.

"Don't be smart! What's she like?"

"Don't you have the questions?" Dusting off her hands, Jorden watched Margo reach up to the wicker basket above the refrigerator and pull out several photos. "Here's one of them taken in Columbus, Georgia." She handed the picture to Sarah.

"She's lovely. They make a nice looking couple."

Jorden smiled at the compliment.

"Why are you hesitating? You're holding something back. What is it?" Sarah looked at Margo.

"I don't know."

"You can do better. Spit it out. You're troubled."

"I'll be straight with you. Jorden isn't Catholic. She's Protestant. Methodist, I believe. Alex says she has agreed to convert and raise their children in the Catholic faith, but ..."

"But what—sounds like she is being reasonable. Give her a chance, at least for Alex's sake."

"Bravo for Sarah!" Jorden mumbled under her breath. She almost clapped, but then she remembered she was hiding behind the bushes.

"I don't know. It just worries me. Jorden seems so young and naive. I wonder if she realizes what she has committed to. Saying you will convert is one thing and believing in Catholic doctrines is another. It's not a light decision, and I don't know if she has given it enough thought. I'd hate to see any of my boys split away from the Church. What if she converts and then decides it's not right for her or their children. It's a burden."

Jorden couldn't argue with his mother; she worried about the same thing.

"What do you mean?" Sarah asked, looking directly at Margo.

"It's not just me. Steven refused to be here this weekend. He doesn't want a southerner in our family—much less a converted Protestant. You know Steven has always been tough on Alex, expecting more from him. Now, Alex is coming up short again."

"Talk to him."

"Steven's impossible. He will never budge. He says this girl and her family aren't our kind. He wants better for Alex. How do I deal with him?"

Jorden's mouth dropped open, but she pressed her head closer to hear.

"Stand up for Alex. Be there for your son." Sarah took her eyes off her crocheting and looked at Margo. Open your eyes and see Jorden for what she is."

"Amen!" Jorden murmured.

"He won't listen to me. I try, and Steven shuts me out. Alex's Dad has always been hard on him."

"Listen to you. You disappoint me. Support your son."

"I don't know if I want to. I really wish he'd marry his own kind from the North. You know, a good Catholic. Alex can do better."

Jorden gasped. The words hurt—stung! She felt defeated. To stop the tears, Jorden concentrated on the baby blanket—anything but Alex's mother.

Sarah checked her blanket. "I can't believe I forgot to change colors." She pulled out the last row. "I think you're wrong. Have you told Alex what you think?"

"No. I don't want him going to Vietnam upset . . . thinking we disapprove. He might just do something foolish and marry her now.

I made Steven promise he wouldn't say anything. At least he agreed not to."

"Good. You're right not to get Alex upset, but I think you're wrong about Jorden. You should try and get to know her better."

Jorden lost her footing and slipped down the incline. She'd heard too much! Crushed, she couldn't listen to another word. This time, she couldn't stop the tears. No matter how hard she tried to fit into Alex's family, she knew prejudice ruled. Alex's father hadn't even met her, and he already had his mind set against her.

Mrs. Whelan's words hurt the most. "Alex can do better." She knew Mrs. Whelan's words were only meant for her friend, but the reality of the situation struck Jorden hard.

Alex called up to Jorden, "Looks like the tire is okay—they all seem fine."

Jorden wiped the tears away with a determined swipe before she scurried back down the steps.

Alex looked toward Jorden. "What were you doing in the bushes? Are you all right?" He seemed to notice a difference in Jorden.

"I'm fine. I lost my footing and slipped off the top step. I heard voices and looked to see where they were coming from." She could never tell him what she just heard—at least not now.

"Come on! Let's go in." The aroma of the Cornish hens filled their noses as they entered the kitchen.

"There you are," Alex's mother said. "Come in, Sarah's here."

Margo introduced Jorden to Sarah. Jorden tried to make small talk, doing her best to conceal her anguish. Jorden couldn't stop Margo's words from running through her mind and tearing her apart. She couldn't look at Alex's mother.

After a half hour, Sarah excused herself. "I've got to run. I promised my daughter I'd pick Jeremy up at five thirty. It was nice to meet you, Jorden. I'm glad you'll be joining this family."

"Thank you." Jorden wanted to hug Sarah; if only, Alex's mother felt the same as her friend. At least Jorden knew where his parents stood. Alex would be gone for months—time was on her side. She wouldn't give up!

Soon after, Sarah left. Alex and Jorden made their way upstairs to change for dinner.

As Alex turned to head up to the third floor, he stopped. "Oh, Scot and Carrie will probably get here around six."

Jorden kept her head down.

"What's wrong?"

"Nothing. I'm just nervous."

"Don't be. They're just family."

Chapter 41

January, 1970

The plane flew to Los Angeles as did Jorden's memories of Saturday evening. She couldn't get the tightness in her stomach to ease up.

***

Previous Year – Saturday evening, Albany, May17, 1969

"Just family," Jorden mumbled. She stood at the threshold of the guestroom. The name fit. She was a guest—not family. Now she had an inkling of what she had to face. Mrs. Whelan said it plain as day to her friend. Jorden doubted whether Alex's mother or father would ever accept her. She loved Alex and wanted the marriage to work despite their differences. Maybe after a year his family would come around and see her in a different light. She was going to do her best to turn them around.

A knock at the door startled her. "I'm on my way down."

"Thanks, Alex, I'll be right there."

As soon as Jorden reached the kitchen, Alex got up and moved by her side. Mrs. Whelan and Carrie were doing last minute preparations while Scott and Alex had been sitting at the kitchen table talking.

"Come on over! I want you to meet Jorden," Alex called to his brother and his sister-in-law.

Jorden saw how the brothers favored each other. Scott was taller but had the same slim build. His blue eyes contrasted with Alex's hazel ones. Scott seemed to resemble their mother.

"We're glad you're here. Alex couldn't stop telling us about you."

"I hope all good things."

"Glowing," Carrie replied.

"Great to hear." Jorden smiled.

Carrie, barely five feet tall, was perky, with fair skin, blond hair, and light blue eyes. She definitely looked pregnant—possibly more than six months. "How was your trip?"

"Great. It didn't take long," Jorden replied.

"We're happy to have you and glad we could get together tonight." Carrie glanced toward the kitchen. "Looks like Mom needs me—I better get back."

Jorden was surprised when she heard Carrie refer to Mrs. Whelan as Mom. Obviously, Carrie felt accepted by the family.

"Can I help?" Jorden offered.

"No, we have it under control, but thank you."

Jorden looked in awe at how well Margo worked with Carrie. If only Alex's mother would come to accept Jorden's help. She would be ecstatic.

"Where are you from?" Scott asked.

Jorden remained lost in her thoughts for a moment after Scott had asked her a question.

"I told you. Jorden's from Trenton, New Jersey," Alex replied.

"I hope Alex has been showing you a good time. I told him he'd better." Scott slapped Alex on the back and gave him a brother-to-brother look.

"The best," Jorden piped up.

"Come on. We need extra hands to get Mom's wonderful dinner on the table," Carrie called out.

Jorden and the others helped carry dishes to the dining room table. Taking her seat, she noticed the white roses were on the top of the antique chest. Pleased, she smiled. But, sadly they were not in the vase she had given Mrs. Whelan. Two of the rosebuds had opened while the third one remained closed. Jorden had been deeply immersed in her thoughts when she realized all of the family was seated.

"Scott, will you say the blessing?" Margo asked, bowing her head. They all crossed themselves. Jorden tensed, not knowing what to expect.

"Bless us O Lord, and these thy gifts, which we are about to receive, from thy bounty, through Christ, our Lord. Amen." Jorden looked on as each one at the table crossed themselves once more. This was so different from her family's dinner blessing. Would she ever fit in?

After the prayer everyone relished the meal. Not hungry, Jorden did her best to make a polite effort of eating. Compliments were given, including one from Jorden, raving about Margo's excellent dishes.

"The Cornish hen is so tender. How do you do it, Mom?" Carrie asked. "I'd love to have the recipe."

Margo smiled. "I'd be happy to write it down for you."

Carrie reached for another serving of the Cornish hen, plus two heaping spoons of saffron rice, and another dinner roll. Everyone watched, including Scott.

"Carrie, what are you doing?" Scott asked.

Carrie replied without appearing to be taken aback by his remark. "I'm starved. I haven't eaten since early this morning, besides—I'm eating for two."

Scott chuckled. "You look like you're eating for twins." He reached out his hand to stroke her bulging belly.

"Don't touch!" Carrie slapped at his hand, but an affectionate smile played on her lips.

Jorden couldn't help but smile at Carrie and Scott. In spite of Scott's rude comments, Jorden sensed the couple enjoyed prodding each other. This time Carrie seemed the winner, with Scott on the verge of an apology.

"Let her be, Scott," Margo piped up. "She's hungry. Let's change the subject, shall we? How are your house plans coming along?"

"You're building a new place?" Alex asked with a note of surprise in his voice.

"The plans are done and the construction begins early June."

"I can't wait," Carrie said, glowing. "I'm going to have a fabulous kitchen with all state of the art appliances and lots of space."

The conversation continued to center on the couple's construction plans. Jorden found Carrie and Scott entertaining as they tried to outdo each other. Alex got in a few comments, but Jorden didn't say two words—and no one attempted to bring her into the discussion. For her, it was a relief when the meal ended. Her nerves eased, and the flutters in her stomach settled down.

Jorden helped Mrs. Whelan and Carrie clear the table. Alex and Scott pitched in as well stacking dishes onto a cart from the butler pantry. Carrie proceeded to wash the dishes, Jorden dried, and Mrs. Whelan put them away.

"Well, Mom, can you believe we're already done?" Carrie raised her voice, apparently to make sure the men overheard her. "See what happens when everyone chips in?"

"Thank you all! I'll be right back. My feet are killing me; I need to change into my slippers." Margo turned and climbed up the back stairs.

"Jorden, can you do me a favor?" Carrie asked.

"Sure."

"Help me take these serving dishes to the butler pantry. They go in the lower cabinet under the bar area. Thanks. I'll be right out with the rest." Carrie handed Jorden three large platters.

Jorden carried the dishes to the pantry, but she wasn't sure which cabinet Carrie meant. Jorden opened the one closest to her. There she found an assortment of wrapped gifts. Her eyes stopped when she saw familiar wrapping paper. She drew closer, thinking it must be an optical illusion. It wasn't. A distinctive blue and white wrapped box topped with a violet bow was on the shelf. Directly under the box lay a note. Unable to resist, she bent down and read the card. "A pale blue vase—nice for a wedding gift."

"Oh! You have the wrong cabinet. It's the one on the left."

Startled by Carrie's voice, Jorden jerked up and dropped one of the platters. The antique dish cracked right down the center, reverberating loudly on impact. Jorden panicked. Now what would Margo Whelan think?

"What happened? Did something break?" Margo called out from the kitchen.

"It's nothing, Mom. All's under control," Carrie called back. At the same time, she lifted her index finger to her lips to warn Jorden to be quiet. Then, Jorden watched Carrie pick up the cracked platter and stash it in the furthest corner of the cabinet. Jorden stared at Carrie in amazement.

"Hand me the other platters." Carrie placed them in front of the cracked one. "This was Mom's favorite—came from her Aunt Eleanor. Don't worry! I'll have it repaired, and she'll never know. For now we'll keep it out of sight. Next week, when Mom's busy in the garden, I'll sneak it out. I know the right person to make it look like new."

"Thank you! But . . . why are you doing this?" Jorden looked at Carrie in disbelief.

"I like you, and Margo Whelan has quite a temper. Of course she won't show it in front of you, but believe me, we'd hear about it. It's hard to fit into this family. Only since I've become pregnant has Margo finally come around to accepting me. Alex's father still holds me at arm's length. I was raised in the Catholic faith but my family's wealth is considered nouveau—you know beneath Alex's father's upbringing and status."

Slowly Carrie rose up, hindered with the added weight of the baby. "The cabinet you opened contains Margo's stash of presents. She's always buying items she thinks would make nice gifts. Speaking of Margo, I'd better get back to the kitchen." She touched Jorden's shoulder with obvious affection as she spoke, "Don't worry about the platter. No one has to know but us." Carrie winked and returned to the kitchen.

Speechless, Jorden stood there staring at the cabinet. Carrie had rescued her from a disaster, and Jorden was grateful to have an ally.

She had broken Alex's mother's favorite dish while discovering at the same time her vase would just be re-gifted. Jorden didn't know whether to laugh or cry.

Alex came up behind Jorden. "Oh—here you are. I wondered where you were hiding. What are you doing out here?"

"I was helping Carrie bring plates back to the pantry."

"Come on, let's go back to the kitchen before Scott and Carrie leave." Alex nudged Jorden back into the kitchen just as Scott slipped on his jacket.

Scott leaned over and hugged Jorden. "It was great to meet you."

Carrie also gave Jorden a hug. "Come back whenever you get a chance. Don't worry about the dish," Carrie whispered.

Jorden nodded a silent thank you and gave Carrie an extra squeeze to seal their secret. The pair waved as they left through the kitchen door.

"Why don't we sit in the sunroom," Alex suggested. "What did you think of Scott and Carrie? I could tell they liked you."

"They are nice." Jorden's mind was on the broken platter, but she knew this wasn't the time to mention it or her re-wrapped vase. Instead she simply said, "I enjoyed them. Scott is lucky to have Carrie for a wife."

Jorden wanted time alone with Alex; she wanted him to hold her. "Let's go for a walk; I never got to see the garden."

"It's too dark out there. I'll show it to you in the morning."

Jorden flipped on the outside light before stepping out to get a glimpse of the flowers. Losing her footing, she fell against the side of the house.

"I told you. It's too dark!" Alex seemed irritated Jorden wasn't listening to him.

Mrs. Whelan came into the adjacent den to turn out the light. "Oh, I didn't realize you two were out here."

Margo stayed, making small talk. "You know, I don't think Scott meant to upset Carrie tonight. He's just worried about her—this is their first child. Maybe she ate so much because she really was hungry. She's always been thin and has never had a weight problem." Mrs. Whelan's chatter seemed to go on abnormally long.

Frustrated, Jorden decided to excuse herself. "Thank you, Mrs. Whelan, for the wonderful dinner. I certainly enjoyed meeting Scott and Carrie." She turned to Alex. "I'm tired. I'll see you in the morning."

The distance between Jorden and Alex seemed to increase with each passing hour. They were still under the same roof, but she may as well have been back in Columbus, Georgia. What a way to end their last night.

Chapter 42

January 1970

"Fasten your seatbelts. We're landing in Los Angeles." Jorden looked out the window and saw the urban sprawl. Though on a much larger scale, it reminded her of the view of Albany last May.

***

Previous Year – Albany, Sunday morning, May18, 1969

Jorden tossed and turned Saturday night, praying for sleep to ease her sorrow. She didn't like feeling this way. By nine on Sunday morning, she carried her bags down to the kitchen. Alex and his mother were having coffee and reading the newspaper. Jorden watched them, thinking how different they looked. Alex must take after his father, the one she never met. What a strange family, so different from her own close-knit one. Why hadn't Alex walked with her in the garden last night? Such a simple gesture would have made all the difference.

Alex looked up. "I could have gotten those bags for you. I didn't expect you to bring them down."

"They weren't heavy, besides, I had to come down anyway." Jorden tried to make a joke, but she could see the irritation in his unsmiling eyes.

"Let me get you some coffee," Mrs. Whelan offered. "I made scrambled eggs, bacon, tomato slices with Parmesan cheese, and muffins. Help yourself. They're staying warm in the oven."

"Thank you, Mrs. Whelan." Jorden knew she was just trying to be nice to ease the tension. She didn't look directly at Alex, but she could feel his eyes on her.

"I hope you slept well," Alex commented.

"Fine," Jorden replied. The last thing she wanted was to show her true feelings. Besides, he probably didn't have a clue how much he had upset her last night.

Jorden fixed her plate and poured a glass of orange juice. Amazed by the freshness of the juice and her own thirst, she gulped down half of the glass before she spoke. "This is the best juice I've ever tasted!"

"I make it from fresh oranges. I've spoiled my family and can't get away with buying frozen juice anymore," Margo replied.

Jorden was glad Alex's mother spoiled someone. But, she had to admit his mother was a gourmet chef. "Everything is wonderful, especially the tomato slices."

"I'm so glad you like them," Margo said, brightening.

Alex broke into the conversation. "What time should we leave for the airport?"

"My flight's at two fifteen, so we should probably leave around noon," Jorden replied.

"Good, we have an hour. I can keep my promise and show you the garden."

"Thank you," Jorden replied, thinking it was better later than never.

"What a great suggestion," Margo added with enthusiasm. "I'll get my shoes and join you. It's a perfect time to walk in the garden."

"Mother, you've seen it a trillion times," Alex said with a shake of his head.

"Nonsense. I'd like to show it to Jorden. It's my showcase."

Jorden noticed how his mother seemed to open up with the knowledge Jorden would soon be leaving. Relief, even a hint of joy, played on Margo's face. Following her future mother-in-law, they set off. The path was lined with rose bushes. Jorden could imagine how majestic it must look and smell when the roses were in bloom. The walkway led to a circular opening and a large wooden deck. A barbeque grill was permanently installed next to a large circular table.

"In the summer we often have picnics out here." Mrs. Whelan seemed to pause and reminisce. "When the boys were young, they would race around the deck and terrorize everyone. I wish this awful war was over." Margo turned to look at her son.

For once, Jorden was moved by his mother's words. Her youngest son would soon be off to Vietnam. Jorden knew this must be tearing Mrs. Whelan apart—just as it was her.

"We've been out here almost an hour. We'd better head back," Alex declared. His voice brought them back to reality.

Jorden soaked up the warm sunrays and the scent of flowers as they walked back to the house. If only she could hold onto this moment and set her hurt aside. It would be over a year before she would see Alex again. Within minutes they reached the sunroom, and Jorden went upstairs to freshen up. She took one last look at the guest suite, remembering her time with Alex in the canopy bed. Now it seemed eons ago.

When she arrived downstairs, Alex and his mother were again waiting at the kitchen table. Jorden turned toward Mrs. Whelan, trying to find the right words in the awkward silence. "Thank you for a delightful weekend. I had a wonderful time—so good to meet you, Scott and Carrie."

"I'm glad you could come. I know we're both going to miss Alex. We'll have to keep in touch."

"We will." Jorden intended to keep up her end of the agreement. Maybe this would be one way to get closer to his mother. Both women would miss Alex and pray for his safe return. Jorden wanted to reach out and gain his mother's trust and hopefully one day her acceptance. Hugs had always come with farewells in her family—but none came from his mother. A hint of respect seemed to linger in her look during their final goodbye.

They said little as Alex drove to the airport. After parking, he pulled Jorden close to him. "I don't want us to part like this."

Jorden looked at her hands. She had been dreading this moment—saying goodbye.

"I love you. Believe me, I'm going to miss you more than you know," Alex said as he leaned over and kissed Jorden—a long, lingering kiss, but still not enough to erase the knot in her stomach. She wanted more time with him . . . why didn't he understand? The last few moments were the hardest.

"I have to go," Jorden finally stated simply.

Alex waved to Jorden as she boarded the plane. Upset, she waved back, knowing this would be the last time she would see him before he left for this ugly war.

Chapter 43

January 1970

Heading toward the boarding gate for Atlanta, Jorden walked past a rowdy bar. The patrons were cheering for the Los Angeles Lakers. Elgin Baylor had just made a game-winning jump shot. The crowd went crazy, chanting his name over and over. It reminded her of the wild, surprise call from Alex last May.

***

Previous Year - Columbus, May 21, 1969

The phone rang shortly after Jorden had turned off Scott O'Brady's evening program. She was glad Madison hadn't been there to hear the latest troublesome news from Vietnam. Reaching for the phone, she could barely hear over blaring music and piercing voices. Ready to hang up, she decided it must be a crank call. But—wait—she thought she heard a familiar voice.

"Hello . . . Jorden . . . Are you there?" Alex shouted.

"Yes . . . I can't hear you. Where are you?"

"I'm . . . in a bar outside of Albany . . . with Peter. We're waiting for his girl to get off work. We stopped . . . for a burger . . . and a beer."

"I almost hung up." Jorden was annoyed he was at a bar rather than with her in Columbus.

"I'm . . . coming!"

"What? Speak louder, I can't hear you." Jorden wasn't sure if she had heard him right.

"I'm coming to Columbus! I have to see you before I leave."

"When?"

"I'm flying in Saturday. How about a date?"

"Gosh, I think I'm busy," Jorden replied with a laugh.

"You're what? Your voice is . . . breaking up."

Jorden changed her tune—no more joking. "What time are you getting in? I can't wait to see you!"

"Jorden are . . . you there? You're breaking . . . up again. I'll call you tomorrow. It's so loud in here . . . I can't hear my own voice. I . . . love you." Then the line went dead.

Tears of joy slid down Jorden's cheeks. She couldn't believe it. Shaking, her hands flew up to her face.

"What's wrong?"

Not realizing Madison had come in, Jorden jerked up. "Alex is coming!"

"When?"

"I don't know. No—I mean, Saturday. I just don't know what time. He'll call back tomorrow."

"At last he's come to his senses."

"I can't believe it. I just knew I wouldn't see him again."

"Why don't you know when he's getting in?" Madison looked curious.

"A bad connection; he called from a bar. It was so loud I couldn't hear him."

"What was he doing in a bar?"

"I don't know. Something about being with Peter and waiting for his girlfriend to get off work."

"Whose girlfriend?"

"You sound like a lawyer. His friend's. Peter's."

"Sorry, but I came in here and found you in tears. What am I supposed to think?"

"Just be happy for me." Jorden sent her roommate a pleading look. Madison was her closest friend, but sometimes she just didn't get it, or did she? Jorden had to admit—Madison was usually right.

Alex called the next night. His flight would arrive Saturday afternoon a little after four. Jorden couldn't believe he would be with her a whole week. Seven days seemed like an eternity. For the first few days Jorden was on the top of the world, but by Friday evening her nerves were frazzled.

"Calm down. You're getting me hyped up." Madison looked at Jorden as she dried the last glass in the dish rack.

"I can't help it. I'll have Alex to myself for a week. Of course I still have to teach, but the rest of the time will be for us!"

"He's staying here?"

"Is this a problem?" Jorden frowned as she finished wiping off the counter top.

"No. I don't have a problem, but I worry. You need to be careful."

"Not this again." She knew Madison was right. Birth control continued to be a huge problem between them. Alex refused to use condoms and didn't want her to use birth control pills, and she didn't have a solution.

"I'm going home tomorrow, so you'll at least have Saturday night without me here."

Jorden hugged Madison. "Thank you."

Saturday afternoon, Jorden left at three thirty to meet Alex's flight. Time seemed to stand still until she spotted him. He moved with ease through the crowd and when he saw her, a radiant smile erupted instantly. Jorden's heartbeat quickened as she watched him pick up his pace. He beamed, lifting her upward.

"I can't believe you're here!" Jorden kissed him.

"Well I am, and I'm yours for the next seven days."

Twenty long minutes elapsed between leaving the airport and arriving at Jorden's place. Small talk kept them busy until they stepped into her apartment. Closing the door sent Jorden and Alex into their own private world.

Early Saturday evening, Alex drove Jorden's car to Amore's for dinner. Antonio spotted them as they walked in. "What a nice surprise. I haven't seen you two in a long time. Have you tied the knot?"

"Not yet—next summer." Alex grinned.

After an enjoyable meal, Alex reached for Jorden's hand and touched the bracelet he had given her. "How about next August?"

"Next August?"

"Have you already forgotten?" Alex teased. "Our wedding."

"How could I? But, August is so far away!" At the moment, Jorden wished they could slip off and get married tonight, but she knew Alex wanted to wait.

"A year will go by quickly—you'll see. It'll be hard, but it will make us even stronger. Then we haven't rushed into marriage." Alex squeezed her hand.

They slept late the next morning. Jorden made her pancake specialty, with maple syrup and fresh fruit, to try and impress him.

"Yum tasty, almost as delicious as you." Alex grinned and gave her a kiss. "Thank you."

Jorden blushed. "You're welcome." This was the side of Alex she loved, the one she always wanted to be with.

He sipped his second cup of coffee, looking toward the window. "It's a beautiful day. What about Callaway Gardens?"

"Callaway Gardens. Hmm . . ." Jorden glanced outside. "It's hot enough; we could go swimming."

"I don't have a swimsuit."

"So? We'll buy you one."

"You're nuts!" Alex laughed.

But they did. Jorden talked Alex into buying a swimsuit at Columbus Square before they drove north. Callaway Gardens was packed, but it didn't matter. They enjoyed swimming, walking around the lake, and having dinner at the Callaway Garden Lodge. To Jorden it was a perfect day, except she ended up sunburned.

Mornings were the hardest for Jorden—having to leave for school. Alex would eat with her and then send her off with a wave. Friday, their last day, arrived too soon. She took a day of personal leave; luckily her principal approved it. If he hadn't she would have called in sick. It meant everything to her to spend her last day with Alex.

"I wish we had your Mustang for this gorgeous day," Jorden complained. Instead Alex drove Jorden's Volkswagen Bug south of Columbus.

"Do me a favor. Check the map, Miss Navigator. What's the next town?"

"Cusseta. From there we could bear to the right to Louvale, Lumpkin, and Richland or turn left to Renfroe and Brooklyn."

"What's your pleasure?"

"You are!" Jorden grinned.

"Never heard of U-R!" Alex laughed. "Listen to my navigator—she doesn't know where she's going."

"I do too!"

"Promise you won't get us lost?"

"Never!" Jorden replied.

Alex drove past small farms dotting the country landscape while Jorden listened to "My Girl" playing on the radio. It made her nostalgic for their past as Alex drove through several small picturesque towns. Each one had a main street with large colonial style homes, set back with deep lawns. Wrap-around porches or verandas with one or two swings were common features. In the heat of the day few people were outside.

Jorden enjoyed having Alex drive. She became mesmerized as she watched a young mother and her baby. The woman pushed her stroller along the sidewalk with the top up, shielding the baby from the sun. Jorden's imagination took over. One day she could see herself doing the same. If only the war was over, and Alex wasn't leaving for Vietnam tomorrow morning.

"Where are you? You look miles away."

"Daydreaming."

"Hope I'm there with you."

"Always!"

By the time they reached Richland, it was almost four. Outdoor activity increased. People were out, traffic was heavier, and the town was waking up. Jorden saw a group of boys playing baseball and small children on swings in a nearby park.

"It's getting late; we should go back." Alex drove back through Brooklyn and Renfroe taking in the scenery before reaching Cusseta and finally heading north to Columbus. That night Jorden clung to Alex. She knew such a moment would not come again for a long time. The nagging worry of something happening to Alex was always with her.

Morning came. With sleep still in her eyes, Alex gathered his things and packed them into his duffle bag. Jorden dressed, applying no make-up. Tears slid down her cheeks as he drove. After pulling into the airport parking area, he held her a long time. Lifting her chin, he spoke softly. "I have to go."

"I hate it. I hate the war!"

"I know." Alex brushed his lips against hers. "I love you. I'll write soon," he whispered. "Don't cry. It won't be long." She knew it wasn't true. The flight he was taking would ultimately lead to Vietnam and his twelve month tour of duty.

Chapter 44

January 16, 1970

Jorden arrived at the Atlanta airport at six in the morning. The return flight to Columbus was scheduled for eight fifteen. Alex seemed ages away—now letters would have to suffice. Almost twelve hours separated them. Morning for Jorden in Georgia meant evening for Alex in Vietnam.

After finally touching down in Columbus, Jorden took a cab back to her apartment. She had the weekend to get back into her daily routine. Routine made her think of Matt. Tennis on Wednesday and a movie Saturday night had been their routine. "But, no more!" she scolded herself. How could she even think about Matt?

Emma Lynn's blue Chevrolet sputtered into her parking spot around midafternoon. She looked up and waved wildly when she spotted Jorden at the window. Her roommate grabbed her second graders' papers before hurrying up the stairs.

"How was Hawaii? Tell me all." Darby soon joined them.

"You two are wearing me out. Let's make dinner, and I'll tell you more."

"It's Friday night—no cooking!" Kyle and I will get hotdogs at the basketball game. Why don't you join us? Darby and Chip are coming. I bet Matt will also be there."

"I'm beat! Besides, I want to write Alex."

"Aren't you the spoilsport? Are you going to hole up like you did after Alex left last May?" Darby rolled her eyes.

"You two are incorrigible! You have me stepping out—when I just got back from Hawaii and the man I plan to marry."

Emma Lynn threw up her arms. "Be stubborn. You're only young once, and I'm going to make the most of it! What can a basketball game hurt?"

"Look, I just don't want to go," Jorden replied. Her roommates didn't understand. She had just left Alex, and she didn't want to see anyone, especially not Matt.

"We don't mean to pressure you," Darby replied. "We just think you should get out and enjoy yourself before you're married."

"Thank you. I know you have good intentions."

"We'll let you off tonight," Emma Lynn said with a smirk. "But—we're not done trying."

***

February 14, 1970

Weeks passed. This year Valentine's Day conveniently landed on a Saturday.

"You are coming with us tonight whether you want to or not. No backing down now," Emma Lynn declared.

"I don't need to be going to a party," Jorden stated.

"It's been almost a month. You spend your time grading papers, writing Alex, and occasionally seeing Madison. You need an outing."

"I said no and I mean it. You two go and have fun. I'm fine right here."

"Neither of us will take no for an answer." Darby led Jorden to her closet.

"Amen!" Emma Lynn joined in. "Want to wear my red dress?"

"No!" Jorden said with a scowl. "If I go, I'll wear my own things."

"Good!" Darby smiled in triumph. "We're walking over in a half hour."

"I'll help you pick out an outfit?" Without waiting for a response, Emma Lynn threw open Jorden's closet. A red and white blouse next to a pair of black slacks caught her eye. "Here. This is perfect."

"Thank you, but I can make my own choice," Jorden replied. In a way, she looked forward to getting out; a Valentine party couldn't be so unfaithful to Alex.

"I'm only trying to help. Wear what you want. You've got fifteen minutes."

"Hey! You said a half hour."

"You wasted half your time. Stop talking and change."

Jorden stared at her closet. Actually, she agreed with Emma Lynn's choice.

"We're ready!"

"Give me five more minutes. Go on—I'll catch up."

"We're not budging!" Emma Lynn stamped her foot. "You'll pull a fast one and not show up. I know you."

Jorden ignored her remark. She touched up her makeup, lightly dusting her cheeks with blush.

"I'm ready."

"It's about time," Emma Lynn replied.

Jorden could see a glint in Emma Lynn's eye when she saw Jorden was wearing what she had suggested.

Music drifted across the parking lot as the threesome walked to the recreation room. "Mr. Bojangles" was playing when they entered. The night was still early. Couples were dancing, others were mingling. Kyle and Chip waltzed in around nine. No Matt. It was for the best, Jorden kept telling herself.

Chip appeared with drinks. "Watch out. These may be strong. The bartender had a heavy hand pouring the rum."

"Wow! What a punch!" Darby almost spit it out, but Jorden knew she wouldn't want to embarrass Chip. "I'm getting a taller glass. Come on, Jorden, there's an opening at the bar." Darby picked up a tall glass and a can of Coca Cola. She poured her drink into the taller glass, filled it with the Cola and plopped in a couple of ice cubes. She took a sip. "Much better."

Jorden promptly handed Darby her glass and watched her roommate repeat the process.

Jorden took a sip. "Not bad, thank you." She watched the couples dance while tapping her foot to the music. Emma Lynn was dancing and flirting with Kyle. Darby had returned to Chip, and they were now dancing as "Sweet Caroline" played. Jorden noticed the front door opening out of her peripheral vision. There stood Matt, but he couldn't see her. Trembling, she sipped her drink, not uttering a word. What would she do if he saw her?

Matt stepped forward and weaved through the crowd. Jorden didn't budge. She watched him move toward the bar and order a drink. The lights were low and the music loud. Slowly, he turned his head, and their eyes met. Matt smiled and waved at Jorden before promptly walking in the opposite direction. She couldn't believe he didn't come over and at least say hello. Instead he approached an alluring, petite blond and asked her to dance.

Jorden hadn't seen Matt since mid-December—what was wrong with him? Feeling betrayed, but mostly hurt, she gulped down her drink, dashed past Matt, and out the door. At first she walked, then ran, and finally sprinted up the steps up to her apartment.

Jorden paced back and forth from the kitchen to the living room. "What is wrong with me? Why am I so upset?" she jabbered. The strong drink didn't help her state of mind. Without thinking, she lifted the kitchen's wall phone and dialed the number of the recreation room. After one ring she hung up. She repeated the process two more times, still hanging up. She mounted her courage and dialed the number one last time. By some fluke in the connection, Matt's voice came on the line.

"Jorden?"

She jumped back when she heard her name. "Who is this?"

"Matt. I've been trying to call you. Why did you leave?"

Silence.

"Say something. I'd like to see you." Jorden didn't know what to say.

"Jorden, are you there?"

"Yes. I'm here."

"I'll be there in a few minutes. Stay put. Please."

Shaken, Jorden hung up. She stood in front of the window and watched Matt cross the parking lot. Her heart raced when she heard the main door open and the doorbell ring.

Jorden looked through the peephole. There was Matt. She cracked the door.

"Are you going to let me in?"

"I should leave you right there. It's what you deserve."

Matt pressed the door and met no resistance, so he continued to push until the door opened.

Jorden stepped back.

Matt broke the silence. "How've you been?"

"Good." Jorden stretched the truth. "And you?"

"I've wanted to see you." Matt reached for her hand.

Jorden backed away, afraid to touch him. "You sure have a funny way of showing it—ignoring me and asking the blond to dance."

"I knew you needed space—that's why I've stayed away. I don't know why I asked her to dance . . . I guess I wasn't sure how you would respond to me. I almost didn't come tonight, but I hoped to see you. I wish . . . wish we could enjoy what little time we have left?" Matt reached out again. This time Jorden didn't back away, but a quiver ran through her at the touch of his hand. Next, she heard Darby and Chip's voices on the stairs. Saved! Jorden didn't trust her feelings.

"Good. I see you two connected," Darby declared as she opened the door. "Jorden, I had no idea you had left." Darby then looked from Jorden to Matt with a curious expression.

Jorden knew the look. Before Darby could say another word, Jorden steered Matt out the door. "Come on, I'll walk you down to your car."

Matt looked puzzled. "You're walking me to my car?"

"Let's at least walk around the apartment complex and get some exercise. Then you can walk me back." Jorden knew she wasn't making much sense.

Halfway around the complex, Matt stopped. "Would you like to go to church with me in the morning? I like the Episcopal Church in Columbus."

Matt's words caught her off guard. It dawned on her, she and Alex had never gone to a Catholic service. She hesitated—what harm could it be?

"I guess."

"Good. I'll pick you up at ten thirty. The church service begins at eleven." Matt squeezed her hand. "Thank you. It'll be nice to have your company rather than be alone."

Jorden smiled. "It's late, I'll walk you back." At the top of the stairs Matt kissed her cheek. "See you at ten thirty."

Jorden watched him drive off. She wondered what she was getting herself into.

Chapter 45

February 1970

The alarm blasted off Sunday morning at nine. Half-asleep, Jorden slammed down the snooze button. Church—an Episcopal Church, she remembered. Her hand darted to her head. Rum and Coke had left her with a slight headache.

Jorden listened for the snooze alarm, but it never rang. She stretched out and pulled the clock's face toward her—a quarter to ten. Oh no—she must have shut the alarm button off instead of turning on the snooze. She leaped out of bed and hustled to the bathroom. Pulling the medicine cabinet open, she took two aspirins, splashed cold water on her face, applied makeup, and dressed. She swept into the kitchen to start a pot of coffee.

Darby and Emma Lynn hadn't gotten up. Thank goodness. Now she didn't have to listen to cracks about Matt.

Matt arrived at ten thirty. Jorden caught herself staring. He looked so different in a sports jacket and a tie; she liked the transformation.

"Want some coffee?"

"Not enough time. Parking is tight."

Jorden took one more sip. "Okay, I'm ready."

After finding a place to park, Matt and Jorden walked a block to the church. She looked up with wonder. Trinity Episcopal Church was an impressive structure, located in the heart of Columbus.

"It's regal—don't you think?" Matt asked.

"It's amazing!" The height of the church steeple astounded her. "My Methodist Church is modest compared to this."

As Jorden entered the church, the sight of the huge oaken trusses supporting the roof was overpowering. Matt pressed on her elbow and led her to a pew near the rear of the church's sanctuary. "I like to sit here."

Jorden relied on Matt to lead her through the service. She tried to listen to the sermon but her eyes strayed to the striking brass pulpit set against the brilliant stained glass windows.

"The service was so intense! I couldn't have followed it if you hadn't shown me when to read, sing, and get on my knees," Jorden exclaimed.

"It's easy once you get the hang of it. This church is much more formal than mine in Alaska. I like it though—it's peaceful. I'm glad you came." Matt squeezed her hand. "What about next Sunday?"

Jorden hesitated, not sure what to say.

"I can add a sweetener—I'll treat you to lunch after the services, starting today."

Jorden's stomach growled at the thought of food. "Then—how can I refuse?"

"Good. Have you ever been to the Plantation House?"

"No, never heard of it."

"Major Hawkins told me about it. It's north of Columbus, in the direction of Callaway Gardens but a little closer." Jorden and Matt chatted about their Christmas holidays while he drove. The two month hiatus didn't seem to exist for Jorden.

The Plantation House lived up to its reputation. Over dessert, Nora's name came up.

"How's she doing? Is Eloise still working at your office?"

"Eloise is well—even happy. I keep forgetting how long it's been since we've talked. Eloise and the major seem to be an item. I predict a marriage proposal in the near future."

Jorden leaned forward. "Does Nora like the major?"

"I'm not sure. Nora came by the office late last Friday afternoon. I was finishing up an old project when I heard them argue. I tried not to listen but couldn't help but hear them."

"What were they arguing about?"

"Major Hawkins, I think. I shouldn't say anymore."

"Please do," Jorden responded. "I really want to know how Nora is doing."

"Eloise and Nora didn't know I was there. I couldn't hear everything—just when they raised their voices. Nora seemed terribly upset," Matt admitted.

"Go on, please," Jorden insisted.

"Well, Eloise wanted Nora to spend the night with her friend, Lisa, so she could go out to dinner with Major Hawkins. This didn't set well with Nora. I think she is afraid of her mother getting involved with another man. You remember when I told you how Sam almost destroyed their lives?" Matt looked at Jorden.

"I sure do."

"He's still a real threat and it's not a good situation, from what Major Hawkins tells me."

"How awful," Jorden uttered after Matt finished.

"Enough about them. It's a great day—let's go for a drive." Cheerfully, Matt led Jorden to his Dodge Dart.

Chapter 46

February 1970

Nora arrived at her mother's office late Friday afternoon. She was upset and threw her book bag on the floor next to her mother's desk. Eloise looked up. "There you are! I'm glad Cheryl's mother dropped you off before six. I hope you thanked her for the ride."

"Of course I did, I know how to be nice." Nora scowled at her mother.

"What are you trying to tell me?" Her mother looked clueless.

"Mama, how can you do this to me? I don't want to spend tonight with Lisa! You don't think I know what's going on with you and Major Hawkins, but I do. He's over at our place every day, eating dinner with us on a nightly basis."

"The major's here for our protection—ever since Sam got out of jail. The major's been good to you."

"Yeah! So was Sam when he wanted something." Nora didn't think there was such a thing as a good man. "Why do I have to spend the night at Lisa's?"

"Because the major and I want to go out and I'm not leaving you alone."

"I'm fourteen, old enough to be alone!"

"I know. That's what worries me!"

"I'm not stupid; I know what the major wants from you." Nora rolled her eyes. She figured he just wanted to get her mother in the sack.

"Enough. Lisa picks you up at seven." Before Eloise could finish her sentence, Nora yanked up her book bag, ran out, and slammed the door.

Furious, Nora rushed down the stairs. Her mother made no sense. Nora tripped on the last step as tears blurred her vision. Disgusted, she picked herself up, brushed off her knees, and threw open the outside door. "I'll show Mama . . . I'll show everyone!"

Nora raced down the sidewalk until she noticed blood running down her shin. The bright red stream made her slow down. Spotting an empty bench, she threw down her bag and sat down to inspect her knee. Pulling out a hanky, she blotted her knee to ease the flow.

Her mother made the worst decisions. She and Lisa tried to warn her last year about Sam, but her mother wouldn't listen. Those times stirred up ugly memories, ones she wanted to forget but couldn't.

***

Previous Year, January 1969

Sam did everything he could to persuade Eloise to come back to him. He completely remodeled the house, painted it inside and out, and replaced the roof. He was an excellent carpenter and knew how to cut expenses. Gutting the kitchen, he put in new flooring using materials from a job he'd just finished. He refurbished the cabinets and put in new appliances left over from previous construction sites. He replaced all the old flooring with practically new hardwood floors. The once shoddy house had a new makeover.

In spite of all of Sam's efforts, Nora still wasn't convinced. Lisa also tried to talk sense into Eloise. Pretending to be asleep, Nora listened and learned a lot, especially the night her mother decided to return to Sam's remolded house.

Lisa stood at the kitchen sink washing the remaining dinner dishes while Eloise dried and put them away.

"You don't need to leave. Give it more time." Lisa tried to persuade Eloise.

"I've been at your home over three months, and Sam's been perfect this whole time. You saw the house. It's beautiful!"

"I agree. He does do good work, but you need to think of the quality of your life. What happens if he turns violent again?"

"It won't happen. He promises he's changed, and I believe him."

"I hope you're right for your sake and Nora's."

"Believe me. I am right."

"Listen to me. Don't let him take over your pay check. Right now you're depositing it into your own bank account. Keep it the same way. It's important you establish parameters before you move back in with him. Do you understand?"

"I do and I will."

"You'd better. More than likely, he's going to try and drag you down further. You need to keep control."

"I've already told him if I returned I would need to know about our financial situation."

"Most of all, you need to be in charge of what you earn. Remember, I'm here. Keep talking to me. You can always move back here if you need to."

"I know, but . . . I won't need to. He's a different man. But, thank you." Eloise touched Lisa's hand in gratitude.

"When are you going to tell Nora? You know, she's not going to like it."

"It's hard for Nora to understand, and it makes it difficult for me to tell her."

Sam kept his word. There had been no drinking and he continued to work full time. Even Christmas had been pleasant. He appeared to be making a serious effort, which Nora grudgingly admitted, but she still had strong reservations about them returning to live with him. What if he changed back to his old ways? Was this only an act?

It took a while, but in time Eloise talked Nora into moving back with Sam. If he backslides, her mother promised, they would leave. Eloise and Nora moved in with Sam the last weekend in January of 1969. The first three months were almost picture perfect. Sam outdid himself even helping with the housework. Nora liked how he had redone her room. Her closet had a door, along with hardwood floors, and a built-in desk. Life in their remodeled home had much improved. She even heard laughter between Eloise and Sam.

Eloise became accustomed to the good side of Sam. When he started to slip, she refused to admit it. At first, he stopped helping with the dishes or taking out the garbage and other little things. Eloise didn't want to rock the boat so she didn't say anything. Nora also enabled Sam by pitching in and taking over many of his tasks. Neither mother nor daughter would admit something might be wrong.

Nora also noticed her mother didn't mention Lisa anymore. Sam resented her mother's friend. Nora remembered the night she overheard Sam talking with her mother about Lisa.

"Who are you calling?" Sam asked, taking his eyes off the television.

"Lisa. I don't see her much at work. We're on different shifts. I wondered how she's doing."

"You don't need to call her." Sam stepped forward and put the receiver down.

"How dare you hang up. She's my friend, and I want to talk with her."

"Lisa means trouble. I don't want her in our lives. For the sake of us, I don't want you calling her." Sam moved in front of the phone.

"Please move aside; I mean to call Lisa," Eloise stated.

"No, you don't."

"She's my friend, and I'll talk with her if I want to."

"I'm your husband. I come first." Sam held Eloise at arm's length.

Sam's tone frightened Nora. She had been listening to them from the kitchen. Putting the last plate in the cabinet, she walked into the living room. Sam held Eloise by her shoulders.

"What's happening?" Nora asked.

"Nothing. Your mother and I were having a discussion. Right, Eloise?" Sam released his grip.

"Its fine, Nora. Sam and I were talking about Lisa." Eloise turned away from Nora. "I'll think about what you said. You may be right." Eloise tried to placate Sam.

"Good. I know I am." Sam gave Eloise a hug.

Nora looked on. Warnings sounded loud and clear, but she didn't say anything.

The next morning after Sam had left for his construction job, Nora confronted her mother at breakfast. "Mama, what happened last night? I didn't like the looks of it."

"Oh, it didn't mean anything. Here, have some orange juice and make yourself some toast. You need to eat something before school. You know Sam isn't fond of Lisa, and he didn't want me to call her. No problem, I'll just call her when he's not around."

"You should be able to call her anytime. Don't let Sam bully you."

"Please don't start in on me. Sam has been wonderful these past months, and I want to keep it that way. He apologized to me last night, and said he didn't mean to upset me. I believe him."

"I don't. If he ever hurts you again, I don't know what I'll do."

"It'll be fine. Now eat some toast. Here, have a piece of mine, I'll make some more."

Nora watched her mother closely and prayed to God she was right—but she wasn't. The situation finally escalated on a hot night in July.

***

July, 1969

Nora picked up the phone, assuming it was her friend, Cheryl. "Oh. Hi Lisa. Hold on I'll get Mama."

Eloise lifted her index finger to her mouth, motioning for Nora to be quiet. She lifted the phone out of Nora's hand and tiptoed into the kitchen. Eloise spoke softly to Lisa.

"Hi. Sam is here and it's hard to talk. I should have told you to call before seven. Can you meet me tomorrow morning at eleven at Mender's Flea market? I need to talk with you."

"Sure, I can meet you. I won't keep you. Hang in there."

"Who was on the phone?" Sam asked as he entered the kitchen to get another beer.

"Lisa."

"I thought you stopped seeing her. You know I don't like her!"

"She called. It would be impolite not to speak to her."

"Well, better to be rude since she's a bad influence and always putting crazy ideas in your head!"

"I can hear the beer talking." Eloise couldn't keep her eyes off the trash can. "How many is it tonight? This morning I counted eight cans."

"So now you're counting the cans. You are something! I'll drink as many as I want! Why don't you see how many this one makes?" He picked up the trash can and dumped the contents out in the middle of the kitchen floor.

"Now start counting!" He grabbed for her arm.

Eloise moved faster and escaped his reach.

"I said, count those cans!"

Defiantly, Eloise fled the room.

"Don't turn your back on me!"

Enraged, Sam slammed down the beer, stormed forward, and grasped the scruff of her neck.

"Stop it! You're hurting me. Are you going to beat up a pregnant woman?"

Sam stopped. The statement startled him. "What?"

"You heard me."

Sam's demeanor changed. He wanted a child, but Eloise didn't. He reached out, but she pushed him away, walking out in disgust.

Nora could hear them. She peered over the top of the stairs. She watched Sam pick up the trash, mumbling under his breath. Her mother's words had surprised him as well as her. Was her mother really pregnant? Maybe she said that so he wouldn't hurt her.

In the morning Nora crept down the stairs. Her mother wasn't in the kitchen. Nora knocked on her door. "Mama, please come out."

Silence.

"Mama . . . Mama. Come out. Talk to me!"

Nora heard the bed frame creak. The doorknob turned and Eloise stepped out. She looked awful. Her eyes were red and puffy from crying.

"Talk to me, Mama. Come out to the kitchen and I'll make some pancakes for you." Nora gave her mother a hug, trying to comfort her.

Eloise started the coffee. She sat at the kitchen table with her hands over her face.

"Mama, I heard you and Sam last night. Is it true, about the baby?"

Eloise hung her head. She avoided looking at Nora. "It's ... true."

"Are you sure?"

"I saw a doctor last week. He confirmed it. I'm pregnant." Eloise's voice cracked as she stood up. Tears filled her eyes. For Nora's sake, Eloise put her arms around her daughter.

"Oh, Mama. When?"

"Late February."

"What are we going to do? Sam's no good. You can't expect him to give you any help with the baby."

"Mind your tongue. Sam is the one who wanted this baby. He has to provide for us."

"I hate him. He'll get even worse after the baby comes!"

"Somehow, we'll make it work. We have to. . ."

"We can't stay, Mama. Sam will hit you again. He scares me!"

"The baby complicates everything." Eloise didn't know how she could support Nora and the baby. "I'll eventually have to quit work. Oh, Nora, I don't want you to worry about this." Eloise figured she'd work it out some way. This was the main reason she wanted to see Lisa; she needed her point of view.

"Can't we stay with Lisa again?"

"I wish it were that simple. Sam wants this baby. I'm going to see if I can get him to quit drinking; anything to help. I'm sorry Nora. You're too young to have to go through this."

"I'm fourteen. I know more than you think I do. You could stop this and not have the baby." The stricken look on her mother's face made Nora wish she could take the words back.

"Don't ever say such a thing. Shame on you! This is a little brother or sister you're talking about."

"Mama, I'm sorry. I'm just worried." Nora knew she had stepped over the line.

"We'll work this out somehow. Please don't worry." Eloise hugged her daughter.

***

Nora heard footsteps. It was getting dark. Tense, she sat up straight. She knew she shouldn't have run out on her mother, but Mama should try and understand her better. The footsteps quickened. They had a familiar sound. She smiled when she saw her mother off in the distance.

Chapter 47

February 1970

Eloise spotted Nora on the bench. She cried out, "You had me worried sick! It's almost dark. Where were you going?"

The tension in Nora's shoulder's eased when she heard her mother's voice. Relief came, but then she remembered she was supposed to be mad. "Nowhere. I just needed time to think."

Eloise looked down and saw the dried blood on Nora's leg. "What happened?" Eloise kneeled down to check the scrape.

Nora shrugged. "It's nothing. I slipped on the stairs."

"Let's go home and clean up your knee. It's after six o'clock. Lisa will arrive soon."

"Do I have to go? I like Lisa, but I don't feel like seeing anyone tonight." Nora pushed up off the bench and grabbed her bag.

"Come on, Honey. Please don't argue with me. The car's about a block away." Eloise grabbed Nora's unresisting hand.

Nora didn't utter a word in the car as her train of thought continued to drift back in time. It was ironic she was going to be with Lisa tonight, just like the morning in Mender's Flea Market last July.

***

Previous Year, July 1969

"Thanks for coming." Eloise hugged Lisa.

"You knew I would. Are you okay? You look awful," Lisa replied.

Nora gave Lisa a hug before her mother could answer. "We've missed you," she whispered. "Please help Mama." Nora quickly stepped aside. She pretended to be interested in demitasse cups on a display table.

"How are you? How is it going with you and Sam?"

"Not good." Eloise's lip quivered as she lowered her voice. "I'm pregnant."

"Oh!" Lisa's jaw dropped. "Is this what you want?"

"No. I shouldn't have let it happen. But it did. Sam wants a child . . . or so he says."

"I haven't talked with you in ages since we're not on the same shift anymore. Every time I call, Sam says you're out—I was lucky Nora answered last night."

"I'm not surprised. You aren't Sam's favorite person."

"Yes. I've figured that out."

"You know he's drinking again. Its beer, not the hard stuff, but he still gets drunk. I hate it!" Agitated, Eloise slammed her hand against a shelf.

Nora watched Lisa steer her mother to the end of the aisle. Nora stayed back but near enough to hear them.

"Listen to me. You may need to leave him," Lisa declared. "I'm not saying today or next week. Maybe never, but you need to have a plan. Drinking is a bad sign. It will escalate. Believe me, I know after going through a horrific divorce from an alcoholic."

"What about the baby? What happens when I have to quit work?" Eloise knew she couldn't support Nora and the baby on her own. Tears filled her eyes.

"You still have time. Sam may be all right, but I don't think so. I think it's going to get worse. Let me help you make a plan in case you need to leave. If Sam becomes violent, you need to be prepared."

"What do you have in mind?" Eloise looked up at her friend.

Lisa covered the main points. "First, make sure Sam can't have access to your paycheck or bank accounts."

"I have. My bank account is still in my name only," Eloise replied.

"Good, for a start. Don't tell anyone at work you're pregnant, hold off as long as you can. Build up a cash fund and have your bags packed."

"How can I be packed with Sam around?"

"Store your clothes at my house. You can bring a load over each Saturday when Sam is working. I'll make sure you have a key in case I'm not there."

Eloise looked overwhelmed. Her mind was going in all directions. How could she do all this?

"Don't worry. I know this is a lot to absorb. Let's get together next Saturday, and we'll work out the details." Lisa seemed to know Nora was listening, so she maneuvered Eloise to the other side of the market. "I don't want Nora to hear us, but I'd like you to think about handgun training. We could do it together—think about it."

Nora didn't pursue them. She'd heard enough.

Eloise followed up on Lisa's suggestions. She had two bank accounts, one for checking and another one for savings. Faithfully she deposited each paycheck with a portion going to her savings account. She got a raise but never told Sam about it. Several Saturdays, while Sam worked, Eloise went to Lisa's with clothes and other items she and Nora would need if they had to leave in a hurry.

But as time passed, Sam began to backslide into his bad ways. Nora couldn't forget the horrific Saturday last September as memories flooded back into her mind.

***

Previous Year, September 1969

The first Saturday of September Nora and Eloise were busy gathering items to fill the car. "I think this is all for the time being." Eloise closed the trunk lid. There were also boxes in the backseat stacked up high.

"Hop in. Let's go." Eloise didn't want to get back too late. She had cut it too close last Saturday.

"I'm coming." Nora put a bag in the back seat. As they backed out and started down the alley, they saw Sam's truck coming, bouncing over the gravel. Eloise froze. Nora jumped forward in her seat.

"Mama, look!"

"I see."

Sam's truck blocked their car in the narrow lane. He stared at them before opening the door and sliding out. With his hands on his hips, he strode up to their car.

"What's going on?" Sam leaned into Eloise's window.

"We're taking some of our old clothes to St. Joseph's Mission. They've been on the radio all week, requesting listeners to give whatever they can spare for the needy. Haven't you heard them?"

"No." He stepped back and pulled open the back door and reached for the last bag Nora had thrown in. He peered in—whatever he saw seemed to satisfy him. "You should save them. I almost got fired today, but my boss needs me, so I'm not worried."

"Oh Sam, I'm sorry to hear you had a bad day," Eloise softly responded. "Do you want us to come back to the house with you? Don't worry about these old clothes; they aren't worth keeping. We can deliver them another day."

"Go on. I'll manage. Don't be long—I want an early dinner." Sam returned to his truck, backed up, and let them pass.

"Mama, you're a genius. How did you think of St. Joseph's Mission?"

"One of the women at work told me about it." Eloise sighed. "I hate to think what Sam would do if he knew what we're actually doing. What was in the bag to convince him?"

"Just my old slippers and a worn out blue nightgown," Nora replied.

"Thankfully, he didn't look further."

"Mama, why don't we just leave Sam? We live like a cat and mouse, and Sam's the cat."

Eloise ignored the comment. This would be her last load, at least for the time being. Besides, Lisa was running out of space in her spare bedroom—the one she and Nora had shared for three months until they moved back in with Sam at the end of January.

Nora and her mother got back home a little after six. Before Sam had even opened his mouth, Nora could tell he'd been drinking. He was pacing back and forth the way he did when he got drunk.

"I thought I told you I wanted to eat early."

Eloise plopped down a bag of hot fried chicken with gravy, mashed potatoes, and slaw. "I have dinner right here." Eloise and Nora continued to pretend there wasn't anything wrong. They didn't want to do anything to raise Sam's temper.

Later in the night, Nora lay in bed and listened to them fighting. Eventually her mother's bedroom door slammed shut. Nora hoped her mother had locked him out. In the meantime, Nora could hear Sam sneak out the back door. She assumed it was for the bottle of whiskey he had stashed in the shed. He'd probably drink himself into a drunken frenzy.

The house became eerily quiet except for the patter of rain against the window panes. A slow drizzle lulled Nora to sleep, but a loud crash woke her. Sam had kicked her door open. He rocked from side to side in the doorway.

"I'm not good enough for your Mama, so I'll have to settle for you." He could barely get his words out without slurring them.

"Get out!" Nora yelled.

Sam stumbled forward. "Don't scream—you're no better than your Mama. I'll teach you a lesson you'll never forget!" He leaned down and grabbed the front of Nora's nightgown.

"No you won't! Take your hands off Nora!" Eloise stood in the doorway with a .38 caliber Special. Nora had never heard her mother speak with such force, especially to Sam.

"You can't stop me." Sam sneered. "How are you going to shoot a gun? You've never even held a one."

"Watch me!" Eloise raised her arms to show she meant business. "This bullet is for you. Believe me. I'm good! I've been taking lessons."

Sam grabbed Nora as a shield. "Now what are you going to do? Shoot Nora?" He laughed in a high, inebriated pitch.

"Let her go. Now!" Eloise shifted her weight to emphasize her determination.

Nora's nerves raced. Adrenaline kicked in. She jammed her foot into Sam's shin bone, throwing him off balance. He stumbled backward, losing his grip. Nora raced forward, hiding behind her mother.

In the flurry of activity, Eloise panicked and pulled the trigger. The bullet shattered a lamp; broken fragments grazed Sam's hand. His eyes flashed with disbelief as blood sprayed from his hand to his face.

"You could have killed me!"

"That's the point. Get out of here or you're a dead man!" Eloise cocked the gun again, prepared to pull the trigger a second time.

Sam looked at the blood on his hand, and the fire in Eloise's eyes and bolted. Nora watched him sprint down the stairs to escape to his truck.

"Mama—you did it!"

"We did it! Come on. Let's go. We're never coming back. Sam is out of our lives! It's just you and me and . . . the baby!"

***

"Nora, wake up. We've arrived at our apartment." Eloise nudged her daughter. "Let's go in, it's almost six thirty. Remember, Lisa is coming tonight to pick you up."

Startled by her mother's voice, Nora realized she had relived the horrible night from last September when Sam tried to attack her. She reached out for her mother's hand. She never wanted to go through anything like it again. Sam was a monster!

Chapter 48

February 1970

Nora looked up at her mother with pleading brown eyes. "Why can't I stay home? I won't cause any trouble. I promise."

"I know you won't. But, I'm afraid Sam might show up. I don't trust him." Eloise knew what a drunk he was—no telling what he could do. She hugged her daughter. "Lisa should be here soon. I'm not having you stay with her to punish you; it's for your safety. Please believe me."

"We have a restraining order. Sam can't bother us," Nora begged softly.

"It's just a piece of paper. I wish it could guarantee our safety—but it doesn't!" Eloise replied.

Ten minutes later, the doorbell rang. "Lisa must be here." Eloise opened the door, surprised to see the major. He gave her a squeeze.

Nora watched them hug. Their closeness struck a nerve. She didn't want to lose her mother yet to another stepfather. "Doesn't Mama know it's too soon?" she mumbled.

"Hi, Nora," the major called out.

She sat on the couch and didn't say a word.

Eloise looked at her daughter, expecting a response. "Aren't you going to greet the major?"

Nora got up and gave him a limp wave. She turned and walked to her bedroom. "Let me know when Lisa gets here."

"I'm sorry. Nora's unhappy with me. She wanted to stay tonight, but I'm having her go to Lisa's." Eloise knew Nora wasn't happy with her spending time with the major, but she couldn't tell him so. Eloise also understood how destructive Sam had been to Nora over the last year. If only she had the money to help Nora psychologically, but a professional was too far out of Eloise's reach.

A short while later, Lisa arrived. "Sorry I'm late. There was an accident on Victory Drive. Where's my girl?"

"She's in her room. Mad at me!" Eloise admitted.

"I'll cheer her up. Thought we might catch a movie. *True Grit* with John Wayne is playing. Think Nora would like to go to a show?"

"I would!" Nora strode into the living room with her overnight bag. "Let's go. I'm ready." She didn't look at either her mother or the major.

"I'll have her back tomorrow by noon. Is that okay?"

"Noon is fine. Thank you, Lisa."

Eloise gave Nora a hug. "Be good now!"

Nora shrugged her shoulders.

Driving to the movie Lisa asked, "What's going on with you and your mother? I know you've been having a rough time, especially since Sam's vicious attack this past September and his arrest at Thanksgiving. Lisa glanced at Nora trying to find the right words. "Your mother is trying to do her best for you."

"Maybe, but Mama doesn't think I can take care of myself. Also, why is she seeing the major so much? Don't you think it's too soon after all the trouble with Sam?"

"Sam attacked you six months ago, and now it's February—it's been a while. Your mother has been through a lot. You both have. Remember, the baby would've been due about now?" Lisa touched Nora's hand.

"How could I forget? It was only a week after Sam attacked me when Mama ended up in the hospital. She never told me what happened but, two weeks later, she lost the baby. Do you know what happened?"

"Your mama should be the one to tell you, but knowing Eloise, she won't."

"I just want to know. Please tell me."

Lisa hesitated before she spoke . . . "Your mother had just gotten off her shift at the mill. She was walking to her car to go home. I had gotten there early for my shift. Sam's truck was parked close to your mother's car. At first, I thought he was trying to apologize to your mother to get back into her good graces. When I heard his garbled words, I knew he wasn't." Lisa stopped.

"Tell me more," Nora pleaded. "I need to know!"

Lisa didn't want to share anymore with Nora. She still couldn't forget Sam's drunken words to Eloise.

"Your worthless! How dare you shoot me—you could have killed me," Sam shouted a string of obscenities.

"You were going to rape Nora," Eloise roared back. "Why don't you report me to the police?" she challenged him.

"I'm here to take the law into my own hands. You don't have a gun today, do you?" Sam laughed, swiping his hand across his face—a telltale sign he had been drinking. Wild-eyed, he raised his arm and struck Eloise. He smashed his foot into the side of her belly as she lay on the ground.

"Stop!" Eloise screamed, curling into a ball.

Sam let out a blood-curdling howl. "Now you know how I felt!"

Lisa looked at Nora. She couldn't repeat those words. Instead, she summarized the details.

"Sam attacked your mother. It happened in a split second. I screamed out the window of my car for him to stop. I think I startled him. Someone from inside the mill must have seen what had happened. Minutes later, a police siren blared out. Two police cars zoomed onto the scene. The policemen grabbed Sam, cuffed him, and shoved him into a squad car. An ambulance arrived; paramedics swarmed around your mother."

"I followed the ambulance to the hospital." Nora hung onto Lisa's words. "Your Mama is strong. I was with her in the hospital that September night when they told her she would recover, but she might lose the baby. They warned her to take it easy. Your mother was released from the hospital the next day. She took a week off work, but still she had the miscarriage."

"Why didn't Mama tell me?"

"She didn't want to worry you, or have you feel any guilt about the baby."

The reality of losing her little baby brother or sister finally began to sink into Nora.

Lisa patted Nora's hand. "This has been hard on your mother. You have to try and understand the major is helping her. He's a good man—nothing like Sam. Give him a chance for your mother's sake."

"I hate men!"

"Well, just try and like him," Lisa said with a strong, compelling voice.

Nora stammered, "I don't want to! But . . . for Mama's sake, I'll . . . I'll try."

"Good, that's a much better attitude!" Lisa sighed with relief. "Now, let's go see *True Grit*. It starts in fifteen minutes."

Lisa squeezed her hand. Nora squeezed back.

Chapter 49

February 1970

Winter marched forward. It was the end of February, with rainy days and cold nights. Jorden listened to the wind howl through the trees behind her apartment. She thought about Matt. She'd been seeing him since she had gone with him to the Episcopal Church service. Now, she imagined how miserable he must be leading patrols of soldiers on training details through the swamps of Georgia over the last four nights. She laughed at his description of how he wrapped his poncho around him to stay warm and dry. She wondered if the poncho really worked. Just thinking about it made her shiver. Bending her knees, she pulled her blanket up and gathered it around her neck.

Jorden kept telling herself she and Matt were just friends. Rationalizing, she kept Alex and Matt in separate compartments. Alex was her future. Matt? Matt was fun. No complications—made seeing him easier.

The last few nights had been dedicated to writing Alex. Yesterday Jorden had mailed him a care package—easing guilt from seeing Matt. Alex's tour of duty would be over at the end of May, and they would finally be together. She finished grading papers and concentrated on Alex's latest letter.

I'll be happy to leave in May and be with you. I know it will be beautiful. The army put me in Columbus, Georgia which was good. Meeting you makes being in Vietnam worth it. Soon we'll be married—well, some months off. I think about it a lot. Marriage is a big step, but it's so right. I love you. You love me. It's a good feeling. You have such an effect on me. You make me happier than anyone ever has. The first year of marriage is so important—a good chance to start off right. The short week in Hawaii was heaven. Our marriage will be the same.

Jorden sat back and remembered their five days in tropical paradise. "Heavenly" did describe their time together.

That same night, Jorden talked on the phone with her mother to discuss the wedding invitations. Jorden had already placed an order to have them printed and delivered to her home in New Jersey. August seemed a long way off but in reality it really wasn't.

A knock on Jorden's door startled her. "Come on in."

Darby popped her head in. "Mama wants to know if you're interested in the wedding dress she made for me. You know—for me and Nate. She'll sell it to you at the cost of the materials. Of course she'll also make adjustments for nothing. It's a beautiful dress. For fifty dollars it's yours!"

Emma Lynn pushed Darby further into Jorden's bedroom. "If you don't go for it, I will!"

Jorden smiled. "Are you keeping something from us? Did Kyle pop the magic question?"

"No. But I hope he will. I'm patiently waiting, but no hint so far."

Darby looked solemn. "I hate to see you get your hopes up too high. Kyle doesn't look like he's ready for wedding bells with Vietnam at his heels."

Emma Lynn didn't know what to say. "Never mind. I withdraw my offer but, Jorden, you should go for the dress. I can imagine it's gorgeous."

"We could all go down to my home. If you like it, Mama can make the adjustments and I can bring the dress back after Easter weekend. The Alabama Gulf Coast is about fifteen miles from my home. March isn't very warm, but it would be fun to walk on the beach and look for shells."

"Oh, let's do it!" Emma Lynn exclaimed. "I love the beach!"

Jorden's mind reeled. The price of the dress couldn't be beat. What a deal. Jorden knew Darby's mother was an excellent seamstress and each stitch would have been made with love. Why not try on the dress? "What a great idea. Let's do it."

"Good. I'll tell Mama. Let's decide which weekend to go." The three roommates huddled around the hanging cloth calendar in the kitchen. "The end of March is Easter, so it has to be at least a week before then. Mama will need time to make the adjustments if you decide you want it. What do you think, Jorden?" Darby asked.

Emma Lynn piped up before Jorden could answer. "I can't go the first weekend in March. Kyle and I are going to a concert. How about the next, Saturday, March 14."?

Jorden leaned in toward the calendar. "Okay with me."

"Well, we'll have to leave right after school on Friday. It takes at least four and half hours to get to my home. If we leave by five, we should get there by nine thirty, not too late. Jorden can try on the wedding dress Saturday morning. If you like it, Mama can measure for adjustments. We'll have the afternoon free for the beach." Darby looked from Jorden to Emma Lynn. "What do you think?"

"Let's go for it!" Jorden beamed.

"I can't wait. I haven't been to the ocean in ages." Emma Lynn squealed.

"I'll call Mama back to check and see if March 14, works for them."

Jorden wrote a long letter to Alex. She told him about the possibility of the wedding dress. "I can't wait!" she wrote. The dress and the ordered invitations seemed to lock in the reality of their future. But, at the same time, Jorden felt butterflies in her stomach as she thought of the coming wedding. She blamed it on nerves.

Chapter 50

March 1970

Friday, March 13, arrived. Darby, Emma Lynn, and Jorden were on their way by four thirty to the Alabama Gulf Coast. Jorden soaked in the bright sun as Darby drove across the state line into Alabama.

"What's going on with you and Matt? I declare you two are never apart."

Jorden turned and eyed Emma Lynn. "Nothing! Just friends."

"Baloney!" Darby remarked as she drove her reliable 1967 yellow Camaro through the narrow paved Alabama roads. "Looks like more than a friendship to me."

"You two are terrible! What's wrong with a good friendship? That's all it is!" Jorden leaned forward looking from Darby to her left and Emma Lynn in the backseat. "No more on Matt."

"Yeah! Right! We hear ya." Emma Lynn giggled. "Our lips are sealed—for the moment."

"Not mine! I don't believe it. Friends—humph! I see lots more. We hardly see you anymore. Either you're off playing tennis or who knows what? We love you—but you can't fool us," Darby said, emphasizing her words.

Night came. Jorden looked out the window as the light from the moon illuminated the pavement. Darby concentrated on driving while Emma Lynn had drifted off to sleep in the backseat, and Jorden sifted through her roommates' comments. She knew Darby was right. Her relationship with Matt was becoming more than just a friendship. Still, she refused to admit he meant anything more to her than an enjoyable way to spend time before Alex returned.

By nine thirty they were winding down a curvy rural road to Darby's home. Emma Lynn stirred. She sat up in the backseat and stared ahead. "What's lying in the roadway?"

Darby flipped on the high beams. "Only . . . only a snake! Good eye, Emma Lynn."

Jorden became mesmerized by the long black snake moving in curling motions. Darby swerved the car to the left to avoid it.

"Watch out!" Emma Lynn warned.

"We're fine. You worry too much!" Darby laughed as the car flew by the snake.

"How can there be a snake in the middle of the road in March?" Jorden asked.

"The sun must have been hot today and snakes tend to come out for the warm pavement." Darby slowed down as she approached her gravel road. "Hey, there's Mama on the porch." Darby rolled down her window and waved.

"Hi, y'all!" Darby's mother greeted them. "We've been expecting you. Come on in." Mrs. Simms gave her daughter a big hug. "Your daddy's gone to bed—he has an early start tomorrow. Come on! I have some cookies and freshly made iced tea. I hope you like it sweetened."

Jorden nodded her head yes.

"Yum! Mama. Did you make your famous chocolate chip pecan cookies? I can smell them from here." Darby raced to the kitchen to look for the tasty morsels. A large plate of cookies sat in the middle of the kitchen table. She grabbed the top one, with Emma Lynn on her heels.

Jorden noticed Mrs. Simms looking at her. She assumed she must be assessing the differences between her and Darby. Her daughter was several inches taller than Jorden.

"You must be Jorden. Mrs. Simms motioned to the porch swing. "Have a seat. I love to sit out here on warm nights. Where are you from?"

"New Jersey. I grew up back East but my roots are in the South."
Jorden looked out from the porch and listened to the crickets. "Are
you from here?"

"Seems like it. After all these years this is now my home. Like
you, I grew up in a different part of the country. My people are from
the west. I used to wonder what my life would have been like if
I hadn't married Darby's father. His life is here with the land and
farming—he loves this rich Alabama soil. I have to admit I do, too.
It grows on you." Soon, they could hear Darby's voice.

"Where are you? Come on in, Mama. Have you captured Jorden?
You have the rest of the weekend to get to know my roommates!"
Darby stepped out on the porch, laughed, and ushered them into
the kitchen.

Mrs. Simms opened the refrigerator for the pitcher of iced tea.
The four of them sat around the table chatting and laughing for
almost an hour. Before Mrs. Simms left, she caught her daughter's
attention. "Tomorrow, after breakfast, I'll start on the dress." She
turned to look at Jorden. "Young lady, do you think you'll be ready to
try on the wedding dress? I think it will be perfect for you."

"Can't wait!" Jorden replied.

Darby's home was comfortable with a lived-in atmosphere.
Jorden liked Darby's mother. She was easy going, unlike Alex's
mother. The three roommates shared Darby's bedroom—two in her
double bed and the other on a cot. It felt more like a sleepover from
Jorden's school days.

The next morning they had a southern breakfast of grits,
scrambled eggs, ham, and coffee. Afterward Jorden, Emma Lynn,
and Darby followed Mrs. Simms to her sewing room. The wedding
gown was carefully hung in a clear plastic garment bag. A professional
seamstress's mannequin stood in a corner of the room. Jorden
assumed its measurements were set for Darby's figure.

"Okay. Let's get this on." Mrs. Simms removed the dress
from the garment bag. Oohs and aahs escaped from Jorden and
Emma Lynn.

"I want it! It's lovely. Oh, Mrs. Simms, you're fantastic!" Emma
Lynn's hands flew over her mouth.

"Mama's good. I have the best mama in the world!" Darby gave her a big hug.

"I can't wait!" Jorden slipped off her sweatshirt and corduroy pants, pulling the dress over her head.

"Mama. Come help us with this."

"Move back. I'll get it." Mrs. Simms zipped up the back of the dress. Jorden turned around and looked into the mirror. She gasped. "It's beautiful!" The scooped neck, bodice, and light puffy sleeves had hand-stitched lace with seed pearls. The back of the gown had a slight chapel train. Simple but elegant. Jorden couldn't take her eyes off her image in the mirror—it gave her shivers, a thrill of excitement. She could see herself walking down the church aisle, holding onto her father's arm and gliding toward Alex.

"Turn around and face me. Stand up straight and watch the wall clock," Mrs. Simms stated confidently in a gentle manner. She cocked her head to the left, seeming to hesitate a moment before she put the first pin through the satin fabric. Jorden's eyes dropped. It had to be hard to alter the dress she had made with such love for her daughter. The length of the dress and the sleeves needed to be adjusted and shortened. Mrs. Simms spent almost an hour carefully measuring and rechecking the length. Jorden wondered how this must be affecting Darby.

After a while, Darby and Emma Lynn seemed to be getting restless. "Mama, are you almost done? I don't think the dress can hold many more pins." Darby squirmed. "The more I look at this dress on Jorden, the more I think about different scenarios."

Emma Lynn fidgeted in her seat. "What are you talking about?"

"Think about it, Emma Lynn. Use your insight and you'll figure it out." Darby grinned.

Emma Lynn jumped up. "Oh I get it! Matt Ulster. Who else? Yes! Yes! The dress is meant for Matt."

"You love Matt as much as I love Kyle. Admit it!" Emma Lynn clapped.

Mrs. Simms looked up at her daughter in a questioning manner. "Who is Matt?"

"Matt is Jorden's friend," Darby replied. "He calls himself her escort, but we know they are more than just friends. We're crazy about him and think he's perfect for her."

Jorden shot Darby a petulant look.

"Of course, we don't know Alex, so we're partial to Matt. Mama, it's okay. We're just kidding Jorden. I promise."

"This is a serious matter—nothing to joke about. Jorden, I hope you know who this dress is for?" Mrs. Simms looked up from the hem and made eye contact with Jorden.

"Yes! This is for Alex! No more mentioning of Matt!" Jorden reached down to touch Mrs. Simms shoulder. "Really—this is for Alex and no one else!" Jorden shot fiery looks toward Darby and Emma Lynn.

After a tense moment Mrs. Simms sighed. "Okay. Good, no more nonsense. Now hush up, girls! I'm trying to get the finishing touches. You can have your picnic at the beach while I start working on these adjustments. We'll have supper at six."

"To the beach we go," Emma Lynn chanted while she twirled around the sewing room.

"Watch out, Emma Lynn! You're going to knock over Mama's mannequin."

Emma Lynn stopped. "I'm not." She couldn't help herself and twirled around the room one more time. "I just wish Kyle would pop the question!"

"I wish he would too for your sake." Darby looked at Emma Lynn with sympathetic eyes. "I know he cares for you."

"We're finished. Come on, Jorden. Let's get you out of this dress. It's time for you girls to head to the beach," Mrs. Simms said.

A furrow nestled between Darby's eyebrows. "I hope my favorite spot is still there. Hurricane Camille came crashing through here last summer. I remember the day Camille was classified a Category 5 hurricane—the worst level. It was August 16, 1969."

Jorden remembered the Mississippi coastline got hit the hardest. Winds, as high as two hundred miles per hour, were reported. The destruction was unbelievable, especially at Long Beach, Gulfport, and Biloxi. "What happened here?" Jorden asked.

"We got twenty-seven foot tidal surges but nothing compared to the damages to the Mississippi coastline."

As Darby drove closer to the coast she exhaled. "What a relief; it looks much the same."

Jorden could see there was a lot of driftwood blown in by the hurricane, but otherwise it probably wasn't much different. It was too cold for swimming but they had a picnic and walked on the beach.

Supper was at six, just as Mrs. Simms had announced earlier. Jorden joined the others as they sat in the dining room around a large sturdy oak table. This time Darby's father joined them. Before he sat down, he gave his daughter a big bear hug. "How's my best girl?"

"Oh, Daddy! You're embarrassing me!" Darby laughed affectionately.

Like Darby he was tall, a strapping man, with angular features and a commanding presence. His bronzed complexion must have come from running a farm and being outside so much. Mrs. Simms served a delicious spaghetti dinner with meat sauce, followed by pound cake and sliced strawberries. They finished by seven and gathered in the living room to watch Lawrence Welk on the television. Jorden smiled as Darby's father raved about his favorite show.

They departed after breakfast the next morning. Mrs. Simms turned to Jorden before they left. "I'll have your dress ready when Darby comes home for Easter. Two more weeks and it will be yours!"

"Thank you." Jorden beamed while she gave Mrs. Simms a check for fifty dollars.

Darby's mother gave them all hugs. She waved as Darby backed up, calling out, "Y'all come back with Darby anytime. We enjoyed having you."

After stopping for lunch, they arrived in Columbus around four Sunday afternoon. Driving up to their apartment building, a young woman with disheveled hair, a very short skirt, and a skimpy blouse showing expansive cleavage skipped out of Kyle's apartment. She turned and blew him a kiss. "Call me soon."

"Sure thing!" Kyle yelled back as he stepped out his door. He turned and saw the girls. Three sets of eyes stared at him. Jorden could see a deep flush rise up from his neck to his face.

Obviously furious, Emma Lynn bolted out of the car. "Who was that? Your sister?"

The young woman leaned over to open her car door. When she heard Emma Lynn's voice, she stopped in her tracks, turned around and simply simpered, "Honey—you can be sure I ain't his sister!" The woman chuckled. She slid into her car, tossed her head back and revved the engine.

Emma Lynn stormed up to the front landing. "How dare you! I'm gone just two nights and you're out with whatever comes along. I hate you!"

"Emma Lynn!" Kyle reached for her. "Settle down please. I can explain."

"I bet you can. Don't touch me!" Emma Lynn shook with tears running down her face. After a moment she allowed Kyle to lead her into his apartment. Jorden didn't see Emma Lynn until the next morning.

Things changed after Sunday night. At first, Emma Lynn and Kyle seemed reconciled. He still came to the apartment each night for the next week—then suddenly he disappeared. Jorden couldn't believe her eyes when she watched Kyle move his things out of the apartment below them, and another young soldier moved in. Emma Lynn was off doing errands when Kyle departed.

Emma Lynn was crushed when she heard Kyle had left. If Jorden hadn't known her so well, she might not have noticed the huge difference. Emma Lynn maintained appearances and never was late for work. If anything, she put more time into teaching and school activities. But, underneath Jorden could tell her emotions were raw with sorrow. Darby and Jorden did their best to help her. Over time, Jorden knew Emma Lynn would bounce back.

Chapter 51

March 1970

"What are these rumors I'm hearing? Chip said Kyle moved out. Is it true?" Matt looked out the window. "I see Kyle's car isn't here. What's going on?"

"It's true. Kyle moved out; Emma Lynn's devastated. He gave her no warning—kinda like you did to me after Christmas." Jorden raised her eyebrows at Matt.

"What are you talking about? You're the one who's going to desert me. I'm going off to war, and you're ditching your escort."

"You're awful! You know perfectly well I'm getting married. You will be gone before then and will have forgotten me."

"I'm teasing. Let's change the subject. What are your plans for Easter weekend?" Matt asked.

"Nothing in particular. I'll probably go over to Madison and Luke's for dinner. Aren't you going to see your aunt and uncle?"

"No. I drove down to see them the weekend you went to Darby's home, but . . . I have a better idea. How's the beach sound? I'm envious of your trip to the Gulf. What do you think about going to Panama City, Florida? It's also on the Gulf of Mexico on the Florida Panhandle. We could leave early Saturday morning and return Sunday evening."

"How can I possibly go? Darby and Emma Lynn would have a field day with such an excursion. They'll never stop teasing me. Right now they already give me grief all the time. Are you crazy?" Jorden watched Matt's grin expand.

"So? They won't be here. I've heard you say they're both going home for Easter. They'll leave Friday afternoon. Don't tell them your plans. If they ask, tell them you're going to Madison's."

Warning alarms pounded in her head. This was the last thing she should do. Alex would never forgive her if he found out. In fact, he'd hate her.

"I can't!"

"Why not? This escort won't bite. We can walk the beaches, have a relaxed dinner, and enjoy time together. Sounds like fun to me—an innocent escape."

Jorden fidgeted in her chair. She couldn't think of a response. It didn't sound innocent to her.

"Besides—we don't have much time left." His eyes never left hers.

He hit a nerve. They didn't have much time. Jorden couldn't ignore his last bit of logic. What could it hurt? Giving in, Jorden, blurted out, "Okay . . . but don't let me regret this!"

"Never. I promise!"

Jorden watched his soft brown eyes, and she knew they didn't lie. Still, she carefully avoided mentioning the trip to Darby, Emma Lynn, and especially Madison. None of them would understand. She and Matt didn't have much longer, she kept telling herself, but her decision still haunted her.

Jorden was semi-truthful with her roommates. Before they left late Friday afternoon, she told them she and Matt were going to a movie.

"Have a good Easter. Try to remember my wedding dress," Jorden teased.

"Mama would never let me forget." Darby paused. "You know, you should get your priorities straight. Really, who do you think the dress is right for? Open your eyes and focus. Hear me?"

Emma Lynn reached for Jorden's arm. "Don't let Darby bug you. We all know you and Matt care a lot for each other. All we're saying, is don't throw away what could be. I know you think you're not the perfect match—but who is? Think about it. Even though I don't know Alex, I wonder if he's the right one for you."

The words struck with force. Jorden watched each roommate drive off. Why did they keep pushing her? Did they see something she was missing?

To console herself, Jorden reached for Alex's latest letter—only to find this wasn't the best decision, either.

> *Hon, don't be disappointed, but I think it's best if I fly home to Albany first, get my car and then drive down to Columbus. It will make everything much easier. I'll have time to see my family and get the Mustang ready for the long trip. This will give us more time together in Columbus with no pressure from my family. I'll call you as soon as my flight arrives in California. Please try and understand. I know you want me to come to Columbus first—but trust me—this is for the best.*

Jorden knew his words were logical, but they were also hard to accept.

Saturday morning Matt drove into the apartment complex at seven sharp. No one else was driving in or out of the parking area at the time. Jorden purposely wanted to get an early start to avoid anyone seeing them drive off together. She didn't want rumors to get back to her roommates. Jorden looked out the peephole; Matt was wearing blue jeans and a sweatshirt, just like her. Not wanting to carry much, she took a small tote bag filled with makeup and two changes of clothes. The weather forecast predicted rain. Right now the sun beamed into the apartment's front window. She could feel the warmth on her neck when she opened the door.

"You're ready! I'm impressed—just one bag!"

"Thank you. Let me get my hooded jacket. It's probably going to be chilly. We should take this warm sunshine with us."

Matt had the door open when Jorden reappeared. "Ready now?"

"Almost." Jorden stepped into the kitchen. Last night she had washed and dried all the dishes, even the coffee pot. She knew the checks and re-checks were being used as a stalling mechanism. Was this all a terrible mistake?

"What's keeping you? I thought you wanted to leave early."

"I'm coming."

Matt grinned as he drove off. "I don't think anyone saw us. You're safe; no one knows you're running off with your wild escort."

"You tease too much! Please . . . I just want some coffee—not your wisecracks."

"Okay. We'll get you coffee."

"Thank you. Look! There's a Krystal. Turn in there!"

Matt swerved to the right, down-shifted to slow his Dodge Dart, and slid into an empty parking slot. Jorden held onto her seat. She was tempted, but held back any snide remarks.

Matt delivered her a large coffee with cream. "I hope this is okay."

"Yes. Thank you. Just the way I like it."

Matt got back in the car with his black coffee in hand. "It's about 180 miles to Panama City. We're making great progress—we only have 177 miles to go."

Jorden ignored his comment. When they reached Eufaula, Alabama, she finally spoke. "Are we getting closer?"

"No, silly. We've gone about forty-six miles—nowhere near the coast. Just shut your eyes and relax."

Jorden didn't resist, resting her head against the headrest. Matt continued driving and, forty minutes later, he passed through Newville. Her eyes fluttered open, as she adjusted them to avoid the sunlight.

"Hey, look at the sign!" Jorden said suddenly.

"What sign?"

"Look. There's another one: "Headland Municipal Airport." I can't believe it!"

Matt spotted the sign off to the right. "Why is it special?"

"You wouldn't believe me if I told you."

"Give me a try. I deserve an explanation."

"I could have been killed." Jorden stated matter-of-factly.

"What are you talking about?"

Jorden wasn't surprised how easily the story came to mind, even though it had happened six years earlier. She hesitated before she answered.

"Anna Reynolds, my friend, saved my life when she looked at my parachute and freaked out. She saw the pins had been left in the static line. The trainer also went ballistic and immediately removed them—otherwise, my parachute wouldn't have opened. I did have a smaller reserve chute, but there's always the chance I'd have panicked and not pulled it." The memory drained the color from Jorden's face.

"You did what?"

"Parachuted!"

"Whatever possessed you?" Matt asked.

"No one ever believes me. When it does sink in, they think I'm crazy. I've purposely avoided the subject. Look at you. Do you see how you're reacting? You don't believe me?"

"You astound me." By then they were in the small town of Headland, Alabama. "Let's stop and get something to eat. I need a break—besides, you can't leave me hanging."

"It doesn't amount to much. The Headland Municipal Airport sign caught me off guard and brought it all back."

Matt found a small local diner, pulled off and parked. It was almost nine fifteen. Not many people were milling around the town on a Saturday morning.

A waitress ambled up to their table. "You two passing through?"

"We're on our way to the beach."

"Weather report says it's gonna be windy and rainy. Better take raincoats. Now, what can I get y'all? Eat hardy. You'll need it."

Matt ordered a full breakfast. Jorden ordered an English muffin and coffee.

"You're not hungry?"

"Not really. Lost my appetite."

"You can have some of mine. Now tell me about your parachuting days."

"Not much to tell."

"Come on. Start from the beginning. I'm curious." Matt stirred his coffee in an effort to cool it.

"It was my first year of college. Part of the freshman orientation included an introduction to the different clubs on campus. The Parachute Club happened to be one of them. Sounded exciting. My friend Anna, talked me into joining. She and I practiced PLF's on almost a daily basis."

"What are those?"

"Oh. Sorry." Jorden laughed. "PLF means parachute landing falls. Anna and I jumped off car hoods and practiced rolling over on our landings. We also went through additional hours of training and instruction. Afterward, we went to an Army/Navy surplus store and bought secondhand orange jump suits and worn combat boots. Ugly! What a sight we were!"

"And? Your first jump? Were you scared?"

"Terrified—but exhilarated!"

"Well go on," Matt encouraged her.

"My first jump took place in mid-October around five thirty in the afternoon. The small plane took off and circled until it reached the right altitude—probably around three to five thousand feet—I'm not sure, can't remember." Jorden lifted her coffee cup, put her elbows on the table, and took a sip while she thought.

"What else do I remember? I climbed out of the airplane, stepped onto the wheel, held onto the wing and looked down. After what seemed like an eternity—I pushed off. It was terrifying! Soon I felt a jolt and jerked upward. The static line had opened the parachute. The sight was unbelievable. Farm land spread out below me with the drop zone off in the distance." Jorden looked up at the diner's wall clock and remembered—time seemed to stop as she floated downward.

"I felt motionless—as if I were suspended in the air," Jorden laughed. "Foolish me, I started pulling on the toggle lines to change direction. I pulled one to turn left and the other to the right."

"You were supposed to land on a target? Right?"

"Yes, a big X. But I had fun changing directions and of course I went way over the target. While I floated down, the ground appeared to rise up. Before I knew it, the land beneath my feet seemed to rush up and smack me! Anyway, that's what it felt like. I ended up in a pasture next to a pond where a horse was grazing. Lucky I didn't land in the water." Jorden's blue eyes sparkled, her skin glowed and excitement rang out in her voice.

Matt reached for her hands. "Seems like you enjoyed it."

"Oh, I did. After the third jump, my parents found out and went crazy—another story." She chuckled.

"Amazing!"

Jorden looked up at Matt, trying to read his thoughts. "You don't believe me?"

"I do. Maybe we can compare notes—I've got airborne training in May. Deal?" Matt polished off his last bite of ham.

"Deal." Jorden smiled and gobbled down her muffin, hungry after all. Matt went up and paid the bill. He left a good tip.

The waitress smiled and pocketed the money. "Thank you. You might try the hardware store down the street for rain slickers. They're the only place you'll find them in Headland. They're cheap and will help with the coming rain."

"Thanks. We'll try them. Which direction?"

"To the right."

Matt and Jorden left and sure enough they went right.

"You're going to look for the slickers?"

"You bet I am. Probably will work like a champ—like my poncho in the Georgia swamps."

"What if it doesn't rain?"

"We'll use them another day."

They bought two sets of bright yellow slickers, rain boots, and hats. Matt laughed. "We'll look like characters from the Beatles song "Yellow Submarine.""

Matt amazed her. He had suddenly turned her mood 180 degrees—from anxious to jubilant. In hindsight, she didn't think she'd ever mentioned parachuting to Alex. In fact, she knew she hadn't.

Chapter 52

March 1970

The clouds darkened the further south Matt drove. Raindrops hit the windshield with increasing speed.

"It looks like the weather forecast was right."

"Can't stop us. We've got rain gear," Matt replied, squeezing Jorden's hand.

"How much longer? Seems like you've been driving forever." Jorden squirmed in her seat.

"We should be there by one thirty. The last town we passed was Highland City, so we're still in Alabama, but we'll soon be in Florida."

Jorden wondered where they would stay. She hoped it wouldn't be a dilapidated place like the Chelsea Retreat Motel where she, Alex, and Tom had stayed. She remembered the three of them sharing one bed. It still made her smile. Thinking of Alex, she twisted his bracelet around her wrist. What was she doing? It wasn't right. She had to keep the two sides of her life separate. Alex, her future husband, in one compartment and Matt, her friend, in another compartment—never touching.

Matt drove up to a traffic light in Panama City. "We made it. We're in Florida!"

"At last!" Jorden exclaimed.

"We need to find a place to stay. What's your preference? Beach front or further back?"

"On the beach. I'll share the cost," Jorden declared.

Matt didn't answer. "Remember, it's Easter weekend. There shouldn't be a lot of people here—especially with this miserable weather. Let's drive down the main beach road and see if there are vacancies. People usually stay home for the holiday." It was close to two when Matt drove onto the beach frontage road. Most of the motels they passed had a vacancy sign. Many looked weather-worn. Jorden figured Hurricane Camille probably hit here last August, just as it had in Darby's area.

The motels became fewer the further Matt drove. A sign for the Drift Inn stood out. "How about this one? Looks like we'll soon run out of road. I'll go in and register."

"I'll go with you." Jorden knew Matt could only afford one room, but at least she would pay her share. She was about to jump out of the car when the intensity of Matt's glare stopped her.

"It's better if you wait here. Would you say we look like a typical couple from this area? We're of different races."

Jorden couldn't disagree, but something about it upset her. Grudgingly, she slid back into her seat. Irritated, the landmark civil rights decision *Loving v. Virginia* popped into her mind. The Supreme Court had legalized interracial marriages in 1967. She remembered she and Justin, her old boyfriend, had a fight over the decision. He adamantly opposed the ruling while she agreed with the legalization.

Now look at her. What was she doing? But the decision didn't really affect her, so why think about it? She would never marry Matt—Alex was the one. She thought about other changes during the 1960s, like hippie subculture in Haight-Ashbury, San Francisco and Woodstock Festival in New York. The lifestyles and cultures of many young people were slowly gaining acceptance.

Matt grinned as he left the office with the key dangling from his fingers. "We got a deal. Winter rates are still in effect for a couple more days. Can you believe $16.99? Higher rates begin in April—of course summer rates are even higher."

"Let me split it with you."

"My treat. I mean it. It's not every day we get to do this. I wonder if we're the only ones here; I don't see any other cars. The office clerk didn't ask many questions—just wanted my money."

"Which one is ours?" Jorden glanced at the red brick building with white wooden trim.

"We're in 15-B, the last one on the right." Matt drove down and parked in front of their unit. Jorden's thoughts wandered in all directions. This can't be happening. Was she crazy? She was playing with dynamite. This could destroy her relationship with Alex.

Matt grabbed their bags. "Come on. It's starting to rain again." He unlocked the door and waved at her—she got out and joined him.

"We're really at the ocean. Look at this view!" Matt opened the sliding glass door. She could hear the sound of the waves crashing against the beach. Jorden noted that the motel was austere but looked clean. She picked up her tote bag and carried it further into the room. There were two beds. Her nerves settled down with a rush of relief. She knew Matt wouldn't push her, but still—she didn't completely trust herself.

"Let's go for a walk. Dress warmly," Matt suggested.

"Where are you going?" Jorden watched him open the door to the parking area.

"To get our yellow slickers. They're in the trunk."

She slid open the glass door and looked at the rolling waves while watching seagulls overhead. "What am I doing here?" Jorden shouted at the foreboding sky. If only she could fly off with the seagulls. Instead, she made a pact with herself. Don't spoil what little time you have left with Matt. Let go and enjoy these last moments. With her mind made up, she joined Matt.

"Are we nuts?" Jorden laughed. They trudged over the sand wearing the yellow slickers, boots, and rain hats with warm clothing underneath it all. No one was on the beach except for a few seagulls. The sea pounded heavily against the white sand. Up ahead, another quarter of a mile, they spotted a large sand dune.

"Let's go for the dune. Maybe it'll offer some relief from this wind and rain," Matt called out.

With her head down Jorden tried to avoid the sting of the blowing sand, putting one foot in front of the other, determined to get to the dune. They sat on the leeward side, partially sheltered from the elements. Huddled together, they held onto each other to keep warm. Their rain hats covered their faces.

The sound of the surf hammered into the beach in a continuous pattern. The scenery was bleak but the chemistry between them was anything but dreary as Jorden watched Matt pull up the yellow flap of her rain hat, lift her chin, and gently kiss her. Raindrops splattered off their faces but she didn't feel them. A seagull squalled overhead while she let her head rest on his chest. They sat still until she started shivering.

"Let's get your blood moving. Come on, I'll race you back."

"You're on!" Jorden jumped up but quickly lost her footing. Matt caught her and pressed her against the sand dune to steady her. Suddenly a gust of wind caught the edge of her hat, sending it down the beach. Jorden scrambled to catch it but the wind and rain were too strong. The yellow hat landed in the surf. A large wave surged forward then rushed backward, taking the hat further out to sea.

Matt jumped into the water, almost reaching the hat, when a huge wave slammed against his legs. He went down with the surging surf.

Jorden couldn't stop laughing. "You do look like The Beatles' 'Yellow Submarine,'" she yelled over the howling wind.

Matt jerked around, regained his footing and ran up the beach to avoid the next set of waves. "You're no help. How dare you make fun of me! I gallantly tried to recover your crown."

"Oh! Now it's my crown?"

Matt pushed her; she pushed back. The tug-of-war began. Eventually, Jorden ended up in the sand.

"I quit!" Jorden lay back, the rain drenching her face and grains of sand becoming imbedded in her hair.

Matt pulled Jorden up. Laughing, they ran back to the motel a half mile down the beach. Matt threw off his rain gear; he was soaked. He took everything off except for his shorts and gave his clothes a good shaking.

"Come on. You're next!"

"I'm not taking this all off!" Jorden scoffed.

"No one can see you." Matt laughed playfully.

"You can!" Jorden scowled.

"You're soaked. Here, I'll help you." He proceeded to lift up her sweatshirt.

"Don't touch! What do you think you're doing?"

"Your underwear is just like a two-piece bathing suit. You're full of sand. The sooner you get it off the sooner we get inside."

"No way!"

"I promise I won't look."

"Turn around." Jorden stripped down to her underwear. She shook out her sand-laden clothes and then covered herself with them loosely. "Okay. You can turn around."

Matt opened the door and let them in.

"So much for your rain gear," Jorden remarked.

"I have a solution. Let's take a hot shower." Matt dropped his clothes next to the door and took Jorden's out of her arms before she could protest, exposing her bra and panties. Her mouth dropped open.

Matt pushed her toward the shower, pulled back the curtain and lifted her in. Quickly, he turned the water to warm. At first the showerhead sprayed cold water.

"Get me out of here! You're crazy!" She pushed away from Matt, but the warm spray came on strong. She stopped, soothed by the water. Matt slid his arms around her waist and let her lean against him to get the full impact of the warm water. They stayed that way as the bathroom steamed up. He turned Jorden around and leaned down for a lingering kiss. His arms moved up her back. Jorden lost her footing, reaching for the shower tile when the silver chain of her bracelet clanged against the hard surface. Images of Alex shot through her mind.

"I can't do this. I want to . . . but . . . I can't!" Jorden whispered loud enough for Matt to hear.

He stopped. Slowly he dropped his hands while he looked down at her with a slight smile. "We can kiss, can't we?" Before Jorden could open her mouth Matt pushed her toward the shower nozzle.

"Let's at least rinse the sand out of your hair." But, somehow, one thing led to another and of course it didn't end there.

***

They got back to Columbus around nine thirty Sunday night. Darby and Emma Lynn's cars were in their usual parking spots.

"Keep my bag. I can't walk in there carrying this. Remember, we went out to dinner tonight. Maybe they'll believe me. You think?" Jorden looked over at Matt.

"Of course they will. I've walked you up, but I'm not going in."

"You're going to leave me to the wolves?"

"Yes!" He leaned over and kissed her before skipping back down the stairs.

Jorden waited a few minutes. She watched Matt drive out of the parking area before taking three deep breaths to give her the strength and confidence to face her roommates. "Then again, she mumbled, "why should I be feeling guilty?" She couldn't let the moral views of her mother rule all her actions. Stop the guilt, she told herself.

To Jorden's surprise, Darby and Emma Lynn were quietly talking at the dining room table.

"We didn't think you would ever get back. Go look in your closet." Darby smiled.

"My dress! Is it here?"

Her roommates couldn't contain themselves and followed Jorden back to her bedroom. Jorden swung open her closet door. The garment bag from Darby's mother's sewing room hung in the center of her clothing rack. Jorden's fingers quivered. She zipped it open.

"Put it on!" Emma Lynn prompted. "I can't wait to see it!"

Jorden climbed out of her jeans and sweatshirt. She remembered what she'd worn on Saturday—those sandy clothes were in the tote bag in Matt's car.

The wedding dress fit perfectly. "It's beautiful!" How could she justify her time with Matt? She pushed the thought aside—she couldn't deal with it now.

"Mama will be so happy to know her adjustments couldn't be better. Turn around. It's lovely on you."

Emma Lynn threw up her arms. "Stunning! Elegant! Exquisite! I wish it were mine." Her arms dropped. "But I know—it's not my time."

"I'll call Mama tomorrow and tell her the good news." Darby gave Jorden a hug, followed by Emma Lynn.

Neither of her roommates questioned her about the weekend. Jorden wanted to keep it to herself. She never told Madison. Still, guilt surrounded her, but Jorden had to admit that the clandestine adventure was fun—but no more! Nothing could interfere with her marriage to Alex; she was determined to make it work.

Chapter 53

April 1970

The doldrums of winter had evaporated; temperatures were warmer, the dogwood trees and azaleas were blooming, and Emma Lynn had lightened up. She began dating again, along with Darby. Jorden and Alex's wedding plans were underway. The date was set for Saturday, August 22.

One evening, Jorden's mother called. "They're here!"

"What's here?"

"The wedding invitations. They're perfect. We'll have to start addressing them when you come home in June. Do you think I should start them now?"

"No, Mom. They can wait until I return to Trenton. I need to get names and addresses from Alex for his family and friends. I wrote his mother but she hasn't answered." Jorden looked down when she thought of Mrs. Whelan. What few letters she had received from her were short and to the point.

"Okay. I'll wait. But . . . I could get started on our side of the family."

"They'll wait," Jorden reassured her.

"I heard from Father Capello. All the arrangements have been made at St. Joseph's. Even, your Pre-Cana classes are set up for you to attend. I never knew there was so much involved in marrying a Catholic. Are you sure this is what you want?"

"Mom! How could you even ask? You're a worrywart! Nothing is stopping me from marrying Alex."

"Good. Glad to hear your confirmation. We haven't heard from his parents but the wedding is still over four months away."

The muscles on Jorden's forehead tightened when she remembered Mrs. Whelan's words: "Alex can do better." She would never tell her mother.

Jorden wrote Alex the latest details for their wedding.

> *We're making progress on our wedding plans. The invitations arrived in Trenton this week. Mom is anxious to start addressing them. I told her to wait for us in June. I also wrote your mother for names and addresses from your family, but I haven't heard back. The next time you write her, can you drop a helpful hint? It won't be long now until you return to the States. I'm counting the days—forty-six, give or take. Your return will be a glorious time . . .*

Matt had been out on ranger training duty the past four days, which gave Jorden time for catching up on lesson plans, grading papers, and writing Alex. She heard the kitchen phone ring from her bedroom. She checked her watch; it was after nine. Darby caught it on the third ring. Jorden picked up part of the conversation.

"Sounds like fun. I'd love to go. Okay, I'll check with Emma Lynn. Hold on, I'll get her. Jorden—phone for you."

Jorden figured it must be Matt. She had hoped to hear from him tonight.

"I've got great news! Mark down today's date: Thursday, April 16," Matt exclaimed.

"What is it?"

"I can't tell you over the phone. We're all going to celebrate tomorrow night. You and I, Chip and Darby, Lyon and, I hope, Emma Lynn. We'll have dinner and then go dancing at the Chattahoochee Club in downtown Columbus. It's bohemian, literally it is down under the street level. You won't believe it. You can come—can't you?"

"I wouldn't miss it, but what's up?"

"I'll tell you tomorrow. Six thirty? Okay?"

"I guess." Jorden sounded perturbed. "Why can't you tell me now?"

"I will. Tomorrow. See you then."

Jorden slapped the counter top when she realized he had hung up. Reaching for the phone to call Matt back, she spotted Alex's letter on the floor. What was she doing? She had just written Alex about their wedding plans. Was she a bumbling idiot? Alex was her future—Matt was not. But, she knew, hoped, and prayed she had the situation under control. Matt would soon be part of her past.

Darby stuck her head into the kitchen. "Emma Lynn just told me she can go tomorrow night. What's the occasion? Matt sounded upbeat!"

"He wouldn't tell me—he ticks me off."

"I'll get to see Chip. It's been a while." Darby had been dating Matt's roommate off and on since January.

Friday evening brought a welcome change. The girls dressed up for the occasion. Chip and his other roommate Lyon pulled in ahead of Matt. Chip was in rare form, full of wisecracks. His light blue eyes danced under his thick, bushy brows. He set the mood for the night's adventure. Lyon and Emma Lynn were a mismatch, but they didn't seem to mind.

"Meet you at the Officers' Club. I made reservations for six under my name," Chip announced.

"We'll be right behind you," Matt replied.

Jorden rode with Matt while the other two couples went in Chip's car. "Well? I'm waiting."

"You'll hear it at the Officers' Club."

"You're going back on your word?" Jorden asked.

"Can't you wait?"

"No! I'd like to hear it before everyone else."

"Okay. I don't know where to begin. I got my orders yesterday. Of course there were other names on the list, but—mine was different. My destination, APO address, had been crossed out."

"And? What do you mean?"

"A new APO address replaced it." Matt slowed down for a traffic light. "At first I wasn't sure. But . . . later in the day . . . I found out." Matt stepped on the brake and came to a stop for a red light.

"Found out what?"

"Korea! . . . I'm . . . I'm going to Korea—Not Vietnam!" A huge grin exploded on his face.

Jorden's fingers dug into his. She shouted, almost jumped out of her seat, and kissed him. "Yes! . . . Yes! . . . I . . . can't . . . I can't believe it! Now I won't have another year of worry. What a relief!"

"Do you hear yourself? You'll be married, and I'll be the last thing on your mind. You're silly—but I'm glad you might worry about me."

"Of course I'd worry about you. I want you to be safe. I'd never want anything bad to happen to you. You mean the world to me. You're the best friend I've ever had." Jorden stroked his cheek, moving her fingers over his chin.

A car horn blasted. "Move it, you idiots! What do you think this is—lover's lane?"

Startled, their eyes moved back to the road. A bright green light glared at them. Matt shifted gears and stepped on the gas. Jorden laughed as the Dodge Dart sped forward.

At the Officers' Club they ate, drank, and toasted to Matt's good fortune—Korea rather than Vietnam! Jorden figured it must give his roommates hope they also could be so lucky. After dinner the plan was to meet at the Chattahoochee Club.

"Chip, you need to give me directions to this famous club of yours. Jorden and I have never been there."

"Here, I've written it down for you, but first I need to stop by a liquor store. The laws down here are crazy. You can't buy booze at a bar—you have to bring your own bottle and leave it at the bar."

"It sounds idiotic, but I know you're right." Darby's eyes flashed.

"It's true alright. We're in Columbus, Georgia and the Muscogee County doesn't let a bar sell liquor, only the setups—mixes like soda and tonic water. Sounds nuts to me," Chip replied as it began raining on their way out.

Jorden watched them get into Chip's car. "My roommates are something else." Jorden's eyes softened. "I heard them talking last night about leaving Columbus. They've gone through a lot this year—Darby's broken engagement and Kyle leaving Emma Lynn."

"You're kidding. They're leaving Columbus? I thought this would be the best place to meet and date interesting men. Look at your apartment, every night it's filled with guys from all over the States." Matt turned the key in the ignition when Jorden slapped his forearm.

"What's that for?" Matt replied.

"Listen to you! Do you think we're here only to find men?" Jorden scowled.

"You took my words in the wrong way. Besides, you already have one lined up."

"How dare you!" Jorden looked straight ahead. She was glad Darby and Emma Lynn couldn't hear him.

"Please, let's not argue. We're out to celebrate. You're supposed to be happy for me, at least tonight!" Matt reached for Jorden's hand. At the same moment, the radio announcer came on, "A new song is gaining popularity. What better night than this one for 'Rainy Night In Georgia.'" They sat and listened to the compelling lyrics and melody.

"Come on. Let's go dancing and join the others. They'll wonder where we are. We don't want to give them something more to gossip about. Do we?" Matt's eyes crinkled.

Jorden couldn't help but smile at his devilish grin. "Okay. Let's go!"

The live band was in full swing by the time Jorden and Matt joined the others. The club was filled to capacity. A server appeared. Chip ordered another round of gin and tonics. He had already dropped off a bottle of gin at the bar along with his name.

"Where have y'all been? We've been here a half an hour. Get a flat tire?" Emma Lynn giggled.

"No way, we got stuck in traffic." Actually, Matt had taken a wrong turn but, being a man, he wasn't going to admit a mistake.

"What do you think of this place?" Chip shouted over the loud music.

Matt threw up his thumbs. Soon, their drinks appeared.

"Come on. We can't miss this song." The band started to play "Wild Thing." The dancefloor filled up and the six of them danced and laughed through a couple rounds of drinks. Finally, a slow song began to play, "Crimson and Clover." "I like this one." Matt hummed the melody in Jorden's ear. "After this, let's go. I'll settle with the guys tomorrow. What do you say?"

"Good. I've had too much to drink."

They snuck out before anyone noticed. Rain continued to fall as they raced to the car. It was close to one when they reached Matt's house on Monticello Drive.

"Where are we?" Jorden blinked.

"Thought we'd come to my place. Chip and Lyon probably won't be back for at least another two hours. The three of us rented the house in September. You've never been here, have you?"

"No." Jorden stared at the house and didn't move. "It's late. I thought you were taking me home."

"I just thought we'd have time to ourselves here. Seems like we're always being interrupted at your apartment—but I can take you home," Matt replied, backing out of his driveway.

"Wait, you're right. We never have time alone at my apartment, so let's stay. Besides, I'd like to see your place." Jorden smiled.

"You're sure?"

"Definitely," Jorden replied.

Matt changed gears and drove forward, returning to the driveway. "Come on, I'll give you a tour." Matt helped Jorden out. "Watch your step." He held onto her arm and guided her up the walkway. They entered the foyer while Matt flipped on the light. He led Jorden into a small living room which was sparsely furnished and then into the dining room. There was a large oval table and chairs but little else. "And now, our most used room, the kitchen."

Jorden noticed it was a mess but the appliances looked new. The area seemed three times the size of her apartment's kitchen. She could handle this amount of space. Looking around, she tried to spot a bathroom.

Matt seemed to read her thoughts. "I bet you're looking for the bathroom. It's this way."

Jorden followed Matt down the hallway. "I see it. Thanks," Jorden said as she darted into the room. Her eyes gazed around. It was pretty bad. Towels lay on the floor and clothes halfway out of the hamper. The sink had smears of toothpaste plastered to its edges. Still, Jorden used the facility. She ended up sitting on the closed toilet seat, wondering what she was doing here. She knew she had too much to drink. A loud knock sounded on the door.

"Are you okay? I need to use the bathroom."

"I'm fine. I'll be out in a minute." Jorden got up, washed her hands and put a cool wash cloth on her face. She didn't know who it belonged to—and at this point, she didn't care.

The rest of the night was a blur. Jorden tried to block it out. Only the images and sensations were real. Jorden's eyes fluttered open early, around four. Matt lay next to her. She turned on her side and noticed the outline of their clothes on the floor. He stirred while opening his eyes. Jorden's guilt came through in her voice. "This can't be happening again."

"You're right. We both had too much to drink. I'll take the blame. Let's get you home," Matt offered.

"Let's," Jorden agreed in a softer tone, realizing it wasn't all his fault.

Chapter 54

April 1970

The end of April brought changes for the roommates in Apartment 206. Darby and Emma Lynn decided not to renew their teaching contracts with the Muscogee County School District. Instead, they decided to leave Columbus, Georgia and move westward. At the beginning of July her roommates would drive to Colorado and look for teaching positions. Emma Lynn often danced around the apartment chanting, "Colorado Springs here we come!" Her spirits lifted after she put her relationship with Kyle in the past; at least, she appeared to make a good attempt.

Alex was scheduled to return to the States by the end of May. More than likely he would be discharged from the Army in California. Jorden couldn't talk him into coming to Columbus first. He was determined to go home, get his Mustang, and then drive down. Their wedding plans for August were coming together. The good news, Alex had been accepted at Harvard Law School. A few of his undergraduate professors had given him good recommendations which helped. Jorden planned to look for work teaching in the Boston area. Everyone had new plans.

In spite of all this, Jorden and Matt continued to see each other on a daily basis, or whenever possible. They seemed to be in the eye of a hurricane, never touched by reality. She rarely got back to her apartment before midnight. Her wedding plans were never mentioned. She knew their relationship was escalating, but she refused to acknowledge it.

One night, Jorden and Matt stopped for ice cream cones at Columbus Square. Jorden spotted Nora, Eloise, and, with them, Major Hawkins.

Nora waved first. "Hi, Miss Marshall."

"Hi!" Jorden called out.

Matt and Major Hawkins shook hands.

"It's been a while since I've seen you. Rumor has it you're going to Korea. Did I hear right?" Major Hawkins asked Matt.

"It's a go! I head out in August. I'll take a couple of weeks off in July to spend time at home in Alaska. It'll be a nice break before I head to Seoul."

Jorden's throat constricted; she couldn't catch her breath. Matt's future plans hit her like a ton of bricks. He wouldn't be a part of her life anymore. Stop it, she told herself. Accept it—you're getting married in August.

Nora started asking Jorden all sorts of questions. At the same time, Major Hawkins and Eloise chatted with Matt. When Eloise spoke about their upcoming wedding, the word marriage caught both Jorden and Nora's attention.

"So you and Eloise are getting married. Great. When?" Matt asked.

Jorden watched Eloise bubble over with joy talking about their wedding plans. "The ceremony is on base at the Main Chapel on Saturday, May 16 and the reception is at the Officers' Club. We were fortunate to get the Club; they had a cancellation. You and Miss Marshall must come."

"We wouldn't miss it," Matt replied.

Jorden looked at Nora, afraid of what her reaction might be. Instead of looking troubled, Nora's eyes seemed to sparkle. She, surprisingly, was happy about her mother's marriage. Three months earlier, this was not the case; she would have been very upset. But, from February to the present, the situation between Nora and Major Hawkins had begun to change.

***

Three months earlier, February 1970

It started the night Nora and Lisa had gone to see the movie *True Grit*. Nora had been very upset with her mother as she wanted to stay home and not spend the night with Lisa. She was jealous of the major and didn't think her mother should be going out on dates with him. In her young mind, it was too soon. She didn't want to lose her mother to another stepfather.

But Eloise was adamant. She was afraid of what Sam could do in a fit of rage, like his attack on Nora last September. Besides, it was unfair to have Lisa cross the expanse of the city twice in one night. Grudgingly, Nora finally accepted her mother's demands.

Eloise and the major did return to her apartment around ten that evening. "Can I get you some coffee?" Eloise offered.

"Love some. Black is good." A loud street noise caught the major's attention. He spread the curtains open as a dark truck flashed by. It stopped at the end of the street, turned around and drove back, passing slowly in front of Eloise's apartment before it came to a stop. The driver had a baseball cap pulled down over his face.

"Could he be Sam? What is he doing?" The major muttered as he watched the man roll down his window.

Eloise walked into the room with their coffee. "What are you mumbling about? What's happening? Is it Sam?" Eloise shivered. She yanked the curtain further back.

Sam appeared to recognize her. His voice rang out loud and clear, "No one can protect you . . . remember that!"

The major pushed her behind him while the truck sped off. "You shouldn't have to live like this. I'm calling the police."

"No! Don't . . . I can't handle the police tonight. I don't want any more trouble from Sam. I'm fine." Eloise hung onto the major's arm, her eyes pleading with his. She was thankful Nora was at Lisa's for the night.

"I'm staying with you tonight! Not a word against it."

"You can't. Nora would have a fit if she knew you were here. Right now she doesn't trust you or any man."

"Nothing you say can persuade me to leave, but I'll make sure I'm gone before Nora returns tomorrow. Tell me this. Do you still have your .38 caliber Special?"

"I do. Once a week, Lisa and I go to the firing range. Believe me, I'm good now, better than in September and I'm improving each week!"

"Where do you keep it?"

"It's in the nightstand next to my bed. Nora knows about it. She's promised not to touch it and I believe her. I always make sure the safety is on." Eloise led him into her bedroom. She opened the drawer and pointed down at the handgun.

The major picked up the gun and inspected it. "Good the safety is on. Guns can get you into trouble. Sam's a big man—he could wrestle it away from you in an instant. Who knows what he could do to you or Nora. There has to be a better solution!"

"I have to have it. It's awful living in constant fear of Sam, especially for Nora. How could I have ever married him? I was a fool. Thankfully the divorce is final!" Eloise looked at the major and sensed his thoughts were elsewhere.

"You know . . . I have a friend in the FBI at the Atlanta office. We became close at West Point. I bet he can help. I'll see if he can look into Sam's background."

The same Friday night, Sam was pulled over again for another DUI. The police slammed him back into jail. Another incident helped to get the ball rolling to start an investigation. By March, substantial information had been gathered on Sam—enough for the FBI to open an official investigation.

***

April 1970

In early April, Nora overheard her mother and the major talking. They were caught up in their conversation and seemed to forget she was in the apartment.

"Listen to me, Eloise. There is startling news. It's all happened so quickly. My friend from the FBI contacted me today. I don't have all the details but enough. Sam is a fugitive, running from his past. Please sit next to me and I'll explain."

Eloise shuddered as she slid next to the major on the couch. He held her hand. "Sam Butler is really Jason Cartiere from Mississippi. Right now there is a warrant out for his arrest in Biloxi, Mississippi. He's been on the run for over four years. He changed his identity and blended into this sprawling community of Columbus. He even fooled you—you married him."

"What did he do?"

"Murder!"

"Who?" Eloise's voice rose.

The major paused. "His wife."

"How?"

"In a fit of rage—he beat her to death. I heard it was gruesome. An older neighbor witnessed the murder from her second floor bedroom window. She's the one who called it into the authorities. But, somehow, Sam managed to escape capture. You know the rest."

Eloise shook. "I married a monster! How could I have been so foolish?"

"Hold on! Here's the good news. He's been arrested and sent back to Mississippi for arraignment and trial. It'll be in tomorrow's paper, but I wanted you to hear it from me first."

Eloise collapsed against the major. "I can't believe it. God has answered my prayers. He can't hurt us anymore."

"No, he can't. He'll probably be serving a life sentence—hopefully without parole." The major pulled Eloise closer. "I want you to know I'm here for you and Nora. In time I hope Nora comes to accept me."

"I hope so—more than anything! She has been through so much. You know Nora comes first—I can't let her down again!" Eloise's voice trembled.

The major held Eloise gently. "I know—I understand."

The conversation she just heard stunned Nora. She knew Sam was a devil and this information proved her right. Still in shock, Nora rocked back and forth as her mother's words played back in her mind, "Nora comes first—I can't let her down." Tears streamed down her face as she hugged herself, relieved Sam would finally be out of their lives.

Chapter 55

April 1970

That spring Major Hawkins did his best to gain Nora's affection. Every night he came for dinner bringing flowers or small gifts for both Eloise and Nora. They had fun trying to guess what he would bring them. One night he arrived empty-handed.

Nora spoke up first. She looked at the major, circling him before their eyes met. "Nothing? You didn't bring anything?"

"Nora, don't be rude. The major doesn't have to bring something every night. He's been spoiling us." Eloise reprimanded her daughter but, at the same time, winked at the major.

"Oh, but I do have a surprise. Since it's getting warmer, I thought Nora and I could walk to Shelley's Ice Cream Parlor and buy an ice cream treat after supper. Yesterday I noticed the new shop had opened. It's not far from here. What do you say, Nora?"

"Can I pick out the flavor?"

"Sure thing," the major agreed.

A new ritual began. Eloise cleaned up the dishes while Nora and the major surprised her with a different flavor of ice cream each night. After a couple weeks, they became comfortable with their evening walks.

"Have you ever married?" Nora asked one night.

The major was silent for an awkward moment. "Yes, I married soon after I graduated from West Point. Ginny Upton swept me off my feet. We were high school sweethearts." He grinned as he remembered his young wife.

"What happened? I can tell you were happy," Nora said without thinking.

"I was happy. We were married three years and expecting our first child. Ginny was beside herself with the baby coming. I can picture the bloom on her face, her eyes filled with joy." He paused and looked down. His smile disappeared, replaced with a deep furrow between his brows.

"What happened?" Nora looked up, sensing his distress.

"I haven't mentioned Ginny to anyone in so long, not even your mother. Oh, she knows I was married but I never told her more, and your mother didn't ask. It's very hard for me to talk about. But . . . I'd like to tell you." The major motioned to a nearby bench. "Let's sit for a moment."

Nora sat next to the major. She could tell it was difficult for him to speak. His eyes seemed to concentrate on stray blades of grass sprouting up from the dirt.

"It happened in the spring. We had a week of heavy rain. Ginny had been shopping for the baby." He smiled. "You name it and our baby had it." Then, he stopped. He covered his face with his hands. Nora wanted to comfort him but she couldn't move or say a word.

Then, his words spilled out. "The rain drenched the roads; visibility was poor. Ginny's windshield wipers must have been going at full speed. She stopped for a red light. As soon as the light turned green, she stepped on the gas. At the same time, the driver in the other lane ran the light. She never saw the car smash into the side of her door. Ginny . . . she . . . died instantly."

A tear welled up in the major's eye. He brushed it aside with the palm of his hand and shook his head as if trying to clear his thoughts.

"What about the baby?" Nora asked, in full innocence.

"The baby, a girl, didn't survive. It was the hardest time of my life." The major reached for Nora's hand and gave it a squeeze. "Thank you."

Nora looked down as the major held her hand. For the first time, she felt a connection between them. More, a subtle light opened her narrow vision of men. He was her friend.

He smiled at her. "Enough sadness. We have a mission. Let's get the ice cream. How about strawberry?"

"How about butter pecan?" They ended up with a carton of each.

April became a whirlwind of activities for Nora, Eloise, and the major. It made all the difference since Sam was out of their lives. Their time together became a melody of memories, movies, dinners, walks in the park, and even a weekend at the beach.

Nora remembered the warm breezes from the ocean, the sunshine, and the waves racing up the sandy beach, splashing their toes. The major held their hands; Eloise to the right, Nora to the left. All of a sudden, he stopped, dropped to his knees and released their fingers. A large grin spread across his face as he looked from Eloise to Nora.

The major's words came slowly. "I love you both. I hope to be a part of your lives." He looked first at Eloise. "Will you be my wife?" Then he turned to Nora. "Will you let me be a father to you?"

Eloise and Nora looked at each other and back at the major. They each beamed. The major pulled them down to his level, kissed Eloise and hugged Nora. There was no resistance from either.

He looked at them. "Yes?"

They nodded in an apparent agreement and each gave him a kiss on opposite cheeks.

The major gathered them into his arms with an embrace that seemed to never end.

Chapter 56

May 1970

Saturday, the day of the wedding, arrived. Jorden and Matt sat on Eloise's side of the chapel. The bride wore an elegant and simple full length ivory satin gown, with an empire waist and delicate, laced short sleeves. Nora and Lisa wore similarly styled dresses in light baby blue. The major's brother and his good friend, the FBI contact, completed the wedding party. At first Eloise had wanted a simpler wedding. Her first marriage at age nineteen had been a sham. Her second marriage to Sam occurred at the courthouse as a mere formality. The major wanted this wedding to be special for Eloise and Nora. He went all out.

The occasion celebrated a new beginning for Eloise, Nora, and the major. Jorden thought of her own upcoming wedding and hoped she would be just as happy. After the chaplain pronounced them husband and wife, the major kissed the bride. Matt squeezed Jorden's hand.

The reception followed at the Officers' Club. Jorden and Matt greeted the newlyweds in the receiving line. Music played while guests mingled and snacked on finger foods before the official cutting of the wedding cake.

"Hi, Miss Marshall. Isn't Mama something?" Nora's eyes drifted in her mother's direction.

"She is and so are you. I've never seen you look happier." Jorden embraced Nora.

"I believe this is the best day ever!" Nora couldn't stop smiling.

"Where are Cheryl and her family? I thought they would be here."

"They're in Memphis. Cheryl's uncle died. I promised her I'd take lots of pictures."

"How sad. Give my regards to her family." Jorden recalled her uncle's death last year before Christmas. She couldn't forget Alex's reaction when she told him she couldn't drive north with him. The apartment felt like an arctic breeze had blown through when he had left abruptly. She put her hands down on the table top to steady herself. Her vision began to blur. She tried to focus on the flat surface of the table.

"Miss Marshall . . . are you all right?"

"Oh! I . . . just lost my balance for a second."

Matt watched from a distance before he slipped through the crowd to join her. "Are you okay?"

"I feel a little faint. Maybe some fresh air will help." Jorden turned toward Nora. "If I don't get to speak with your mother or the major before they leave, please give them my best."

Nora gave her a thumbs up.

"Thank you!" Jorden waved as Matt led her to the door.

"What happened to you? You look pale."

"I don't know. I think I'm overwhelmed. It's the end of the school year and there's so much to do."

Matt didn't push further. "We can leave now. It's almost six. Where would you like to go?"

Jorden took several deep breaths until she gave a slight smile. "You'll think I'm nuts!"

"Try me."

"Think you could show me where your airborne training takes place? I'm curious how the military does it. Remember, you promised to show me."

"Easy to do. Come on. It's just a few miles from here."

Matt stepped on the gas but didn't drive too fast on the base as the MP's were often around the corner. After ten minutes, the training area appeared. A high tower stood off in the distance.

"Watch your step. The ground is uneven." They made their way to the running track which passed in front of a massive structure used to practice parachute jumps. An open field lay in between, providing a convenient area for exercises.

"It's impressive. Have you done any jumps yet?"

"Not yet. We train first. We're still in the first stage." Matt eyed Jorden. "You're gloating, aren't you?"

"Me? Never. You always beat me at tennis, but now I'm ahead of you by three jumps. This is a nice change if it holds before we part." Jorden regretted the words as soon as she said them.

"It will be a sad day." Matt turned to walk back to the car.

"I'm sorry!" Jorden caught up with Matt and tugged at his arm. "I take it back."

"You can't take some words back." Matt widened his stride. "I know we don't have much longer. It might help if I knew how much time we actually have left."

"I wish I knew more myself. I'm not even sure when he gets back to the States."

"I don't understand. Why don't you know?" Matt seemed puzzled.

"Alex hasn't given me a specific date. He says he can't be sure when he'll get a flight out of Saigon his last week in May. I understand he can't control his departure time—but when he does return to the States, he plans to fly home first. He's determined to get his car ready before he drives down here. So, you tell me. I'd like to know," Jorden snapped.

"Now, you know how I feel," Matt replied.

Jorden did know and she didn't like it either.

Chapter 57

May 1970

The days flew by. Jorden's students couldn't wait for the school year to end. It was already Friday, May 22. Alex should be back from Vietnam within a week.

Startled by the phone, Jorden caught a glimpse of Darby answering it.

"Jorden, its Madison."

Guilt struck! She realized she hadn't talked with Madison in almost a month. Matt had been taking most of her spare time.

"Hey. What's up? Have you left town?" Madison joked.

"No. Just busy. You know, the end of the school year—trying to tie up loose ends."

"Sounds like a weak excuse to me. How about having supper with us tomorrow night? Nothing fancy, I'll make spaghetti. Luke wants to hear the latest on Alex. When's he coming?"

"I'm still not sure. I'd love to come, but I promised Darby and Emma Lynn I'd go to the James Brown concert with them." Jorden knew she stretched the truth, but she couldn't handle Madison's questions. She had only mentioned Matt's name once before Thanksgiving.

"Oh, James Brown—so he's more important than us?" Madison laughed. "Just kidding, I'd go see him anytime over us. How about next Tuesday night? That's the twenty-sixth."

"I can come then." Jorden pushed her hair behind her ears. She knew there would be time to see Matt afterward.

"Good. I'll hold you to Tuesday. Come around five thirty."

***

Four days later, Luke answered the door. "It's about time you came. You must think we have the plague."

"Of course not." Jorden hugged Luke. "Yum! Smells good." She inhaled aromas as they drifted from the kitchen. "I'm starving. I missed lunch today. One more week to go! I can't wait for next Tuesday—school will be out."

Madison walked out of the kitchen with a ladle in her hand. "Do you mean you don't have to go in after Tuesday? I'm jealous! My last day is Friday, June 5."

"I meant when the students are gone. My official last day is the same as yours." Jorden slipped off her sunglasses; it had been a hot, sunny day.

"Oh, you're right. My second graders will also be gone. Good. I feel better." Waving her hand in the air, Madison orchestrated the ladle back to the kitchen and into the spaghetti sauce.

"There's my wife, conducting the New York Philharmonic. Now, how about ladling us some scrumptious sauce." Luke blew Madison a kiss while he filled the glasses with iced tea. Madison winked and piled the meat sauce over the spaghetti. Parmesan cheese topped it off.

"Delicious!" Jorden declared after taking her first bite. Conversation slowed as they finished their dinner and ate the last slices of crisp garlic bread.

"Where's Alex? It's already the twenty-sixth—shouldn't he be here soon?" Luke asked.

"You tell me—I'd like to know. Alex's last letter said he hoped to get a flight out of Saigon this week."

"You never can tell. I was delayed several days before I got out last August," Luke confirmed. "Is he coming here first?"

"No. He wants to go back to his home in Albany before he drives to Columbus." Jorden looked at her plate, avoiding eye contact with either Luke or Madison.

"Good logic when you think about it. He'll have his car when he heads down here," Luke replied.

"I'll just be glad when Matt gets here," Jorden muttered in a frustrated voice.

Silence. "Who's Matt?" Luke's eyebrows went up.

Stunned. Jorden couldn't believe her ears. "Oh, I meant Alex." Embarrassed, she didn't know what to say. "You know, there are so many different men at our place every night, I get confused."

Luke looked skeptical but let it go. Jorden couldn't believe her blunder. If Luke hadn't caught it, she never would have known she had switched names. What was wrong with her? Unable to concentrate, Jorden fabricated an excuse to leave.

"It's still early. Don't go," Madison pressed her.

"Remember it's still a school night; we haven't been set free yet." Jorden waved on her way to the door. "Thank you for the great meal."

"Don't stay away so long next time. Call me this week. Hold on, I'll walk you out." Madison held the door open. Jorden knew Madison couldn't resist questioning her on the way to her car. "Is this the Matt you played tennis with? I haven't met him, have I?"

"No, and yes. He's the one who helped me with my tennis game, and no, you haven't met him. It was a senseless slip. I'm tired and not getting enough sleep," Jorden mumbled.

"I hope it's not more." Madison looked doubtful. Jorden knew she hadn't convinced her friend. If anyone could size up her situation accurately, it was Madison. But, she had made a harmless mistake Jorden rationalized.

After Jorden returned to her apartment, she called Matt. The cloth calendar caught her attention as she dialed his number. There were five days left in May—she still hadn't heard from Alex. Any day he could be on his way back from Vietnam.

"Hello . . . anybody there?" Matt's voice rang out.

Startled, Jorden almost dropped the phone. "It's me. Sorry. I got distracted." Her eyes still lingered on the calendar.

"How was your dinner? I feel like I know Madison and Luke. What's up? Keeping me at arm's length from them?"

Jorden ignored his comments and didn't answer.

"How about a Coke? I can pick you up in fifteen minutes."

"I'm on." Jorden continued to stare at the calendar. She wished Alex would let her know when he was coming.

Most nights Jorden got home before midnight. Tonight, though, she and Matt were tired and accidently fell asleep at his place. It was close to two thirty when Jorden crept into her apartment. Rarely had she been this late. The apartment was silent. A good sign. Darby and Emma Lynn wouldn't have anything to tease her about.

The alarm rang at six fifteen. Jorden struggled to open her eyes. The clock slipped out of her hand and continued to ring. She finally smashed the alarm button with her fingers. By then Jorden could hear Darby running water in the kitchen. Emma Lynn's alarm wouldn't go off until six forty-five.

Darby had the coffee going by the time Jorden entered the kitchen.

"Where were you last night? Alex called around two and woke me up."

"What are you talking about?" Jorden panicked. "What did you tell him?"

"I didn't know what to say. I checked your bedroom—you weren't there."

"What . . . what did you tell him? I can't believe he called and I wasn't here," Jorden's hands flew to her face.

"I told him you couldn't sleep, and you and Emma Lynn went to get Krystal burgers. I didn't know what to say. I didn't think you wanted me to tell him you were out with Matt—as usual." Darby's eyes flashed.

"No! Thank you—you did great! Do you think he believed you?"

"I don't know. I tried to sound convincing."

"I'll call him now."

"He might be in the air. He said his flight to New York left in a half hour." Darby poured a second cup of coffee. "Want some? You look like you need it."

"So, he's going back to Albany first." Jorden's eyes darted to the calendar. "He probably won't get there until later today. I hoped he would at least stop here for a day," Jorden muttered to herself.

Darby frowned. "I don't think you have much of a bargaining chip at this point. It doesn't look so good you weren't here."

"You're right. But—I do have to call Alex. I'll wait. I don't want to talk with his mother before I speak with him." Jorden paced the kitchen.

"You better get dressed. We're late. I just heard Emma Lynn's alarm."

Jorden had a hard time concentrating on her classes. Her students didn't seem to notice as they were also restless. The same question kept going through her mind. How could she have been so late? The one night Alex called, she should have been there.

After school, Jorden raced back to her apartment. Her papers landed on the couch, sliding from one end to the other as she darted to the kitchen. She phoned Alex. No answer. She was pacing the kitchen when the phone rang. Startled, she jumped back before answering it with a shaking hand.

"Hi Hon! I'm back." Alex didn't sound angry. She couldn't believe it.

"Oh, Alex! I'm so sorry I missed your call last night. I couldn't sleep. Emma Lynn and I went to get something to eat."

"It's okay. I just got in from the airport and wanted to hear your voice."

"When are you coming? I wish you could fly here right now."

"I'll be there soon, but I need time here. I also need to get the car worked on before driving south."

They talked over an hour. Jorden tried, but couldn't persuade Alex to change his mind. He wouldn't budge. He planned to leave Friday, June 5 and get in early on Sunday, June 7.

After the call, Jorden hung up in defeat. But, on the bright side, she and Matt would have extra time. Now she could let Matt know what was happening. She marched back to the kitchen and counted the days. Twelve days until Alex arrived. Eleven more days with Matt—a gift in time.

Chapter 58

June 1970

Reality struck! Jorden and Matt had reached Saturday, the eleventh day, their last one together. Her relationship with Matt seemed straightforward at first. What happened? She wanted the ending to be the same—not tearing her apart.

"Are you okay?" Darby asked. "You look upset."

"I am. I'm not prepared for this. How do I let go? What would you do?"

"I don't know. You say you love Alex—have you changed your mind? Or, are you seeing the light and questioning your relationship with Matt?"

"No—no! I've waited a year for Alex. I don't know what's wrong with me. My relationship with Matt has always been temporary. I just hate to say goodbye."

Jorden's stomach churned when Matt's white Dodge Dart drove into the parking area. Seconds later the doorbell rang.

"Come on in. The door's not locked," Darby yelled from the kitchen.

"Ready?" Matt's eyes met Jorden's as soon as he entered the apartment.

"I'll get my purse."

Matt drove—neither spoke. Finally he broke the silence. "How about lunch?"

"I don't feel much like eating." Jorden shifted positions in her seat.

"Are you okay?"

"No. I'm not okay." Jorden bit her lip. "I guess we could try Fiona's. Do you remember when we went there?"

"It was after we had gone apartment hunting with Eloise. Now, it seems so long ago."

Restless, Jorden shifted her position again. "It was last October. How different life was then. I don't know, maybe we shouldn't go there. Memories are too hard to deal with. I can't believe we're down to our last day." She looked away—anywhere but at Matt. Tears welled up in her eyes. "I thought this would be easier."

"Eating should help. I bet you haven't had anything, have you?"

"No, but I've lost my appetite. I don't think I can sit in a restaurant. Do you think we could pick up sandwiches and go to a park?"

"Sure." Matt turned right at the next stop sign and entered Columbus Square. "Tealand Deli is good." Matt squeezed her hand. "I don't think times like this ever get easier."

Jorden looked at his hand on hers. The contrast stood out.

Matt brushed aside her tears. "I hate this as much as you do. I never thought it would be this difficult."

By the time Jorden opened the car door, she had composed herself. Tealand Deli was off to the right after entering the mall. A lunch crowd had lined up to place their orders; Matt and Jorden followed behind them. Heads turned to look at them. Typical, Jorden thought. She ignored their looks of curiosity.

"What would you like?" Matt asked.

"Surprise me. I'll have whatever you order. I think I'll look at the teas." Jorden stepped out of the line to browse through the various selections. None of them registered. Her eyes could not focus. A half hour later they were on their way to the park. The clouds were getting darker. The threatening weather seemed to thin out the number of people at the park.

"There's an empty picnic table." Matt pointed it out as they walked along the path. He placed the sandwiches and beverages on the table. "Turkey or roast beef? What's your pleasure?"

"Turkey's fine."

Matt handed Jorden a sandwich and a Coca Cola. "Cheers!" He lifted his Coke, attempting a toast.

"What are we toasting?"

"To a good future."

"What an odd toast," Jorden mused.

"It is and it isn't. I wish the future held us but we know it doesn't. Still, I wish you the best." Matt swung his leg over the bench. Jorden felt his thigh next to hers—it felt good. Right now she couldn't think of the future. She only wanted to hold onto the moment.

Off in the distance, two small children chased each other. The shrill laughter resonated in the air.

"You're not eating," Matt observed.

"Neither are you," Jorden replied.

"I guess I've also lost my appetite. We're quite a pair, aren't we?"

"I'll say," Jorden agreed.

Matt placed his hand on top of hers. They sat still, watching the children play. Within minutes the sky darkened and drafts of air swirled, causing the trees to sway back and forth. Droplets of rain hit the table top. Parents scurried after their children, gathered their belongings, and ran to the parking lot. Lightning flashed, followed by a heavy burst of thunder.

"Let's go. I'll race you to the car." Matt threw their lunches in the bag. They were drenched by the time they reached his Dodge Dart.

"Aren't you a sight?" Matt laughed.

"You're not any better," Jorden quipped. The laughter helped relieve the tension.

"Let's go to my place to dry out. Chip and Lyon are gone. Besides, we can put our clothes in the dryer."

They spent their last few hours in his familiar bedroom on a rainy afternoon. Jorden didn't want to leave. Tears slipped down her cheeks. Matt held her close, appearing to deal with his own loss.

"It's almost six," Matt said softly. "I need to drive you back to your place."

"I don't want to go." Jorden's voice shook.

"I know, but we have to ... let go ..." Matt's voice trailed off.

Jorden knew he was right. This was it. She let her eyes roam his four walls and the hardwood flooring for the last time. Matt was tidy. Even the hardwood floor shined. These thoughts kept her mind busy, stopping the tears as they left his house. But pain hit when she watched him drive away from her apartment building. Tears rolled onto her blouse. Then, uncontrollable sobs rocked her.

Darby and Emma Lynn had gone out so Jorden had the apartment to herself. She needed this time to reflect. The phone rang around nine. Jorden ran to the kitchen. "Hello?"

"Hi, Hon. It's me. I'm in Spartanburg, South Carolina, almost five hours away."

"Are you driving to Columbus tonight?"

"I'd like to, but I'm beat. It's raining hard and visibility is zero. I'm in a motel right now." Alex sounded tired. "I can't wait to see you, but looks like I won't get there until around noon tomorrow."

Jorden relaxed. She tried to find the right words. "Just get here in one piece. I've waited this long—I can wait a few more hours. I love you." The words almost stuck in her throat.

"I love you, too. See you soon."

Jorden hung up. How was she going to do this—make it work? She showered, cleaned her face and decided to read one of Alex's latest letters before trying to sleep.

> *Not long now. I can count the days on my fingers. I like to think about our plans. After our wedding day, a week in the Pocono Mountains sounds wonderful. Then we can stop by my house in New York and yours in New Jersey.*

Jorden had never been to the northeastern part of Pennsylvania, especially the Poconos.

> *It's good we have two months before we get married. I can take care of the little details and you'll have the same opportunity at your home in New Jersey. I'm looking forward to visiting with people I haven't seen in the last year and just having time off.*
>
> *After we're married, don't let me get into bad habits. We'll be able to talk and be honest with each other. You're important*

and deserve the best. I want us to have a good time, especially the first year. I can't believe I am so lucky to fall in love with someone like you. You mean the world to me. I realize falling in love is beautiful, but we have power over each other. All my life, I will try to be the best husband. I promise I'll try and make you the happiest ever. My hopes and dreams all look forward to seeing you soon and our coming marriage in August...

Jorden hated the complexity of her feelings as she read his words. She wanted her marriage to Alex to work—it had to succeed. But .. . how did she expect her feelings for Matt to fade away? That's what she prayed would happen.

Chapter 59

June 1970

Jorden woke Sunday morning with a start. Sunlight streamed through the split in the curtain and settled on her face. She reached for the clock; it was six forty-five. Relieved, she turned over—there was plenty of time before Alex arrived. But, sleep eluded her. To distract herself, she changed from one outfit to another, trying to find the perfect combination . . . but nothing seemed to work. She felt like a bundle of nerves.

"Come, sit down. It's almost eleven. It won't be much longer," Darby said with an understanding look.

"You know we would be the same. It's exciting," Emma Lynn proclaimed.

"I'm so nervous. I can't help it. I've been waiting a year for this. Are you sure you don't mind if Alex stays here?" Jorden knew they shared an unspoken rule—usually no men stayed overnight.

"It's fine." Darby smiled.

The doorbell rang. Darby and Emma Lynn backed away. Jorden hesitated. She looked out the peephole. Alex. She froze for a moment before she grabbed the doorknob and opened it. Awkwardly, they looked at each other. It was almost like they were feeling their way, but then Alex pulled her into his arms. They kissed and held each other until they heard the lower entrance open and footsteps on the stairs.

"Come on in." Jorden reached for his hand. Alex looked thinner than he had in Hawaii, but he had the same boyish grin. "Come meet my roommates. Hey, you two! Alex is here."

Emma Lynn bounced out of the kitchen with Darby on her heels. "Finally, we get to meet. We've heard so much about you. It's like we know you."

"Same here." Alex nodded. "You were often in Jorden's letters. It's good to meet."

After a few minutes Darby and Emma Lynn excused themselves and went to their bedroom. Alex reached for her hand. The bracelet he had given her dangled against his wrist. He focused on the emerald. "I have a place for us."

"You have what?" Jorden looked confused.

"I've rented a small, one bedroom apartment. I wanted us to have our own place."

"Where?"

"Buena Vista Apartments. It's close to Fort Benning. It'll be good for us."

A shadow clouded Jorden's expression. She remembered Eloise and Nora had chosen the same apartment complex. Were they still there? Jorden stretched her memory. Yes, Matt had mentioned the major and Eloise decided to stay two more months. They didn't want to disrupt Nora's school year. No problem. She and Alex would probably never see Nora. If they did, so what?

"What's wrong?" Alex shifted his position. "We'll have the whole place to ourselves and you won't have to worry about your roommates. I paid for the first week and, if we need longer, I'll cover another week."

Jorden shook her head. "Don't pay attention to me—my mind's wandering. Of course I'm happy. It'll be great to have our own place. Give me fifteen minutes. I need to pack." Jorden brushed her hand over his shoulder.

"Don't be long," Alex said with a wink.

Twenty minutes later Jorden was stepping into the familiar red Mustang. "I've missed this car, I've missed you—I'm so happy you're back." But she knew she would have been happier if they had married last year—then Matt wouldn't be an issue. Jorden stretched out her legs and slid her hand over the dashboard. "I'm glad you didn't sell it."

"I toyed with the idea, but this car has too many great memories." Alex squeezed Jorden's hand.

Soon they reached Buena Vista Apartments. Jorden's heart beat faster as they turned into the complex. She hadn't written Alex she was back on birth control pills. She stretched the truth at the doctor's office and said she was married. After an exam the doctor had given her a prescription for a year's supply. Jorden looked around. The apartment complex was large with four separate buildings. "Which one are we in?"

"The fourth one—10D." Jorden remembered Nora and her mother were in building B, specifically 12B. She was thankful they weren't in the same building. Alex drove around each building until he reached D.

"How'd you know about these apartments?" Jorden asked.

"Tom. He ended up moving here after I left last spring. Our apartment was too expensive for him. This is where I stayed when your mother came last April."

"I had assumed you were back at your other apartment. What happened to Tom?"

"He's back in New York. I actually saw him at the airport on my way to Albany. It was quite a coincidence. He looked gaunt, but he was his same old self. Enough about Tom. Let's get our things and check out our new place."

They spent the next several hours getting reacquainted. Exhausted, they eventually fell into a light sleep. Jorden's eyes fluttered open an hour later. She looked around the small bedroom with one large empty dresser. They still hadn't unpacked. Easing out of bed, she was careful not to disturb Alex. First, she showered, before exploring the apartment and ending up in the tiny kitchen.

Alex surprised Jorden by closing his arms around her waist. "Are you thinking about cooking us something?"

"Oh! You startled me."

"I have a suggestion. Let's go to Amore's. Maybe we can surprise Antonio."

"What fun. I haven't been there since you left," Jorden replied.

On the way out the door, arm in arm, Jorden and Alex strolled down the walkway to the street. A green Chevy approached. She could see two people in the car. Her eyes gravitated to the front passenger. A pair of dark brown eyes stared back at her. To Jorden's surprise, she heard her name.

"Miss Marshall! It's me. What are you doing here?" Nora shouted as her head slipped out the side window.

"Mama, stop. It's Miss Marshall," Jorden could hear Nora saying to her mother.

Jorden didn't know what to say as the car came to a crawl. "Hi, Nora. What a surprise to see you."

Eloise waved from the driver's seat while she spoke to Nora. "We need to get home and not bother Miss Marshall." Eloise looked at Alex. Jorden and Eloise exchanged glances, after which the latter pressed on the gas pedal.

"Mama, stop! Who's that? Where's Matt?" Jorden heard Nora's words as the Chevy pulled away with increasing speed.

Alex's eyes darted from the car back to Jorden. "What was the young girl talking about?"

"The girl was Nora—a former student of mine."

"I mean who was she talking about? Who's Matt?" Alex's jaw seemed to tighten.

"No one special. He helped me with my tennis game last fall."

"If there is more to this, I need to know." He turned toward the apartment. "Let's go back in and talk about it."

"No!" Jorden grabbed his arm and pulled him back to her. "Honestly, there is nothing to talk about. Matt and I are only friends. He knows I am getting married and in a month he goes overseas. Please. I don't want anything to come between us." Jorden's large blue eyes pleaded with him.

"I want to believe you." Alex appeared to hesitate. "I want to. Okay . . . I'll take your word for it."

"Thank you. I love you." Jorden squeezed his hand.

***

"Mama! What's wrong with you? Why didn't you stop for Miss Marshall?" Nora scowled at her mother. "Who's that man?"

"Her fiancé. They plan to marry in August. I'm sure they heard you. He must be wondering who Matt is! I didn't want you to say any more or cause problems."

"What about Matt?" Nora asked.

Eloise faced her daughter. "From what the major has told me, Miss Marshall and Matt are just good friends. Matt has known all along Miss Marshall planned to marry someone else."

Nora looked straight ahead, absorbing her mother's words. "I don't believe it. There is more than friendship between Miss Marshall and Matt. I just know it."

"It's none of your business—so let it go. Hear me?"

"Whatever," Nora replied.

Chapter 60

June 1970

Amore's looked the same, but Antonio no longer worked there.
"When did he leave?" Alex asked the hostess.

"He's been gone almost a year. He moved to Gainesville, Florida last summer." The hostess looked at her calendar. "Here it is—he left in July." Jorden remembered how she avoided Amore's so he wouldn't see her with someone else . . . like Matt.

"Too bad. We were fond of him."

"I'm sure you'll like John. He's very good. This way, please." The hostess led them to a quiet section.

"This is nice. Thank you," Alex said with a nod.

She handed them menus after they were seated.

Jorden smiled. "This still looks the same even after a year."

"May I help you? My name is John. I'll be your server. Oh, I didn't recognize you. Where's . . ." he stopped and looked at Alex.

Startled by the waiter's voice, Jorden looked up. He looked familiar. She soon realized he was the attendant from the tennis hut. He took their money—Matt's money. Without a ball-cap or shorts he looked a lot different. This must be his second job.

They ordered dinner and enjoyed a leisurely meal with sorbet for dessert.

"I'm disappointed Antonio isn't here. It's not the same. What was the server saying to you about tennis?"

"Nothing really. I couldn't place him at first. He works at the park and collects fees at the tennis courts. He looks much different here."

"Is he at the park where you and your tennis coach go?" Alex scowled.

Jorden didn't reply.

"Well? Am I right?" Alex pushed.

"Yes. My tennis lessons were at the same park. It amounted to nothing—only lessons. Let's drop it."

"I'm just curious about this character. He seems to keep popping up."

"I already told you, there's nothing to it. In your letters you told me I should get out. He was a safe outlet. We're different. He's an American Indian—we come from different backgrounds."

"Safe? Hmm ... he doesn't sound safe to me."

"Would you like to meet him? I'm sure he'd be happy to set your mind at ease."

"No. The last thing I want is to meet him. Were you with him the night I called from California? I remember you weren't at your apartment. It was after two. Don't you agree it's late to be out?"

Jorden watched Alex's face turn angry, the look unbalanced her. She had dreaded this question. How did she answer? She would have to keep to the original story. "I couldn't sleep, but I have to admit I was upset that you decided to go to New York first. Emma Lynn couldn't sleep either, so we went out for Krystal burgers. If you don't believe me, I'm sorry." Jorden hated to lie, but the truth would open up more questions and stir up too much trouble.

"It's hard for me to believe you would go for burgers at two o'clock. I imagined all sorts of scenarios. What am I supposed to think after the young girl asked her mother, 'Where's Matt?'"

"Either you believe me or you don't. What about you? Is there anyone in Albany? Is that why you went there first?"

"That's crazy and you know it!"

"Is it?" Jorden stood, poised to leave.

"Look, believe me, there is no one in Albany except my family. Let's stop fighting. I'm trying my best to understand." Alex walked around the table and put his arm over Jorden's shoulder. "Come on, let's go," he said in a somewhat gentler tone.

Neither said a word on the drive back to the apartment. Thoughts swirled through Jorden's mind. What was he thinking? The palms of her hands felt clammy. Alex reached Buena Vista Apartments and drove by the B complex. If Nora hadn't come along none of this would have been stirred up.

Alex parked the car. He placed his hand over hers. "We're okay, aren't we? I love you?"

"Yes, we're okay. You know I love you." Even while saying it, Jorden knew something was missing. What was wrong with her? Where was the magic? Buck up! This is the man she would marry.

"Let's put this behind us."

She leaned into Alex's shoulder. They sat there for several minutes, each lost in private thoughts.

"Let's go in and make up for lost time," Alex whispered. Jorden lifted her head off his shoulder and placed a kiss on his cheek.

Chapter 61

June 1970

Madison and Luke had them over for dinner the night before but now, Wednesday, Jorden felt isolated again. The apartment didn't have a phone. She didn't have access to her car, hadn't seen her roommates since Sunday, and Matt haunted her thoughts. "Put him out of your mind!" she cautioned herself. "Think about tonight!"

Jorden had planned a special dinner for Alex. After lunch they drove to the grocery store. Feeling adrift, she roamed aimlessly around the Piggly Wiggly, barely aware of Alex by her side. The list of ingredients for his favorite lasagna dinner acted as a guide, a crutch for her dazed mind.

"Let's start in the cheese section. I need ricotta, cottage cheese, mozzarella, and sharp Cheddar." Jorden stared at the cheese selections while her mind shifted into slow motion, unable to concentrate. What was happening to her? She felt on edge, her stomach churned. Miraculously, the cheeses ended up in her grocery cart.

They moved onto the meat section. "A pound of ground beef is all we need." Jorden looked for the best quality of hamburger she could find.

Breathing easier, she suggested the pasta section next. "We need lasagna—the wide, flat-shaped pasta." With an upbeat voice, she tried to hide the anxiety pulsating through her. Her eyes darted back and forth between spaghetti, angel hair, and egg noodles.

She couldn't find the lasagna pasta. Her thoughts wandered to Matt. Where was he? Would she see him again? Jorden tried to shove the thoughts away.

"Is this what you're looking for?" Alex held up a box of long, flat pasta.

"Yes. Where did you find them?"

"Right in front of you. Maybe you need to get your eyes checked." Alex put the box in the cart.

"Maybe."

They spent the next thirty minutes looking for the remaining ingredients. Jorden tossed a carton of ice cream into the cart without thinking.

"Anything else?"

No answer.

Alex tapped her on the shoulder. "Did you hear me?"

"I'm sorry." Jorden checked the cart. "How about a nice bottle of red wine?"

"Good idea. I'll check out the wine section. You go ahead and get in the check-out line."

The cashier rang up their last items just as Alex rejoined Jorden. "Let me get this. I buy and you cook. What do you say?"

"Deal."

Alex pushed the cart to the parking lot and placed the bags in the back seat of his Mustang. Jorden looked over her shopping to-do list. All the items were checked off—except picking up her car. She couldn't stop thinking about it.

"Don't forget I want to get my car. Let's swing by my apartment before we drive back to our place."

"Shouldn't we get these groceries home first? It's hot out," Alex commented as he turned on the car's air conditioner.

"The groceries will be fine in your car. My car must feel like an oven. I haven't driven it in four days."

"Why not tonight? We can drive over after dinner. Your roommates should be there."

Jorden forced herself not to clench her teeth. Before she could think, the words spilled out. "Nighttime isn't a good time.

Our apartment is a gathering spot and there are always men stopping by. I won't get to talk with Darby or Emma Lynn."

"Oh. You never wrote about all the men. What else haven't you told me?"

Jorden fought for patience. "I never wrote about their male visitors as I was always in my bedroom writing you. I didn't think you would want to hear about Darby and Emma Lynn's soldier friends. Please, I just want to get my car."

"You don't need your car. I think you should sell it. I can take you wherever you need to go. It's crazy to drive north in two cars."

Jorden's mouth dropped in disbelief. "I don't want to sell my car!"

"We can talk about it later."

"Look, I want to get my car!" Jorden stared out the windshield.

"You are stubborn, aren't you? Have it your way. I'll take you to your apartment."

"Thank you," Jorden replied.

Neither spoke on the drive. Jorden contemplated other difficult moments with Alex. Her thoughts went back to the first time, a year and a half ago, when Uncle William died. Alex shut her out when she told him about his death. The second time occurred at the Twelfth Week Party for the OCS candidates, and the last time was on the visit to his family's home in Albany.

Jorden kept quiet. When they reached her apartment, she quickly slid out of the car.

"Thank you. I won't be long."

Alex didn't bother to answer. He stepped on the gas and backed out. Jorden watched him speed around the pool and turn right at the exit heading back to their apartment.

"He can't make me sell my car," Jorden murmured. Was he always this domineering? In the meantime, she looked around but didn't see Darby or Emma Lynn's cars. She opened her Volkswagen's door. The heat blasted out like an inferno. She swore when she touched the steering wheel. After the heat dissipated, she rolled down the windows.

No one was at the apartment. She was disappointed; she had hoped to talk with at least one of her roommates. Entering the kitchen, she passed by the phone and couldn't resist lifting up the receiver. She hesitated, but then dialed Matt's number. No answer. Next she called Madison. Again there was no response. No roommates. No Matt. No Madison.

Jorden waited a half hour. Neither roommate returned. While waiting she went back to her bedroom and picked up some clean clothes. She thought about Alex; he wanted to leave Columbus midway through next week. She wanted to wait another full week. The thought of leaving Columbus made her feel sick. If only she could talk with Matt once more.

Jorden left a note for her roommates. It was three thirty when she drove by a phone booth. At the last second, Jorden made a sharp turn and pulled into the Shell station. She looked around and recognized the area. Their apartment was about a quarter mile away.

Jorden pulled open the phone booth, inserted change into the coin slot, and dialed Matt's number. It rang six times. Frustrated, she was about to hang up when an out-of-breath voice answered.

"Hello?"

"Matt?" Jorden's hand shook.

"No. This is Lyon. Matt's not here."

Jorden's shoulders slumped. "Oh. Thank you." She hung up. His roommate didn't seem to recognize her voice.

A tapping sound startled her.

"Miss Marshall? I thought I saw your car."

"Nora! You surprised me."

"I ride my bike around here a lot. Our apartment isn't far from here."

"You're right," Jorden agreed.

"Who was the man you were with the other day? Mama says it's none of my business, but are you really going to marry him? What about Matt?"

"My, a lot of questions," Jorden replied as she left the phone booth. "Matt is a good friend. Alex, the man I was with on Sunday—I plan to marry."

"Oh." Nora seemed to hesitate. "Promise you won't tell my Mama I asked you."

"I promise." Jorden realized how wise she was for her age.

"Thanks. I'd better go." Nora hopped on her bike and waved as she peddled away.

***

The lasagna dinner went well. Alex didn't say a word about their dispute regarding her car. It was as if they never had a disagreement. He helped Jorden clean up the dishes before they had ice cream sundaes.

"A great dinner. You get an A+."

"Thank you." Jorden sat back and tried to relax, but her nerves were frazzled. She couldn't sit still.

"I have an idea. Let's put the Mustang's top down and go for a ride. It's a clear night and still warm outside," Alex suggested.

"Great idea." The thought of getting out in the open air gradually eased Jorden's anxiety.

Millions of stars glittered above them as Alex drove. Jorden threw her head back and let the wind blow her hair every which way. She looked up at the sky. "It's beautiful. I wish this moment could go on and on." She squeezed Alex's arm.

"These moments will go on and on." He placed his hand on Jorden's knee as she sat close to him.

If only she could divide herself in half. Half for Alex and half for Matt—not unequally divided as they were now. But that could never happen.

Chapter 62

June 1970

Early Thursday afternoon after they had lunch, Jorden contemplated driving to her school. She wasn't sure how to broach the subject. Absent-mindedly, she reached for her purse.

"Going somewhere?" Alex asked.

"To my school." This time, Alex didn't argue. "Want to come?" Jorden wanted to get the rest of her things and look at her classroom one last time.

"No. I'll let you have your time to reminiscence. I think I'll drive around the base—see if Fort Benning has changed much in the last year." Alex pulled out his car keys. "See you about four. Will that work?"

"Fine." Before Alex could get out the door, Jorden gave him a kiss. "Thank you."

"You're welcome," Alex replied, kissing her back.

Jorden's shoulders relaxed. The tightness in her stomach eased as she watched him drive away. A half hour later, she pulled into her junior high's parking lot and checked her watch. The drive had taken ten minutes more from the Buena Vista Complex.

Jorden sat at her familiar desk while her eyes wandered over her students' empty seats. She looked at the desks Nora and Cheryl had sat at during her first year of teaching. They had been in her fifth period math class. She couldn't forget their bright faces when they learned they had won the stock market contest.

Old memories were continuing to flood Jorden's thoughts when she heard voices off in the distance. The principal and his secretary were still working. She glanced at the wall clock. It was a little after two. She gathered the last few items from her closet and put them into a cardboard box. Then she walked down to the principal's office to thank him for his support over the past two years.

"I'll be looking for another teaching position in the Boston area. Can I use you as a reference?"

"Of course. Any time. I wish we weren't losing you," Mr. Rinehart replied.

"Thank you. I'll miss your help, the kids, and the school." What she couldn't say was how lost she felt, but she couldn't even explain the reason to herself. Driving away, she spotted a gas station with a payphone. She couldn't resist pulling over. First she dialed Matt's number. No answer. By now she expected nothing. Next, she called Madison.

"Hello?"

"Madison?"

"Yes, it's me. Who else, besides Luke, do you think would be answering my phone?"

"Don't give me a hard time. I tried to call you yesterday and you didn't answer."

"Luke and I were shopping. You sound stressed. Want to go for a Coke?" Jorden knew how well Madison could pick up on her state of mind.

"Love to. I'll meet you at Shoney's. We can have a Coke and fries for old time's sake. I have to be back by four, but this will work for me. Thanks," Jorden replied.

She spotted Madison as she entered the restaurant. The air conditioning brought instant relief from the humid, ninety degree weather.

"Over here," Madison called with a wave. "What's up? Why aren't you with Alex? Did you have a fight?"

"No. Nothing so serious. Civilized disagreement is more like it. Plus, I needed some time and space. I got my car at last. Alex wasn't keen on picking it up."

"Slow down. I can see you're upset. Take a deep breath. Hold it. Now exhale." The commands coming from anyone else would have irritated Jorden, but Madison had a calming effect.

"Better." The muscles in Jorden's shoulders relaxed.

"Now, what's this about your car?"

"First, Alex doesn't think I need a car. He said I should sell it so we can drive up north together. He forgets we're going to two different states before we're married. Trenton, New Jersey is at least two hundred miles away from Albany, New York."

"I can see his logic," Madison interrupted. At the same moment the waitress brought over a tray. "Oh, I ordered for us. I knew we'd be short on time." Madison pushed back her chair to give the waitress additional room.

"Two Cokes and fries. If you need anything else, let me know."

Jorden glared at Madison as she waited for the waitress to leave. "I can't believe you're siding with Alex. You think I should sell my car? What am I supposed to do? Our wedding isn't until late August and I'll be stuck in New Jersey with no transportation. My mother is working now, so both my parents will be using their cars."

"Have a french fry." Madison pointed at the heaping plate.

"I can't believe your nonchalance." Jorden pushed the plate toward Madison. "You eat them. You're supposed to be my friend and sympathize with me."

Madison looked directly at Jorden. "Something's not right. You shouldn't be this upset over a car. It's your car—so don't sell it. You should be happy. Tell me what's going on. Are you and Alex having problems?"

"No!" Jorden automatically replied.

"Then what? I know you. What aren't you telling me?" Madison touched Jorden's arm.

"I'm cut off from everyone."

"You don't sound like a woman in love. I couldn't get enough of Luke after he got back from a year in Vietnam. He was the only person I wanted to be with. Remember how you were when you visited Alex in Albany? You were so upset you didn't get to spend more time with him. Tell me what's going on."

"Nothing. It's nothing. You've helped me. I won't sell my car. It's settled." Jorden looked up at Madison. "I have an idea. Let's all go out Saturday night. We can have dinner at Amore's and then catch a movie. What do you think?"

Madison watched her friend. She seemed to know she probably couldn't get the truth from Jorden until she felt comfortable enough to share it with her. So she replied, "What a good idea. I'll check with Luke and give you a call."

"We don't have a phone."

"Right. What a bummer. Let's just plan on it. I'm sure it'll be okay with Luke."

"I can call you from a payphone tomorrow," Jorden offered.

"No. We'll meet you at Amore's at six. It'll be fun."

Jorden looked at her watch. "I better go. Thanks, Madison."

The friends walked out together. Jorden felt a little better.

Chapter 63

June 1970

Over breakfast Friday morning, Alex lit a fuse in Jorden.

"I think I've found a buyer for your car. Yesterday, I ran into Colonel Harris at Fort Benning. I was surprised he remembered me. Anyway, we got to talking and it seems his wife is looking for a smaller car. They want to take a look at your Bug this weekend."

Jorden looked down at her plate, trying to control herself. "I never said I wanted to sell my car. You said it—not me. I specifically remember saying I didn't want to sell it."

"Come on, Honey. It's crazy to drive north in two vehicles. I'll help you buy another car after we're married. It makes more sense."

"I'm not selling it." Jorden simmered. She wondered if he ever listened to her? "You need to respect my wishes."

"I do, Jorden. But—it's impractical. Right now all we need is one car."

"Sell yours," Jorden said, reversing his logic.

"What a crazy idea. My Mustang's worth much more than yours. Just let Colonel Harris and his wife take a look at your car. I already told them they could come by Saturday morning."

"Call and cancel. I'm not selling my car!" Jorden pushed away from the table, leaving her half-eaten breakfast.

Alex followed her. "Please be reasonable. Let's not fight over this."

"I'm being reasonable. You're not." She stepped away from Alex.

"Have it your way, but I can't call him. You know we don't have a phone. I don't even have his phone number." Alex pivoted on his heel, picked up his car keys, and stomped out.

This was yet another argument since he had returned. Jorden walked to the window and watched him drive off. She lifted her wrist to look at the silver bracelet. Where was the man who gave this to her? Then . . . Matt came to mind. She couldn't think about him—he wasn't a solution.

Jorden stressed for the next two hours. She resolved to speak her mind. She would let Alex know how much he had provoked her. But, unexpectedly, Alex opened the door with a dozen yellow roses poking out of white tissue. He immediately apologized. "I was wrong. I got a hold of Colonel Harris and canceled tomorrow. We'll keep your car," Alex said with such a gentleness—like his old self. "Please take these as a peace offering."

Jorden couldn't resist and gave into his charm. She knew calling Colonel Harris had been hard. Even though, Alex was no longer in the Army, he still respected the colonel's rank. Her resolve to speak her mind vanished when she reached for the roses and hugged him. "Thank you."

***

Saturday flew by. Alex seemed pleased with the idea of joining Madison and Luke for dinner. They arrived a little late.

"Hi y'all," Madison called out. "Hey, you're almost on time. Good for you, Alex, you're improving."

"I see you haven't lost your sense of humor," Alex replied.

"Never." Madison laughed. "Hope you brought a good appetite. Dinner's on us tonight."

"No. It's our turn," Jorden protested. "You had us over the other night. Besides, I was the one who suggested we get together."

"I second it—I'm buying," Alex insisted as he held a chair for Jorden to sit down. The comfortable atmosphere of Amore's added to the ease of conversation—especially since their previous waiter, John, wasn't there.

Luke looked across the table at Alex. "How does it feel to be out of uniform?"

"Great!"

"Have you gotten used to civilian clothes yet?" Luke asked.

"I don't miss those fatigues at all, but I have to admit it felt odd being on base dressed as a civilian. Most of all I'm just glad to be back in the States with my best girl." Alex nudged Jorden in a loving way. Madison seemed delighted to see Jorden and Alex looking happy.

The dinner ended with a scrumptious dessert of cheesecake and fresh strawberries. "Have we chosen a movie?" Madison asked, finishing her last bite.

"I know what I'd like to see," Luke said before anyone could say a word, "*A Man Called Horse*, with Richard Harris. I read an excellent review of it. There are a series of scenes which take place on the Rosebud Indian Reservation in South Dakota. Actually, some of the Lakota Sioux tribe members act in the movie. It's set in the early 1800s. What do you think?"

"Sounds good. I'm up for it." Alex nodded.

"I've never heard of the movie, but I like Richard Harris. I vote for it," Jorden added.

"A consensus. Let's go." Madison stood up.

Jorden became immersed in the storyline. At the end, the young Indian woman died and the Englishman departed with a broken heart. Discreetly, Jorden brushed tears aside. The movie brought Matt and his Native American heritage to life. Of all the movies currently playing, this was one she should have seen with Matt—and not Alex. "You can't think about Matt," she scolded herself. "He's out of your life."

"The movie was excellent, but sad," Madison commented as they walked out.

Luke began to talk about the time period, the South Dakota location, and the Rosebud Reservation. He went on and on, full of details.

"Come on, Luke. It's late. We need to let Jorden and Alex go."

Luke scowled. "I was just getting started."

"I know. That's the point." Madison looked at Jorden, sensing something wasn't right.

Luke didn't seem to notice. "This was fun. Are you two free for bowling tomorrow night? We go most Sundays."

"Sure we are." Alex answered for both of them.

"Meet you at seven. It's Kempton's Bowling Lanes. Jorden, you know where it's located, don't you?"

"What?" Jorden hadn't been listening. Her thoughts were still focused on the movie.

"Come on, Jorden. Have you heard a word?" Alex chided her.

"It's okay." Luke repeated their plans. "You know where Kempton's Lanes are, don't you?"

"Of course I do. We'll meet you there around seven." Jorden did her best to appear cheerful. "Sounds like fun."

Chapter 64

June 1970

Jorden barely said a word on the drive back to their apartment. "Are you okay?"

"I'm just thinking about the movie. It troubled me. I can't get it out of my mind."

"I'll cheer you up, I promise. We still have plenty of time; it's not quite midnight." Alex held Jorden's hand until they arrived back at their place. After he escorted her inside, his eyes strayed toward the bedroom.

An hour or so later, Alex stirred from a light sleep. Feeling his movement, Jorden sensed his gaze. "What is it Alex? You look so serious."

"I'm worried. Don't you think we are taking too many chances? I know you don't want to get pregnant before the wedding. You need to let me know when it's safe for us."

"Aren't you a little late asking that question?" Jorden countered.

"I'm serious, we need to talk about this." Alex let a long lock of Jorden's soft hair slip through his fingers.

Jorden remained silent. How would he react if she told him she was on birth control pills?

"What is it?" Alex looked directly at her in the dimmed light.

Jorden watched Alex's chest rise and fall rather than focus on his eyes. She took a deep breath. "We are safe. I saw a doctor in April ...

and . . . I got a prescription for birth control pills. I was going to tell you."

"When? Is this how it's going to be after we're married? You're going behind my back?"

"No! You're being so unfair. Of course I won't be. I'm being open with you now," Jorden countered.

"I don't want you taking those pills. You need to stop them! Finish out this month's supply, and promise me you'll throw the rest out."

Jorden felt cornered. Her eyes narrowed with resentment. "I . . . I want to be safe during our first year of marriage. You'll be in law school and I hope to be teaching. This isn't a good time for us to have a baby. You wrote the same in a couple of your letters."

"Not this way. This is against my beliefs. You know how I feel. We've talked about this before. I went along with you in Hawaii because I didn't want you to get pregnant while I was in Vietnam. But now I'm here, so it's different." Alex became louder. "I . . . I just don't want you taking those pills!" His voice vibrated as he spit out the words.

"And—What? It's your way—or no way?" Jorden lashed back.

"Don't put it like that. I can't force you to stop taking them, but it upsets me." His cold glare repelled her.

Jorden turned and sat on the edge of the bed with her back to him, looking down and covering her face with her hands. She flashed back to memories from last summer.

***

Summer of 1969

At the end of May, after Alex had left for Vietnam, Jorden took a couple of graduate courses at the university. All seemed well—until two missed periods changed everything. Frightened, she just knew she was pregnant. Her life began to spiral out of control. How would she face her own family, or even more, Alex's family? The timing spoiled any happiness a baby should bring. Alex would still be in Vietnam when the baby was born.

Jorden's thoughts went in all directions. The most extreme was not legal and definitely was not an option. Never, she reiterated to herself.

Jorden couldn't bring herself to confide in her roommates. Finally, though, she broke down and called Madison. Of course, her friend laid it out in practical terms.

"See a doctor first to determine if you are pregnant," Madison simply stated.

"And if I am—what then?" Jorden glared at the phone. "Please don't tell me you told me so. I was a fool. Now I'm paying for it. If only we had gotten married. But no, Alex wanted to wait. I want this baby, but the timing is rotten. Alex won't even be here. I figure the baby will come sometime in February. What am I going to do?" Jorden appealed to Madison.

"Married or not, if you're pregnant you'll lose your teaching position as soon as you start showing. That's Georgia State law—and how the system works."

"I know, but I keep hoping my period will come."

"You need to make a doctor's appointment. Do it soon. Remember, I'm here for you," Madison said encouragingly.

"I know. Thank you. I'll . . . I'll have to go back to my parent's home. It's really the only solution. Mother and Dad will flip, but what else can I do?" Jorden looked defeated.

"Try and be positive. See the doctor first and go from there," Madison firmly stated.

Jorden figured she must have conceived in May at Alex's home in Albany. Continual spotting gave her hope she might not be pregnant. She still hadn't seen a doctor—excuses came up too easily. She didn't write Alex about her fears. By July, Jorden let her imagination run wild. She visualized a small being—a baby boy, a little replica of Alex. She named him Lexie. He had become a part of her. At times she even talked to him.

During July, Scott O'Brady filled the news with the excitement of Apollo 11 and the much anticipated lunar landing. The walk on the moon was set for July 20. O'Brady highlighted the life of each astronaut. Their names were etched into Jorden's memory.

Neil Armstrong was the Commander to be assisted by Buzz Aldrin and Michael Collins.

By Sunday night her roommates, like millions of others, were glued to the television, waiting for the astronauts to set foot on the moon. Jorden wasn't with them. She lay curled up on her bed. The spotting and pain increased. Deep down she had an inkling of what was happening. She had read everything she could find on pregnancy, which also covered miscarriages. The rest of the night became a blur as the heavy bleeding began and the pain became hard to bear. But—still maybe her period had finally come through and all her worry had been unjustified. She would never know.

The next morning Jorden made it to her ten o'clock class. She walked the same route every morning, only now she felt a loss, but at the same time she couldn't help but feel relief. Jorden managed to get through the long hot summer. She finally wrote Alex about her missed periods and the fears and worry she had gone through. She anxiously awaited his response and was disappointed in his lack of concern. Madison seemed to show more compassion than Alex ever did.

***

June 1970

Sitting on the side of the bed, Jorden felt Alex shaking her shoulders. "What is it? Say something." His fingers pressed firmly into her shoulders.

Jorden lifted her head. She took a few deep breaths. "You know . . . we weren't exactly careful last spring. You remember, don't you?" Her voice turned to ice.

"Why are you so concerned about last year now?" Alex looked at her with disdain.

"It didn't seem to matter to you then if I became pregnant before you left for Vietnam, so why are you so concerned now? Don't you wonder why I was so determined to take birth control pills before I joined you in Hawaii? It wasn't to go against your religious beliefs; it was to protect me. I could never go through what happened last July again." Tears gleamed in her eyes.

"But you wrote you were okay." Alex pulled her toward him.

Their eyes met. "That's not the point. I thought I was pregnant and it scared the wits out of me. When I wrote you about my worries, you didn't seem to care. Last spring you weren't very concerned about me getting pregnant. I should have been stronger but I was so much in love with you."

The more she spoke, the angrier she became. As if a revelation came over her, she knew they weren't going to work—too many doubts had taken hold and shattered her illusions. "I can't listen to any more of this." Without thinking, Jorden scrambled into her clothes, found her shoes, and purse.

"What are you doing?" Alex grabbed her.

Jorden jerked out of his grip. "Right now I need space to think." But, what was there to think about, she asked herself.

Brushing the tears from her face, Jorden rushed out the door. She drove away in a daze. Going back to her apartment wasn't an option. She couldn't face Darby or Emma Lynn. The next half hour Jorden drove aimlessly, trying to decide what to do. She was approaching an intersection when the traffic light turned red. The streetlight reflected off the emerald in her bracelet. What happened to the man who gave this to her? She unlatched the silver chain and let the bracelet slip from her wrist.

The light turned green. Jorden stepped on the gas. They had too many differences. Finally, she could see it wasn't going to work. It is better it happened now—just keep driving," Jorden told herself.

Chapter 65

June 1970

"It's over! No wedding!" Jorden declared. She drove without direction until she noticed she was close to her apartment complex. Still, she couldn't face her roommates and drove past the entrance. After several miles she realized she was headed back toward Fort Benning. At the next intersection she instinctively turned right when the light turned green.

As she drove, the streets and houses began to look familiar. She knew the area. A streetlight illuminated her watch; it was late, almost two thirty. She drove through the neighborhood and stopped when she came to the house on Monticello Drive. Jorden never thought she would see Matt's place again. His white Dodge Dart was parked in the driveway. What was she doing? At this moment, she didn't care as she steered her VW Bug to the curb, running over it slightly. Her heart raced while her eyes darted from Matt's car to the one story house. No lights were visible. What now?

Jorden's hand trembled when she opened the car door. Silently, she approached the rear of the house, hoping not to alert the neighbors. The shrill sound of crickets sent a chill through her; she didn't want to be reported to the police.

Matt's bedroom had two windows. The side window was too high, so Jorden crept up to his back window. The window pane had been pulled halfway up. She jumped up but couldn't reach the windowsill. Frustrated, she searched for pebbles. Close to the foundation, moonlight reflected off a pile of rocks. Those were too large. A couple steps to the right she found smaller stones, ones able to wake him without breaking the window.

Jorden stepped back and pitched a single pebble. It hit the wall. She aimed higher. The second pebble hit the upper glass pane.

"Matt, are you there?" No answer. She hurled several more pebbles. Still no response.

Jorden was ready to leave when she spotted a sawhorse in the shadows among other construction materials close to the house. Dragging it under the window, she steadied two of the legs against the back of the house and climbed on. She placed her hands against the house and grasped onto the window's ledge. Now she could see in, but she couldn't see Matt. Standing on her toes she tried to get a better view.

Matt stepped into his bedroom. Startled, Jorden almost lost her balance. She called out, "Matt . . . over here. Help me!"

Matt abruptly stopped. He turned toward the window.

"It's me. Jorden."

Dazed, Matt stumbled to the window. He appeared to do a double take. "What are you doing here?" His eyes widened. "Is this for real?"

Jorden could see him trying to focus on her. The unsteady sawhorse rocked backward again. "Help me . . . I'm losing my balance . . . give me your hand!" Jorden leaned forward with her right hand stretched out while holding tightly to the windowsill with her other hand.

Matt pushed up the window, grabbed her hand, and yanked her up and forward. They flew backward and ended up on his bedroom floor. Matt started to laugh.

"What's so funny?" Jorden couldn't help but laugh herself as she lay on top of him.

"Unbelievable! This is the first time a woman ever visited me through my window." Matt howled.

A whiff of his breath overwhelmed her. "Are you drunk?"

"If I am, it's your fault. Serves you right for leaving me!" Matt rolled over and away from Jorden.

She sat up. "You look awful! You haven't even shaved."

"You don't always bring out the best in me. I've been smoking cigars, drinking, and feeling sorry for myself." Matt struggled to his feet. "Here, give me your hand." Reaching down, he helped Jorden up. "I must smell awful. Don't go away, I'll be right back." He staggered to the bathroom.

Jorden stood there, gazing at his familiar bedroom—she missed it.

Matt returned and put his arms around Jorden's slim waist. "I'm not feeling the best. Do you mind if I lay down." It wasn't a question. He slipped back onto the bed. In an instant, he was out for the rest of the night.

Jorden laid down next to Matt, closed her eyes, and listened to the early morning birds chirping outside. She drifted into a fragile sleep. She stirred first and watched him doze. He didn't look so bad now; at least, he had shaved and brushed his teeth last night.

Matt stretched and groaned; his eyes met hers sheepishly. "Sorry about last night. It's obvious I had too much to drink. You did that to me—I never thought I'd see you again." He touched her face. "You're a beautiful sight. What happened? I was stunned to see you."

"Alex and I . . . we had a fight. Words not to be taken back. I tried this week, but it's not meant to be."

"Does this mean the wedding is off?" Matt's eyebrows lifted.

"It's off." Jorden tenderly touched the outline of Matt's face.

"You are amazing. Tell me I'm not dreaming." Matt buried his face in Jorden's neck and held her gently.

"No. This is reality."

They lay there holding each other until they heard one of his roommates moving around.

Jorden rose and sat on the side of the bed. "I should get back to my apartment."

"What are we going to do?" Matt touched Jorden's shoulder.

"I don't know . . . only I know it's not going to work for me and Alex."

Louder sounds came from the hallway. "Listen. I hear someone moving around. I better go. Think I can sneak out?"

"Don't be silly. Lyon won't care, but he may wonder how you got in here." Matt grinned as he reached for his cutoffs. "Come on, I'll walk you out."

Jorden peered out the door. "The coast is clear. I think I can hear Lyon. It sounds like he's in the kitchen." She pulled at Matt's arm. "Come on." She took his hand and dragged him down the hallway and out the front door. Jorden laughed with a sense of relief when they reached her VW Bug. "We made it." She got in behind the steering wheel.

Matt held onto the open door. "What next? We need to talk. You can't leave like this."

"Get in. Let's talk."

Matt stepped to the other side and slid into the passenger seat.

"Move in with me . . . I . . . I love you." The words slipped out of Matt.

"I can't. It's just not right." Jorden protested before his words even registered. She touched his hand; love had been a forbidden word.

"We've been blind." Matt squeezed her fingers. "Tell me . . . tell me you don't love me."

Jorden looked confused. She was speechless. In the beginning, love didn't fit into their relationship. All this time she had been in complete denial, refusing to acknowledge what was happening between them. Thinking about it made her tremble. Shivers ran through her as she allowed herself to focus on the word. Finally, she opened up to herself and Matt. "I can't deny it. We both know . . . I love you." Those simple words said it all.

"There's your answer. Just move in with me."

"I can't . . . I can't. Maybe we should end this—go our separate ways."

"Do you really want us to split up?" Matt watched her closely.

She looked down. "No."

"What if we get married?"

Jorden looked up, surprised by his words. "Are you serious?"

"Yes."

"What if . . . it doesn't work?" Jorden replied.

"If it doesn't work, then we can part."

"Sounds crazy. We can't get married—it's too sudden!" Jorden protested.

"No, it's not. It's a great idea. It's what I want. Be honest. Don't you?"

Jorden thought about it. "Well, if it doesn't work—we can go our separate ways, making the decision easier."

"Is that a yes?" Matt pressed.

She hesitated, then the corners of her lips moved upward. "Yes!" Her eyes brightened. "When?"

"Soon. We don't have much time before I leave for Korea. We have a couple weeks to work out the wedding details. Let's start with Lyon. Come on, I'm sure he won't believe it."

"Wait before we tell anyone—I have to talk with Alex. It's only fair."

"You're right. You should talk with Alex first. Just don't let him change your mind." Matt reached for Jorden's hand.

"Never!"

Chapter 66

June 1970

Jorden raced up the stairs to her second floor apartment.

"Jorden?" Darby called out. "There you are. Alex called this morning. He wants to meet you later this afternoon, specifically at five. What happened? I thought you were with him. In so many words, I told him I hadn't seen you since last Sunday."

"It's over."

"What's over?" Emma Lynn stepped out of the bedroom.

"Alex and I. I left late last night." Jorden reached for the side of the couch for support.

"Left for where? You didn't come here," Emma Lynn said.

A smile danced on Darby's face. She grinned at Emma Lynn. "Only one place."

"Matt's!" Emma Lynn shrieked. "Tell us all."

Jorden looked from one roommate to the other and debated what to tell them. "I need to talk with Alex first. How did he sound?"

"Hard to tell. Distant, disconnected . . . for as little as I know him." Darby replied.

Jorden looked at her watch. "I better call Matt and let him know what's happening."

At five, Jorden stood before the apartment's picture window, waiting for Alex's Mustang to pull up. She had decided to meet him outside. The red Mustang rounded the corner of the parking area.

She sucked in her breath, summoned her courage, and made her way down the stairs to the walkway. He was already there.

"What's going on?" Alex was clenching his jaw and tightening his neck muscles. Jorden knew the look—hard and impenetrable. "So where were you last night?"

Jorden hesitated. "Last night—I drove senselessly. I was so upset. I didn't want to face my roommates and their questions. I didn't want to face my own answers."

"I don't believe you. You weren't here when I called this morning. You're avoiding my question. Where did you go?" Alex glared at her with unflinching eyes.

Jorden's stomach churned, she felt sick—she wanted to run.

"You were with him. You've slept with this character, haven't you? Don't lie to me."

Her throat constricted. She couldn't speak.

"That's where you were the night I called from California. I should have known. I thought you were above this." Alex grew colder. "No wonder you're on birth control pills—very convenient. When were you going to give me the details—after we were married?"

Jorden choked. "You're not fair."

"And you play fair? Give me a break," Alex responded, raising his voice.

"This isn't about playing fair. This is about you and me. Everything has to be your way. Religion . . . no birth control . . . when we marry . . . where we live . . . what I can and can't do . . . and . . . even down to selling my car. Control is what this is about. I can't live like that!"

"Live however you like—just not with me!" Alex twisted away and yanked her bag out of his front seat. "You left these behind last night." He hurled her stuff to the curb.

Dumbstruck, Jorden watched him speed away. Just like that—it was over. Those were the last words Jorden ever heard from Alex. Tears ran down her cheeks as she slowly slid down to the curb. Time seemed to stand still until she saw a car in her peripheral vision—a white Dodge Dart. In spite of herself, Jorden smiled when Matt reached her side. He immediately pulled her into his arms.

Comfort was just what she needed. Moments later, they climbed the steps to her apartment.

Darby and Emma Lynn just stared at them as they entered. "Well, what's going on?" Darby blurted out.

Jorden then leveled with her roommates and told them, before anyone else, of their wedding plans.

"I knew it!" Emma Lynn exclaimed.

Darby smiled. "I'm not surprised. I always knew the wedding gown was meant for Matt."

"I concede you were right," Jorden replied.

"What are you talking about? What wedding dress?" Matt rotated his head. Three sets of eyes stared at him.

"Nothing you need to know," Emma Lynn said with a laugh. "This is between us girls!"

Matt shrugged his shoulders. "Come on, Jorden, we've got calls to make."

"Call my mother?" Jorden rolled her eyes. Her head exploded. Her heart raced.

Twenty minutes later they were at Matt's place. His roommates seemed happy for them but somewhat dubious. Matt called his grandmother first, then his aunt and uncle and a few close friends. Jorden listened to his side of the conversation, wondering what she would tell her parents.

When Matt finished, he backed away from the phone. "Now it's your turn."

"I think I should wait a few days."

"Jorden, the wedding is less than three weeks away. You have to let your parents and family know." Matt slid the phone over to her.

She forced her fingers to dial the number. The phone rang three times before her father answered.

"Hi, Dad."

"Hi, Honey. What's up? Are you and Alex leaving soon?"

"Dad. Alex already left. There's . . . there's been a change. I'm marrying . . . Matthew Ulster in three weeks.

A long silence followed, with faint words in the background. Next thing she knew her mother had come on the line.

"Jorden? What's this nonsense your Dad is saying? I think he needs a hearing aid. When are you and Alex driving to Trenton?"

"Mom. We're not. I'm not marrying Alex. I'm going to marry Matthew Ulster. I think I mentioned him at Christmas—the Native American."

"I don't understand. What happened to Alex?"

"We broke up. I'm with Matt right now. I know you'll like him. I met him last October so it's really not sudden. I hope you, Dad, Bobbette, and Mark can come. We don't have the details worked out yet, but I'll let you know as soon as we do. We're looking at Sunday, the fifth of July."

"I don't know what to say. This seems awfully sudden. I want to be at your wedding—really . . . I want to come . . ." Silence . . . then the line went dead.

Matt's eyebrows darted upward. "Well?"

"Mom hung up on me." Jorden rested her head in her palms. "For once Mother didn't know what to say."

The next three weeks were a whirlwind of activities. Darby and Emma Lynn immediately took over. Exuberantly, they set up checklists of what needed to be done. Jorden smiled—she had her own wedding planners. Her roommates clashed at times over the wedding arrangements, but on the whole, they worked well together. Matt tried to reserve the Episcopal Church in downtown Columbus; however, it had a year-long waiting list. He managed to get a chapel on base but the Officers' Club wasn't available. As good luck would have it, a fellow officer volunteered his house for the reception, and also his expertise as their photographer.

In the midst of all the activities, Jorden's parents kept calling. She couldn't forget her father's words. "Jorden, your mother wants you to get help—talk with someone. She thinks you've lost your mind. Even Bobbette is worried. Have you thought this through? Marriage can be difficult even when you come from the same race, but being so different can pose all sorts of problems." He stopped just short of calling her crazy.

She was thankful Bobbette agreed to be in her wedding. Her sister tried to explain the home front. "I doubt Dad will come.

He's even more upset than Mom, but she won't miss the wedding. Of course it's a given Mark and I will be there."

The hardest call to make was to Madison. Jorden delayed for a couple days. Actually, Madison called her first. "What's up? When are you and Alex driving north?"

"Alex left last Sunday," Jorden replied simply.

"Why are you still here? I knew something wasn't right when Alex canceled bowling last Sunday. What happened?"

"It was devastating." Jorden went into a long explanation before telling Madison about Matt and how they planned to be married.

"Wow! I should have known. I wish you had told me about Matt—but I can see why you didn't. I hope you'll invite us to your wedding."

"You're first on my list—only I was afraid you wouldn't want to come. My dad's not even coming. He thinks I've lost my mind. I really want you to be there. Be one of my bridesmaids. Please."

"I don't even know Matt," Madison replied.

"So? You'll get to know him. He'll grow on you. Please . . . you have to do this for me!" Jorden begged.

After continuous pleading, Madison conceded. "Okay—for you I will."

"Thank you! Come with us tomorrow; we're looking for bridesmaid dresses. My color theme is yellow. Yellow for the sun. It's bright and how I want our wedding to be. We'll have fun!"

Chapter 67

July 1970

Wedding preparations continued. Darby and Emma Lynn postponed their departure date until July 10. Jorden and Matt planned to rent the apartment for the remainder of July. Matt would be deployed to Korea in the middle of August. Jorden still hadn't decided what to do while Matt spent the year in Korea.

"Meet us in Colorado Springs," Darby suggested. "You can find a teaching job."

"It's perfect. Join us after Matt leaves." Emma Lynn clapped. "It'll be fun; besides, you'll help with the rent."

Jorden mulled it over. How could she go back home when her father wouldn't even come to her wedding? "I like the idea. I'll do it."

"Great! It's settled. Now, when's your mother's flight arriving in Atlanta?" Darby asked.

"Tomorrow." Jorden pointed to the kitchen calendar—Wednesday, July 1. "Matt and I plan to pick Mom up at the Atlanta airport tomorrow afternoon."

"Is she staying with us?"

"No. Thankfully, Madison offered to have her stay in their extra bedroom. I just hope Mother doesn't give me a hard time." Jorden's stomach rolled.

Emma Lynn joined them in the kitchen. "Your mother will adore Matt. Everyone does."

"I hope you're right."

Jorden and Matt left early Wednesday afternoon for the Atlanta Airport.

"Don't be nervous. I'm sure Mom will be on her best behavior. Bobbette called last night and said Mother was getting excited about the trip."

"Is your dad still not coming?" Matt asked. Jorden noticed Matt tighten his grip on the steering wheel while his knuckles turned whiter.

"No. He's not coming. Bobbette says it's his stubborn streak. But she said Mark would walk me down the aisle. I told her, if Dad's not here, no one can take his place. My dad's brother also offered, which was sweet of him. At least they'll be at my wedding—thank goodness some family is coming." Jorden looked up. "There's the sign to the Atlanta Airport."

A half an hour later they were waiting at the arrival gate as they watched the Boeing 727 land. Neither Jorden nor Matt spoke when the passengers deplaned directly onto the tarmac.

"There's Mother. Stay right here. I'm going to stand next to the man over there." Jorden pointed in the direction of a skinny man in his twenties with long greasy black hair, a scruffy beard, and tattered jeans with his shirttails hanging out. She had a hard time suppressing a laugh. Matt looked at her as if she were nuts.

Mary Marshall seemed to do a double take. Her eyes widened and focused on the man next to her daughter. Her pace slowed, she lowered her head and slid behind the burly man in front of her.

Jorden waved. "Mom! Over here." As her mother approached, Jorden stepped back next to Matt with his short military haircut, clean shaven face, and neat appearance. Relief seemed to wash over Mary Marshall. Briskly, she walked up to her daughter and Matt.

"Hi, Mom." Jorden enveloped her mother. Matt automatically reached for her carry-on bag. "Mother, this is Matthew Ulster."

"It's so good to meet you." Mary smiled with approval after her first scare. Jorden noticed the eyes of the scruffy looking young man. He seemed to follow them before vanishing into the crowd.

"Good to meet you, Mrs. Marshall." Matt stretched out his hand to shake hers.

"Please call me Mary."

The awkward introduction gradually changed to easy laughter between Matt and her Mother on the drive back to Columbus. Mary Marshall never seemed to be at a loss for words.

Over the next few days, invitations to the wedding were spread directly or by phone calls. Relatives and friends from both sides would be there. Bobbette and Mark drove in early Saturday afternoon.

Jorden threw her arms around her sister. "Thank goodness you're here."

"We held off as long as we could. I thought Dad might change his mind. I swear he almost gave in and came with us."

Jorden and Matt didn't have much time alone with the continual buzz of activity. The wedding rehearsal went well. It would be a simple ceremony in the same chapel where the major and Eloise were married.

During a quiet moment Jorden asked Matt, "Did you remember to invite the major, Eloise, and Nora?"

"Of course. They'll be there. Nora was delighted we ended up together. Sounds like she's been having fun teasing her mother about it."

"I'm so glad they're coming."

Sunday morning proved extremely hectic. Darby and Emma Lynn were at the officer's home where the reception was being held, getting everything set up.

Bobbette called Sunday morning. "Jorden?"

"Yes. What's up?"

"You won't believe this! Guess who's here?"

"Who?"

"Dad! He flew in late last night. I wanted to surprise you at the church this afternoon but thought it might be too much of a shock. Mom's beside herself. She can't believe he came."

Jorden slid down onto the kitchen floor, cradling the phone against her ear. "Say it again. I don't believe you." Tears glistened on her face.

"It's true. Dad's here. He's off with Mom right now or I'd have you talk with him."

***

The day went on. All the planning, even in the short span of time, paid off. By four, Bobbette, Madison, Darby, and Emma Lynn had Jorden's makeup and hair ready. Within thirty minutes, her entourage arrived at the chapel's dressing room.

The dress and veil hung perfectly on Jorden's slender frame. She couldn't believe the reflection in the mirror. She touched her face and ran her fingers along the creamy white satin material. "This really is me."

Darby affectionately squeezed Jorden's shoulders. "My mother would be proud. This dress was always meant for you and Matt." Darby placed one more hairpin in the veil to secure it. "It's your day to shine and you will." Emma Lynn straightened the train on the wedding gown with her eyes tearing up. Darby reached down and touched Emma Lynn's forearm. "Come on, we all need a hug to celebrate this special day." The bridesmaids encircled Jorden.

For the finishing touch, Madison handed Jorden her wedding bouquet. White roses and daises were interspersed with baby's breath.

"How gorgeous!" Jorden grinned at Madison. "No catching this one—you've got Luke."

At the same moment Nora barged into the dressing area. "Oh, Miss Marshall, how beautiful you look. I knew I was right about you and Matt."

Jorden gave Nora a bear hug. "You sure were."

"Oh no! I'm squashing your flowers. I better go before Mama catches me." Everyone laughed as Nora bolted out the door. The organist began to play.

"Our cue," Darby spoke up. "We need to begin the wedding procession."

Emma Lynn blew Jorden a kiss.

Bobbette reached out to Jorden and pointed to the door. "Dad's waiting in the hall."

"Thanks." Jorden nodded as her sister followed the others out.

Grant Marshall greeted his daughter with a huge embrace. "Honey, don't cry. You'll mess up your pretty face." He reached down and kissed her forehead. "You know I couldn't stay away."

Jorden hugged her father back tightly—then her nerves exploded when she heard the organist begin the wedding march.

Her father smiled at her. "It's your time."

A huge smile lit up Jorden's face. She grabbed her Father's arm. "Let's do this."

Arm in arm they walked down the aisle toward Matt and the wedding party.

***

At the end of the reception, Jorden and Matt drove off in his white Dodge Dart with a Just Married sign attached to the bumper.

"Well, Mrs. Ulster—we did it!"

Jorden leaned over and kissed his cheek. "Yes we did!"

Epilogue

Years Later

Jorden looked up at the gathering and smiled. Matt was chasing Jamie, the one grandchild who was too quick for him.

"Come on, Dad, are you going to let my twelve year old beat you?" Their daughter yelled.

"Never!" Matt called out. "I'm still winning."

Jamie stepped up his pace and quickly passed his grandfather. "Too bad, Pops, you don't have it anymore. I'm faster!"

"Admit it, old man," Jorden laughed.

"Not me. I'll never slow down!" Matt circled back to Jorden and grabbed her. "I can still catch you."

"Good thing. I don't know how you would have gotten through all these years without me," Jorden chided.

Matt couldn't argue with her logic as he held onto Jorden.

***

Jorden thought back on their life together. They had celebrated numerous holidays with their family of five, including two sons and one daughter. Sadly, Jorden's parents had passed, but Bobbette still kept in touch on a weekly basis. Now there was the sweet addition of three grandchildren with another one on the way. They had settled in the Northwest and made this their home over the past years.

Strangers still stared at them and their obvious differences, but it couldn't stop them from smiling.

But things had changed quite a lot from the late 1960s. Jorden was thankful the draft had been eliminated in 1973. Matt didn't have a choice when he was drafted to serve back in 1968, but now their sons could choose. Post-Traumatic Stress Disorder (PTSD) was finally recognized in 1980; however, Vietnam Veterans did not have the advantage of that diagnosis in the 1960s and earlier 1970s. Jorden never forgot one of the soldiers at their Julian Apartment complex the fall of 1969. He would sit at the pool in a daze, never speaking. His friends would supply him with drinks and sandwiches, doing their best to watch out for him. At the time, Jorden and her roommates didn't understand what was happening to him.

Her roommates had been good about writing and now e-mailing, texting, or using Facebook for their latest news. Emma Lynn eventually found her special love. They were married and settled outside of Atlanta. She had a circle of grandchildren whom she loved to spoil. Talented Darby branched out into writing. She became a bestselling author, now living in New York City with her well-known, renowned husband and two daughters. Proud of Darby's success, Jorden savored her friend's novels and had them on the shelf above her desk.

Of course Madison, her close friend, came back to mind. Madison and Luke, who had known each other since their early teens, continued to be happily married with two children and four grandchildren. Jorden still bounced ideas and problems off of Madison since she always gave good, straight answers which Jorden relied on.

Eloise and Major Hawkins ended up in Massachusetts after he retired as a Lieutenant Colonel from the U.S. Army. Nora grew into a sharp young woman who made a big splash on Wall Street. She did so well she received a write-up in The New Yorker magazine. Jorden was delighted for Nora and followed all her accomplishments. Of course, Nora would always hold a special spot in Jorden's heart; she had been Jorden and Matt's most powerful cheerleader.

Jorden turned and stretched as she looked at her husband. He winked back with the same magic she had first seen years ago.